Praise for Claire Allan:

'Amazing. I read it in one go.'
Marian Keyes

'Utterly addictive! Literally couldn't put it down all day!
Compulsive, twisty, tense. And LOVED the ending.'
Claire Douglas

'A powerful and emotional psychological thriller that will
keep you guessing and leave you breathless.'
C.L. Taylor

'SUCH a good read! It made me feel so uncomfortable,
but I still kept gobbling up the pages.'
Lisa Hall

'*Her Name Was Rose* is heck of a read! It's a psychological
thriller with a heart, it's taut, emotionally challenging and,
unlike so many thrillers, each twist and turn is there because
it deserves to be and not for the sake of it.'
John Marrs

'An exciting debut that I couldn't put down, *Her Name
Was Rose* got under my skin in a way I wasn't expecting.
An intriguing and menacing page turner.'
Mel Sherratt

'The depth of characterisation and its fast pace is what
makes *Her Name Was Rose* stand out as a thriller.
It had me hooked until the end.'
Elisabeth Carpenter

DISCARDED
From Nashville Public Library

D0111085

'A tight and twisted tale with a set of seriously complex characters – kept me guessing right 'til the end. This is going to be one of 2018's smash hits.'
Cat Hogan

'All I can say is wow! Such a great concept, expertly delivered to keep you turning the pages. This book toys with the reader until the last page. Trust me, this will be THE book of 2018!'
Caroline Finnerty

'Mesmerizing to the point of complete distraction. I was totally engrossed in this book.'
Amanda Robson

DISCARDED
From Nashville Public Library

HER NAME WAS ROSE

Claire Allan is a former journalist from Derry in Northern Ireland, where she still lives with her husband, two children, two cats and a hyperactive puppy.

In her eighteen years as a journalist she covered a wide range of stories from attempted murders, to court sessions, to the Saville Inquiry into the events of Bloody Sunday right down to the local parish notes.

She has previously published eight women's fiction novels. *Her Name Was Rose* is her first thriller.

When she's not writing, she'll more than likely be found on Twitter @claireallan.

CLAIRE ALLAN

HER NAME WAS ROSE

avon.

Published by AVON
A division of HarperCollins*Publishers*
1 London Bridge Street,
London SE1 9GF

www.harpercollins.co.uk

A Paperback Original 2018

18 19 20 21 22 LSC 10 9 8 7 6 5 4 3 2 1

Copyright © Claire Allan 2018

Claire Allan asserts the moral right to
be identified as the author of this work

A catalogue record for this book is
available from the British Library

ISBN-13: 978-0-00-830014-2

This novel is entirely a work of fiction.
The names, characters and incidents portrayed in it are
the work of the author's imagination. Any resemblance to
actual persons, living or dead, events or localities is
entirely coincidental.

Set in Bembo by Palimpsest Book Production Limited,
Falkirk, Stirlingshire

Printed and bound in the United States of America
by LSC Communications

All rights reserved. No part of this publication may be
reproduced, stored in a retrieval system, or transmitted,
in any form or by any means, electronic, mechanical,
photocopying, recording or otherwise, without the prior
permission of the publishers.

For more information visit: www.harpercollins.co.uk/green

To my parents,
Peter and Karen Davidson,
for all that you are, all that you do and all that you have
taught me.

Chapter One

It should have been me. I should have been the one who was tossed in the air by the impact of a car that didn't stop. 'Like a ragdoll,' the papers said.

I had seen it. She wasn't like a ragdoll. A ragdoll is soft, malleable even. This impact was not soft. There were no cushions. No graceful flight through the air. No softness.

There was a scream of 'look out!' followed by the crunch of metal on flesh, on muscle, on bone, the squeal of tyres on tarmac, the screams of onlookers – disjointed words, tumbling together. The thump of my heart. A crying baby. At least the baby was crying. At least the baby was okay. The roar of the engine, screaming in too low a gear as the car sped off. Footsteps, thundering, running into the road. Cars screeching to a halt as they came across the scene.

But it was the silence – amid all the noise – that was the loudest. Not a scream. Not a cry. Not a last gasp of breath. Just silence and stillness, and I swore she was looking at me. Accusing me. Blaming me.

I couldn't tear my gaze away. I stood there as people around me swarmed to help her, not realising or accepting that she was beyond help. To lift the baby. To comfort him. To call an ambulance. To look in the direction in which the car sped off. Was it black? Not navy? Not dark grey? It was dirty. Tinted windows. Southern reg, maybe. It was hard to tell – muddied as it was so that the letters and numbers were obscured. No one got a picture of the car – but one man was filming the woman bleeding onto the street. He'd try and sell it to the newspapers later, or post it on Facebook. Because people would 'like' it. A child, perhaps eight years old, was screaming. Her cries piercing through all else. Her mother bundled her into her arms, hiding her eyes from the scene. But it was too late. What has been seen cannot be unseen. People around me did what needed to be done. But I just stood there – staring at her while she stared at me.

Because it should have been me. I should be the one lying on the road, clouds of scarlet spreading around me on the tarmac.

★

I stood there for a few minutes – maybe less. It's hard to tell. Everything went so slowly and so quickly and in my mind it all jumps around until I'm not sure what happened when and first and to whom.

I moved when someone covered her – put a brown duffle coat over her head. I remember thinking it looked awful. It looked wrong. The coat looked like it had seen better days. She deserved better. But it broke our stare and an older lady with artificially blonde brassy hair gently took my arm and led me away from the footpath.

'Are you okay, dear?' she asked. 'You saw it, didn't you?'

'I was just behind her,' I muttered, still trying to see my way through the crowds. Sure that if I did, the coat would be lifted in a flourish of magic trickery and the lady would be gone.

Someone would appear and shout it was an elaborate trick and the lovely woman – who just minutes before had been singing 'Twinkle Twinkle' to the cooing baby boy in the pram as we travelled down in the lift together – would appear and bow.

But the brown coat stayed there and soon I could hear the distant wail of sirens.

There's no need to rush, I thought, she's going nowhere.

'I'll get you a sweet tea,' the brassy blonde said, leading me to the benches close to where the horror was still unfolding. It seemed absurd though. To sit drinking tea, while that woman lay dead only metres away. 'I'm fine. I don't need tea,' I told her.

'For the shock,' the blonde said and I stared back blankly at her.

This was more than shock though. This was guilt. This was a sense that the universe had messed up on some ginormous, stupid scale and that the Grim Reaper was going to get his P45 after this one. Mistaken identity was unforgivable.

I looked around me. Fear piercing through the shock. There were so many people. So many faces. And the driver? Had I even seen him? Got a glimpse? Could it have been *him*? Or had he got someone else to do the dirty work, and he was standing somewhere, watching? It would be more like him to stand and observe, enjoy the destruction he had caused. Except he'd got it wrong. She'd walked out in front of me. I'd let her. I'd messed with his plan.

I'd smiled at her and told her to 'go ahead' as the lift doors opened. She'd smiled back not knowing what she was walking towards.

A paper cup of tea was wafted in front of me – weak, beige. A voice I didn't recognise told me there were four sugars in it. Brassy Blonde sat down beside me and nodded, gesturing that I should take a sip.

I didn't want to. I knew if I did, I would taste. I would feel the warmth of it slide down my throat. I would smell the tea leaves. I would be reminded I was still here.

'Let me take your bags from you,' Brassy Blonde said. I realised I was gripping my handbag tightly, and in my other hand was the paper bag I had just been given in Boots when I'd picked up my prescription. Anxiety meds. I could use some now. My hands were clamped tight. I looked her in the eyes for the first time. 'I can't,' I said. 'My hands won't work.'

'It's the shock. Let me, pet,' she said softly as she reached across and gently prised my hands open, sitting my bags on the bench beside me. She lifted the cup towards me, placed it in my right hand and helped me guide the cup to my mouth.

The taste was disgustingly sweet, sickening even. I sipped what I could but the panic was rising inside me. The ambulance was there. Police too. I heard a woman crying. Lots of hushed voices. People pointing in the direction in which the car had sped off. As if their pointing would make it reappear. Beeps of car horns who didn't realise something so catastrophic had held them up on their way to their meetings and appointments and coffees with friends. Faces, blurring. Familiar yet not. They couldn't have been.

The tightness started in my chest – that feeling that the air was being pushed from my lungs – and it radiated through my body until my stomach clenched and my head began to spin just a little.

He could be watching me crumble and enjoying it.

The noise became unbearable. Parents covering the eyes of children. Shop workers standing outside their automatic doors, hands over their mouths. I swear I could hear the shaking of their heads – the soft brush of hair on collars as they struggled to accept what they were seeing. Breathing – loud, deep. Was it my own? Shadows moving around me. Haunting me. I felt sick.

'I have to go,' I muttered – my voice tiny, distorted, far away

– as much to myself as to Brassy Blonde, and I put down the teacup and lifted my bags.

'You have to stay, pet,' she said, a little too firmly. I took against her then. No, I wanted to scream. I don't have to do anything except breathe – and right now, right here, that was becoming increasingly difficult.

I glared at her instead, unable to find the words – any words.

'You're a witness, aren't you? The police will want to talk to you?'

That made the panic rise in me more. Would they find out that it should have been me? Would I get the blame? Would I become a headline in a story – 'lucky escape for local woman' – and if so, what else would they find out about me? I couldn't take that risk.

I consoled myself that I probably couldn't tell them anything new anyway.

No, I didn't want to talk to the police. I couldn't talk to the police. The police had had quite enough of me once before.

Chapter Two

A hit and run, they said. That was the official line. A joyrider, most likely. Joyrider is such a strange name for it, really. There was no joy here. The words of the police did little to comfort me. After I ran from Brassy Blonde, I checked the locks three times before bed, kept the curtains pulled on the windows of my flat and for those first 48 hours I didn't go out or answer my phone. The only person I spoke to was my boss to tell him I was sick and wouldn't be in. I didn't even wait for him to answer. I just ended the call, crawled back into bed and took more of my anti-anxiety medication.

I tried to rationalise my thoughts and fears in the way my counsellor had told me. A few years had passed since Ben had made his threat; five to be exact. Life had moved on. He had moved on. Moved to England, if my brother Simon was to be believed. Simon, who I secretly suspected believed Ben about everything that went wrong with us.

Simon, who most definitely, did not believe that his former friend was waiting in the wings to destroy my life for a second time in his twisted form of revenge.

'You're letting him win every day,' my counsellor had told me. 'You're giving him power he doesn't deserve.'

But she didn't know him. Not the way I did. I spent those two days in a ball in my bed, sleeping or at least trying to sleep, and compulsively checking Facebook to find out as much as I could about the woman who had died when it should have been me.

There was no fairness to it. She had everything going for her while I, well, if I evaporated from this earth at this moment no one would really notice. Except perhaps for Andrew who would be waiting to give me a final written warning.

I had to go to the funeral. I was drawn to it. I had to see the pain and let it wash over me – to salve my guilt perhaps or to torture myself further? See if she really was as loved as it seemed.

I needed to remind myself just how spectacularly the gods had messed this one up.

Perhaps I was a bit obsessed. It was hard not to be. The story of her death was everywhere and I had seen her life extinguished right in front of my eyes. Her eyes had stayed open – and they were there every time I closed mine.

Her funeral was held at St. Mary's Church in Creggan – a chapel that overlooked most of the city of Derry, down its steep hills towards the River Foyle before the city rises back up again in the Waterside. It's a church scored in the history of Derry, where the funeral Mass of the Bloody Sunday dead had taken place. Thirteen coffins lined up side by side. On the day of Rose Grahame's funeral, just one coffin lay at the top of the aisle. The sight stopped my breath as I sneaked in the side entrance, took a seat away from her friends and family. Hidden from view.

All the attention focused on the life she'd led, full of happiness and devotion to her family and success in her career. I thought of how the mourners – the genuine ones dressed in bright colours (as Rose would have wanted) – had followed the coffin to the front of the church, gripping each other, holding each other up. I wondered what they would say if they knew what I knew.

I allowed the echoes of the sobs that occasionally punctuated the quiet of the service to seep into my very bones.

I recognised her husband, Cian; as he walked bowed and broken to the altar, I willed myself not to sob. Grief was etched in every line on his face. He looked so different from the pictures I had seen of him on Facebook. His eyes were almost as dead as Rose's had been. He took every step as if it required Herculean effort. It probably did. His love for her seemed to be a love on that kind of scale. His grief would be too.

He stood, cleared his throat, said her name and then stopped, head bowed, shoulders shaking. I felt my heart constrict. I willed someone – anyone – to go and stand with him. To hold his hand. To offer comfort. No one moved. It was as if everyone in the church was holding their breath, waiting to see what would happen next. Enjoying the show.

He took a breath, straightened himself, and spoke. 'Rose was more than a headline. More than a tragic victim. She was my everything. My all. But even that isn't enough. As a writer, you would think the words would come easily to me. I work with words every day – mould them and shape them to say what I need to say. But this time, my words have failed me. There are no words in existence to adequately describe how I'm feeling as I stand here in front of you, looking at a wooden box that holds the most precious gift life ever gave me. When a person dies young, we so often say they had so much more to give. This was true of Rose. She gave every day. We had so many dreams and plans.'

He faltered, looking down at the lectern, then to Rose's coffin and back to the congregation. 'We were trying for a baby. A brother or sister for Jack. We said that would make our happiness complete – and now, knowing it will never be, I wonder how life can be so cruel.' He paused again, as if trying to find his words, but instead of speaking, he simply shook his head and walked, slowly, painfully, to his seat where he sat down and buried his head in his hands, the sound of his anguished sobs bouncing off the stone walls of the church.

There was no rhyme or reason to it. No fairness in it. I tried to tell myself that Rose had just been spectacularly unlucky. I tried to comfort myself that on that day luck had, for once, in a kind of twisted turn of fate, been on my side. I needed to believe that – believe in chance and bad luck and not something more sinister. I had to believe the ghosts of my past weren't still chasing me.

I tried to tell myself life was trying to give me another chance – one that had been robbed from me five years before. It was fucked up. George Bailey got Clarence the angel to guide him to his second chance. I got Rose Grahame and her violent death.

I got the sobs of the mutli-coloured mourners. And I got the guilt I had craved.

It might have helped if I'd have found out Rose Grahame was a horrible person – although the way she sang to her baby and smiled her thank you to me as I let her go ahead of me out of the lift and into the cold street had already told me she was a decent sort.

I wondered, selfishly, if this had been my funeral, would I have garnered such a crowd? I doubted it. My parents would be there, I supposed. My brothers and their partners. My two nieces probably wouldn't. They were young. They wouldn't understand. A few cousins, a few work colleagues there because they had to be. Some nosy neighbours. Aunts and uncles. Friends – maybe, although many of them had fallen by the wayside. Maud may travel over for it from the US, but it would depend on her bank balance and the cost of the flights. They would be suitably sad but they'd have full lives to go back to – busy lives, the kind of life Rose Grahame seemed to have had. The kind of life that allows you to pick up the pieces after a tragedy and move on, even if at times it feels as if you are walking through mud. The kind of lives with fulfilling jobs and hectic social calendars and children and hobbies.

Not like my hermit-like existence.

Five years is a long time to live alone.

Of course, being at the funeral made me feel worse. I suppose I should have expected that. But I hadn't expected to feel jealous of her. Jealous that her death had had such an impact.

I crept from the pew, pushed past the crowds at the back of the church, past the gaggle of photographers from the local media waiting to catch an image of a family in breakdown, and walked as quickly as I could from the church grounds to my car, where I lit a cigarette, took my phone from my bag and logged into Facebook.

Social media had become my obsession since the day of the accident. Once I had got home, and I had crawled under my duvet and tried to sleep to block out the thoughts of what I had just seen – what I had just done – I found myself unable to let it go.

I didn't sleep that day. I got up, I made coffee and I switched on my laptop. Sure enough the local news websites were reporting the accident. They were reporting a fatality – believed to be a woman in her thirties who was with her baby at the time.

A hit and run.

A dark-coloured car.

The police were appealing for witnesses.

The family were yet to be informed.

The woman was 'named locally' as Rosie Grahame.

No, it was Rose Grahame. Not Rosie.

She was thirty-four.

She was a receptionist at a busy dental practice.

Scott's in Shipquay Street.

The child in the pram was her son – Jack, twenty months old.

She was married.

Believed to be the wife of local author, Cian Grahame, winner of the prestigious 2015 Simpson Literary Award for his third novel, *From Darkness Comes Light*.

The news updated. Facebook went into overdrive. People giving details. Offering condolences. Sharing rumours. Suggesting a fund be set up to pay for the funeral and support baby Jack, despite the fact that, by all accounts, Cian Grahame was successful and clearly not in any great need of financial support.

Pictures were shared. Rose Grahame – smiling, blonde, hair in one of those messy buns that actually take an age to get right. Sunglasses on her head. Kissing the pudgy cheek of an angelic-faced baby. A smiling husband beside her – tall, dark and handsome (of course). A bit stubbly but in a sexy way – not in a layabout-who-can't-be-bothered-to-shave way. He was grinning at his wife and their son.

It was all just an awful, awful tragedy.

Someone tagged Rose Grahame into their comment saying, 'Rose, I will miss you hun. Always smiling. Sleep well.' As if Rose Grahame was going to read it just because it was on Facebook. Does heaven have Wi-Fi?

Of course I clicked through to her profile. I wanted to know more about her – more than the snippets the news told me, more than the smile she gave me as I held the door to let her through, more than the gaunt stare she gave me as she lay dead on the ground, the colour literally draining from her.

I expected her profile to be a bit of a closed book. So many are – privacy settings set to Fort Knox levels. But Rose clearly didn't care about her privacy settings. Perhaps because her life was so gloriously happy that she wanted the whole world to know.

I found myself studying her timeline for hours – scanning through her photo albums. She never seemed to be without a smile. Or without friends to keep her company.

There she was, arms thrown around Cian on their wedding day. A simple flowing gown. A crown of roses. A beautiful outdoor affair. The whole thing looked as if it could be part of a brochure for hipster weddings.

There she was, showing off her expanding baby bump – her two hands touching in front of her tummy to make the shape of a heart. Or standing with a paint roller in one hand, the requisite dab of paint on her nose, as she painted the walls of the soon-to-be nursery.

There were nights out with friends, where she glowed and sparkled and all her friends glowed and sparkled too. Pictures of her smiling proudly with her husband as he held aloft his latest book.

And then, of course, the baby came along. Pictures of her, perhaps a little tired-looking but happy all the same, cradling a tiny newborn, announcing his birth and letting the world know he was 'the most perfect creature' she had ever set her eyes on.

Pictures of her bathing him, feeding him, playing with him, pushing him in his buggy, helping him mush his birthday cake with his chubby fists. Endless happy pictures. Endless posting of positive quotes about happiness and love and gratitude for her amazing husband and her beautiful son.

The outpouring was unreal – I hit refresh time and time again, the page jumping with new comments. From friends. From family. From colleagues, old school friends, cousins, acquaintances, second cousins three times removed.

And then, that night, at just after eleven – when I was considering switching off and trying to sleep once again, fuelled by sleeping tablets – a post popped up from Cian himself.

My darling Rose,

I can't believe I will never hold you again. That you will never walk through this door again. You were and always will be the love of my life. My everything. My muse. Thank you for the happy years and for your final act of bravery in saving our Jack. I am broken, my darling, but I will do my best to carry on, for you and for Jack.

I stared at it. Reread it until my eyes started to hurt, the letters began to blur. This declaration of love – saying what needed to be said so simply – made me wonder again how the gods had cocked it up so spectacularly.

Poor Cian, I thought. Poor Jack. Poor all those friends and family members and colleagues and second cousins twenty times removed. They were all plunged into the worst grief imaginable. I felt like a voyeur and yet, I couldn't bring myself to look away.

So that was why, then, even outside the church, fag in my hand, smoke filling up my Mini, I clicked onto Facebook and loaded Rose's page again. The messages continued. Posts directly on her timeline, or posts she had been tagged in.

'Can't believe we are laying this beautiful woman to rest today.'

'I will be wearing the brightest thing I can find to remember the brightest star in the sky.'

'Rose,' Cian wrote. *'Help me get through this, honey. I don't know how.'*

I looked to the chapel doors, to the pockets of people standing around. Heads bowed. Conversations whispered. A few sucking on cigarettes. I wondered how any of us got through anything? All the tragedies life throws at us. All the bumps in the road.

Although, perhaps that was a bad choice of words. A black sense of humour, maybe. I'd needed it these past few years. Although sometimes I wondered if I used it too much. If it made me appear cold to others.

Cian had changed his profile picture, I noticed. It was now a black and white image – Rose, head thrown back, mid laugh. Eyes bright. Laughter lines only adding to her beauty. She looked happy, vital, alive.

I glanced at the clock on my dashboard. Wondered if I should wait until the funeral cortège left the chapel to make their way on that final short journey to the City Cemetery as a mark of respect. I could probably even follow them. Keep a distance. Watch them lay her to rest. Perhaps that would give me some sort of closure

I took a long drag of my cigarette and looked back at my phone. Scrolled through Facebook one last time. A new notification caught my eye and I clicked on it. It was then that his face, his name, jumped out at me. Everything blurred. I was aware I wasn't breathing, had dropped my cigarette. I think it was only the thought of it setting the car on fire around me that jolted me to action. I reached down, grabbed it, opened my car door and threw the cigarette into the street; at the same time sucking in deep lungfuls of air. I could feel a cold sweat prickle on the back of my neck. It had been five years since I had last seen him. And now? When my heart is sick with the notion that he could finally be making good on the promise he made to get back at me, he appears back in my life.

A friend request from Ben Cullen.

In a panic I looked around me – as the mourners started to file out of the chapel. I wondered was he among them. Had he been watching me all this time? I turned the key in the ignition and sped off, drove to work mindlessly where I sat in the car park and tried to stop myself from shaking.

14

The urge to go home was strong. To go and hide under my duvet. I typed a quick email to my friend Maud. All I had to say was 'Ben Cullen has sent me a friend request'.

Maud would understand the rest.

Andrew – my line manager in the grim call centre I spent my days in – wouldn't understand though. He wouldn't get my panic or why I felt the need to run home to the safety of my dark flat with its triple locks and pulled curtains. As it was, he thought I was at a dentist appointment. He had made it clear the leave would be unpaid and it had already been an hour and a half since I'd left the office. I was surprised he hadn't called to check on me yet. If I were to call him to try and verbalise the fear that was literally eating me from the inside out, he not only wouldn't understand, he would erupt. I was skating on perilously thin ice with him as it was. My two days' absence after Rose's death had been the icing on the cake.

But my head hurt. I saw a couple of police officers in uniform as I drove and momentarily wondered whether to tell them Ben Cullen had sent me a friend request and I thought there might be a chance he was caught up in all this. Saying it in my head made me realise how implausible that would sound to an outsider; but not to me, I knew what he was capable of.

I had to get away from here. I wanted to go home but I needed my job. Maybe I would be safer at work anyway? Desolate as it was, we had good security measures. I made sure all the doors on my car were locked and I drove on, the friend request sitting unanswered on my phone.

Chapter Three

Rose

2007

Rose Maguire: is thinking this could be the start of something new! :)

I knew – the minute I saw him – that there was a connection there. It wasn't like a bolt of lightning or a burst of starlight, just a calmness that drew me to the dark and brooding figure sitting hunched over a table at the library, pen in hand, scribbling into a leather-bound notebook.

A Styrofoam coffee cup at his side, his face was set in fierce concentration and I knew – even as I stood there returning the books I had borrowed – that he was going to mean something to me. Maybe my brain was a little too turned with the romantic novels I had been reading, but it felt right. It just felt like it was meant to be. I couldn't help but look at him – wonder what had him scribbling so intently into that notebook. I clearly stared a little too long, or a little too hard, because when he looked up he caught me and stared straight back, his expression at first curious, serious even, then he smiled and it was as if I saw the real him.

The strong jaw, the twinkling eyes, the slightly unkempt hair that was just messy enough. If Disney drew a modern prince, one who hung about in libraries looking intense and wearing checked shirts, they would do well to model him on the man in front of me.

I should probably have looked away when he caught me staring. Ordinarily that's exactly what I would have done – but something about him made me keep staring. I didn't even blush. Not really – although I did feel a little flushed.

I tilted my head to the side, smiled back. Flirtatious, I suppose. As soon as the librarian had scanned the books I was borrowing, I walked over to him. I never expected to find any sort of connection here of all places. The Central Library – close to work. A functional building that lacked any charm. It had the air of a doctor's waiting room about it but as I approached him, and he stood up, I felt something in my core flip. I blushed then, of course, wondering if he could read my mind – see how my breath had quickened just a little at the sight of him.

'Leaving?' I asked him.

'My coffee's gone cold,' he said, gesturing to the cup on the table. 'I thought I'd nip out and get a fresh one. Want to join me? We could walk up to Java? They do great cappuccinos. You look like a cappuccino kind of a girl.'

'You're right, and I'd love to,' I said.

'Good.' He smiled before extending his hand to shake mine. 'I'm Cian.'

'Rose,' I replied.

It wasn't how I had thought my weekend would start. I had been planning on curling up on my sofa, throw over my knees, cup of tea in my hand and losing myself in the books I had borrowed. The last few weekends had been hectic – this one was for regrouping. Having time to myself.

It didn't work out that way. It started with two hours over

coffee where we talked about all sorts of everything and nothing. He told me he was a writer, working on his first novel. I blushed a little when I told him I worked in a dental surgery – nowhere near as glamorous or creative as his job, but he smiled and said people would always want good teeth.

I asked if I could read any of his work but he was shy, bowed his head. It wasn't ready to be seen by anyone else yet. He wanted it to be more polished, he said. I knew it would be good though – he oozed a brooding intensity that no doubt came across in his writing.

We left the coffee shop having exchanged phone numbers, and he sent me a text later that night asking if I wanted to meet him the following day – a picnic in St. Columb's Park, just across the river, he suggested. The weather was to be lovely and he always felt more inspired outdoors.

Giddy at the thought, I got up early and went to the Foyleside Shopping Centre to buy something that looked picnic casual but still a bit alluring. I showered, spent time making sure my hair was straightened to within an inch of its life, applied a 'no make-up make-up' look and made some pasta salad to take as my contribution along with a bottle of wine that had been chilling in my fridge.

The picnic was everything I hoped it would be. We walked through the wooded pathways of the park, down as far as the riverbank away from the noise of the play park. He took my hand. We chatted. We sat beneath the dappled shade of the trees and he read some of his favourite poems to me – and even though poetry had never, ever been my thing, I found myself completely entranced by him. The emotion he found in the words – the way he made the lines that had always baffled me before suddenly make sense. He didn't sneer when I asked a question – he answered.

He asked about me too – about my life. My work. My

18

friends. My family. The music I liked, the films I watched. He wasn't ever going to be a huge Nora Ephron fan, he said – but he could see the appeal. After a glass of wine and some food (he said my pasta salad was delicious), when the afternoon sun had made us both feel a little sleepy, we lay side by side on the blanket listening to the sounds of families playing close by and the chatter of teenagers, feeling liberated by the sunshine. He took my hand and told me he'd had the best afternoon he'd had in a long time. I looked at him – there was something there – an expression I couldn't read. I tried to find something to say, but before I could, he raised himself up on his elbow and leaned across, kissing me so tenderly I thought I might just float away.

I know it sounds sickening, but it felt so right. So right that he came back to my flat and we kissed some more, and talked, and laughed and drifted in and out of sleep in each other's arms until we couldn't actually resist a proper sleep any longer and he followed me into my bedroom. We slept curled around each other until morning.

It didn't feel awkward or odd when we woke up. It didn't even feel weird that we had spent the night in bed and hadn't, you know, had sex. Not that I didn't want to – but he said we should take our time. Enjoy the kissing stage, he said. The promise of it. It made me feel special. Cherished. Turned on.

We spent Sunday watching old movies – one of my choices and one of his. Well, I say watching old movies, but that's when most of the kissing took place. It was a wrench when he went home that night – and we had kept up our chatter through text messages, which turned into a phone call, that turned into a happy Facebook status just before I went to work. I knew I couldn't wait to see him again.

Chapter Four

Emily

My heart was in my mouth all the way back to my office – a stark, concrete building on the main road out of the city towards Donegal with tinted glass in the windows lest any of us peek out of the window and see the world in all its true colour and wonder. I wanted to get there and to immerse myself in the routine of my day-to-day life to the point where I couldn't think about everything else that was going. Rose, Ben, it was too much to take in.

I thought of how I had passed the last five years sitting in my cubicle, in front of my computer screen, tapping on my keyboard, lost in a routine that suited but didn't challenge me. It was all I could manage in the aftermath of him leaving. Somewhere I could sit and do my work, go home at five and be done with it until the following morning. It was boring. Soul destroying even. But it was safe.

I wondered about Rose Grahame. Had she enjoyed her work? Had it fulfilled her or had it simply been somewhere she hid away from life? I couldn't imagine she wanted to hide from anything. Colour marked her funeral, just as I imagine it marked her life.

'All good?' Andrew asked when I got into the office, before I had so much as hung my coat up.

'Yes. Yes, fine,' I lied. I missed Maud at that moment. Wished she was still here and I could drag her into the kitchen and weep on her shoulder and have her reassure me in the way only Maud could.

'You were gone a long time. I wondered, did you need a few fillings? Or an extraction? Or perhaps an entire new set of teeth chiselled out of enamel there and then by Capuchin Monks or similar?'

Andrew was younger than me by a good eight or nine years. While in his mid-twenties, he still looked as if he only needed to shave once a week and even then, only with a fairly blunt razor just to make him feel more manly. Short in stature and slight, he favoured slim-fit clothes, which far from flattering his petite physique made him look like a child playing at being a grown up.

'No. Nothing like that,' I said before breaking eye contact and walking across the room to my desk and hoped he wouldn't follow me. It had been hard enough trying to keep it together as it was without him being on my back.

My desk was in a particularly bleak spot, devoid of any access to natural light. Management had a strict clear desk policy, with no personalisation of our cubicles allowed. It was supposed to increase productivity, but instead it just made each workspace feel cold and clinical. Like we were battery hens. I plugged myself into my computer terminal, watched the beeping light on my keyboard tell me a caller was waiting and wondered how long they would keep me chatting.

Rose would be buried by now. Part of me wanted to go online and hunt through the pictures of the funeral. See more of her life. See if I could spot Ben among the mourners. A bigger part of me was terrified to look in case he was. And that friend request was still waiting. I felt a headache start to build behind my left eye, warning me that a migraine was on the way.

I was, admittedly, less patient than usual with the man on the other end of the line who seemed unable to understand my most basic of requests. He was muttering madly, in a panic about how he didn't know how to switch his router off, or even which piece of hardware his router was.

It was one of those times when I felt angry. Frustrated. Cross at the mundane nature of people's lives. How could they get flustered over broadband when a woman was dead? Killed. Wiped out.

People could carry on even though the police hadn't found her killer. When he was still out there. When he could be sending friend requests to ex-girlfriends on Facebook. Paranoid, I told myself. I was just being paranoid but as the man wittered on about what lights were and weren't flashing on his finally located router I couldn't stop thinking about Rose's killer.

I wondered if, as they ploughed into Rose, they had looked at the other people in the street? Had they seen me? Mouth agape? Eyes wide with fear and shock?

The man on the phone barked something into my ear which pulled me from my thoughts. I apologised and asked him to repeat himself.

'Oh you are still there then?' he said, scorn dripping from every word. 'I thought you'd gone for a nap, or maybe a holiday.'

'I'm terribly sorry, sir,' I repeated, trying to diffuse the situation. These calls were monitored and the last thing I needed was for this to end up in a training session at the end of the month. 'You have my full attention now – let's get this problem solved.'

Ten minutes later he was appeased and I was able to hang up the call and take a moment to rub my temples; to try and regain focus on what I was being paid to do.

Thirty seconds, that was all it would take to check online for pictures. Then I could settle myself and get back to work. Properly.

I picked up my phone, refreshed the internet app and happened upon a picture of the weeping relatives, their bright colours looking garish, standing at a graveside. Jack, thumb in mouth, being carried by an older woman wearing a bright pink coat who looked as though she was resisting the urge to hurl herself into the grave. Cian — ashen faced — was captured tossing a cream rose into the hole in the ground that now contained his wife. She was gone. It was done. But looking at the faces of the mourners, I realised it was just beginning for them.

★

I had put my phone away and answered another call when I saw Andrew walk over towards my soulless desk. He was trying his very best to look intense and managerial, but the unmistakable glint in his eyes implied he was about to impart news that made him feel important. He stood a little too close while he waited for me to finish the call I was on, and just as I was about to answer the next call waiting in the queue, he lifted the headphones from my ears and forced himself into my direct eyeline.

'A word?' he said, head tilted to the side.

'Any word or had you something particular in mind?' I said, a weak attempt at a joke.

As feared, it went right over his head and he looked at me as if I was a puzzle he couldn't figure out. A human Rubik's Cube. 'My office?' he said, an eyebrow raised. He led the way. A bad feeling washed over me. Nothing good ever, ever happened in Andrew's office. Still a part of me lived in hope he was going to break the company-wide tradition of demoralising and humiliating staff and offer me a pay rise or a promotion or both.

'Close the door,' he said as he took his seat behind his desk. He probably imagined he looked foreboding – but he didn't. He was too small, too fine a creature, too weedy to intimidate me. I wondered whether his mother still took his trousers up for him.

'Sit down,' he said, and I did, straightening my skirt and taking a deep breath. I looked at him.

'So the dentist?' he said.

I shrugged, unsure what he wanted me to say.

'You were there this morning?'

I nodded. 'I told you that, and I took unpaid leave.'

'Is your dentist a very Godly person?' he asked, and I was sure I could see the hint of a sneer.

'I can't say we've discussed theology,' I replied. Tone light. Not rattled.

'Well, it's just you seem to have been in church this morning, so I wondered was your dentist moonlighting as a priest? Confession and tooth removal a speciality?' A wave of dread shot right to the pit of my stomach.

I willed myself to think fast.

'Who? What? I don't know . . . what?' I stumbled, feeling the heat rise in my face as my cheeks blushed red.

He turned his computer screen towards me, and I saw my image frozen in pixels, creeping from the church ahead of the mourners. Looking shifty. Ducking out of view – but clearly not enough.

'I had to go to the funeral,' I stuttered, 'and I knew the company policy about compassionate leave being only for immediate family. I took unpaid leave. It doesn't really matter, does it?'

That was clearly the wrong thing to say.

'Of course it matters. We have targets to hit and you took time off on the premise of a medical issue and instead you were getting a nosy at the big funeral of the year. Did you even know her?'

'It's not like that,' I said. The blush in my cheeks was now so hot, I could almost hear the roar of the blood rushing to my face. 'I saw it. I saw the accident. I was a witness. I had to go. I had to get closure.'

The words were spilling out. My hands were shaking – maybe not enough for Andrew to see but I could feel them jittering as I tried to get enough air into my lungs between my short, sharp sentences. I willed the panic not to take hold.

I saw Andrew shake his head. Heard him sigh. I wanted to scream at him.

'You know we can't carry dead weight here, Emily. We've talked before about this. About your attendance. About your attitude to being here and being part of the team. You've had enough warnings. We can't keep giving you chances. And lying to management? That constitutes gross misconduct.'

I stared at him. 'But I had to go. Don't you understand?'

He shook his head again. I wanted to grab him and shake the rest of his weak, puny body along with his stupid head.

'And you never mentioned it before now? Really? You want me to believe that?' He snorted. A short, derisory laugh that made the room spin a little more. All sense of balance, of calm, was leaving me. 'Regardless, Emily, you know that it's not good enough. I have no choice but to dismiss you with immediate effect. You've had more chances than most. More chances than you deserve, if I'm being honest. I am very sorry it's come to this but really, you have no one to blame but yourself.'

He sat back in his seat, either oblivious to or unmoved by my growing distress. I tried to find the words to reply, but my

25

tongue felt heavy in my mouth. 'No one to blame but yourself' reverberated wildly around my head.

Blame.

It was all down to me. It was always all down to me. Isn't that what Ben had always said? That I brought things on myself? Then and now – it was a fault I couldn't escape.

I could hear a faint humming; he was talking again. Muttering about clearing out my desk and leaving immediately. HR would be in touch. He hoped I wouldn't make a scene.

'Don't make it worse for yourself,' he said, head tilted to the side. False compassion that made me want to cry more than any true compassion would have.

I felt my nails dig into my palms – the sharp, scratchy sensation at least making me feel grounded in the room that was becoming increasingly stifling. I willed myself to get up, to remember the breathing techniques I had learned in hospital. I willed my tongue to loosen – to tell him to go straight to hell. I willed myself to turn sharply on my mid-heeled court shoe and slam his office door behind me. But my legs were like jelly.

No one to blame but yourself.

I stood up, using the back of the chair for leverage. I was vaguely aware that Andrew was still talking but I couldn't hear. All I could hear was the humiliation pounding through my veins.

Sacked. At thirty-four. With rent to pay on a flat I didn't even like that much and credit card bills that were already a struggle.

No one to blame but myself.

And Rose, I suppose. For taking my place. For walking in front of me and getting hit by the fucking Toyota Avensis.

But I had let her, hadn't I? I had smiled at her beautiful curly-haired baby and, touched by her cooing and singing and

26

the baby's toothy grin, I had said: 'Mothers and children first' and let her walk through the door before me.

No one to blame but myself.

I could have stayed and talked to the police. Had some sort of proof to show Andrew I had been there. But I had bolted. Like I wanted to bolt now. Or faint. Or throw up. React in any of the ways one would normally react to a shock.

At least, I thought, as I shovelled the contents of my desk drawer into my handbag without making eye contact with anyone else in the office, the company's bleak clean desk policy meant I didn't have much to pack up. A Cup–a–Soup that was long out of date. A mug with our faded company logo on it. A strip of paracetamol. A strip of Buspirone (my anti-anxiety medication, rarely used at work but a safety net in case a panic attack crept in, as they were prone to do, with no warning). A couple of faded business cards. Forty-seven pence in loose change. Three paper clips, two salt sachets and a torn, half-empty pepper sachet, spilling its dusty brown contents in my drawer. A button from a long-forgotten clothing item. Two pens.

Not much of a life. I popped two Buspirone from the packet and threw them back with a mouthful of water. They would knock me a little silly – take the edge off. Probably shouldn't drive though. Wouldn't be safe. Wouldn't be right. And we all know how driving dangerously ends, don't we?

Might as well have a drink, I thought. End the day on a big fat high of having no one to blame but myself.

Chapter Five

I missed the smell of smoke in pubs. The comforting mix of stale smoke mixed with stale alcohol was a signal to the senses that they were about to be soothed. Now I had to buy my drink and stand outside, hopping from foot to foot, cradling my drink to me in a bid to keep warm while I sucked on my cigarette.

Vodka was the drink of the day. I hadn't had it in a while – but desperate times called for desperate measures. Lots of 35ml measures of impending oblivion.

Jim, the barman, had looked at me oddly when I walked in from the bright winter sunshine to the cosy gloominess of Jack's Bar, just a short walk from my flat on Northland Road.

'Early doors today?' he asked as I took a seat at the bar.

I looked at him quizzically.

'Is it not early to be knocking off work? Time off for good behaviour, eh? Teacher's pet?'

I couldn't help but snort at the irony of the words. 'Yes, something like that,' I said. 'Double vodka and a Diet Coke.' He raised his eyebrows but didn't speak, just lifted a glass and carried it to the optic where I stared as the numbing clear liquid poured out.

'The hard stuff, eh?' he asked, as he added ice and popped open a small bottle of Diet Coke. He didn't pour it. I imagined he knew as well as I did that the soft drink was really only for show. I would add a splash; enough to colour the vodka but not enough to dilute its potency.

'Hard to beat,' I said, raising my glass before tipping it back, allowing the sharp taste of the alcohol to warm my throat and sink to my stomach where it would settle the growing sense of unease.

'I thought you were going off the booze for a bit?' Jim asked, as I pushed the glass, now empty, towards him and gestured for a refill.

'I did,' I said. 'It's been a few weeks.' I knew as well as he did that it had been just over a week, but he didn't correct me.

'Are you sure you want another? It's still early and last time you were in you told me—'

'Never mind what I told you,' I said, making a conscious effort to keep my tone light when all I really wanted was for him to pour me another drink. 'Look, Jim. You can pour me another drink – and maybe even another after that – or I can take my business elsewhere. But if I'm honest, I like it here. It's quiet and most of the time you're not a pain in the ass.'

Jim shrugged and poured my drink. To try and make him feel a little better I added more than just a splash of my Diet Coke to the glass and nodded towards the beer garden, where I headed with my drink and my smokes to imbibe nicotine along with the alcohol.

I knew I shouldn't be drinking. Of course I did. Not least because of the double dose of anti-anxiety meds dissolved in my system. Ones that came with a big 'Do Not Consume Alcohol' warning on the front. But the alternative was not appealing. Go home to my flat in the half-light of the afternoon, work out just how many weeks' rent I could afford to pay before I was officially broke. Broke and homeless. With a mild drink problem, an addiction to prescription medication, in hiding from a man who wanted to cause me actual physical harm and nursing a very heavy dose of guilt about the death of Rose Grahame.

Standing shivering in the beer garden beside a plant pot festooned with cigarette butts and some fairy lights that no longer twinkled, I felt the first wave of negative feelings towards Rose and her perfect life. Had she not the sense she was born with? The sense to look both ways before crossing the road? She was pushing her baby in a pram for the love of God. If she had just looked up I wouldn't be tormented by the abnormal angle of her neck and her left leg when she fell. I would be able to escape that glassy-eyed stare. I wouldn't have felt compelled to go to the funeral and I wouldn't have had to lie to Andrew and I wouldn't now be unemployed and feeling slightly fuzzy headed as the last dregs of my vodka and Diet Coke slid down my throat.

I'd have one more – and then go home. I stubbed out my cigarette, left it teetering on the pile of butts on the plant pot – all playing a dystopian version of Buckaroo, and walked back into the bar. I pushed my glass in Jim's direction and he shook his head but poured another double measure anyway. 'I'll get you a toastie made. Some soakage,' he said, but I shook my head.

'I've dinner plans,' I lied. 'I'll be good,' I lied again.

He walked away, knew he was beat. I poured the remainder of my Diet Coke into my vodka glass and took out my phone, clicking back into Facebook. I stared at the dialogue box asking me 'What's on your mind?' – it had been just over five years since I had shared what was on my mind, but I couldn't bring myself to delete my account. I hadn't always been so reticent to share what I was thinking, of course. I used to share everything.

My life on view for whoever wanted to see it and even a few people who didn't. When things were better, of course. Or at least when I thought they were better. The fool that I was.

★

My keys clattered onto the floor as I kicked the pile of letters away from the door and stumbled into my flat, wondering who had moved the light switch a few inches to the left. I had been true to my word. I had left after my third drink (that it was a double wasn't important). Now though, stumbling towards the moving light switch and feeling my stomach – empty but for the alcohol – churn, I decided I'd had a little too much. I needed to sit down and try to stop the room from spinning. My head had started to hurt. I knew I needed a glass of water and a few painkillers, so I made my way to the kitchen and pulled out a packet of pills, taking two small yellow and green Tramadol capsules out and throwing them back with water from the tap. I didn't need painkillers this strong any more; they were given to me for backache a few months ago. I probably should have returned the remainder to the chemist, but I liked how they made me feel. Not only would they sort out my headache, they would knock me into the oblivion I desired – the kind of oblivion where, if I was lucky, I would dream of happy endings and nice things. An escape from my reality and of the face of Ben Cullen that haunted my notifications. Perhaps dreams of a sexy, stubbly husband called Cian, and a chubby cheeked baby called Jack and a life where I felt I had something to contribute to Facebook after all. A life worth mourning. Pinching the bridge of my nose, I kicked off my shoes and lay down on the sofa, pulling a blue chenille throw over me and drifting off into a hazy sleep.

I was woken with a start at 2.37am, my blurred eyes trying to focus on the shadows drifting across the room, cast by a car driving by. In my half asleep, slightly drunk, Tramadol–induced state, I was sure I saw her, standing, head still twisted at an unnatural angle, eyes glazed, blood dripping from her hands. But smiling – because life was perfect. Because even dead, it was still better than mine. My heart froze, I pulled the blanket over my head and concentrated on trying to steady my breathing, aware of the thumping of my heart in my chest, trying to chase away the ghosts of the sound of the car crunching into her, the noise and the screams of those around her. For the first time I heard my own scream join the mêlée. Had I screamed that day? I didn't know any more.

I woke again when it was just getting light and my phone was beeping incessantly. I glanced at the low battery warning, and spotted five missed calls and six text message notifications.

Rubbing my eyes and spreading the dregs of yesterday's mascara across my dry skin, I tried to focus on the screen. The missed calls were, all but one, from my friend Maud. The other was from Andrew; I gave my phone the finger at seeing his name. I scrolled down my messages. Five from Maud, panic increasing in each of them.

Ben Cullen? WTF?
Called work. You're not there? Kieran said you were let go. WTF happened?
Tried calling you. You're not answering.
Emily, call me. I'm really worried.
ANSWER YOUR PHONE.

The one from Andrew was a simple: *HR would like to see you on Monday morning. 10am.*

I swung my feet around and stood up, fighting the nausea in the pit of my stomach. I wandered to the bathroom, used the loo, splashed cold water on my face and pulled my hair back in a loose ponytail. I looked at my reflection in the mirror. I was a fetching shade of grey, dark circles under my eyes. I gulped water directly from the tap and brushed my teeth before going back to my bedroom and peeling off my clothes from the day before. I pulled on some tracksuit bottoms, a T-shirt and a pair of mismatched socks and walked through to my kitchen where I made toast (after cutting the slightly mouldy corner off the bread) and a mug of tea before walking back into my living room, sitting cross-legged on the sofa and calling Maud.

The phone rang twice before she answered, her voice thick with sleep. Remembering it was only 3am in New York – I immediately apologised for waking her.

'Jesus, Emily. I've been worried to death. Ben? And then you going off grid? And work? What the hell is going on?'

Maud could be confidently called my one true friend. And Andrew's predecessor at the call centre. She'd taken me under her wing when I started at CallSolutions. I liked to think she saw something fixable or loveable in me; but whatever the reason, she helped me find my feet again.

She kept me (just) on the right side of the company's many policies. The day, 17 months earlier, she announced she was moving to the States to head up the opening of a new call centre for our multinational company was the day my time with CallSolutions started to slide towards the inevitability that one day I would end up eating stale toast and wondering where it had all gone wrong.

'I went to Rose's funeral. Told Andrew I was going to a dental appointment. He fired me.'

I heard her sigh. 'Jesus, Emily. Was that wise? To go to her funeral? And to lie about it?'

Ignoring her question as to whether I should've gone to the

funeral, I told her I had lied to Andrew because he wouldn't understand why I needed to go. If Maud couldn't understand it, there was no way Andrew would.

Her sigh was heavier this time. Before I'd told Andrew, Maud had been the only person who knew I had seen the accident – she had told me to look into counselling, or at least talk to my GP if I felt my mood slipping or my anxiety growing. Actually, she had made me promise I would talk to my GP *and* look into counselling.

'He would have understood, if you'd told him. You know that. Anyone would have understood. You witnessed a major trauma,' she said, cutting through my thoughts.

I shook my head. 'I didn't want him to know. I don't want anyone to know. They'll make me go over it all again, or talk to the police . . .'

'And Ben, how does he come into all this?'

'He sent me a friend request, I told you that.'

'Did you accept it?' she asked.

'No, of course not,' I almost shouted, without letting her know it was still sitting ignored in my account.

'So just ignore him. Leave it at that. Nothing to worry about.' She sounded so sure that I wondered was I overreacting or simply going mad?

'But what if he wants back in my life?' I asked her, omitting the fact that I feared he already was and that he might be tied up in the whole Rose situation. I knew what she would say. She would rationalise it to nth degree – but little about Ben Cullen was ever rational. He was just one more big reason why I couldn't and wouldn't go to the police myself. They had been so firmly on his side before – willing to believe whatever he told them. Everyone believed Ben over me. Everyone. I couldn't go through being made to feel like a liar again.

'Do you want me to talk to Andrew?' Maud interrupted my thoughts. 'Perhaps I can persuade him to give you one last chance? Although, he has given you enough chances before.' Her tone was soft, but I still felt the judgement in her words. Yes, he had given me chances but then any other decent boss – like Maud had been – wouldn't have made such a big issue over such little infractions anyway.

'God no. No, it'll be fine. I'll get another job. It will work out. It was probably about time for a change anyway. It's not been the same since you left,' I said with more confidence than I felt.

'Hmmm,' Maud replied. 'Well maybe this is the kick up the bum you need? And I say that with love in my heart. You can do so much with your life, Emily. You need to go out there and grab it by the balls. Maybe you were too comfortable in CallSolutions. It didn't challenge you. It was easy – which is what you needed at the time, but comfortable isn't rewarding, is it?'

I stifled a laugh. I was never comfortable in CallSolutions – not really comfortable. I found most days unbearably dull and I lived with the constant feeling of being the odd one out. The co-worker who was never invited for Friday drinks, or Saturday nights out and who wasn't even invited to be part of the Lottery Syndicate. But Maud was right – it didn't challenge me in any way. It had been a safe place when I needed to feel safe. Now, even though I still needed medication to switch my mind off at night and help me sleep, I needed more than safe.

'What could I do?' I asked.

I heard Maud yawn. 'I don't know, honey. But you could try your hand at anything. Get online – see what's on offer.' Then she stifled a laugh. 'Oh I'm going to hell for saying this, but I'm pretty sure there's a post for a dentist's receptionist that's just been made available?'

I laughed back, said my goodbyes, told Maud I was sorry for waking her and for worrying her.

'Don't apologise, Emily. And most of all try not to worry about Ben. It was a long time ago. Everything got a bit out of hand back then. Maybe he just wants to say sorry? Now, try to keep calm and carry on, as the saying goes. You've got this. This is your new start.'

I ended the call and sat on the sofa, the tea going cold at my feet, and wondered if this was all some strange karmic intervention. Maybe I was meant to see Rose die so that I could move on to a job where I would be happy and fulfilled, and where everyone would be lovely and friendly and supportive? Maybe Maud was right – she always could talk me down. Ben may just, finally, be saying sorry. That this apology came at the same time as Rose's death was more than likely just a twisted coincidence. I chided myself for being so paranoid. Thought about my options.

There really wasn't anything to stop me from applying for Rose's job, was there? In fact, given that Derry ranked among the top three unemployment blackspots in the UK, it was probably wise that I did. I had experience in customer care. I had, years ago, gained all my admin qualifications. I could answer phones with cheeriness – even when people were being complete pains in the ass. I could do it. I knew I could.

And even if contemplating taking over a dead woman's life – or a facet of it – was a tad morbid, it wasn't as if she had use for it any more.

Chapter Six

Scott's Dental Practice operated out of shiny bright offices on Shipquay Street, one of the city's main thoroughfares.

The old Georgian façade had been updated – it was now glass fronted and everything inside was decorated in soft white tones, from the comfy sofas to the reception desk and the calla lilies in their clear glass vases on every table. With light marble floors and soft music piped through the room, it felt more like a hotel lobby than a dentist's waiting room. Except, that is, for the unmistakable smell of dentists – a kind of minty disinfectant smell mixed with sheer fear.

I'd had my hair done that morning. Asked the hairdresser to slip a few blonde highlights into my otherwise mousy brown hair. I had spent money I could ill afford on a nice suit – a pencil skirt, blazer and a soft silk blouse – which I wore with a classic pair of nude patent heels. I had taken extra time applying my make-up. I had seen enough pictures of Rose Grahame and her colleagues to see that they were all the well-groomed type. Contoured, plucked and preened – and of course with glistening white smiles – they looked as if they spent their days in the boutiques of Milan rather than in a busy dental surgery, answering phones, making appointments and staring down the throats of countless patients.

If I was to fit in – and I wanted to fit in – I had to look the part. I had to be Rose, mark II. And I wanted to be Rose, mark II. Although it had been three weeks since her funeral, I had not yet beaten my addiction to her Facebook page. People hadn't stopped posting on it – even though she had been laid to rest and the news columns had largely moved on. Except for the occasional appeal for information about the car's driver, Rose Grahame's tragic demise had become yesterday's news. Except to those who loved her. People still shared pictures. They still expressed their shock. They still wrote about how they missed her.

Cian posted almost every day – pictures, love quotes, messages that would take tears from a stone. Sometimes he sounded so utterly lost that I found myself wondering if anyone was there just to give him a hug and tell him that it was going to be okay. Sometimes he sounded angry – not at Rose of course – but at the injustice of the situation. At other times there was an underlying fatigue behind his words, as if he was tired of waking up every morning and realising, once again, that she was gone and not coming back.

I read every word. Facebook had become my window on the outside world – a world I was starting to feel like I could become a part of again. Ben's Facebook request still sat in my inbox but it didn't scare me the way it had. I'd heard nothing more from him and reassured myself that all reports still had him living in England. I reminded myself what my counsellor had said to me over and over – to deal with the facts and not catastrophise every situation.

So I focused on what I knew. I lost myself in what decent men were like. Men like Cian, who wasn't afraid to share his vulnerability and grief. His posts garnered him a host of responses, 'likes' and words of comfort. I hoped he listened to them and I hoped they helped. I wondered how the girls at Scott's Dental Practice felt, as I was waiting for my job interview. Were they too still wading through the metaphorical mud of each day, trying to make sense of their grief? Certainly, the bright (dazzling, definitely paid for) smiles on the faces of the two ladies at reception would con a person into thinking no sadness had ever visited them in their lives.

But it was when I was brought through to a small staff kitchen and offered a cup of coffee while I waited for Owen Scott that I saw evidence of a workplace in mourning. On a small table by another white wall sat a framed picture of Rose, a candle lit in front of it along with a small posy of flowers. The receptionist who had let me through the kitchen must have spotted that I was gawping at the picture.

'That's Rose,' she said. 'She died a few weeks back. She left very big shoes to fill.'

The receptionist sniffed slightly. I put her in her mid-forties; her auburn hair was swept back in a glossy ponytail, make-up perfect, dressed in her white tunic and trousers, which helped show off her perfectly applied fake tan. I could see her eyes filling. I tried to think of something to say but I was caught in the moment of looking at the picture of Rose, here in her workplace where her presence and her absence could be keenly felt.

'I read about that,' I stuttered. 'It was awful.' I decided not to tell her I had actually witnessed the moment the life had been knocked right out of her on the cold tarmac.

I watched a tear slide down her cheek, leaving a trail through her foundation. She reached in her pocket for a tissue and dabbed her eyes with it. 'I'm so sorry, I'm giving you a really bad impression. We knew today would be tough – having people in interviewing for her post. We wanted to wait a bit longer but we're busy and we can't afford any downtime. You must think I'm an awful bitch – all that big shoes to fill stuff.'

I shook my head. I didn't think she was a bitch. I knew Rose Grahame wasn't far from sainthood.

'Don't worry,' I said, rubbing her arm. 'It must be very hard.'

The woman nodded. 'I'm Donna,' she said. 'Sorry, I haven't even introduced myself. Thanks for your understanding.'

My mind whirled. Donna. Probably Donna O'Connor, who posted on Rose's Facebook to say that no day would ever be the same without her smile. I didn't have a visual to go by – as almost all of Rose's friends had since changed their profile picture to one of their deceased pal in some bizarre act of solidarity.

'Were you very close?' I asked.

Donna laughed, then sniffed back more tears. 'We were the closest. I called her my work wife. She was the person I could always go to when I had a tough day, or was tired, or the kids had kept me up all night and I was on my last nerve.'

'It must be so hard,' I soothed, watching this perfectly put together woman unravel in front of me. 'I can't imagine,' I lied, because I had clearly spent much of the last three weeks imagining.

'Thank you,' she muttered, taking a long, shuddering breath to settle herself. 'You don't think things like this actually happen. You hear of it, but you don't think it will happen to someone you know. It's just wrong. Everything about it is wrong.'

Did it make me a bad person that as I watched this woman deal with her grief in front of me, my primary thought was that here was a woman who could use a friend and I could be that friend to her? I could walk in here and work with someone who had already confided in me, who I had seen at her most vulnerable, and we could bond. Maybe *I* could be her new work wife? Maybe she would come to me when she'd had a tough day? Maybe we could go for drinks after work (I'd be good, I promise!) and take selfies to fill my poor, neglected Facebook page with? A bubble of excitement started to fizz in the pit of my stomach. I pushed it down. I wasn't there yet. I had to impress the man who made the decisions.

★

Owen Scott was not a man I recognised from any of the group pictures on Rose's Facebook. He was the kind of handsome that creeps up on you. At first glance, I saw this slightly greying, craggy-faced man, with a dimpled chin and a mild look of irritation on his face. He looked uncomfortable as he took a seat behind a messy desk in what must have been the practice's admin office. He swore quietly under his breath as he rifled through some paperwork to find just what he was looking for, and my confidence from just five minutes before started to fade.

I clenched my fists at my side, rubbing my fingers across my palm to fight off the clammy sensation I was feeling. I tried to steady my breathing. Reminded myself that it was okay. I could do this.

I looked at the top of his head, the sprinkles of salt and pepper colour through his dark locks, which really could have done with a trim. Watched him run his hands (no wedding ring) through his hair before he sat upright and looked at me, taking a deep breath.

'I should have been more prepared,' he said. 'Things have been a bit difficult here lately.' He looked tired and I nodded.

'I spoke to Donna. She told me about Rose. I'm very sorry for your troubles.'

With sad, grey eyes he nodded. 'Rose kept things running fairly smoothly here – I'm afraid we've all kind of let things go a bit since . . . well, since.'

'That's understandable,' I said. 'It must have been a great shock.'

He nodded again, but didn't answer. He didn't need to. The shock was written all over his face.

He took another deep breath, cleared his throat and pinched the bridge of his nose.

'Now, Emily D'Arcy?' he began.

I nodded.

'Obviously I've looked at your CV. It's been a while since you worked directly with the general public, but your qualifications seem to be in order. This is a very busy practice, we rely on people who can work well, and under pressure at times. We value good organisational skills – how can you sell yourself to us?'

I had rehearsed my answer carefully. 'I'm hard working and diligent. Yes, the last few years have been spent helping people remotely, but I believe if you can deal with sometimes irate callers, while timed and on script, you can deal with almost anything. I also like to think my age is an asset in circumstances such as these. I bring a certain maturity and appreciation of what being a good team player means with me.'

He nodded, looked down at the sheet in front of him and back up at me. He sighed, and I clenched and released my hands by my side to ease the tension creeping through my body.

'And your last job? Why did you leave?'

I tried to keep my face non-expressive. Now was not the time for an exaggerated eye roll or badly timed grimace. 'I craved working directly with the public again. Doing something to help people. I found CallSolutions wasn't really offering me a challenge anymore. I decided to take a leap of faith. I mean, you never really know what's ahead of you, do you? And I thought I could stay there and continue to feel uninspired and demotivated or I could push myself into making a change by making a big gesture and hoping it paid off. So I quit – and I took a chance because sometimes in life, you just have to take chances.'

I knew I was being horribly, terribly manipulative. I had anticipated this question because I'm not totally stupid, and I had decided to play on the recent tragedy in Owen Scott's life, which may just have focused his mind on the whole 'life is too short' thing. I was playing dirty, but my intentions were from a good place.

It was almost imperceptible but I saw something in Owen's eyes after my answer. Something that made his features soften, his face look less worn, his handsomeness creep up on me a bit more.

'Look,' I said, 'I know this must be a very difficult time for everyone here and it can't be easy having someone come in to take over a job that was previously held by someone you all clearly held in such very high esteem. I can't imagine how you are all feeling right now – but if you give me a chance, I promise you won't regret it.'

I was surprised to find I actually meant what I was saying. Even more surprised to feel a lump form in my throat and tears spring to my eyes. I hadn't cried since Rose Grahame died. I didn't think I had a right – even though what I had seen had been traumatic and awful and sometimes when I woke in the night I could still see her eyes staring right at me.

But there, sitting across from Owen – noting that small, tiny change in his demeanour – the softness in his gaze, the realisation that I really, really did want and need to change my life hit me. That, far from this being just a speech I was giving to earn me a job where Rose had been happy, I realised this was a place I could be happy. I willed the tears to stay where they were. I took a slow breath in, and then, shuddering just lightly, I exhaled.

Owen was looking at me. I wasn't actually sure if he had spoken after my emotional outburst or if he was, like me, wondering what on earth to say next.

'I'm sorry,' I muttered, reaching for my bag.

'For what?' he said, looking genuinely baffled.

'For getting a little emotional,' I lied. 'It was unprofessional of me.'

But what I really wanted to say was that I was sorry that it was me, and not Rose, who was sat in front of him. That I was sorry she, and not me, had died.

'We're all a little emotional around here these days,' he said softly, a small, comforting smile playing on his lips. 'We get the whole life is short thing. And we get that some people need second chances.'

★

Second Chances. I almost wrote a blog called that. A secret blog that I wanted to start when it all went wrong. It would be private, anonymous. It would be a therapy of sorts. No one would need to know about it. Not even Maud. Maud would have thought it was a spectacularly bad idea. It would have made her worry. I didn't want to worry her anymore.

That's maybe why I decided against it, in the end. That and the fear that things always get out. We share too much, you know. All of us. Even those of us who swear we don't. We let it out in our behaviour. What we like. What we don't. The pages we follow. The clothes we wear in our pictures. Our inspirational quotes. Our lack of inspirational quotes. The music we share. The things we write when we're tired. Or emotional. Or drunk.

The life we let people see. The life we let ourselves believe. It's strange how we can convince ourselves our Facebook life is our actual life – because we want it so desperately to be. I did anyway.

I found my Facebook life, where things were good and glossed over, very difficult to let go of when it all ended because I knew people – who I had perhaps done my best to make jealous – would enjoy some sort of Schadenfreude when it all went tits up.

That expression flashed through my brain again. *No one to blame but myself.*

I had been too open. Believed too much in sharing. Believed the world to be a good place. Believed people had the same motives as I had. I had believed in the power of love. I had believed I could make him love me as much as I loved him. That I could change him. No, not change – fix. Heal. Heal him with love.

I tolerated so much because I believed, in my heart and in my soul, that Ben Cullen was a good person. A damaged soul. A bit battered, but I could soften his rough edges. I could love him into being the person I knew he was beneath his thorny, gruff exterior.

Beneath the outburst – the angry ranting, the occasional hand to my left cheek, the pinching of skin, twisting it so it turned white, blanched of blood, before his grip loosened and the purple of a bruise started. Upper arms. Upper thighs. Hidden bruises from a misunderstood man. He was hurting too; I was sure of it. Even when his anger shifted gear – when he became lazy about making sure the bruises could be hidden so easily, or when his tongue loosened a little too much in company. Not that we kept much company. We enjoyed 'another cosy night in together' too much – well, according to my Facebook posts we did.

But I loved him. I did. I adored him. I wanted so badly to make it better for him, for both of us. I believed with all my heart that I could.

Then I got a message on Facebook from someone I didn't

know. Someone who had a picture of the man I so smugly, desperately, passionately, soulmate-ingly loved with his tongue down another woman's throat and his hand up her skirt. If there was any doubt it was him, the second picture, one which showed his face twisted in orgasmic ecstasy as the object of his affections knelt in front of him, did away with all of that.

I knew the shirt he was wearing. I had bought it for him for Christmas. The last Christmas we were together. The first Christmas we had been an engaged couple.

He had betrayed me. My soulmate. The man who I had tried to help. Who I had let take his rage out on me in the hope that one day he would be spent of it all. But he had betrayed and humiliated me – although I knew the worst of the humiliation was still to come when the news spread. When people started talking. Leaving 'supportive' messages on my Facebook page. Inspirational quotes. Songs. When I unpublished the dream wedding Pinterest board and the beautifully filtered Instagram pictures of us walking along the beach. When I realised, or accepted, what a lie it had all been.

When I knew that it had been my fault for wanting it as much as I did. For letting him do to me what he did. Because I thought we could be happy. I had no one to blame but myself. Those words were so true.

And of course, I'd love to say those moments – that night and the days that followed when I dismantled my real life, along with my virtual existence – were the lowest I sank. But they weren't, of course.

The worst would come later.

Chapter Seven

I was shocked and surprised to find out I was being offered the job at the dentist's. Okay it was a much lower salary than I had been paid in the call centre (and that had been a shockingly low salary to start with) but it did offer me the new start I had been longing for.

I sent a quick email to Maud to thank her for both the suggestion and the reference. And for persuading Andrew to give me a reference that probably led him to spending a good hour in Confession for all the lies he told. Not that they were really lies – I was a good worker. Or I could be.

Maud had been mildly horrified when I told her I'd put her name down as a referee.

'I was only joking when I said you should apply for the job,' she'd said, her voice solemn.

'Maybe you were, but you had a point. There's a job there and I need a job. Why wouldn't I throw my hat in the ring?'

She had paused, a soft humming coming over the phone line. 'Do you not think it a bit odd?' she asked. 'I mean, you saw that woman die. And now you're applying for a job in her old workplace? Her job?'

'Hmm,' I shrugged. 'Maybe if I had known her. But I didn't. I mean, yes I saw what happened and it was horrible but it shouldn't hold me back. This could be a real chance for me and I need one now that Andrew has turfed me out. It's not like this place is overflowing with jobs either, is it? Beggars can't be choosers.'

So I persuaded Maud to not only give me a reference but also to speak to Andrew and ask him to back her up. I knew it was cheeky, but I also knew Maud had pull. I had long suspected Andrew had a crush on her and would do anything she asked.

I smiled as I tapped out the email to her on my laptop. 'This is going to be a new beginning,' I told her. 'I know I haven't always got it right in the past but I can get it right now. You have to meet these people, Maud. You would really like them. They're so genuine. I think I will really fit in there.'

I was still smiling when I hit send, and when I got up and started to declutter and clean the flat. This would be a new start and I would put myself in the best place possible to make the most of it. I threw open the curtains for the first time in weeks and whizzed round, vacuuming everywhere, even under the sofa and along the skirting boards. I stripped my bed, put the sheets in a boil wash and tried not to think about the last time I had changed them. I dusted. I bleached. I swept the pile of magazines and junk mail from the coffee table and put them in a pile by the door for recycling.

I cleaned out my cupboards and my fridge. I threw out a lot of food that was past its sell by date, and anything with mould went straight in the bin. Then I grabbed my shopping bags and took myself to the M&S Food Hall where I put a decent shop of fruit and veg and low-fat meals on my credit card. And bottled water. I bought a lot of bottled water. It seemed like the thing to do.

The old me was just that: old, in the past, and gone. This would be the new me – a better version than any previous model. Lessons learned, rock bottom hit, and I had pushed myself away from it again, swimming upwards towards fresh air. The last few weeks – the Ben Blip as I would call it – would be just that. A blip. I showered when I got home, then made myself a dinner of low-fat bolognaise served with butternut squash noodles and poured myself a long glass of mineral water. Then I sat on my freshly plumped and vacuumed sofa, pulled my laptop onto my knee and logged into my Facebook account.

I stared at my long-neglected wall – the account I'd only kept open so I could keep an eye on everyone else. That evening though, I updated my status, picking a quote about life being a big adventure and being grateful for the journey. I clicked into my notifications and finally rejected Ben's friend request once and for all.

Then I clicked onto Rose's profile. There was another message from Cian – and I couldn't resist reading.

Rose,

It's been just over a month since you left me. Since you left us. I know they say time heals, and that no time at all has really passed, but at the moment each day just gets harder.

Jack looks for you. His eyes search you out when he wakes. He calls out 'Mama' – and I know when it's me that peeks over the cot at him he is disappointed each and every day. Every day that disappointment kills another little piece of me. He can't understand where you've gone. How can I expect him to understand when I can't either?

I don't want this to be true. I have begged and pleaded with God to bring you back – I know, it's stupid of me. You know I never even believed in God anyway. But if I thought there

was a chance . . . Rose, I'd do anything. I'd promise him anything.
Everything I have. All the success. All the awards. Everything.
I'd give myself to have you here.

Then again, what kind of God would take you away from
me? Take you away from Jack? What kind of a God would
leave a child without a mother? No kind of God I would want
to know or believe in. That's not a God of kindness – there is
no kindness, no 'bigger picture', no 'plan' in you leaving us.

My arms feel so empty – but so heavy, all at the same time.
They ache for you. They don't understand why you aren't there.
They are without purpose. I am without purpose.

If I had known our time together would be so short, I would
have tried harder. I would have been better. I would have protected
you more. I would never have let you out of my sight. Not even
for five minutes. I'd have fought off anyone who tried to take
you away. Even a god. I'd have fought, and I'd have kept you
safe.

I need to believe you are out there, my one and only. I need
to believe my arms will hold you again.

Always and forever,
Cian

I wiped away a tear, looked at his profile picture. Still the
smiling image of his late wife. I contemplated, very briefly,
sending him a message. Telling him she was still out there. I
believe that. That people don't really leave. Their echoes remain.
Someone as bright and vivacious as Rose – that energy doesn't
just, can't just, disappear. It has to go somewhere.

I wanted to tell him to stay strong – for that beautiful blue-
eyed baby who smiled so brightly at his mother as she sang
to him. The baby who screamed as she pushed his buggy out
of the way of the oncoming car, throwing herself in its path
instead.

But I didn't. I closed my laptop and reached into my bag for one of my anti-anxiety tablets. They would help me sleep and prepare myself for my new beginning. Hopefully they would even stop Rose from slipping into my dreams again — her face pale, her eyes now cloudy and grey.

★

My uniform fitted nicely. I found the conformity of it — the sense of belonging that came with it — comforting. Teamed with a pair of white soft leather ballet shoes and a silver name badge, I looked good. Crisp. Fresh. Professional. I still hadn't contoured my make-up or flicked my eyeliner, but I had made more of an effort than usual.

I looked good, and more than that, I felt good. Both Donna and Owen greeted me when I arrived. Their smiles seemed warm, their welcome genuine. They introduced me to the other staff, whose names I would remember eventually. Although, to be fair, I felt like I knew some of them from their Facebook profiles already. Donna led me through to the staff canteen, showed me where everything was — the teabags, the coffee, the ladies' loos. Then she led me to a small back room that was lined with lockers. 'This is yours,' she said, pointing to one right in the middle of the top row. All the others looked as if they were in use. I wondered for a second whether they were giving me Rose's locker. I wondered whether to ask, but decided against it. Instead, I pushed my bag into the back of it and closed it, taking out the key and slipping it into my pocket.

'Owen doesn't like us having our phones while we're working, but it's fair game at break and lunch. Although, to be honest, we tend to spend more time gabbing than tweeting or Facebooking,' Donna said.

'Do you all eat lunch together then?'

Donna nodded. 'Well, sort of. I mean, we have staggered

lunches because we can't all just disappear for an hour – but we do tend to have a good natter. We ring a sandwich order to the deli down the street every day at 11. You're not obliged to join us, but they are lovely sandwiches. They do paninis, wraps, all that sort of thing. And the most delicious salads and soups.'

'You've me sold,' I smiled, imagining girly gossips over lovely food in that cosy kitchen, where a framed picture of Rose was now hung on the wall, watching over us all.

'You'll shadow Tori for today,' said Donna. 'She's been on reception for a year – was Rose's deputy. She'll show you how everything works. We'll get you a bit of time in the surgeries too, sometimes we have to pull people in from reception to help. Nothing on the squeamish side, but note taking, making sure the records are updated properly. Best to get used to working with the sound of the drill. But Tori will keep you right, show you the system out front. Explain our policies with emergency appointments, missed appointments, and regular bookings.'

She smiled the whole time she talked so it was impossible to feel overwhelmed. It all sounded doable – even working to the sound of the drill.

'That all sounds good,' I said, beaming without having to force it.

Owen was equally welcoming. He smiled and shook my hand, welcomed me to the 'madhouse', made sure I had all the logins I needed for reception, and showed me the filing system in the admin office.

'It's your first day. Everyone gets a get-out-of-jail-free card on their first day. So just take it easy. Don't worry about things. Follow Tori's lead. Don't be afraid to ask questions, and as long as we don't find you sucking on the nitrous oxide between appointments you'll do great.'

He laughed and I laughed back and threw myself into my new work. I felt so light – so inspired.

Donna made sure the pair of us ate lunch together, recommending a BLT from the deli, which she told me had an extra zing thanks to a gorgeous tomato chutney they made in store. We sat at the small table, steaming cups of coffee in front of us, and she told me I had done well. 'I'm sure you will fit right in. Owen knows how to pick good staff, you know.' She smiled then paused, glancing up at the picture on the wall.

'Is this awkward for you all?' I asked softly. 'Someone being here who isn't Rose.'

She looked down at her sandwich, put it down and sipped from her cup.

'Not awkward as such. Strange maybe. I never thought we wouldn't have her here. Even when she was on maternity leave with Jack she would call in all the time. She couldn't stay away. She'd pop in for a five-minute chat and end up offering to sort out some charts for Owen, or help out with a nervous patient. She had a way of calming them. All of us got used to nursing Jack while she did her bit, not that we complained. That baby is a dote.'

Her smile dropped at the mention of his name. I suppose she was imagining him as a poor motherless child – the baby that couldn't understand where his mother had gone according to Cian. I reached over and rubbed her hand.

'I can't imagine . . .' I said.

'She loved it here too. Said we were her family. You know, she didn't have to work – especially after Cian's books became so successful. He wanted her to stay at home with Jack but she said we were all her family too, and while she loved him, she loved us as well. I used to tell her I'd give anything to have a husband who begged me to stay at home – provided for us . . .' Her eyes filled and I gave her hand an extra squeeze. She sniffed and looked up, roughly rubbing her eyes, her perfect eyeliner smudging. 'Yes, but we have to move on, don't we? And God, here you are putting in a great first morning. We don't want you to think you have to try and fill her shoes. You're your own person and we're happy to have you here.'

'I understand that it's tough. What happened to her . . . The shock of it must have been fierce.'

'It was,' she said, putting her coffee cup down and rewrapping her half-eaten lunch. She stood up. 'It still is. Look, if you'll excuse me, I need to go and check my phone – make sure the kids' school hasn't been on to me. There's always one of them forgetting their PE gear or recorder or some other such disaster. I do my best to keep on top of them but, well, I'm only one woman, and not Wonder Woman.' She offered me a smile but it didn't seem to reach all the way to her eyes. As she left the room she glanced again in the direction of the picture on the wall.

'I'm my own person. I'm here on my own merits. I am doing a good job,' I whispered to myself as I forced the last bites of the sandwich down – the zesty tomato chutney now tasting a little bitter.

As I balled up the wrapping from my sandwich, Donna came back in, and took a deep breath. 'Look, see everything here, with Rose, with it all. It's just . . . well, it's complicated, and it's still raw.'

'Complicated?' I asked, raising an eyebrow.

She looked to the door, and back to me. 'Look, it's . . . maybe complicated is the wrong word. There's a lot to try and make sense of is all. It gets on top of me sometimes.'

I would have asked her more, but just as I opened my mouth one of the other girls walked into the kitchen and started asking us about our day. The moment was gone, but the words would stay with me.

That night, changed into my lounge wear, my make-up removed with cleansers and toners and not my usual swipe of a baby wipe, I smiled at a friend request from Donna on my Facebook page, and when Owen sent a quick text to say he hoped my first day hadn't been too off-putting.

I typed a quick reply, put my phone down and sat back and thought of everything that had happened over the last few years. After Ben. My life was divided that way; before Ben and after Ben. The actual 'with Ben' stage didn't even seem to matter so much anymore. It had been a lie anyway.

Was this, this new era at Scott's, a new beginning? I didn't know. I wanted a new beginning. A new start. Friends. A lover maybe. A life.

All the things I had fought in vain for over the last few years. The years that had followed that most public fall from grace. I had been broken. In pieces. Pieces that no matter how patiently, how delicately, I tried to fit them back together, could never be the same as they were before they were broken in the first place.

Sharp edges jutted out. Others, dulled by thick globs of glue – ugly, deformed, misshapen. All the pieces were still there. But they weren't the same. I was not the same. How could I have been? The whole had become both more and less than the sum of all its parts.

Maybe what I had been trying to do these last few years was to break myself again in a stupid attempt to make this break cleaner, hoping the fix would be neater this time. But it just made it worse. The gaps started to widen. So I stuffed the gaps with whatever I could find. First drink, then pills. They made the broken edges softer. They made it more bearable.

Except they also made it worse. They facilitated me making poor decisions. Voicing my hurt to him. To show Ben my anger, and not realise that the truth can often be distorted. He told his side of the story – his lies – to anyone who would listen and they believed him because they saw the drunk I was quickly becoming. Believed I was unstable.

I started to spend each and every minute of darkness in a ball of anxiety, sure that it would never get light again. You can't take these things for granted. When you get complacent things go wrong.

I had thought about suicide. Especially at night when the very act of existing hurt. When even banging my head against the wall didn't silence them. When I missed him so badly that all I could think of was how little effort it would take to make it all stop.

To break myself so badly that no one – not even all the king's horses and all the king's men – could put me back together again.

I even planned it. It was the awful winter of 2010. The snow didn't seem to stop. The headlines were filled with record low temperatures. The River Foyle froze, Europe's fastest-flowing river, now creaking, slow, thick with the effort of trying to break through the ice.

I planned to go the beach. I would wash down some pills with vodka, walk down to the shore front, sit crossed-legged on the sand, and wait for the cold to feel too warm. Wait for the vodka and the pills to lull me to sleep, or to a place where I didn't hurt so much.

Maud thinks I mustn't have really wanted to do it. She thinks it was all a cry for help. Why else would I have sent Ben an email telling him that it was my turn to leave him? That I couldn't live without him.

Maud needed to think it was just a cry for help, if you ask me. Because it was too hard to think it was anything but. And my parents? I don't think they have ever forgiven me. I let them down. How could I have done that to them? As if I had done it just to spite them. Our relationship has never recovered. I have never recovered.

Chapter Eight

2007

Rose

Rose Maguire: is in a relationship with Cian Grahame

There's a freckle about two inches under my left breast that Cian loves. I'm not sure I even paid attention to it before he told me how cute he thought it was. Before he circled his finger around it as we lay in bed together before leaning across to kiss it, so tenderly that I could only hold my breath.

'Even your imperfections make you more perfect,' he had whispered, and my heart had soared. I was falling in love with him. Properly in love. Not just lust, or desire or those feelings that aren't real that just rush in at the start of something to make people obsessed with each other. This was something more. Love that I'd read about, where you feel invincible; as if you have met the other half of yourself that you didn't quite know was missing.

I knew that I ached when we weren't together – although he sent me flowers to work, called me at lunchtime, sent romantic text messages telling me he couldn't wait to be with me again. When I went home he would come and make me dinner – and he finally let me start reading what he had been working on.

It was so different to what I normally read – but it was good. *He* was good. He had talent to burn. I wanted to tell everyone about him – about his writing – but God, he was so shy about it. So secretive. It had to be just right he said. I felt so privileged that he let me read it.

But more than that, Cian wanted me to keep him company while he wrote round the clock. I was his muse, he said. Imagine that. Me? A muse! It made me feel unique and special, even if sometimes it seemed that a muse's role was not to talk much but supply cups of coffee and Custard Creams when needed.

Of course I got to be there when the doubt started to creep in too – doubt, it seems, having a habit of creeping in with writers quite frequently at 3am when I was trying to sleep. But I loved him enough not to mind waking to soothe him, to calm him with a kiss. To tell him how good he was. It made me feel special, and he would hold me tighter and tell me he didn't know how he ever wrote without me, how he felt as if he was on the cusp of his life finally coming together, both personally and professionally. He was getting all he ever wanted – and taking me with him.

There was a hotshot agent interested in representing Cian and this book so the stakes were high on him getting this just right. It was incredible pressure to work under. Not like my job where I went in, sorted out people's teeth, and went home again. I didn't have to think about my job morning, noon and night. Cian said the book was always with him. Always. I'd laughed, asked him if it was with him even when we were, you know . . .

He looked at me very intently and I felt that familiar curl

in the pit of the stomach – the one that made me want to forget the run of myself and have noisy, messy sex with him right there and then.

'It's always with me,' he had said and then he'd kissed me so passionately, with such an intensity it almost took my breath away.

If he became a little distracted from time to time I reminded myself it was, as he called it, just part of the creative process. I remembered how it came and went – how when things were going well for him he became almost euphoric with the joy from it and I encouraged those good times and was suitably sympathetic when he had a bad day.

And I revelled in the highs – in the way he kissed that freckle just under my left breast and told me that my imperfections made me more perfect.

Perhaps it was the same with him? And God, I was falling so in love with the perfect and the imperfect parts of him that I don't think anything could have stopped me.

Chapter Nine

Emily

A man was arrested in relation to Rose Grahame's death two weeks after I started work at Scott's Dental. I say a man, but he was more of a boy. Nineteen years old. A 'frequent flyer' at the local Magistrates' Court, according to the prosecutor who oversaw his first appearance. Charged with a host of offences, including Aggravated Vehicle Taking and Failing to Stop and Report an Accident, Kevin McDaid wore a greying shirt with a black tie – probably the only tie he owned, bought for funerals – along with a cheap suit as he stood in the dock. The pictures in the local media showed him trying to hide his face as he was led in handcuffs from the court building to the waiting police van. Remanded in custody. Bail denied. But his solicitor made it clear he would appeal that decision in the High Court. There was every chance he'd be out on the street in days. A young lad who had a penchant for stealing cars, driving them too fast and leaving them abandoned somewhere. He'd never offended on this level before, his solicitor said. 'Racked with guilt, my client has been unable to sleep and has turned once again to alcohol and drugs.'

He had 'simply panicked' when he hit Rose and had driven

on in that state of panic. He knew there were people around who could help Rose. He didn't think he'd hurt her. Not really. Not enough to kill her.

It probably made me a bad person that I sagged with relief at the news. He was admitting it. It had been an accident. I had overreacted thinking it was anything more sinister than that. Maud had been right. Things had been crazy with Ben. That he had got in touch again so close to Rose's death was nothing more than a coincidence.

Kevin McDaid 'wouldn't trouble the court' his solicitor had said, indicating his client would be pleading guilty to all charges. It should have made things easier. Possibly even make us feel some compassion of sorts for Kevin McDaid. Kevin McDaid, who hadn't even shaved before his court appearance, if the pictures were anything to go by. His stubble, unlike Cian's, was the kind that was borne out of laziness and not any kind of a style statement.

Although there was a trace of utter wretchedness about him – in the way he walked, the scuffed trainers on his feet, the panicked look on his face – I couldn't bring myself to feel sorry for him. Even though I, of all people, knew that people could fuck things up.

He was nineteen. Even if he got a heavy sentence, he would still be out and walking the streets in his early thirties. He would still have all the years Rose didn't have.

The news of the arrest and of the court appearance saw a dip in mood at Scott's. It made me feel a little guilty that it had brought me a sense of relief I hadn't felt in weeks. At least I didn't have to sneak around trying to see what was happening; everyone in Scott's was talking about it. Everyone, naturally enough, was obsessed by it. Even Owen took time out from a patient to watch the lunchtime news report, and to shake his head when Kevin McDaid appeared on screen.

'Isn't he one of ours?' Tori had asked, and a room of horrified faces turned to look at her. 'I think he's one of our patients – or was. There's something about him?'

Donna had gone to the office to check our records and came back a few minutes later, ashen-faced. 'He was a patient here before. Lapsed now. Was here as a child; hasn't been since he was sixteen.'

Owen walked out of the room, slamming the door so strongly behind him that tea from a cup that had been sitting beside me shook and spilled onto the table. For the rest of the day he went about his work saying only what he needed to and no more. The rest of us walked on egg shells around him, all the while lost in our own thoughts about how the foolish actions of a nineteen-year-old could change the lives of so many.

★

On the day Kevin McDaid was brought before the court, I found myself itching to get on Facebook to try and see how Cian was coping. Was he angry like Owen? Was he a bigger person than many of us? Had he found compassion for his wife's killer? Did he have a sense of closure? A victory that, bar sentencing, the man who had taken his wife from him was being brought to justice?

I found he hadn't written much. No letter to Rose. No rant at the judiciary. No angry words aimed at Kevin McDaid. In fact, just four words.

From Darkness Comes Light.

It was the title of his most successful book to date. I hadn't read it, to be honest. I wasn't much of a reader. Didn't have the concentration span for anything more than reading bite-size portions of news and stories. Still I clicked onto Amazon, searched Cian's name and the book title.

The blurb didn't enlighten me much. I was able to ascertain, amid the flowery language, that it was a story about redemption, of a flawed detective who found he was losing all he held dear, and who battled to make his life his own again.

I clicked to buy it, wondering if Cian and I were more kindred spirits than I had ever thought before; if he would understand, in a way few could, that flawed people can find the light again.

When I asked the girls at work a bit more about Rose and Cian, being so very careful to make sure I didn't reveal just how much I had gleaned about them from my hours on the internet, Tori told me they had been the most in love couple she had ever set eyes on.

'He would come and pick her up from work each day. He used to tell me he couldn't wait a minute more to see her. And that wee baby of theirs? Well you combine the genetics of that pair and you get a baby that could be a model. Rose was such a good mum to him too. She doted on him.'

I wondered what that was like, to have someone come to collect you from work because they just could not bear to be away from you for five more minutes? Oh, to have someone love me like that and mean it.

So when I read Cian's posts on Facebook, when I thought of a man who feared losing it all more than anything in the world, I thought of Tori's words – the dreamy look that came across her face when she spoke of him – and I thought how unjust it was that someone with so much love to give had been left with this gaping hole in his life?

On occasion, when I closed my eyes at night in my bed, I allowed myself to picture his face. Allowed myself to think he was saying those love-filled words to me. That he would look at me with such an intensity that I would fear my breath would catch in my throat forever. That maybe he would kiss me, the roughness of his stubble rubbing against my chin and my face so that when he pulled away I would feel that I had been thoroughly kissed. I tried to not allow myself to think about that very much because it felt a little wrong.

But sometimes, in the darkness of my bedroom at night, it felt very, very right.

*

It was an unusually quiet Tuesday morning when the door of Scott's Dental Practice opened and a man pushing a buggy edged his way in backwards out of the rain.

I was at the reception desk dealing with patients, beside Tori who was answering the phones. I looked up when the door opened, an instinctual reaction to the gust of cuttingly cold air that rushed in and made me shiver where I sat. Fat droplets of rain ran from the man's coat to the non-slip mat underneath his feet. His hair was matted to his head and his jeans bore a tide mark from where they had soaked up the moisture from the ground. He brushed the excess water from the top of the rain cover on the buggy, sending it splashing onto the street below before he turned around and closed the door behind him.

I knew him immediately. Even though he was soaked and tired-looking. Even though his face was thinner than it had been before, more drawn.

Cian Grahame. I felt myself suck in the air around me, my hands tense, my brain screaming at me not to welcome him by name. To fight the urge to run up to him and hug him and tell him I was so, so sorry for his loss. That I found his letters to her moving and genuine and heartbreaking. That I had started to read his book, that I felt enchanted by the lyrical language, by the sense that he knew me, that he was talking about me in his fluid prose. I held my breath as he walked towards me. I peeked over the top of the desk to see a sleeping toddler lying back in his buggy and then I raised my head to look at Cian, directly into his eyes. I prepared myself to welcome him in the most professional way possible. He didn't know who I was and I, as far as everyone knew, did not know him.

I was just about to speak when I heard a gasp from Tori beside me.

'Cian!' she cried out, the two patients sitting in the waiting area looking up at the commotion. She jumped from her seat and moved out from behind the desk at lightning speed and threw herself at him, pulling him into a giant hug. He took a step back, but she followed him, not letting go of her grip. He let her hug him, his arms limp at his side before she pulled back and glanced down at the buggy, tapping on the rain cover and cooing loudly at the baby inside.

'Oh Cian, it's so lovely to see you here! And Jack too.' Stunned from his slumber, Jack blinked at her through the prisms of raindrops. I watched him rub his eyes with chubby fists as Tori whipped the rain cover off and lifted him out of his pram and into her arms. He started to cry, but Tori, oblivious to being the cause for the child's distress, just pulled him close to her and kissed the top of his head, telling him it was okay. Cian stood watching the scene, not interjecting. He looked worn out. I fought the urge to reach out to him and offer to help him in whatever way I could.

Tori continued to coo at Jack while Cian spoke, his voice soft and low. 'I know Rose was intending to register Jack here so I wanted to do what she wanted. His first teeth are well through so it's time to start doing things, isn't it? I thought I would bring him here for a check. Sure, he knows you all anyway.'

At that he turned to look at me. He narrowed his eyes, looked me up and down as if trying to place me.

'Hi,' I said softly. 'I'm Emily. I'm very sorry for your loss.'

I extended my hand to his, but his arms remained by his side. He just looked at me, his eyes vacant, and I grew wildly uncomfortable.

'When did you start here?' he asked, blinking at me.

'A month ago, something like that,' I answered.

'You're her replacement then?' he said, his voice sad but I couldn't help but notice a new tension in his jaw. 'Owen didn't waste much time, did he?'

I blushed, blinked. Didn't know what to say. 'I'm sure it wasn't like that. I've heard Rose was irreplaceable,' I offered.

'Clearly not,' he said, any softness gone from his voice.

I couldn't find any words. I just stood and looked at him and then to Tori, hoping to catch her eye, but she was lost cooing over Jack who had stopped his crying and was looking around him, taking in the sight that must have been so familiar to him at one time.

I felt awkward. The blush that had started at the back of my neck turning into a slight sweat. I felt stupid. Self-conscious. Unwanted. Angry too – if I'm honest – at his response. Still he looked at me, his gaze filled with disdain. I tried to jolt myself into action, remember I was here to be professional.

'You wanted to register your son?' I muttered.

'Is Donna here?' he answered. 'Or Owen himself? Or would he not come and talk to me, the husband of one of his most beloved employees?' His voice dripped with scorn.

'They're with a patient just now, but I'm sure they would be happy to see you. In the meantime, I can help you with the paperwork you need to do?' I offered a small smile, which wasn't returned.

'I know how to fill in a registration form,' he said, as I attached one to a clipboard and handed it to him with a Scott's Dental pen.

He stalked to the seating area. The two waiting patients

gawked at him, having given up the pretence of looking at their phones to watch the scene unfolding before them. Tori, who was now singing 'Humpty Dumpty' to Jack, was lost in her own happy world. Clearly, she never really thought about how tragic it was when all the king's horses and all the king's men couldn't put Humpty together again.

To my shame I felt tears prick at my eyes and a lump form at the back of my throat. I realised my hands were clenched as a wave of anxiety threatened to buckle me. This was not the Cian I had come to know from his Facebook posts. This was not the man I had felt so sorry for. He was mean and cruel and I suddenly felt like the outsider again. How could he not be the person he let the world believe he was? Then again, Ben had turned out to be someone, something, I never could have dreamed possible.

When I heard the surgery door open and saw Donna walking out, leading a patient to reception, I sagged with relief. She could deal with him now. She could listen to his aggression about how Owen had the audacity to replace his dead wife, the dead wife who, the cruel part of me wanted to tell him, clearly wasn't even one bit fit for work. I needed some air. I watched as Donna caught sight of Tori with Jack, how she looked at the waiting area where Cian sat with his head bowed over the form, scowling in anger. I watched as she turned back to me as if to give herself a chance to take in what she was seeing and I nodded.

'I need my break, Donna,' I said. 'I'm feeling a bit faint,' I lied, walking straight through the door to the staff kitchen and locker room before she had the chance to stop me.

I pulled my bag from my locker, rummaged through it until I found the strip of anti-anxiety pills that would bring me a little calm, and pressed two out into my hand. Running water from the cooler, I threw the pills back and gulped the water to wash them down and then sat on a chair, under the beatific picture of Rose, trying to still my hands from shaking.

I don't think I ever thought I would actually come face-to-face with him. Of course, I knew he was a real person but he had taken on a different kind of status in my mind. He was my romantic lead. The man who wrote beautiful, heartbreaking, impassioned letters to his late wife. Not this gruff, wan-looking man with his steely eyes looking at me like I was a piece of shit he had just wiped off his shoe. Not this man who was angry at me just because I existed. Because I stood in the spot his wife once did. I knew he was grieving. I wasn't stupid. I know grief makes you say and do things that perhaps you probably wouldn't normally, but I hadn't deserved for him to dismiss me in that manner.

I sipped from my glass of water and wondered whether it was worth going outside for a quick smoke. Remembering the sheets of rain battering against the glass front of the practice, I decided against it. Besides, I was really trying to cut down – the cool and beautiful girls of Scott's Dental didn't smoke. Two of them vaped but that was different, of course. That didn't leave a funk of stinky smoke on their clothes. It didn't turn their professionally whitened teeth yellow.

I was just about to put my bag back in my locker and return to work when the door to the staff kitchen opened and Donna shooed Cian in in front of her.

'Emily, could you put on a cup of tea for Cian here? Just while Owen and I finish with our next patient.'

I wanted to scream, No! I wanted to say could they not find someone – anyone – else to do it instead of me, but I couldn't do that. I couldn't throw a strop. It wasn't befitting of someone in a white uniform with perfectly preened hair and a silver name badge. So I smiled and said yes, and set about my task without making eye contact with him. I heard Donna tell Cian she and Owen wouldn't be long, and that the girls were having a wonderful time seeing baby Jack again and maybe a cup of tea would help him settle his nerves. Then she left, all soothing tones and hushed voice, leaving me wishing the kettle would explode and kill me outright and save me having to talk to Cian again.

'Her picture,' he said. I'm not sure if he was talking to me, or the room, or no one. I kept my back to him, setting out a cup and dropping a tea bag into it while waiting for the kettle to boil. I should offer him a biscuit too, I supposed. I lifted down the tin from the cupboard and took the lid off.

'I'm sorry for before,' he said to my back and I felt myself tense up. I walked to the fridge and took out the milk.

'I . . . well . . . it's been very hard even coming here. I didn't know if it was the right thing. I don't think I know what the right thing is anymore. Rose, she did all these things, you know. Dentists. Doctors. Childminders. And music with mammy classes. No one wants to see the sad widower come along with a grouchy toddler.'

I turned to face him then.

'So I'm left to try and do all this and I don't really know what I'm doing. I thought coming here might make me feel closer to her. That was stupid of me, I realise that now. I mean, Jesus, it's just one more place she isn't anymore, isn't it? And I saw you, and you know, the world is moving on without her. Everyone else, they've cried their tears and worn their black clothes and, even here, they closed their doors on the day of her funeral, but life goes on, doesn't it? Even the man who was driving the car – did you know the High Court let him out on bail? He's walking the streets like he never hurt anyone in his life. And it's only me, stuck in this fucking mess.'

He was swearing but his words weren't angry. They were sad and his eyes had filled with tears. My earlier hurt evaporated.

'It can't have been easy, coming here,' I said hesitantly. 'People haven't really moved on if that's any consolation – everyone talks about her all the time, you know? They miss her.'

He put his head in his hands, running his fingers through his still wet hair. 'I didn't mean to come here and make a tit of myself. Rose would kill me if she could see me now,' he said.

'I'm sure she would understand,' I offered. 'Milk and sugar?'

He looked up at me as I poured the boiling water into his mug. He looked so wretched I had to fight the urge to put down the kettle, walk across the room and just hold him. He looked like he desperately needed to be held. To be comforted.

'I'm sorry this happened,' I offered.

'Thanks,' he said, sniffing, and I handed him a piece of kitchen paper to blow his nose with. 'And no milk but two sugars. Rose used to give out about that. Working here and all.' He forced a watery smile, which melted my heart even more as I spooned the sugar into the mug and stirred it.

'Even Owen takes sugar in his tea,' I said smiling, and offered him the cup.

'I thought he would be sweet enough,' Cian said, sipping from his cup.

I laughed at the remark. But he didn't laugh with me. He just rubbed the stubble on his chin and sighed, before taking another sip of his tea. 'You make a good cuppa,' he said.

'One of my few skills,' I muttered, blushing, offering him the biscuit tin. He reached in and I noticed not only the glint of his wedding ring, but the solid strength of his hands. I sat the tin on the table, moved back across the room. A safe distance.

For a minute we said nothing. I tried to find something to say that wouldn't make me sound like a complete eejit, but my tongue was tied. Every time something did enter my head it related to something I probably shouldn't have known about, something I had gleaned from my evenings reading his posts to Rose on Facebook.

'Your little boy is gorgeous,' I offered eventually.

He smiled again. 'He's what's keeping me going right now. I think I'd have given up without him. He's such a great little boy. So loving. So funny. He gets all his goodness from Rose, of course.'

'I'm sure that's not true,' I said, thinking that the goodness – the love for his son – was oozing right out of him.

'Oh it's true,' Cian said. 'It's like he got all her best bits – her temperament, her smarts, her beautiful blue eyes. At times when I look at him, he pulls a face or something and it's like looking right at her. It's the nicest thing in the world and a kick in the teeth at the same time.'

'It must be hard, I'm sorry. I can't think of anything to say that will make a difference. It's just rubbish.'

'Yes,' he said, shaking his head slightly. 'It's just rubbish. But Jack, he's good. He's the good in all of this.'

'I'm sure you're a great dad. He's lucky to have you,' I said.

'Thank you,' Cian replied, but he seemed lost in his own thoughts all the same. He put the chocolate biscuit he had selected back in the tin and his cup on the table. I had a feeling he was going to say something more but the door opened and in walked Donna and Owen, the latter holding baby Jack who whooped with delight on seeing his father and threw himself forward, arms wide, towards Cian who pulled him into a hug and kissed the top of his head.

'Cian,' Owen said. 'We didn't expect to see you.'

'I just thought I'd register Jack here. I know Rose intended to so it seemed the right thing to do.'

'Well, I think that's lovely,' Donna said. 'And of course, we're always happy to see this little fella.'

'But if it would upset you and Jack to come here, maybe

another dentist would be a better option?' Owen said, a serious tone to his voice.

I watched as Cian lifted the same chocolate biscuit he had put back in the tin just a few minutes before and handed it to his son.

'Everything upsets us at the minute at one level or another, Owen. If we stopped doing things just because they brought back memories of Rose, we'd never do anything. Not even wake up. She's everywhere. It's good for Jack to be around things that can remind him of her. God knows he won't remember her, not in any real sense – he's much too young. So I'll do what it takes to keep her in his life for as long as possible.'

I couldn't quite pinpoint what exactly felt strange about how Cian spoke to Owen but something was off. Was it his tone? The look on his face? The way he barely blinked as they spoke? All of a sudden I felt as if I was watching something I shouldn't be.

I took the first opportunity I could to slip out of the kitchen and back behind the reception desk to continue with my filing.

Not five minutes later, Donna followed Cian and Jack out of the kitchen and through the waiting area, telling him everyone was just struggling to deal with the loss of Rose and his visit had been a bit of a surprise.

'You're part of the family here,' she said, as Cian strapped Jack back into his buggy. 'And this wee man will always be our lucky mascot.'

Donna crouched down and tickled Jack, who squirmed and giggled back at her. I thought of how he smiled at his mother that day, as she sang to him in the lift. Neither of them knowing what was about to happen.

Cian thanked Donna and they hugged briefly. I tried not to stare, or to think what it would be like if I had his arms around me. 'We'll see you for this young fella's first check-up then? In two weeks?'

'Yes,' Cian nodded, pulling up the collar of his still sodden coat before opening the door and stepping back out into the pouring rain. I looked on as Donna watched him push the buggy away from the practice and towards the main street. As she turned on her heel to walk back to the desk, I put my head down and tried to look as if the only thing I was concentrating on was my work.

'It was nice to see him,' Tori said.

'Yes,' Donna said. 'Look, girls, could you make sure Jack sees Sarah and not Owen the day of his appointment?'

'Are you sure?' Tori asked, and I looked over to them. Sarah, an old school dentist in her late fifties, worked with us part-time, and normally she didn't work with the younger children.

'Yes,' Donna said. 'I'm sure.'

Again, I couldn't quite put my finger on it, but something was off about the whole situation.

Chapter Ten

Of course I had decided to leave my car at home that day, it hadn't been raining that morning and it was often quicker and easier to walk to Shipquay Street than to try and beat the morning traffic from Northland Road. So by the time I got home that evening, I was soaked to the skin. There was nothing for it but to strip off and stand under a hot shower until I warmed up. I had dressed in my pyjamas, wrapped my hair in a towel and was staring into a mug of milky tea when I heard my phone ping with a notification. Hoping it was Maud texting to see if I needed to chat — because I really did feel as if I needed to chat — I lifted my phone and unlocked the screen.

I swear I thought my heart would stop beating when I saw a message request from Cian Grahame.

★

I stared at the name in front of me. The icon beside his name was the same profile picture I had been looking at for the better part of the last two months. It was him. Actually him. The last person on earth I ever thought would message me.

I threw my phone onto the cushion beside me as if it were

suddenly too hot to hold. Cian Grahame was messaging me. I wanted to both read the message and not read the message. I was simultaneously curious and scared. Intrigued and freaked out. I involuntarily muttered a quick 'fuck' and lifted my phone again, turning it round and clicking the accept message button so that his words popped up in front of me.

Emily,

I just wanted to thank you for the kindness you showed me when I came to the surgery with Jack today – and to apologise for the manner in which I spoke to you. Especially when I first arrived at Scott's. I know you understand how hard this is for me – and I appreciate that you listened while I ranted and raged in the staff room after. People, they don't always listen. Not really. Grief gets tired for other people pretty quickly. But you listened – and you listened without prejudice. As an outsider – someone who could perhaps give me a bit of a healthier perspective on things.

You also made a good cup of tea. I'd love to repay your kindness by buying you a cup of tea, or coffee, at some stage. Just a way for Jack and I to show our thanks? And for me to show you that I'm not always an arsehole who gives strangers a tough time.

While my gut reaction was to smile, to feel excited that he wanted to meet me, that he appreciated how I had listened, part of me felt that something about it all just didn't sit right. But I pushed those feelings down because I wanted to feel the happy feelings more.

Perhaps, I told myself, this was just what it appeared to be – that Cian just needed someone to talk to? Maybe he just needed to think about a cup of tea instead with someone he could listen to? Cling to the normal in the incredibly abnormal?

I picked up my phone. Typed a quick response.

No need to apologise. Or to offer a cup of tea. It was the least I could do. This all must be so hard.

I hit send, expected no more. Hoped, perhaps for a response, somewhere deep inside. Hoped that he would talk to me. That he would confide in me – even though I really didn't have any right to assume that. Was that mad of me? I felt confused but unable to step away from it.

It was only a matter of minutes before his message arrived in my inbox.

I think every day will be hard now for us. I'm just trying to keep putting one foot in front of the other. I have to, for Jack. Please say you'll meet us for a cup of tea? It's the least we can do – and to be honest, the distraction, a chance to talk to someone new – would be good.

I felt for him. Imagine the whole world being in your business, watching you, pretending to support you in your grief but ultimately when night fell, he was alone in his house with his son and his thoughts.

I typed back quickly.

Of course. Let me know when suits. And if there's anything I can do?

His response was almost immediate – as was the friend request he sent me so we were officially 'connected'.

Would Saturday suit? Afternoon? Or is that too short notice?

I replied that it would and that I looked forward to it and we agreed to meet at 2pm at Primrose Café.

When I put my phone down, confident that night's exchanges of messages were done, I found I had to make a conscious effort to keep those happy feelings floating at the top. This was okay – it was perfectly normal that he would reach out to someone slightly removed from the situation he was in to find some sort of listening ear. Wasn't it?

Chapter Eleven

I didn't intend to look online again that night. I wanted to exist in my perfect little bubble. One where a day that had tested me had ended well; in fact, it had ended well with the promise of something more, another connection. I went to the kitchen and fished around in the cupboard under the sink for the bottle of vodka I had hidden there. As I had banned fizzy drinks from the flat as part of my ongoing health kick, I settled for a (large) measure of vodka poured over some ice and sipped on it before putting my Foy Vance CD on and laying back on the sofa to listen to it. I wanted to enjoy the moment; celebrate it even. I savoured the tang of the vodka as I felt its warmth slide down my throat and into my stomach.

I closed my eyes tighter. Sipped some more vodka.

My head felt light – a gorgeous wooziness washing over me. I picked up my phone and WhatsApped Maud.

I met him, I typed.

Who? she replied.

Cian! He's so sad, Maud. Like he needs a hug.

Cian? The husband of the woman who died?

Yes, he came into the surgery today. He is SOOO handsome. And so lost & lovely.

You need to be careful.

Of course! Am not stupid!

You know I worry about you.

There's no need. I'm a big girl, I jabbed at the screen.

Sweetheart, I'm at work. I can't get into this right now. But I will call you later. I know you're a big girl. But you know how it is . . .

I knew how it was. I knew that Maud would always feel she had something over me because she had been the one to help me piece myself back together after what happened with Ben had left me broken. But that was the past; I was different now. Stronger.

The next time Maud saw me – when she saw my confidence emerge, when she saw my new healthy, clean-eating lifestyle, when she spotted the highlights in my hair, my newly whitened teeth, the new additions to my wardrobe – then she would see how far I had come. She would be happy for me, and she'd stop worrying.

I got to my feet, perhaps a little less steadily than I would have liked, lifted my glass and the bottle and walked to the kitchen where I poured the rest of the tempting clear liquid down the sink. Filling a pint glass with water, I drank as much as I could and washed down two paracetamols.

Just before settling down to sleep, I checked my phone to find a text message from Tori telling me to check the *Derry Journal's* website.

Through fat fingers and numb thumbs, I found the website and saw they were reporting that the body of a nineteen-year-old male had been recovered from the River Foyle. While the deceased's identity had not been confirmed, he had been named locally as Kevin McDaid, the man currently awaiting trial over the death of Rose Grahame.

I clicked onto Facebook, which was in meltdown. Vitriol aimed at McDaid. Emotional messages to Rose saying she could now be at peace. People pleading with others to be thoughtful of McDaid's family at this time. Swear words and vile pictures and every emotion under the sun typed out by keyboard warriors keen to vent.

Police were not thought to be looking for anyone else in connection with the death, which I knew was police talk for suicide. Kevin McDaid had killed himself. I thought for a second how it wasn't really fair. His death wouldn't have been as violent as Rose's. Don't they say drowning is quite peaceful in the end?

He had escaped justice. Escaped standing in front of Rose's family and telling them all why. Telling them sorry. Looking Jack Grahame in the face and telling him he was sorry for taking his mother away.

But then again, he was dead. Gone. Surely Cian could start to move on now? Surely this provided some closure for him? Surely he would feel a sort of relief in knowing that man wasn't out there living his life, and would never be living his life again. He wouldn't serve a few years in some cosy cell with his Xbox to keep him company, eating his three square meals a day and not having to worry about finding a job, or paying the heating bill or any of those things we had to worry about here on the outside. He wouldn't one day walk out of the gates of the prison, if he even got sent to jail in the first place, and get to start over. He wouldn't get to enjoy new beginnings.

Kevin McDaid wouldn't feel anything ever again. He wouldn't hurt anyone ever again. He wouldn't destroy another life.

I climbed out of bed, walked to the kitchen and poured myself another glass of water, which I drank quickly, as if it would have magical sobering properties. I stood in the kitchen, shivering in my underwear, and tried to read my phone again.

Tried to take in what was in front of me. Someone posted that they had seen him go in. Seen him jump.

Someone else said it was good enough for him.

Another person said McDaid had been drinking and spoofing that he would be out of jail in a couple of years just hours before he went missing.

An anonymous profile – an obviously made up name – said his mother had received a text message from him, had panicked and sent a search party out and this whole sorry state of affairs was about to get really messy.

'You couldn't make it up' someone else had typed.

'Unless you're Cian Grahame. He could make anything up' someone replied, complete with laughing emoji.

All entertainment for the masses, it seemed, this nightmare in people's lives. I had to stop myself telling people they mightn't be so flippant if they had been there.

*

Two things dominated my thoughts the following morning. The death of Kevin McDaid and, if I'm honest, the impact that the death of Kevin McDaid may have on my plans to meet with Cian that Saturday.

I'm not sure what I was expecting in the surgery – a sense of all coming right with the world, perhaps? Maybe some sort of morally questionable glee at the news McDaid was dead? I'm not saying my colleagues were mean-hearted, or the kind of people who would take any pleasure from the suicide of another, but in this instance it would be understandable in the circumstances, wouldn't it? I mean, we would all pretend we weren't feeling that way, but we would be. Because he was a bad man. We'd do our best not to think about the family and friends he left behind. We had probably already judged them as lacking in some way anyway.

But there was no glee – partially hidden or otherwise – at Scott's that morning. People look worn out and tired. The veneer of keeping up appearances for the sake of the clients coming through the doors was wearing thin, so thin it was almost transparent in places. Look hard enough, or even a little, even more than a cursory glance, and the strain was showing.

The door to Owen's office was closed. I could hear voices inside, raised, emotional. Donna and Owen talking. I wanted to put my ear to the door, to listen in properly, but the office was in clear view of the waiting area, where any of our patients could look up and see me clearly being a nosy baggage.

So I took a deep breath and walked on to the kitchen where the face of St. Rose stared down at me. I wondered what she would make of it all? She was the kind of woman who would have probably forgiven Kevin McDaid for killing her before the last breath had escaped from her perfectly lined lips. She wouldn't have wanted a double tragedy to come out of it all. Two families plunged into grief instead of just one. I wondered what she would think of Cian messaging me and asking to meet with me? Would she be as magnanimous about me as she would no doubt be about Kevin McDaid? Some things could be forgiven more than others. I had to remind myself I wasn't doing anything wrong. Nor was Cian. We were just two people meeting for tea. In a platonic way. Even if I allowed myself to occasionally drift into daydreams where he stood, his new book aloft in one hand, my hand holding the other. Smiling from my Facebook page.

I filled the kettle. The need for caffeine was strong, as was the need to eat the jumbo-sized croissant I had picked up in the M&S Foodhall in Foyleside before going to the surgery. I looked in the fridge hoping to find some butter to spread thickly – needing as many calories as possible to soothe my stomach but I was out of luck; I'd have to eat the croissant dry.

And, by the looks of it, drink the coffee black. It wasn't like Donna not to have picked up milk on her way in, but then again, these were extraordinary times. A bit of forgetfulness now and then was only to be expected. I topped up my coffee with cool water and checked my phone one last time before I had to put it in my locker.

A public post from Liz McDaid was being shared widely, complete with a picture of Kevin McDaid, wearing a suit and grinning lopsidedly at the camera, a beer can raised in a cheerful salute to whoever was behind the lens. Although littered with errors and text speak, her message was all too clear.

This is my boy. Youse will all be talking about how he died by now. Everyone in this town likes a gossip and I no there are lots of folk out there who will be smilin at the news of Kevin's death. Shame on u all! He was no angel but he was only 19, his hole life was ahead of him. I no he didn't mean to kill that woman in the accident, but u lot r so quick to judge. He was a good boy. He had his problems but he was a good boy. My only son. And don't listen when people tell you he killed himself. Kevin wouldn't do that. He wouldn't do that on me. He always said he would watch out for me. Me and him were a pair. He wouldn't of left me like that. And youse know he was going to be a daddy soon. He was relly looking forward to that.

People would want to be lookin closely at what happened and ask some questions of the cops. Because my boy wouldn't do that. He wouldnt go in the river. He didn't run from his problems.

Don't be coming round our house to gawk at him and to pretend to be his friend when youse wouldn't of spit on him when he was livin. Where were youse all these last few weeks? When he needed u? Look at urselves. What youse did to my boy. Only his friends are allowed at the wake, and keep away from the funeral to. RIP our Kev. My wee son.

I felt for Liz McDaid. Of course I did. She was a grieving mother, trying to come to terms with the loss of her son and the legacy of hurt he had left behind. But surely she, more than anyone, knew the kind of person he was? His criminal record spoke for itself, never mind that he had admitted killing Rose! A mother's love must really be unconditional, I thought. Then I tried to push out my thoughts on my own mother and our fractured relationship.

It was distasteful that Liz McDaid was speaking so openly over social media given what Kevin had done and that she was trying to pin the blame elsewhere. I knew the sort – the kind that would always, always look to blame someone else rather than point the finger where it really needed to be pointed. It was a shame though, even I had to admit, that McDaid's child would never know his or her daddy – but then again, who wanted a childhood visiting daddy dearest in prison?

I clicked off the link and was just opening my locker when Donna walked into the staffroom. She looked flustered, a pinkish blush on her cheeks that complemented the red tinge around her eyes as if she had been crying.

'Are you okay?' I asked, well aware I was asking the most stupid question in the world and the obvious answer was that no, of course she wasn't okay.

She fixed a smile on her face. I could see it took considerable effort to do so – to pull all her facial muscles into the right shape. 'I am,' she said softly. 'This is all just very strange. I don't know what we're supposed to feel. It makes it raw again, but it's done, isn't it? It's over. It's closure – but we still have to grieve for Rose. None of this brings her back.'

I nodded, rubbed her arm gently, tried to think of something to say.

We were interrupted by Tori arriving, narrowly avoiding walking into the door frame while she gawked at her mobile phone. 'Did you guys see this? This post from Kevin McDaid's mother?'

I didn't answer, didn't want to let even a hint of my obsession out by admitting that of course I had seen it, and read it in detail, but Donna grabbed the phone from Tori and scanned the screen.

'What does it say?' I asked, pretending I didn't know.

'A lot of things – that he was a decent fella.' Tori rolled her eyes at that. 'And she didn't believe he would have killed himself. I wouldn't say he accidentally fell off the bridge though, would you? And I heard they found his belongings, folded neatly on the footpath, plus his mum got a text message. You can't send that kind of text message by accident.'

Donna looked up from the phone. 'Your friend seems to know a lot; the rumour mill in this town would sicken you.'

Donna's voice was harsh, angry – more angry than I had ever seen her. Poor Tori visibly cowered as Donna thrust her phone back into her hand. 'It's all tasteless – chatting about it. He's dead. He killed Rose – our friend Rose. Then he had the decency to kill himself too, which was good enough for him if you ask me. Now I think we should remember we're here to work and get on with being professional – if you remember how to do that.'

Tori looked as though she had been slapped in the face. 'I didn't mean anything . . .' she stammered. 'I just . . . didn't . . .'

'Didn't think. You didn't think,' Donna said. 'Now put your phone away and let's get on with today.'

Donna slammed her own locker shut, turned on her heel and left. I could see Tori's hands shaking as she put her bag and phone away. 'I didn't mean anything,' she said to me, her voice trembling. I could see tears sitting in her eyes. 'I thought we were talking about it. Donna usually talks about things.'

'Try not to take it personally,' I said, trying to soothe her. 'I think the news just has everyone a bit on edge. It's bound to bring up a lot of feelings about Rose and how she died.'

'I loved her too,' Tori said, as she left the room. 'She was my friend too.'

'I know,' I said, and I couldn't think of anything else to say to comfort her because Donna had been out of line. Whether or not her feelings were raw didn't really matter. Tori hadn't deserved that. And still, the horrible inner part of me was even more glad that I hadn't admitted to reading the post myself.

Chapter Twelve

2008

Rose

Rose Maguire: said yes!

The stone in my engagement ring glinted under the bright lights of the dental surgery. I allowed myself a moment to revel in it – the way it caught the light and threw it back at me – before I slipped on my latex gloves and set to work.

We'd kept it quiet for a bit – not because we weren't happy. We were happy, deliriously so, but because Cian said it would be nicer to hold the secret just to ourselves for a while.

I'd wondered if he'd been embarrassed about my ring – even though I wasn't, not at all. But I know he wanted to give me more than he did. The 'diamond' in my ring was a rather lovely cubic zirconia, which to the untrained eye would look no different, but so many people had trained eyes these days. They'd wonder whether it was a platinum or white gold setting when the truth was it was silver. It had cost a little over £100 and he had vowed, on his knee in front of me, that when times got better he would replace it with my dream ring.

I didn't want any other ring, I told him. I was entranced by the romance of it – that this ring was all we needed to say we loved each other. It made our love purer. Didn't it?

'I will get you another ring,' he had said again, a determination in his voice. 'You deserve more.'

I thought all I needed – all I deserved – was to be with him in the room we were in, in our lives together. Our flat. Our easy existence, me going out to work, him writing. I had such faith in him that I didn't mind paying the bills, keeping us afloat. We were a team.

But Cian? He sometimes seemed not only to be embarrassed that I was the primary breadwinner in our relationship, but even resentful about it.

'It should be me providing for you, not the other way around.'

'Don't be so silly,' I'd chided him. 'This isn't the 1950s. We're in this together. It's not like you're not working – you're writing a book, Cian. One I know you'll have great success with.'

He smiled. Seemed content with my answer. 'And when I do, I promise I'll make all this up to you. You'll never have to work another day in your life. I'll take care of you. Give you everything you've ever wanted.'

'I already have what I've always wanted,' I told him, kissing his forehead. 'You, my job, my friends, my family, this ring on my finger. That's all that matters to me.'

I meant every word. Those were our happiest days, strange as it sounds. When we were struggling a little bit. When our world was small – contained. When I still thought he was a good and decent person.

Chapter Thirteen

Emily

We were on egg shells the rest of that day, and by the look on Donna's face it was she who was smashing the eggs. I wanted to take her aside and talk to her, see how she really was, but I was afraid to ask. We had been getting on well, Donna and I. I had a lot of time for her. There was no doubt she had a lot going on in her life. She'd told me she used to look at her work as a break from the stress at home – I suppose it was only natural she was uptight that her calm place was anything but.

I felt sorry for her, which was quite remarkable. It took a lot for me to feel sorry for anyone given the shit show my own life had become. But at that time, knowing my Ben worries had been unfounded, I felt a little freer to feel sorry for others. When I went home in the evening I had no one to worry about or pick up after other than myself. She had three teenage boys, all seemingly at that horrid stage where they treated their mother like their personal slave. Donna did try to make her stories about home sound like some sort of family banter but I knew that behind her too bright smile, she was miserable with her lot. I vowed to give her a bit of space that day, and then maybe over the weekend text and see if she wanted to meet for lunch, or a drink, or just a chat, and I would just listen and nod and not say her boys were ungrateful shites because even though they were, she was the only person allowed to say that.

I was never so glad as when the shutters came down on Scott's and we left the surgery behind, muted calls of 'Have a nice evening' echoing as everyone quickly went in their own directions, no one looking back. Everyone had had enough – of work, of tension, of thinking about Rose and how she died and trying to figure out how we were meant to feel about Kevin McDaid's death.

I made myself pasta and a quick tomato sauce for dinner and sat in front of my laptop, took a deep breath and clicked on the Facebook logo, logging into my account. Liz McDaid's post was still doing the rounds, shared hundreds of times. People suddenly describing him as a decent sort, just a bit of a lad. People saying he should have been given a second chance. He was so young. It was all just an awful waste.

I found myself thinking back to that evening. To the moment his car slammed into her. I tried to think of the sights and sounds and smells. Her face. Did I see his? I don't think so – but I know he barely slowed. He must have seen her. It was a busy street. That alone should have slowed him down. I closed my eyes, could hear the sound of her singing. The swoosh of the lift door as it opened. The noise from the street. The traffic. The chatter. The beeping of a pedestrian crossing letting people know it was safe to walk. Someone was shouting down their mobile phone – they would be late and whoever was on the other end could make their own damn dinner. The sound of feet on the footpath. The clicking of heels. A baby – possibly Jack babbling. The roar. The screech. The thump.

Yes, the roar. Acceleration. There was definitely acceleration.

It couldn't have been an accident. Could it? Could his foot have slipped? No. The roar. Loud enough to block out a scream of 'Jesus Christ' – my scream. My scream as I stood and watched and knew I could do nothing.

No. Kevin McDaid was not an innocent man. He wasn't to be sainted just because he was dead.

I clicked onto Rose's page – friends, of course, were posting that they had been thinking about her all day, that they hoped McDaid was now rotting in hell where he belonged. Cian had said nothing and all that I could think was that he must be so completely thrown by it all that he just didn't know what to say. A wordsmith without words. There was nothing sadder. My heart ached for him, and I stared at his picture imagining what it would be like if I could only comfort him. Hold him. Kiss the top of his head, run my fingers through his tousled hair, tell him everything was going to get easier. I wondered who was comforting him. He seemed so alone at Rose's funeral. Her family seemed to hold each other up, leaving him to wander on his own, looking so hopeless and devastated behind his wife's coffin. Who did he talk to now? Did he have people to call round, bringing him home-cooked meals and making sure he was looking after himself? Were there women waiting in the wings – waiting for an appropriate amount of time to have passed before they made their move? They would never understand what he had been through though. Not like I could.

I decided in that moment that I would message Cian too. Let him know I was okay if he wanted to cancel our plans. Let him know I understood that it must have been a messy, tough, horrible day for him. Let him know I was willing to reschedule whenever he could. Maybe even suggest an alternate date? How long was appropriate to wait? A few days? A week? There wasn't exactly an etiquette for these things.

I was shocked when he replied back, almost instantly.

There's no need to change our plans. Let's meet as arranged x
I tried not to read anything into the 'x'.

★

The following morning I dressed for work, took a little extra time to straighten my hair, fix my make-up, even put on a little eye liner. Not too much. Not enough that I looked overdone. Just that I looked a little more composed. I spritzed on some of my favourite perfume, Chanel No. 5; it always gave me a little push of confidence when I needed it. I had to bide my time, keep doing what I was doing and it would all work out.

But then I wasn't counting on the latest, gut-wrenching twist in the tale. By the time I had arrived in work, news had broken that police were now looking into the death of Kevin McDaid after an autopsy showed signs of injuries inconsistent with a jump or fall from the bridge.

'New information has come to light that gives us cause to look further into the circumstances surrounding Kevin McDaid's death,' a police spokesperson had said, and of course Facebook users were already jumping to their own conclusions. Had someone taken out a hit on Rose Grahame's killer? Had he annoyed the wrong people this time?

Liz McDaid had posted again, railing against the world. Telling everyone the truth would out. She wouldn't rest until she knew what had happened to her son. Until she had justice. Kevin McDaid's picture was everywhere. As was Rose Grahame's. Not just locally – the story was attracting national attention now.

I wondered what the injuries were that were inconsistent with his jumping from the bridge? I tried to think of what that must be like – taking that step, plummeting, jumping – was it a bit like flying? Did you feel a sense of freedom? It wasn't something I had considered, even at my most desperate. Too public. Too scary. Murky water. Dirty water. Being washed away by the speeding tide – away from any chance of being saved, or being found. But he had been found quickly. 'On the glarr', someone said, referring to the sticky, tar-like mud of the river-bank. It could suck people in if you couldn't move. If you had broken your bones with the impact of the fall. The bridge was high enough that even hitting the water could shatter a bone or two. The fall not always predictable. People who had second thoughts and tried to swim to safety could find themselves giving in to exhaustion and the cold as they sank into the bank's thick edges.

I shuddered as an image of him, trying to get to safety, scared, cold, came into my mind. At least Rose had just seconds, if even that long, to contemplate her impending fate. It was merciful really. But Kevin McDaid? Who knew what he had been through. Maybe drowning wasn't that peaceful after all? Dirty water. Mud. Choking. Grabbing for a hold that wasn't there. Sinking into oblivion. Darkness all around. Not knowing which way was up. Which way was down. Trying to find a pocket of air. The white of his eyes stark against the black, the brown and the deep, deep blue.

I tried to shake the image from my head. Tried to find some calm. Reminded myself I was not trapped in this moment. There was air around me. Air I was free to pull into my lungs. I could feel my body shudder as I tried to suck in what air I could. My hands shaking as they fished in my bag. I needed a cigarette. A drink. A breath of air. I could feel the skin dampen on the back of my neck, my skin prickle and my perfectly applied make-up start to slide on my face – now slick with perspiration.

I stood shaking in the staff kitchen as the buzz of my colleagues talking about the news seemed to reach a crescendo. Where was Donna to tell them all to be professional? Where was she to shout the odds, to tell them all to stop talking? To stop gossiping? The noise too much, my stomach turning, I went through to the locker room and out to the back door where I pushed open the fire exit and gulped down what air I could.

I was not expecting to find Donna sitting outside, on one of the patio chairs reserved for the smokers – or the e-cig crowd. She had her coat pulled tight around her, her arms crossed tightly at her stomach and she was staring into space, her phone sat on the small table beside her. Despite the noise, the violence of my bursting out into her space, she stayed still. Her eyes didn't meet mine. Her face looked so pale. So stricken. The pain etched across all her features jolted me into some sort of action. I swallowed my own fears.

'Donna?' I said. 'Are you okay? I heard the news – it's upsetting isn't it? It's okay to be upset by it.' If I focused on making her feel okay, maybe it would help me feel okay too.

Slowly she moved to look at me, her eyes dazed. 'What?' she said, shaking her head as if trying to jolt herself back to some form of consciousness.

'The news?' I said, still feeling my own pulse racing a little too fast. 'You look upset. I assumed the news – the update on the McDaid investigation. You were so out of sorts . . .' I was rambling, I knew that. Donna just blinked at me, her brow furrowed as if I had gone quite mad. Maybe I had?

Slowly, as if it took every ounce of effort she had, she shook her head. 'No. No. It's . . . the boys. Stuff at home. A school thing that has blown up and I have to deal with it . . .' She raised her hand to her forehead as if checking her own temperature and then she pinched the bridge of her nose and continued to shake her head. 'I'll have to go and deal with it. It's not like there's anyone else to sort it out.'

She looked tired. Not her usual groomed self.

'You'll have to deal with whatever gossiping you all want to do without me.' Her tone was sharp. I wanted to shout that I hadn't been gossiping. I wasn't a gossip. But she had already stood up, started to slip her phone in her pocket. 'I need to talk to Owen. Explain.'

'I don't think he's in yet,' I said.

'Oh for fuck's sake,' she said, and I was taken aback because I'd never heard her swear before.

'I could tell him for you,' I offered. 'I'm sure he'll understand, Donna. Why don't you head on?'

She stared at me, as if trying to suss me out. Her look made me feel odd.

'Yes,' she said, nodding. 'Yes.' She walked past me, back into the surgery, and I stood and tried to find my balance again. I'd find Owen. Tell him. Show him I could be good in a crisis. I could hold it together for the team. I just had to control my breathing first.

★

Owen had simply nodded when I told him Donna had gone home. He seemed distracted – perhaps he was struggling with the latest development as much as the rest of us were? I told him I would help cover her duties and he thanked me, then went back to staring at his computer screen, but as I made to leave he called my name.

I turned back to him, realising how tired he looked too.

'Emily,' he repeated, 'Tell me this. What do you think of it all? What McDaid's family are saying?'

'I wouldn't really know . . .'

'But it's all everyone's talking about. You must have an opinion? Do you think there's more to it? Do you think it's about Rose?'

'I think we should wait and see what the police have to say. But I'm sorry for you all – all of you who knew Rose

– that there is more upset. Things are hard enough. I can see that.'

He nodded slowly, sadly. 'It's making it all so sordid.'

'Sordid?' I asked.

'Her death. Seeing her picture everywhere again this morning. People talking about her like she's a minor character in a soap opera now. People writing about Cian. People writing about McDaid. Saying he was a decent sort. Have you seen the hash tag? #JusticeforKevin? It's disgusting. It's cheap and nasty – just like him.'

I didn't know what to say, so I just tried to put a sufficiently sombre expression on my face.

'Isn't it bad enough that we, all of us, her friends and family, have to deal with her not being here any more without him becoming the victim in all this?'

'I wish I had something to say that would make it easier for everyone,' I said.

'You don't think of him as a victim, do you? You don't think anyone who could do what he did could be a victim?'

He was looking directly at me, his eyes focused on mine so that I had no space to hide whatever was going through my mind. I tried to assemble my thoughts quickly – tried to think how to say what I was thinking without aggravating the situation. I took a deep breath.

'In his case? No. I don't think he was a victim in what happened to Rose, but good people can make mistakes – get caught up in something, I suppose. Who knows what he was mixed up in?'

'Whatever it was, I don't think I'll find it in my heart to feel sorry for him,' Owen said. 'I'd just love all this to go away. We all just want to try and come to terms with everything, but how can we? And even here, people come in, ask questions. You know I've already taken calls from the press this morning looking for comment, or insider info, or pictures of Rose they can use? Jesus, it's disgusting.'

'Do you want me to deal with all the calls today? I'll make sure no press get through. You'll be in surgery.'

He nodded slowly. Ran his hands through his hair and stood up. 'I'm sorry for ranting,' he said. 'I'm not making a good impression.'

'It's okay, I understand. And at least it's almost the weekend. You can escape from the public for a couple of days and hopefully this will all settle down a bit.'

'I hope so,' he said, as he made to leave for his surgery. 'I really do.'

★

I changed out of my work uniform. Slipped on a black knee-length pencil skirt with a soft grey cashmere sweater and knee-high boots. I fixed my make-up, keeping it light and neutral, and pulled my hair into a soft chignon. Then I went online and checked the death notices in the local paper and found out just exactly where to go.

I pulled on my coat, sat in my car and smoked two cigarettes in a row, before driving the three and a half miles to Creggan, the council estate where Liz McDaid lived. It wasn't hard to find her house. I parked and as I walked towards the house I saw a small crowd, maybe between ten and fifteen people, standing outside amid a fug of cigarette smoke. They stood, heads bowed, collars up to fend off the cold. Shuffling from foot to foot, the plumes of cigarette smoke mixing with the steam from their breath. The men either wore crisp white shirts, the starched lines from where they had been folded in the packaging peeping out from their good coats, or slightly off-white ones, washed too many times – probably old school uniforms. Black ties, thin, loosely tied, too formal for these men who looked too young to be grieving one of their peers. They spoke in hushed tones, dropping butts on the ground and grinding them out with the heel of their shoes. As I grew closer, I saw two women among their group sat on kitchen chairs in the small front garden, beside the front door, beside the floral wreath that heralded that this was a house of mourning. One, clearly pregnant, held her tummy with one hand, her cigarette with the other, puffing on it as if it were gas and air. The second was staring into the street, a china cup and saucer balanced precariously on her knee, still full. I nodded in their direction as I walked past; gave them a sympathetic half-smile, trying not to feel overwhelmed by awkwardness.

While the hum of whispered conversation hung in the air, the atmosphere was solemn. No press photographers. No TV cameras. No crowds just there for a nosy. Completely different to Rose Grahame's last few days above the soil. More dignified, perhaps? Or maybe people were too scared to get too close to it all. As I stood, waiting my turn to walk into the narrow hallway, waiting to be directed to wherever Kevin McDaid was laid out in his coffin awaiting the procession of mourners paying their respects, I wondered was I mad? Would the other mourners know I didn't know him? Would they know I was just there for a nosy? To see his face – this man who had sent my life into a tailspin?

The talk was muted. Lots of expressions of disbelief. Lots of 'he was so young'. Lots of melancholy laughter at how he was always into mischief. Lots of chat about how 'they' should stay away. I shuffled forward until I was face-to-face with a young man, who could have been anything from seventeen to twenty-five, who was shaking the hands of the mourners, taking in all the I'm-sorry-for-your-troubles expressions and directing us up the stairs to the front bedroom. A brother, perhaps. There was a resemblance to the photo that had been doing the rounds of McDaid that day. I nodded, took his clammy hand in mine, accepted his weak handshake and told him I was sorry for his loss and then step by step I filed with the others up the stairs.

The room in which Kevin McDaid lay was small and cool. A stark bulb hung bare from the ceiling. A chest of drawers had been covered with a white cloth, on which sat two ornate candlesticks, a brass crucifix, a pair of rosary beads and a framed picture of Kevin, still in his school uniform. He couldn't have been more than fourteen in it, his face not yet angular enough to be that of a grown man. No more than a hint of shadow above his top lip. I stared at it while I tried to avoid the eyes of the mourners sat around the room on chairs borrowed from the local community centre – and while I tried to avoid looking at Liz McDaid, sat beside her son's coffin, keening over his body, one hand resting on his chest as she leant her head against the side of the coffin for support. But as much as I tried to resist, I was drawn to the noise of her distress, to the dark wooden edges of the coffin, the shiny satin of the lining. The body resplendent in best suit – the same one he had worn to court no doubt – hands joined. He looked peaceful, though the hint of bruising on his cheek and neck was evident if you looked closely enough. There was something so fake about how he looked – like a ventriloquist's dummy, his face set in place by the undertaker at what looked like hard angles.

It was difficult to think that this man – this child really – in front of me could hurt anyone.

I took a deep breath, which shuddered through my body and set my fight or flight senses on full alert. As I made to leave, I felt a hand grab mine. Instinctively I turned to see Liz McDaid, her face, round, red and wet looking at me. 'Are you okay, pet? You're an awful colour.'

Her concern for me was touching. I felt tears spring to my eyes – tears I tried to blink away but which fell anyway.

'I know, I know – it's awful. It's such a shock. He didn't do this – no matter what they say. He didn't kill himself,' she said, her voice hoarse from grief and exhaustion.

I shook my head, afraid to speak.

A man crossed the room and put his hands on Liz's shoulders. 'C'mon now, Liz. Don't be upsetting yourself again. Or this wee girl.' She shrugged him off.

'We're at my son's wake. I'll upset myself if I want to. Youse are all great standing there telling me you are sorry for my troubles – but will you all fight with me for the truth? He had broken ribs, I'll show you,' she said, standing up and scrabbling at the coffin, starting to unbutton Kevin's jacket until the man pulled her back again, telling her there was no need.

'There's every need. Broken ribs, and bruising, like he was pushed against the railings. Bruising on his ankles. Marks on his hands . . . This wasn't his doing.'

The woman who had been sat outside nursing her cup of tea had now come in and was openly sobbing. 'Mammy,' she cried. 'Please . . . you have to leave it to the police.'

I felt the room close in around me and I wanted to run, but the room was full, the doorway blocked, and it was as if all the air was being sucked from it.

'The police won't do anything for the like of us. They never did. They're just glad to be rid – but I'm telling you, this wasn't suicide. It wasn't. And I'll make you all listen to me . . .'

The woman – who I presumed was Kevin's sister – crossed the room to hold her mother, leaving me space to make my escape. I willed my legs not to run, not to give away that I wasn't just another ordinary mourner. Head low, ashamed of myself for having come, I nodded my goodbyes and left, stopping only to allow someone to pass with a host of china cups rattling on a tray. I swear I didn't breathe in – not properly – until I was outside, past the smokers and the small, rusted garden gate. I sucked the air into my lungs as deep as I could, coughing as it rattled its way back out.

'Are you okay, ma'am?' A deep voice asked. I looked up into the eyes of a uniformed police officer; tall, clean shaven, his expression one of genuine concern – and yet he made me feel nervous. I wondered if he could see through me, know that I wasn't meant to be there.

'I'm fine . . . it was just a shock. It's very sad. All of this,' I said, trying my best to hold eye contact, acutely aware that every movement I made could scream outsider.

'Well, take care of yourself now. Safe home and all,' he said, a female officer at his side nodding at me before they walked on. I made my way as quick as I could to my car where I smoked two more cigarettes before driving home, stripping off my clothes, roughly wiping off my make-up and standing under the shower where I cried for twenty minutes.

Chapter Fourteen

The thought of meeting Cian for tea made the prospect of work the following day much easier. I didn't discuss hair or make-up with the girls at work – who were still too shell-shocked by the events of the last few days to indulge in such light-hearted banter. Their usual Friday chat of after work drinks and weekend plans were muted.

Part of me resented their lack of enthusiasm for their usual weekend activities. It wasn't often that I could join in the chat with them – not really. Not with plans of my own for once. But they were just too busy trying to make it through the day. It was as if their grief had sucked the energy from them – pulling it down through their bodies out of their feet, through the ground. Gone. Leaving these soft masses trying to slip and sludge their way through every day.

I was never so glad to finish up and say goodbye to my work colleagues. To nip into town and pick up some pampering products and a bottle of Prosecco and some candles so that I could soak my troubles away and relax before the big meeting the following day.

When I got home I spent more time than usual looking

through Rose's Facebook page – all her photo albums, especially those in which she was pictured with Cian. I hoped it would give me an insight into what look he went for. Not that I thought he would go for me. But it would be better to be prepared. Just in case.

★

Cian had suggested we meet at 'Primrose on the Quay,' a bijou café on the banks of the River Foyle, for afternoon tea. It was a lovely spot with an on-trend shabby chic design – but with enough little nooks and crannies that it was perfectly possible to have a private conversation without everyone else in the place being able to listen in. Plus, they did good cake. Lovely cake, which I would at most push around my plate afraid of looking like the kind of person who enjoyed it too much. Rose Grahame had the look of a woman who never so much as looked at cake, never mind sprayed it liberally with cream and made orgasmic noises while eating it.

My trawl of Facebook revealed that Rose seemed to have dressed fairly conservatively, but with a chic style that I didn't often manage to pull off. I pulled a black wrap dress from the back of my wardrobe. I had worn it only once before, to my parents' house for Christmas – on a day that hadn't worked out as particularly pleasant for anyone. Teaming it with my knee-high boots, I decided it looked suitably smart-casual for a perfectly innocent cup of tea with a man who was grieving for his wife. I hung a pair of chunky red beads around my neck and spent more time than I should have trying to give my hair that messy but stylish look that other girls – girls like Rose – seemed to be able to pull off effortlessly. (Sea Salt Spray, Google had told me, was my go-to product for such a look.)

I went for a natural look to my make-up. A slick of Mac's Velvet Teddy lipstick, a swipe of mascara. Some blush. I pulled

103

on my old green winter coat and examined myself from all angles in the mirror. I looked good, but not too good. Not good enough that anyone would think I was making a play for the poor widower. Not good enough that, on the chance I would bump into any of my colleagues from Scott's, they would have cause to ask if I was off somewhere fancy.

As I walked alongside the Quay – a walkway that runs beside the river Foyle from the outskirts of the city centre right into the heart of the town – I could feel the cold air pinch at my cheeks and nose. I'd at least have a healthy glow about me when I came face-to-face with him. The café was busy with the clatter of knives on plates, of teacups on saucers, the chatter of old friends gossiping, the serving staff laughing as they made up their teas and coffees and lifted calorie-laden cakes onto plates with serving tongs. I looked around for him – and spotted them almost immediately. Sitting at the back wall, he had Jack in a high chair, running a plastic car along the table and smiling broadly at his daddy. I watched as Cian ruffled his son's hair, blew a raspberry on his cheek. The little boy roared with laughter, grabbing his daddy's face with his chubby toddler fingers before turning his attention back to his toy car. As Jack looked away, I saw the smile slip from Cian's face – just momentarily. It must be exhausting, I thought, to keep up that act for the sake of a child. To pretend to be happy.

He looked across the room and saw me, gave me a smile that warmed my heart. He stood up, his shirt lightly wrinkled, the cuffs rolled up, the top button undone. I tried not to look at the little tuft of hair that poked out below his neckline. A little tuft of hair that made me feel a little weak at the knees.

'Emily,' he said, his voice low and soft. 'I'm glad you came.' He reached over and kissed my cheek. I revelled in the momentary brush of his stubbly face against my skin. Human contact.

Skin on skin – however brief – felt so good. 'We both are,' he said, gesturing toward Jack who was staring at us open mouthed, as if trying to size up who this strange woman was.

I wasn't awfully sure how to act with this cute, wide-eyed toddler in front of me. I didn't have much experience with children. I figured a smile couldn't hurt, so I grinned down at Jack and told him he was a gorgeous little man. He cooed back, gestured his toy car in my direction and I took it from him and drove it across the table, making the requisite 'vroom vroom' noises. This seemed to please him and he giggled loudly.

'You've a fan there,' Cian said, gesturing for me to sit down on the chair opposite him.

'He's very cute,' I said.

'I was going to order afternoon tea for two,' Cian said. 'Does that sound good to you?'

I nodded.

'Great,' he said, waving to a passing waitress to get her attention. He ordered the afternoon tea, and a cup of milk and a biscuit for Jack.

'I should probably have brought a packet of raisins or a banana or something for him. Rose would have done that – but I forgot. Sure a biscuit won't hurt him,' he said.

'No, it won't. I'd say he might even enjoy it.'

Cian smiled at me again, before taking a deep breath and sitting upright in his chair. 'I do want to thank you for listening the other day,' he said. 'You must have thought me a complete arsehole.'

'Not at all,' I said. 'And even if I did, I think you can be allowed a little bit of arsehole behaviour at the moment. Given everything that is happening.'

His eyes darkened a bit. Sadness perhaps. 'It's certainly been intense,' he said. 'And there's no manual in how to deal with stuff like this. Lots of well-meaning people wanting to tell you what to do – but no one who really gets what it's like to be in the middle of it.'

'No, I don't suppose they do. I don't know how you're coping, to be honest. And with what's happened to Kevin McDaid . . .'

He looked down at the table, then brought his hands to his face. For a moment I wondered if he would break down and cry and my heart threatened to crack just a little. He inhaled deeply again and ran his hands through his hair before bringing them to rest on the table.

'This might put me in arsehole territory again, Emily,' he said, 'but I don't much care about what happened to Kevin McDaid, or about what Kevin McDaid did to himself. I don't care about him at all. They say that's the healthiest way to be – to be ambivalent? He got what was coming to him, and that's all I can say about him.'

I admired him. His ambivalence. I'm not sure I could be so cold in the circumstances. I tended to react differently when people hurt me. Go big or go home, wasn't that what they said? Even if I didn't mean to. Even if I tried not to – tried to walk away.

'I can't allow him headspace,' Cian continued. 'Things are tough enough. All the time. Trying to do the things I would have done before without even thinking twice. Waking up. Getting out of bed. It's so fucking hard – there are days when I don't think I can.' His voice was low and angry, he balled his fists, and thumped the table – the teacups jumped and rattled on the saucers – beige liquid splashing onto the table. Jack jumped, a small laugh, then a loud cry as the fright kicked in. 'I'm sorry, buddy,' Cian said, immediately, standing and swooping his son up out of the highchair and into his arms. 'I'm so, so, so sorry for everything.'

It was then I realised he was crying.

People were starting to look round. Just a few, but enough that there was a danger of a buzz spreading through the café. Those who didn't know Cian as the acclaimed author, sure as hell knew him as the widower of that woman killed in the hit and run. I stood up in front of them both, doing my best to hide them from view. Jack quietened down, hugging into his father, putting his thumb in his mouth – his eyes drooping as he cuddled into Cian's chest – which was still shuddering as he cried. 'Oh God,' he muttered. 'People are looking. They'll be talking.'

He looked stricken, I placed my hand gently on his arm. 'You go. Take Jack to the car. I'll sort the bill. He's exhausted anyway.'

'But I promised you a cup of tea at least – and we've hardly had a bite. I'm sorry, Emily. I'm totally useless at the moment. I keep fucking up – this poor wee man deserves better. Not me. Not me who can't do anything right.'

He covered his son's ears as he swore, tenderly kissed the top of his head. He looked utterly broken – in a way that no amount of time or effort could fix.

'You're far from useless,' I said instinctively. 'Where are you parked?'

'Just up beside the toy shop, Smyths,' he said, gesturing to the path I had walked down just a short time earlier.

'Go, take Jack. I'll pay the bill. I'm sure they will box some of this up. You can make me a cup of tea back at yours and I'll be a listening ear for you until this feels a little less daunting. For today anyway.'

He nodded. 'I would argue with you and tell you we'll be fine, but I don't know if we will be.'

'Go to the car,' I repeated. 'I'll see you in five.'

He told me the make and colour of his car and took a now sleeping Jack through the café, ignoring the few open-mouthed stares coming his way, and pushed his way out the door. And I did what I said I would and wondered how I had just managed to invite myself to Cian Grahame's house.

Chapter Fifteen

Rose

2009

Rose Maguire: is getting married today! Looking forward to becoming Mrs Cian Grahame. Love you, Cian, with all my heart and can't wait to start our life together! I feel so lucky to have you love me Xxxx #weddingday #Blessed

It was perhaps a mistake to drink three glasses of champagne the night before my wedding. After a fitful sleep, I woke with a sore head and a mouth as dry as the Sahara. I had to be up early, of course. The hairdresser and make-up artist were arriving at 8.30am and my parents' house was already starting to come alive as the day began. My bridesmaids would be here shortly – and my mother had promised us all a hearty breakfast. Not that I felt I could eat – my stomach was in knots. Nerves were normal, weren't they?

Looking out the window, I saw it was dry and offered up a silent prayer of thanks to whichever one of my relatives had put the Child of Prague in their garden to try and encourage the weather gods to be kind. I knew Cian had been very much hoping that a lot of our day could be spent in the grounds of the hotel, basking in the sunlight and enjoying a relaxed affair. He would be more relaxed himself now that the weather looked as though it would behave itself – and if he was relaxed, then I could relax a bit too. An artist's temperament, he called it – when he got himself wound up about something he couldn't quite control.

For a bloke, Cian had surprised me with his notions of what he wanted our wedding to be. He had very definite ideas. I'd been lucky, a few friends told me. Most men didn't really care and had to be pushed to going out and sorting a suit. Cian was the opposite; he was obsessed with the detail of it all. He wanted a day that symbolised us and what we meant to each other, he said. We didn't need anything big and showy, he said. The most important thing was our marriage, not our wedding day, he said. I couldn't argue with that – even though I suppose I had always dreamed of a big day surrounded by as many friends as we could fit into a decent-sized hotel for a party into the early hours.

Cian was right, of course, when he pointed out that our budget wouldn't stretch that far. Yes, his book had sold and was selling relatively well as these things go – getting him some great reviews – but it seemed that 'relatively well' didn't put a lot of money in the bank. Not that the money really mattered, I had reassured him, but I knew he felt it. Felt he should be providing more.

'I don't want to start the rest of our lives in debt,' he said, 'I'd feel I was letting you, and us, down. Let's just make it about us – and our closest family and friends.'

He talked about it so warmly that I started to relish the idea of something more intimate. Something more low key. Just forty of us, me in a simple dress, my hair dressed with flowers.

I'd even go barefoot if the weather allowed – and we'd skip off early in the evening, forsaking the big evening do, to spend a week in the South of France – a wedding present from my parents.

Cian's guests were small in number – a couple of friends, his agent, a cousin who was acting as best man. His parents didn't keep well and had retired to Cork but they sent their best wishes and a cheque for £500 towards the cost of the day. So we tried to balance the numbers a little – not make it look too uneven. It put noses out of joint for a few great aunts and cousins – but they weren't as important to me as Cian was.

It would be nice not to have the pressure of making all that small talk with distant relatives and neighbours who had only been invited because their postcode matched ours. I actually found myself looking forward to it even if it was different from what I had thought I would want. I closed my eyes and tried to picture the look on his face when he saw me walk up the aisle towards him.

I wondered, would he cry? Would he smile? Would he give me one of his super intense looks?

He had whispered down the phone to me late the night before that I was his – that I would always be his. It would be me and him against the world – and that with me at his side he was sure he could do anything.

'This is forever, isn't it?' he'd asked, and I caught an air of something unfamiliar in his voice. Doubt? Fear? 'I swore I'd never do this if it wasn't forever – for better or worse and all that,' he said.

'Of course,' I'd said, telling myself it was okay to feel a little nervous even if I wanted the lifelong commitment I was about to make.

'Morning, love,' my mother said, rapping on my bedroom door and pushing it open. 'Are you all set?'

There was something about seeing her there – hair in curlers, dressing gown on, familiar and warm and loving, that made me feel a bit weepy. I couldn't help it, and before I could say anything she was sitting beside me, holding me.

'It's a big day,' she said, hugging me and kissing my head. 'You will be happy, sweetheart,' she said. 'But you know you always have a home here. Always. You are always my girl.'

'I love you, Mum.'

Chapter Sixteen

Emily

It was only a short drive to Cian's house. A red-bricked detached house, set back from the tree-lined road in its own grounds off the Limavady Road, which runs parallel to the river in Derry's Waterside. Double fronted. Gravel drive. Manicured lawn. I guessed his books must be selling well. He had been living the kind of life I could only dream about. I think that probably made it all the more tragic.

From the outside, this was the perfect family home – fitting in perfectly with Rose's perfect life. Something in the pit of my stomach twisted just a little bit with jealousy. I willed myself to focus on the task in hand. Cian climbed out of his car, walked round and opened the door for me before opening his front door and directing me – and my takeaway parcel from Primrose – in through the door to the hall, where pictures of Rose and Cian and Jack hung on every wall. I looked around – Rose's eyes on me as I did so. It felt like she was always watching me. Everywhere I looked she looked back. At work. Here. In my dreams. I felt my heart quicken again, looked behind me to see where Cian was – to see him lift Jack from the car and follow me in. 'Go on through to the kitchen,' he said, gesturing to the back of the house. 'I'll put this little one up in his cot.'

I was grateful to walk into the kitchen and out of her gaze – but that's not to say she wasn't there. She was everywhere. It was as if the ghost of her, the essence of who she was, hung heavy in the air.

'What did you start, Rose Grahame?' I whispered as I looked around at the place she had lived in.

Chapter Seventeen

I filled the kettle and switched it on. I would have gone ahead and made the tea but I didn't want to go snooping through the cupboards for tea bags and cups. So instead I opened the fold-down box they had given me at Primrose and rearranged the sandwiches and pastries that were in it. They looked delicious, but my appetite had left me. A knot of tension sat in the pit of my stomach. I was in Rose's house.

Any second now her husband would come back downstairs, and we would sit, most likely at this kitchen island, and drink tea and talk. I would comfort him. I may touch his arm gently again. My skin tingled at the thought and immediately I felt guilty. I shouldn't allow myself to feel attracted to this gorgeous, vulnerable man, but there was a part of me that knew I was already lost and it was his very vulnerability that pulled me to him. I related to it.

I looked around. For a man on his own – a man struggling with the weight of grief – he kept the place remarkably tidy. The worktops were clear except for the kettle, a coffee machine, and toaster. The granite was smear-free. The floor clean. The walls, painted a very pale grey, had no trace of mucky toddler handprints. There was no overflowing laundry basket. No unwashed dishes. No finger paintings pinned to the large, American-style fridge. A family portrait in black and white hung on the far wall above a large, squishy sofa with loose white covers – a grey chenille throw hung over the back of it. The picture was one I had seen on Rose's Facebook page – Rose and Cian, in white T-shirts, jeans, barefoot, sitting close together – and baby Jack, perhaps only six months old, propped between them. A picture of happiness, wide smiles all round. Rose Grahame staring back down at me again.

Apart from the picture on the wall, the only hint to the unknowing eye that a child lived here was a small wicker basket, filled with brightly coloured wooden toys in the corner of the room. I wondered whether Cian sat on the floor with his son and played with them. Or had Rose been the more hands-on parent? Perhaps it had been a joint endeavour between them?

I heard footsteps on the stairs and I looked around as Cian walked into the room. He looked a little brighter. His sleeves were rolled up further and the edges of his hair slightly wet. I imagined he had splashed his face with water, freshened up. Settled himself.

'I didn't know where anything was to make the tea so I just boiled the kettle,' I said as he moved across the kitchen, opened a cupboard and took out two mugs.

'Thanks,' he said, setting about making the tea. With his back to me he said: 'I feel a little foolish now. Crying like that. In public. What must you think of me?'

What did I think of him? I took a breath. 'I think you're a man who has suffered a great loss in the worst circumstances possible and it would be wrong if you didn't have an occasional breakdown. I think anyone would understand.'

'Except for those who think I had something to do with it . . .'

He turned towards me, his green eyes looking straight at me, almost as if he could see everything about me. 'I've seen the comments on Facebook. I've seen people laughing and making snide comments. I've had messages you know – people saying I killed her. Can you imagine that? Can you imagine how that feels?'

'I'm sure anyone who knows you, knows you had nothing to do with it. It's clear you loved Rose very much.'

'I still love her,' he said softly, lifting the two mugs and carrying them to the kitchen island. 'I always will.'

'Of course,' I said, once again a flash of jealousy pinging at me. I chided myself. Of course he would always love her. Of course he still did. What did I think? That less than two months after her death he would fall in love with me? I almost laughed at the ridiculousness of it all – almost.

He rubbed his beard, sighed and sipped from his teacup. 'And Owen? The other girls in Scott's? Have they been chatting about me behind my back? I couldn't help but feel that Owen was off with me when I called in with Jack.'

'Everyone seems very fond of you. I think with Owen, he just felt a bit thrown seeing you. The other girls say Rose's death hit him hard. That he relied on her to keep that place running smoothly. I didn't know him before . . . you know . . . but he, well all of them, I suppose, they really miss her. You coming in probably just added as a further reminder that she was gone.'

'She was very dedicated to her job. To him. To all the staff there. They were all good friends too. Always wanting to go out together – laughing and giggling,' he said. 'I suppose sometimes I forget I don't have a monopoly on grief for her.'

'I think you have more right than most,' I said softly, taking a small sip from my cup. It was scalding hot, burned the back of my throat, and I felt tears prick at my eyes as I waited for the sensation to pass.

'Are you okay?' Cian asked, looking straight at me in that all-seeing way again.

'Can I get a drink of water?' I croaked.

'Oh God, did I make it too hot for you?' he asked, jumping up and pulling a glass from the cupboard. 'Rose always used to tell me off. Said not everyone liked to have the mouth burned off them the way I did.'

He handed me the glass and I sipped from it, fighting the urge to gulp it down. The pain started to ease. 'It's okay,' I offered but he looked bereft.

'See, I can't do anything right.'

I reached out and touched his forearm, the bare skin warm beneath my touch. I fought the urge to close my eyes and breathe in the moment as a fizz of something – lust maybe – shot right to my core. 'You can,' I said softly. 'You are doing things right every day – keeping going, caring for Jack. I see how you are with him, how he looks at you. That's the most important thing you can do, and you do it well.'

I didn't move my hand; I liked how solid and real he felt. Then he placed his hand on top of mine, covering it completely. Making me want to feel him cover me entirely. To consume me.

'Thank you, Emily. You don't know how much that means to me. You really don't,' he said, jolting me back into the moment. Back to the reality that having those kinds of feelings for him was not appropriate. Back to wondering if he felt a little shiver of it too.

*

I felt light and, dare I say it, happy when I went home that evening. I was proud, if that's the right word, that Cian had confided in me. That he had sat with me, in his kitchen, and we had drunk several cups of tea and talked while Jack slept upstairs. He had spoken about Rose, of course, and his grief. He spoke of his love for his son. And he spoke of his life – his writing. How he feared he would never be able to put pen to paper again.

'Isn't it strange? To write about all the complexities of life, the intricacies of the human condition having led a relatively sheltered life? Then something like this happens, something that brings every emotion you ever experienced to the front of your consciousness – raw, real, more visceral than anything I could ever even think to write – and I feel paralysed by it? Christ, my last book was about a man terrified of losing all he held dear and I realise now it was bullshit. It was contrived nonsense. I don't have the words to express this hell. I don't have the ability to accurately depict what this feels like. It's beyond me. So if I can't write about it – about the reality of what this means, how this feels – I don't think I want to write again.'

He had looked stricken at the thought. I'd wanted to tell him I had started reading From Darkness Comes Light and felt connected to him by it. But maybe that would be weird. Still, when I went home I started reading again and I allowed myself to indulge in a little fantasy. The kind where his hand would rest on mine every day. The kind where I would help him learn how to smile again. The kind where I would help him find his voice again – start to write again. He would love me for it. He would move me into his grand house and my pictures would slowly start to replace those of Rose in the hall. Our family portrait, he, Jack, me and perhaps a baby of our own, would hang above the sofa. We'd make sure Jack never forgot his mother of course. We'd speak fondly of her. We'd keep her picture by his bedside. She would be his mother, always. But he would have a new family around him. I would have a family around me. I allowed myself to think about that for a short time before I shook myself out of my reverie – reminded myself just how much he loved her. Would it be possible for him to ever love anyone like that again? Would he ever love me?

Chapter Eighteen

Monday morning arrived and we all ignored the fact that while we set about our work, the funeral of Kevin McDaid was taking place in the same church where Rose had been buried just a few months before.

It would be a different affair, no doubt. No crowds of gawkers weeping at the tragedy of it. The press would be there, I supposed, given the ongoing investigation.

Still, it wasn't something we would discuss in work. We would just set about our business in our usual manner. There was a forced air of niceness about the place. Donna had a tight smile pinned to her face and had made sure to bring in chocolate biscuits from Marks & Spencer along with the milk for morning break.

She still looked tired though. I could have kicked myself as I remembered I had intended to text or call her over the weekend – see how things were going with the boys at home. If I wanted to make a life for myself here I needed to make real friendships. As a pathetic attempt at an apology I helped her make tea and coffee for everyone and poured some of the biscuits onto a plate.

'You're spoiling us,' I said, light-heartedly.

'Everyone deserves a treat now and again,' she said, lifting a round biscuit and taking a large bite. 'Besides, if I left them at home I wouldn't get a look in. The boys would be on them like a plague of locusts.' She half laughed, put the rest of the biscuit in her mouth and chewed.

'Well I'm glad of the gesture – although my hips might disagree,' I laughed back. Everyone gets jokes about diets. Especially women in a work environment on a Monday morning.

'There's nothing to your hips,' Donna said. 'Wait until you've carried three 9lb babies to term – then you'll know about hips.' She lifted a second biscuit and took a large bite, before patting her size 14 hips, hips that gave her a nice curve but that she was clearly uncomfortable with. I wanted to tell her she looked fabulous – hourglass, very Marilyn Monroe, but before I could speak, Tori marched in, her mouth a perfect 'o'.

'The police are outside,' she said. 'They want to talk to Owen. Do you know where he is?'

I shook my head, turned to Donna, who looked as though she had just seen a ghost, or heard of one's impending arrival.

'Donna?' I asked. 'Is Owen in? Have you seen him?'

She shook her head, putting the rest of her biscuit onto the worktop, running a glass of water and drinking it quickly while Tori just looked from me to Donna and back again.

'I haven't seen him,' I said to break the silence.

'He's running a little late,' Donna eventually said. 'Traffic, but he should be here any minute. Did they – the police – did they say what they wanted him for?'

Tori shook her head. 'I didn't think to ask, I suppose I got a little flustered. I'm not used to police landing here.'

'Jesus,' Donna said. 'That's all we need on top of everything else. Police standing in the waiting area. As if people aren't talking about this place enough with everything that has gone on.'

'Should I go and bring them through here?' I offered. 'Get them a cup of tea while they wait for Owen?'

Donna stared pointedly at Tori, before looking at me. 'That would be helpful, thank you,' she said.

'I'll get the surgeries opened up, everything switched on. Tori if you could get reception up and running – and, Emily, if you don't mind, look after the police. I'll go and phone Owen and let him know to get here.'

She stalked off into the admin office, leaving Tori shaken once again. 'I messed up again, didn't I?'

'Don't take it personally,' I assured her, leading the way to the reception area where two uniformed police officers stood, hats on, full bulletproof vests, handcuffs and guns on show. Not the relaxing atmosphere we usually tried to promote.

'Can I help you?' I started, and they turned to look at me – and I knew right there that I had seen the taller of the two before. Just a few days before, in fact, when I had stumbled into him coming out of Kevin McDaid's wake. It was my time to look as though I had seen a ghost, I felt my legs wobble a little. I reached for the reception desk to steady me, trying to look as nonchalant as possible. He may not even recognise me – it was dark, it was a very brief meeting and I was dressed differently, wrapped in a winter coat. But the narrowing of his eyes, the slight tilt of his head, the almost imperceptible pursing of his lips made me think he did.

'I'm guessing you're not Owen Scott,' he said, a smile on his face that didn't quite reach his eyes.

'No. No, I'm one of his receptionists,' I said, making a conscious decision not to tell my name unless asked. 'He's running a little late but I'm told he'll be here soon. If you and your colleague would like to follow me through to the staff

123

room, I'm sure we can get you a cup of tea or coffee while you wait.'

'Well that sounds like a plan,' the taller man said, reaching his hand out to shake mine. 'I'm Detective Sergeant John Bradley, and this is my colleague, Constable Stephen Johnson.'

'Well, Detective Sergeant Bradley and Constable Johnson, we even have a selection of chocolate biscuits on offer.' I tried to keep my voice light, professional, offer no more information than I needed to. I wouldn't even ask what it was in reference to – that was none of my business.

But still, any interlude with the police made me nervous – not just because DS Bradley might be wondering why I had been at Kevin McDaid's wake, but because it reminded me of when things were just so out of control. When I was doing my best to get better and move on but when he – the man I had once thought loved me – seemed determined to destroy me entirely. No, I wouldn't tell these police officers my name unless I had to. I didn't want them looking me up – seeing my file. Making decisions without knowing the full, sorry story.

I lead them through to the kitchen, where I made tea and small talk and tried to ignore the look they gave each other when they saw Rose's picture on the wall.

'So are there many of you who work here?' DS Bradley asked.

'Erm, well we have four dentists here, dental assistants, a hygienist and the admin team; I'm one of them – so fourteen? Some of us are part-time though.'

'And you, are you part-time?'

'No. For my sins I'm here full-time.' I said. 'But I like it. The people are good. Nice, you know.'

'And Rose Grahame?' He nodded to her picture. 'Was she here full-time as well?'

'Yes. Well more or less. I think she worked some family-friendly hours from time to time – to spend more time with her baby.'

'You think?' His eyebrow was raised.

'I didn't work here then. I started after.'

'Ah, you're her replacement?' he said, holding my gaze a little too long. Was it a trick of his – to try and get me to reveal more about myself? Stay quiet, leave a pause, wait for me to speak? Thankfully I was rescued by Owen arriving.

'These men are here to speak to you about Rose,' I told him, at which Bradley shook his head.

'Mr Scott, actually we're here to speak to you in connection with the Kevin McDaid inquiry? If we could have a moment.'

'Of course,' Owen said, but I could see he looked thrown. 'Although I'm not sure what help I can be. I didn't know him. But come through to my office and we can talk. I'll do whatever I can.'

He left the room, the two police officers following him – Bradley stopping just momentarily to nod a goodbye in my direction. I only realised when he left that I hadn't properly exhaled the entire time he had been there.

★

DS Bradley and his sombre-faced colleague nodded in my direction again as they left the surgery half an hour later. Tori and I looked towards Owen's office, expecting him to perhaps walk out and tell us what was going on. But the door remained closed for a few minutes and when it did open, Owen walked straight into his surgery – before buzzing through to tell us to send in his first client and to apologise to anyone waiting for having been delayed. He told us to offer to reschedule for anyone who couldn't wait to be seen. Before saying anymore he hung up, leaving Tori and me staring at each other, more than a little confused. But the increasingly busy waiting room jolted us into action and we sent our first client, an emergency root canal, through to Owen only for our phone to buzz again and Owen to inquire where Donna was.

I had assumed she was waiting for him in the surgery, but as that clearly wasn't true, I went to look for her in the staff room where she was sitting staring at the picture of Rose and sipping from the same cup of tea – now stone cold – that she had made when she arrived.

'Owen's looking for you,' I said.

'The police gone?' she asked.

'Yes, about five minutes ago. Owen just went straight into the surgery, wants to get through the list.'

'He didn't say what it was all about?'

I shook my head. 'But I'm sure he will. If it's anything major. But I think you better go through.'

'Yes,' she said, standing up slowly. 'I suppose I should. Never a dull day,' she said, the smile on her face again not quite reaching her eyes.

'If you need to talk . . .' I said to her back as she left the room, but she didn't answer – just waved her hand in my direction.

By the time lunchtime had hit, we were almost back on schedule. Owen didn't join us in the staff room; in fact he kept himself to himself as the day went on. When I did get a chance to speak to Donna, to ask her if he had told her anything about the police visit, she shook her head.

'Sure we've been knee-deep in clients all day – we haven't had a chance to talk, and from his mood I don't think he's likely to tell me anything anyway. He's like a bear with a sore head.'

She rubbed her temples.

'Headache?' I said.

She nodded. 'I'm not sleeping the best, with everything. I'd scurry off for the afternoon but we are so busy, I don't think it would be fair on anyone.'

'We're almost caught up, you know. I can help Owen in surgery, there's nothing too complicated this afternoon. You have to look after yourself. I know things have been tough, and I know you would normally have spoken to Rose about all this stuff, but I'm here if you need me. Any time, you know. You can talk to me.'

She bowed her head for a moment and when she lifted it again I noticed she was blinking back tears. I reached over and squeezed her hand, congratulating myself on being a good friend.

'I think I will go home,' she said softly. 'Maybe get some sleep while the boys are at school. Shift this headache.'

'I have some paracetamol in my bag?' I offered.

'That would be great,' she said, through a watery smile, and I left to go and retrieve my handbag.

When Donna had taken her tablets, packed up her things and left for home, I told Tori to man reception and I took myself into Owen's surgery, wondering if he would tell me anything about what exactly the police wanted.

'Where's Donna?'

'She's not well again, so I said I would help out, if that's okay?'

He sighed, deeply, as if the thought of me working alongside him was almost unbearable. 'Well I suppose it will have to be,' he snapped and I felt myself pulled upright by the harshness of his tone.

'I'm sorry . . . but she really did seem unwell. Stress at home and headaches and she's not been sleeping.'

'None of us have though, have we?' he said, before catching my eyes and muttering that he was sorry and could we just get on with things.

'If you need to talk at all,' I said as I opened the file for the next patient and refilled the cup of mouthwash by the chair, 'I'm here. But equally, I can just work in silence too.' I forced myself to sound nonchalant, as if I didn't give two hoots if he ever spoke to me again.

'The police – they think there is more to McDaid's death,' he said, sitting down on his stool. 'And they think that means there could be more to Rose's death too.'

'More to Rose's death?' I tried to keep my voice steady but already I could feel my heart rate increasing. A thin film of sweat breaking on my forehead.

'They weren't saying too much – just asking questions about Rose, her friends, her family, Cian. Did she know McDaid, have much to do with him when he was a patient here? That kind of thing.'

'God,' was all I could mutter as I tried to keep my heart from pounding.

'I told them I couldn't think of a single person who would want to hurt Rose, and that's true.'

But there was someone who wanted to hurt me.

'But what happened to Rose was an accident?' I said, flashes of the look of resignation on her face jumping into my head.

'From what I could gather – and please, Emily, tell no one because this is all just me trying to make sense of it – they think it might not have been that much of an accident after all . . . even though, God, that makes no sense at all. None.'

★

Not much of an accident after all.

Not much of an accident after all.

Not much of an accident after all.

Maybe. They think. Perhaps. Several lines of inquiry. He didn't know anymore. He was trying to make sense of it all himself.

But information had emerged to suggest Kevin McDaid driving into Rose was not just a case of a joyride gone wrong.

I wondered what Liz McDaid would think of that? If she pushed for answers and got the wrong ones; ones that made her hate her beloved, now deceased, baby boy?

I wondered what Cian would think. Jesus, how would he react? That there was even the slight hint of a possibility that Rose Grahame was killed on purpose.

I knew what I thought. I knew I had been right all along. There was nothing accidental about what happened except that it had happened to the wrong person.

What if it really should have been me?

I felt my legs turn to jelly, heard someone, somewhere in the distance call my name as everything went black.

★

Back then – when everything was falling apart – I didn't understand how Ben could be angry. I didn't understand why he thought he had a right to be angry. He had been in control, always. He had pulled the strings and I had danced. He had cut the strings and I had fallen – just as he must have known I would. But still and all, he was angry.

Angry that I had feelings that didn't just vanish into a puff of smoke.

I wasn't mean to him. I wasn't cruel. I didn't hurt him – not the way he hurt me. I didn't raise my hand to him. I didn't smash in his car windows, or break into his house and cut one leg off each pair of trousers or put frozen prawns down the back of his radiators. I didn't take to social media to tell anyone what a cheating bastard he was. I didn't share compromising pictures of him. I didn't go to the police and tell them how he had hit me. How he had abused me. How he had forced himself on me. Or had he; was it a fantasy – a consensual thing that got him going every time I said no? Even when I meant no. How could he have known when the lines had been blurred? Because everything inside was a little mangled. Stockholm syndrome? Isn't that what they call it? When a kidnapped person falls for their captor? Not that he had kidnapped me – I had gone of my own accord, freely and in the belief that he loved me and I loved him. And that no one else could ever love me the way he did. No one else *would* ever love me. That's what he told me anyway.

I put up with it because it wasn't always bad. There were times when it was good and I felt like the most cherished woman on the planet and I convinced myself that this was real and this was what life was like. No one was perfect. No relationship was perfect.

So when he took it all away – I didn't know how to react.

I was convinced Ben had made a mistake. So I messaged him. And I called him. I walked around to his house and I stood on his doorstep and rang his doorbell, shouted in his letter box. Begged him to talk to me, until he threatened to call the police.

On one occasion, I walked round to his house, stood on his doorstep and rang his doorbell and shouted in his letter box until he *did* call the police. He didn't even come to talk to me. He told the police I was mad. Mad? I raged so much when they told me that I'm sure I did look mad. I tried to explain everything, but they weren't relationship counsellors. This was a matter between the two of us, they told me, and one we should discuss without disturbing the peace.

They didn't seem to get that Ben wouldn't talk to me. When he had left, outraged that I'd uncovered his infidelity, he had made a clean, brutal cut. He had no interest in discussing anything. No matter what time I called at – morning, noon, night or 3am – he wouldn't answer my calls. Then his line went dead and I knew he had changed his number. So I went to his work, where I sat, bleary faced, still vaguely smelling of alcohol, trying to calm my birds' nest of a hair do into something respectable, rubbing at my eyes, which were red from crying. My hands were shaking, clammy; I realised I'd forgotten to repair the chips on my nail polish. So I sat, nibbling, scratching, pulling at the sleeves of my cardigan to cover my hands. And I waited for him. Waited until I saw him walk in with one of his female colleagues. Before I knew it, before I knew what I was doing or saying I was beside him, tugging on his suit jacket. I was begging him to talk to me. Pleading with him. Telling him in front of everyone – so he knew I meant it – that I forgave everything he had done. All the hurt. All the lies. All the times he lost his temper. All the times he had slept with someone else. Even those pictures. I had sobbed, scraping the rough wool of my cardigan sleeve across my face, make-up from the day before, or the week before, smearing with tears and snot and spit and God knows what.

I knew there were eyes on me – people looking at me – but I was sure if I could make him understand it would be okay. But all I could see was the look of anger on his face. I waited for it to pass, to ease, his muscles to relax into a look of concern. A look of love even, if I'm honest. When I felt his hand on my arm, I momentarily sagged with relief. He was touching me. He was connecting with me. He pulled me into a side room, where I tried my very best to kiss him.

Only he pushed me away. He pushed me away and then wiped his mouth, a look of disgust replacing the earlier anger.

'Emily, for fuck's sake. Get a grip. You can't be here. You can't do this. It's fucking over. Accept it and leave me the fuck alone.'

I wailed and threw myself at him, begging. Pleading loudly. Sobbing while he whispered sour nothings in my ear.

Not if you were the last woman.

Did you really think I would marry you?

I'm glad I left when I did. Look at the state of you.

You disgust me.

You're mad. You mad, ugly bitch.

I sobbed as if each word were a physical punch. Sobbed until I couldn't any more. Sobbed until the police took me away, in front of all his work colleagues. Sobbed as they bundled me into the back of a police car and took me to the station to sober up. Sobbed as my mother told me she was ashamed to know me.

Then I sobbed as he sent me a text message telling me he would never forgive me for humiliating him like that. And one day he would get his own back.

★

'I thought we'd been over this,' Maud said. I could tell she was trying to hide the irritation from her voice. 'Think about it, rationally. Why on earth? Why now?'

It was just after 2pm New York time and I had her assistant pull her from a meeting to talk to me about my emergency. She had come on the phone, breathless, concerned, only to inhale deeply, loudly, when I told her I was sure, sure as I could be, that Kevin McDaid had meant to kill me. That I had been right about Ben all along.

'Because he can now. It's long enough ago that no one would think it was him . . .'

'Because he has moved on. We've all moved on. What happened then was horrible, but it is in the past,' she said.

'But Owen said the police think it might not have been an accident after all,' I said, taking another pill and waiting for the wave of calmness to hit me. I rapped my fingers on the worktop, wondering why Maud couldn't understand my concerns. 'And there is no one in the world that would want to hurt Rose. People love her, everyone. I've not heard a single bad word—'

'You don't know that,' Maud said. 'You know a couple of people from her life and you went to her funeral. It doesn't mean you know everyone loved her, or that she had no enemies. Or that her husband had no enemies. Or that, maybe, the police have it wrong.'

I felt myself tense up. She just wasn't getting it. 'But don't you understand, Maud? I've always known something like this would happen at some stage. I've been watching my back since we split and he threatened me. You don't know what he is capable of. To him I'm nothing more than a liability. A ball fit for kicking. It makes more sense this way, don't you see it?'

'Look, sweetheart,' Maud said, exasperated, 'I know he was a bastard. He is a bastard. But I don't think he would be that bad. That's a whole other level of bastard,' she paused.

I felt the pressure in my head increase. I had told Maud all about him. The way he destroyed me – stripped away every ounce of my confidence not to mention my sanity. How could she not know that coming back into my life just to hurt me was something he was more than capable of? I'd been expecting it. If I was honest, in the earlier days I kind of craved it, craved him coming back and seeking vengeance. I would be near him again. That was back when I didn't fully accept what he had done, what he had made me become. Then I feared it. I tried to run from it. Went through counselling. Support groups.

No one tells you what to do when it comes flooding back unexpectedly though.

'Have you been taking your tablets?' she asked, cutting through my thoughts. 'When was the last time you saw your doctor? Your counsellor? Are you still with the mental health team?'

I rubbed my temples. Just because I had been not strictly sane in the past, that didn't mean this was any kind of madness.

'I'm fine, Maud,' I replied tersely. 'Yes, I'm taking my pills and being a good girl. Doing everything I'm supposed to do . . .'

'If you are concerned about your safety, you could contact the police,' she offered, half-heartedly, but that was the last thing I would do. They would take one look at my file and they too, like Maud, would sigh deeply and tell me it was all in my head.

And maybe it was, and maybe it wasn't. All I knew is that I was scared. Scared and vulnerable and tired of being scared and vulnerable. I just wanted someone who understood. Someone who knew what it was like to lose someone and to be changed forever by it. Someone who was like me.

Someone like Cian.

Chapter Nineteen

Rose

2011

Rose Grahame: Glad rags on – tonight I help my amazing husband celebrate the launch of his incredible book, *Unseen*. Darling Cian, you have excelled yourself this time and I am so proud of you. Love you always, you are my light x #proudwife #buythebook!

Nails (a classic French manicure) done.

Spray tan (subtle) done.

Hair (elegant up-do) done.

I rolled the silky stockings up my legs before dressing in a beautifully tailored knee-length black dress, with a cowl neck that showed off just a hint of cleavage. I slipped my feet into three-inch court shoes. Looking in the mirror, I clipped my pearl earrings on, and a single strand of pearls around my neck. I looked, well, good. I felt elegant. I felt like a proper grown-up – stylish, well turned out.

I felt like someone who would make Cian proud – that he

would be delighted to have me on his arm. That I would look like just the kind of wife who belonged beside him in literary circles – not just 'Rose who worked in the dentists'. Not that I was ashamed of working in the dentists – far from it. Cian had said I could leave if I wanted – his significant six figure deal for *Unseen* gave us a financial freedom we hadn't known before – but I was happy to stay working. After some convincing – making him believe I didn't want to stay because I lacked faith in him, but because I actually enjoyed working and spending time with my work colleagues – he had backed off. However, he had warned me I mightn't have much in common with what he called his 'book crowd'.

So I'd spent the last fortnight reading *The Bookseller* and trying to get myself up to speed with who was who and what was hot in the book trade. I'd prepared for questions about what it was like to live with Cian (told myself not to mention how unbearably touchy he got when in edits) and, of course, I read his book from cover to cover to make sure I was able to talk about it with a degree of authority.

I'd spent a lot of time trying to calm Cian down. To assure him the book would be a success, that his publishers and his agent wouldn't have got behind him in such a big way if they didn't believe in him 100%. In his better moods, he had hugged me and told me he loved me for being so completely behind him. In his worse days, he had railed a bit, told me I didn't understand, could never understand. That how could someone who's ambitions only ever extended to helping clean teeth ever understand the pressure he was under? How hard it was?

His words had cut me to the quick. I'm not afraid to say I cried – but he had apologised over and over again and told me that he was just stressed and he didn't mean it. I had held him, assured him I was okay and that we were okay while he had calmly told me that working at the level he was working at brought so many stresses he had never really thought about before. That I was lucky to have 'a wee nothing job' that I could 'leave behind at the end of the day'.

I suppose in some ways he was right – it was just that I never thought of it like that before. I did my job well. We helped people. We worked together as a team. Okay, no one was going to give me a huge contract to do it. No one was going to review my work in the broadsheets or invite me to talk about it on panel shows where everyone wore tweed and twirled their moustaches. But it mattered to me.

I tried to shake those feelings off as I spritzed his favourite perfume on my neck and wrists and dropped the bottle into my clutch bag before walking out of the bedroom, down the hall of our flat, to where I knew he was waiting in the living room.

With a fairly confident 'Ta da' I walked in and he turned from where he had been looking out the window, waiting for our taxi, to look at me.

I'm not sure what reaction I was expecting – a 'Wow' would have been nice. God, even a 'You look nice' would have sufficed. I knew I had done my best – had scrubbed up well for want of a better turn of phrase – but his face was frozen as he looked me up and down.

'Cian?' I asked, a sinking feeling giving me a sucker punch in my stomach.

I heard a car turn into the gravel drive outside our flat, a horn sound and Cian swear.

'Jesus,' he swore under his breath. 'Rose, now's not the time for jokes.'

'Jokes?' I muttered, my face blazing and tears, to my shame, stinging at my eyes.

'That dress? It's a joke, right? Your tits are practically hanging out of it.'

I blushed harder. Felt a wave of shame hit me as the disappointment radiated off him in waves. Even that word. Tits. Horrible. It made me feel like a tramp. In a dress I thought made me look classy, elegant.

'This is a book launch, not an episode of *Footballers' Wives*,' he said crossing the room in a couple of steps and grabbing my wrist, pulling me towards the bedroom – my shoes slipping on the tiled floor so I kicked them off.

'I can't believe . . .' he said. 'The taxi is here, Rose. Tonight of all nights. Could you not just get it right this one night?'

His words felt like blows – 'just this one night' – had I not got it right before? Did I really look like a joke? I thought the dress gave just the hint of cleavage – the cleavage he loved. He threw open my wardrobe. Pulled hanger after hanger out throwing dresses on the bed.

'Get changed,' he shouted at me, while he cast aside other clothes he deemed unsuitable. Not that I had much to choose from – I didn't have a lot of special occasion clothes. I hesitated, felt a sob rise from my chest and sneak out.

'Oh, for God's sake,' he said, frustrated, as he threw a long sleeved, boat neck maxi dress at me – one I had been meaning to charity shop for a while because I didn't feel it did me any favours. It was as close to a Burka as Western fashion could get and I don't know why I had ever bought it.

'I don't like this one,' I said as my lovely, elegant dress slipped to the floor.

'Put it on, Rose. Stop being such a baby – this isn't about you and what you like. I'll be waiting in the taxi.'

He stormed out of the room – and part of me, the 'Fuck you, Cian Grahame' part considered putting my lovely new dress back on and going out to the taxi, telling him he could deal with it and putting him in his place.

But this was his night and I didn't want to make things

worse. I didn't want to sour the whole evening. I knew this wasn't Cian. Not the real Cian. Not the man I loved and who I knew loved me. I knew he would apologise and feel ashamed for his behaviour. When he saw the bruise that was starting to form already on my wrist, he would be sorry.

I pulled the maxi dress on and quickly patted some pressed powder on my cheeks to cover where tears had spilled.

This was not about me.

This was about my husband and the immense pressure he was under.

You hurt the ones you love, so they say. I was his safe place to let off steam.

Things would settle. Would calm down. I would get my Cian back. My wonderful, loving Cian. Usually loving anyway.

Chapter Twenty

Emily

I had spent the hours before bed checking and double checking that my doors and windows were locked, my curtains were pulled and even going so far as to push my hall table up against the front door. I made sure I had the police on speed dial, and that my phone was fully charged and my bedroom door locked. I had slept with a knife under my side of the bed, just in case. And I had vowed to call my old support worker at Women's Aid the following morning.

I had even clicked into Ben's profile. I'm not sure why. It was unlikely he was going to give away his guilt on his timeline, but I needn't have bothered. His privacy settings were solid.

I googled his name, uncovering a LinkedIn profile that had him working for a bank in Birmingham. It offered me some comfort at least, even though he hadn't updated his details in eighteen months.

When I woke it was just starting to get light and everything seemed, for the moment anyway, a little less scary. Still, I'd make sure to keep the knife under my bed and maybe add another lock to my door.

But for now, I had to pull myself together. I had to think of the present and to the future and not fixate on the past.

Cian and Jack were due in for their appointment that day. That would be my focus. I had moved things around a little the day before to make sure Sarah would need help with record-keeping during the appointment and I'd be the very girl to do it. And even though I never considered myself to be much of a girly girl, I admit I made more of an effort that morning with my hair and make-up. A bit more smoky-eyed, a bit fuller of lip. My hair extra bouncy – but not too much. Not enough to be obvious.

Owen commented that I looked brighter and said he was sorry for sounding off to me and that he was just trying to process all that was happening. He asked me not to say anything more about the police investigation to anyone – not until he knew more himself.

Donna seemed a little brighter, a little more rested as well. The boys had behaved last night: saw she was stressed, cooked dinner and washed up without having to be asked. Her eldest had even poured her a glass of wine. I told her it was okay to have an off day. We all had them.

But today would be a good day. I would bring myself into the moment. I'd message Maud later to tell her I was doing better and when Cian Grahame came into the surgery, I would look every inch the professional, elegant and trustworthy woman he could feel comfortable confiding in again. Because surely that was only one step away from him falling for me – properly.

By the time he arrived, I had butterflies in my tummy. I had to remind myself not to spring from my seat grinning when he walked in. Not to look so needy. Not to be so needy – wasn't that what got me into so much trouble the last time? So I sat at the desk and waited. When Cian saw me, I was sure I saw a hint of a smile on his face.

'Emily,' he said, as he lifted Jack from his buggy. 'It's nice to see you.'

Jack turned around to look at who his daddy was talking to and he smiled widely when I waved at him. 'It's nice to see you, and this little man too. Hi Jack, are you going to show off your lovely toothy pegs?'

He grinned, opened his mouth and shouted 'Ah!' at the top of his lungs.

'I'll bring you through to Sarah now,' I said, smiling. 'You don't mind if I sit in on the appointment, do you? All the girls are busy today but it's a first appointment – so I'll just be getting this young man's notes up and running.'

'Of course I don't mind,' Cian said as I held the door open for him and he walked through carrying a beaming Jack and sat him in the dentist's chair, where the toddler immediately opened his mouth as wide as he could.

Sarah laughed and Cian blushed. 'We might have been practicing a little too much,' he smiled. 'Haven't we Jack?'

Jack nodded and smiled up at Cian while he held his hand and Sarah set about chatting to him. For a dentist who didn't normally take young patients she had a lovely way with him and the pair were soon laughing and giggling as she counted the little white teeth in his mouth.

She called out a series of numbers and letters and I jotted notes in the folder in front of me. I was struggling to concentrate but I didn't want to make a show of myself in front of Cian so I forced myself to pay attention. All too soon, the check-up was done with both Jack and Cian wearing 'I was good for the Dentist' stickers. I watched as Cian bundled Jack back into his coat and made to leave.

I felt deflated. A hint of a smile and a wave from Jack? This is not what I had been hoping for. I followed them through to the reception area, sat behind my desk and tried to hide my disappointment.

I heard Cian say my name and looked up, just in time to catch Jack as he jumped into my arms. 'He wants to say thank you for being the best helper lady.' Jack planted a slobbery cheek on my face, which tickled and I laughed loudly – and that sent Jack into a fit of giggles himself.

'It's so good to hear him laugh,' Cian said.

I smiled. 'He seems a happy little boy, and that's all credit to you.'

'In spite of everything, eh?' he said.

'How are you holding up? I asked. Despite Owen telling me not to talk about the police visit, I wanted to tell Cian about it. Surely he, of all people, deserved to know? But this was not the place.

Cian shrugged his shoulders. 'As you would expect.'

'If you need to talk?' I asked, handing Jack back to him, enjoying the momentary contact with the warmth of his body.

'I'll message you later,' he said, his voice low.

'Any time, Cian. I mean that.'

'Before I go,' Cian said, 'is Owen here?'

I was about to say yes – tell him I would see if he was free when Tori chimed in that no, he had gone out for a late lunch. Cian shrugged his shoulders and, putting Jack back into his buggy, he left.

'It's not like Owen to go out for lunch,' I said, while checking who was next in with Sarah.

'He's not really,' Tori whispered. 'He just told me to say that. Said he didn't want to get caught up in a conversation with Cian.'

'I don't get what's going on between them,' I said. Tori just shrugged her shoulders, and turned back to her computer. She clearly wasn't in the mood for getting caught up in a conversation with me either.

'Who's next with Sarah?' I asked her.

'Louise Flanagan – but she hasn't showed yet.'

'Is there anyone here early we could take instead?'

Tori shook her head. 'Looks like you have a free few minutes. Lucky you. Maybe you could leave these files back in the office for me?'

I lifted the bundle of files and turned on my heel. I have to admit I wasn't particularly enamoured with Tori's attitude, or her ordering me about. I wondered what was eating at her – and then it struck me, she must have seen how Cian looked at me. She was probably suspicious, jealous even. I vowed to play it extra careful over these next few days and weeks. In the meantime, I would do as I was told and be a good little employee.

I hadn't been expecting to find Owen in the office surrounded by a pile of files on his desk.

'I'm just putting these back for Tori,' I said. 'I won't be long.'

He shook his head. I noticed that his eyes looked bloodshot, his face tired. 'If you don't mind me saying so, Owen. You don't look well.'

'I'm fine,' he said tersely. 'Just trying to find something.'

'Can I help?' I offered, trying to ignore the fact everyone in Scott's seemed to have swallowed a grumpy pill that day.

He stood up, lifted two files from the desk and made to leave the room. Only when he reached the door did he stop to look at me. 'You can tidy this lot up,' he said, just as I noticed the file in his hand was labelled with Kevin McDaid's name.

★

I tidied the file room, assisted with a few more appointments, made tea for everyone who wanted it – and by the time home time arrived I was finding it hard to maintain pleasantries.

Everyone was in a fouler of a mood and I started to feel my own slip. As daylight faded, I started to feel uneasy again and all I wanted to do was to get home to the safety of my flat, lock out the world and wait for Cian to get in touch.

As I walked away from the surgery towards the carpark at Foyle Street, I was interrupted by a call of 'Excuse me' from behind. I walked on a few feet, sure whoever was calling couldn't have been looking for me, until I heard it a second time – this time closer. It was a female voice but that didn't make me feel any less uneasy. I picked up my pace and walked on, head down, my keys poised in my hand just in case.

I heard footsteps quicken behind me and I walked a little faster, my heartbeat picking up with every step. I reminded myself to keep breathing. This was a well-lit, busy area. What harm could come to me? Except, of course, when Rose died it had been in a well-lit busy area.

I felt the brush of a hand on my arm, a pull as she gripped my jacket. I turned around ready to shout as loud as I could that she should leave me alone when I saw a rather flustered-looking woman, perhaps in her thirties, hair bone-straight in a perfectly set blonde bob. Minimal make-up – but flawless skin. She wore a full-length military-style coat, and she had pulled the collar up around her neck to keep warm. There was a hint of a pinkish glow to her cheeks and as she apologised for stopping me, she appeared to be a little breathless.

'I'm sorry,' she said. 'I know you are probably really busy but I wondered if you would be able to help me at all, I'm really quite stuck.'

I looked around, tried to see if anyone else was watching or lurking nearby. She seemed to be on her own. I expected her to ask me if she could use my phone, or perhaps give her some money for the bus home – although she didn't look the kind that would ever need to ask for money.

'You work at Scott's, don't you?' she said.

'Yes,' I said, not as calmly as I would have liked. I could still feel my heart thumping. 'But we're closed now. I'm afraid if you're looking for a dentist you'll have to call back in the morning.'

She shook her head. 'No, no. It's not like that. I just need to speak to someone from Scott's. My name is Ingrid Devlin, I'm a reporter for the *Chronicle*.' She fished in her pocket and made to hand me a card but I had no desire to talk to anyone from the press, so I shook my head, said I had nothing to say to her, turned on my heel and started to walk off in the direction of the car park.

'Please,' she called after me. 'I've been sent out here to get something – if I don't come back with a story, I might as well hand in my notice.' Her voice cracked as she came to the end of her sentence. I could hear her footsteps speed up behind me again. 'Look, I've been trying to speak to people – just to do a piece on Rose Grahame – how well she was thought of. That kind of thing. But nobody is talking and I'm running out of leads.'

I turned around to look at her – saw her pleading eyes, as she hastily brushed away tears. 'My boss has told me if I fuck this up, I may as well start looking for another job, so I'm really desperate.' Her head bowed, I watched as her shoulders started to shake.

She looked the perfect picture of misery – the kind of picture of misery I was only too familiar with.

'Look, I'm not sure I can be any help to you. I'm relatively new.'

No doubt sensing she had an in, Ingrid looked at me, a hopeful expression sneaking out from behind her tears. 'Any help at all you could give me would be great. I'm sure you've heard people talking about her? It will be anonymous, you know. I mean I'll know your name and all – but in the story you'll just be a source. No one will ever know it's you. You won't get into trouble and it would really save my life.'

Against my better judgement, I asked what it was she wanted to know.

'Maybe we could have a sit down and a chat?' she said, her demeanour suddenly more chipper. 'Why don't we call in here?' she asked, nodding towards The River Inn, a pub at the very bottom of Shipquay Street. 'Glass of wine on me? As a thank you.'

I looked around me just to check that no one from Scott's was watching, and then I followed Ingrid Devlin into the bar, where she found us a booth within seconds and had ordered a bottle of wine before I had the chance to say I really should just stick to tea.

Of course when it arrived, it looked too good to resist. Condensation formed on the outside of the bottle, drops running in rivulets down the neck into the ice bucket. Ingrid lifted the bottle and poured two generous glasses.

'I don't know about you, but I could really do with this today,' she said, as she fished in her handbag, pulling out her phone, a notebook and a pen. She set her phone to voice record and sat it between us before lifting her glass and gesturing to me to do the same. 'Cheers,' she said, as I half-heartedly clinked my glass against hers. 'To a lifesaver – and girls helping each other out.'

I took a large gulp from my glass – anything to settle the feeling of unease sitting in the pit of my stomach. If Maud were here she would grimace. Tell me I'd gotten myself into another fine mess.

'So tell me,' Ingrid said, 'have there been any whispers around the workplace? Any rumours Cian Grahame is not the man everyone thinks he is?'

I spluttered, sat my wine glass down and looked at Ingrid. Cian? Why was she asking about him? 'I thought this was a piece about how great Rose was?'

'Yes, of course,' she said confidently. 'But you must know there are some nasty rumours doing the rounds about her husband too?'

Nasty rumours? This was ridiculous. 'I'm not aware of any rumours, nasty or otherwise,' I said coldly. 'But I can tell you this – no one at Scott's has a bad word to say about Cian.'

'No one has ever mentioned that he may have a temper?'

Cian Grahame was the most sensitive man I had ever met. A temper? Perhaps regarding the death of his wife, but that's all. Not that it was any of this Ingrid Devlin's business. She was the kind of reporter who gave journalists a bad name. 'I really don't think I should continue with this . . . this . . . whatever it is.'

'Okay, I'm sorry. I won't push it. It's just, you know, when you hear things . . .'

'Hear things like what?' I asked.

Ingrid Devlin leant across the table towards me, put her hand over her mobile phone to muffle what it was she was about to say. 'Look, I have a contact in the police. I'm not supposed to say anything – but I have it on good authority that Cian Grahame is about to come under some serious scrutiny. And not just in relation to his beloved wife – there are questions being asked about a suspicious deposit made into Kevin McDaid's bank account the week Rose died.'

She sat back, hand off her phone, waiting to pick up anything I might say.

'I've never heard anything so ridiculous in my life,' I said, standing up, leaving the wine glass barely touched. 'If you had any idea about Rose and Cian—'

'But I thought you didn't really know them? That you hadn't worked there very long?' she asked me, a little smile – more genuine than any of her previous tears had been – playing on her lips.

'I know enough to know he wouldn't hurt her,' I said before quickly realising I'd better say no more. I wouldn't trust this woman not to twist everything I said and make it into some terrible lie in print. 'I don't think I have anything more to say to you,' I said, turning to walk away, leaving her dumbstruck with the best part of a bottle of wine to drink all by herself.

★

When my phone rang as I drove home from work and I saw my brother's name flash on my screen, my first thought was that something bad had happened to either of my parents. It was a fear I lived with – brought on myself I suppose because I avoided visiting them, not able to cope with the sad, disappointed way they now looked at me. So I mentally settled myself at the thought that any time now I could get a call and my parents – both in their seventies – could have taken ill, or died, or broken a hip and I would be handed another guilt-laden stick with which to beat myself.

Simon never called me. Ever. He occasionally sent a text. Short and to the point. Thanking me for a card sent for his daughter's birthday. Telling me to call mum and dad.

I couldn't really remember the last time I'd heard his actual voice. The big Christmas dinner of disappointment perhaps? Where we had all sat mired in shame, embarrassment and an underlying low-level seething anger – scraping our forks around our plates. The turkey had been too dry – turned to dust in my mouth. I lifted my wine glass to wash it down, all eyes, bar the children's, immediately on mine. How much drink is too much drink on Christmas Day when you've gained a reputation as the town mad woman – the one who always smelled faintly of alcohol, whose skin had a permanent sticky sheen to it?

I had pretended, of course, that I hadn't heard my mother whisper to my father that perhaps they shouldn't have got any alcohol for the dinner. In support of me. Just as I pretended I hadn't heard my father whisper back angrily that he had not reached this stage of life to miss out on a fine Sancerre with his Christmas dinner just because his daughter had made a state of herself.

Part of me wanted to let the phone ring. He could leave a voicemail. Deliver the bad news that way – but a conscience is a terrible thing. I pulled over to the side of the road and answered.

'I was just about to hang up,' he said, his voice strained. No hello. No warm greeting.

'I'm sorry,' I said, immediately hating myself for apologising. He always made me feel like this, as if my very act of existing was enough of a hardship on him that I needed to apologise for it. 'I'm driving. I had to pull over.'

'Are you on your way home?' he asked.

'Yes,' I replied. 'Traffic's heavy. I should be there in about ten minutes – do you want me to call you back when I get there? Is everything okay? Is it mum or dad?'

'Ten minutes,' he said. 'I'll talk to you when you get here.'

With that he hung up and I was left to absorb what he had just told me. I'll talk to you when you get here. Why could he not just have told me what it was he wanted? Why did he have to continue to try and play some sort of mind game where I was the silly little sister and he could talk down to me whatever way he wanted? He didn't drive here, seventy miles from his home, for good news. I felt my hands grip the steering wheel tighter – but at the same time my palms were sweaty, my grip on the wheel and my equilibrium wavering. 'Just breathe,' I whispered to myself as I pulled out into traffic and towards home.

His car was parked on the road outside, half on the pavement. Blocking the footpath for anyone trying to get past with a buggy or a wheelchair or bags of shopping. But that was Simon. He thought mainly of himself. I pulled into my reserved parking space and walked around to the communal entrance where I found not only Simon, but my mother too. Immediately I found myself relieved that she was clearly okay but Simon's lips, pursed in disdain, soon had me feeling uneasy again. I wanted to tell him he looked stupid – all cat's arse pouty. But the tilt of my mother's head and the way she reached out to me and pulled me into a hug, whispering over and over that I should have come to them for help, blindsided me.

Come to them for help over what? I pulled back. 'Mum, lovely and all as it is to see you, there's really no need. I'm fine. I don't need any help. Who's told you I need help?'

I could almost hear the dramatic roll of Simon's eyes in his head, watched as my mother elbowed him into behaving. 'You don't have to put up a pretence with me, Emily. I know what's been going on. But look, the doorstep's not the place to discuss this kind of business.' She whispered 'business' as if it were a dirty word.

I perched uncomfortably on my sofa while Simon made tea, and my mother sat staring directly at me. I noticed the fine lines that were less fine than before. Had her skin looked that delicate and crêpe-like before? If so, for how long? Had I not noticed the paleness of her eyes, red–rimmed with age, framed by wrinkles that didn't disappear no matter her expression? Had I not noticed her ageing?

'You aren't to be cross with Maud,' she started. 'You know she has your interests at heart. She's worried about you. She says you think Ben is after you? Ben? Seriously, Emily?'

I could hear the crack in her voice. The underlying worry that we were going *there* again.

'Look Mum, something happened and it upset me and yes, I got a little carried away . . .' I looked around the room. The curtains pulled. The multiple locks. I realised I probably wasn't looking the most sane.

Simon walked back into the room carrying three mugs of tea.

'I'm going to cut to the chase here because Mum won't – and I don't want to see her and Dad go through what they did before.'

'This is nothing like that,' I said, angrily perhaps. Enough to make my mother stiffen. The fear never far. A small pocket of anger was building inside of me – threatening to release. Simon, my mother – both seemingly more concerned that I was losing the plot again without bothering to ask the nature of my concerns. Without caring about whether or not I actually was in danger. As long as I didn't upset them again.

'They want you to move back home for a bit. Maud told them you left CallSolutions.'

'And I have another job – one I love. I'm not moving home. I'm happy where I am.'

Simon cast a glance around my flat – dark, closed in, safe – and rolled his eyes. 'Really?'

I eyed him back. 'Really!'

Mum took my hand. 'But you . . . you saw that woman die, Emily. That can't be easy. It might have triggered something. It's no wonder you're thinking of Ben and getting a bit . . . well—'

'Obsessed,' Simon cut in.

'I'm not obsessed,' I said loudly. 'But I can't let go of what happened then either. It may not suit you to believe that your friend could treat me so badly, but he could.'

Simon shook his head and my mother looked to the floor. It was clear they still thought I had been the only one at fault when things went wrong. Maybe if I had pushed it? Reported him? Told police about the abuse? But of course I didn't because I wanted him back. I'd made my bed and here I was lying in it.

'Regardless of that,' I continued, 'I'm not obsessed. If I never saw him again or heard mention of his name it would be absolutely fine by me.' I bit my tongue. As much as I wanted to tell them I was scared, I couldn't. They would haul me back up the road to Belfast and put me on suicide watch, fill me with more mind-numbing medication. I couldn't go there again. I wouldn't.

'There's no need to upset yourself,' my mother said, oblivious to the fact it had been both her and Simon's inability to believe I wasn't the villain in all this that was the cause of my upset.

'I'm not,' I said. I took my mother's hand and rubbed it, assured her over and over again that I was honestly, truly okay and I internally wished with all my heart that she believed me, that it had never been me in the wrong back then so that I could tell her exactly how I was feeling at that moment. I wished she believed in me as much as she believed in Ben. He always could win anyone over with his charisma. Even my parents, it seemed. When he came to them, full of mock concern for my mental health after he had destroyed me, they believed that there was no better, more caring man than he. Everyone loved him. There had to be something inherently wrong with me that I had fucked things up so spectacularly with him.

'Ben's not even in the country, Emily,' Simon said. 'Moved to Birmingham. Settled there.'

Would it have made things worse if I said I knew? Would they believe me if I said he had been in touch? I didn't have any evidence to prove he had been. The request had been deleted. So there was little point.

'We just worry,' my mother said and I watched as her rheumy

eyes filled with tears and one rattled down her cheek, skimming over the wrinkles, the soft, fragile skin, the frailness of my beloved mother. 'It was just such a horrible time. For all of us.'

The phrase 'for all of us' jarred but I pushed my feelings aside. It wouldn't do any good to have this argument again.

'There is no need, Mum. I promise you. I promise you with all my heart.'

*

When they left, I got into my car, drove to the nearest off licence and bought a bottle of wine. It had a relatively low alcohol content but would hit the spot – quench the thirst that talking with Ingrid, and Simon and my mother had given me. It would help dull the edges of the anger I was feeling at Maud. She'd spoken to my family, for God's sake, sounded the 'Emily is going off the deep end' klaxon.

I wasn't one minute back in my flat when I unscrewed the lid from the bottle and poured, feeling my heart beat a little quicker as the straw-coloured liquid sloshed into the glass, filling it just shy of the brim. I stood in my kitchen, leaning backwards against the worktop and brought the glass to my lips. I don't think I even tasted the first half-glass – there was no savouring. No gentle swishing of the liquid around the bowl of the glass to release the bouquet. No sniffing. No slight sip and swirling of it around my mouth allowing the subtle hints of fruit and floral tones to burst on my taste buds.

This was simply drinking to drown any notion Ingrid Devlin had tried to plant in my head that Cian Grahame was anything other than a good and loving man.

I felt the warmth in the pit of my stomach as the wine slid down. The second half of the glass helped drown out the worries, the fear, the shame I felt when I looked at my mother. I refilled the glass, knocked back some more and walked to the living room, a slight buzz somewhere in my head. A light-headedness that came with a large glass of wine on an empty stomach. And a few pills, too. Just enough to relax me. To remind me to keep things in perspective. Maud was concerned about me. My mother was concerned about me. Simon was doing a very good job of pretending to be concerned about me – so I should push down the notion to tell them to fuck off. They were good people, beneath it all. Even Simon.

But Ingrid Devlin, my gut told me, was not a good person. She lied. She conned me into talking to her. She was muckraker. A dirt digger. She probably hacked mobile phones of the dead and dying too. I would have no further dealings with her and I would tell them all at work that she was scurrying around, asking questions, saying things she had no right saying.

I picked up my phone and sent Cian a message. A quick hello. We had exchanged the odd message over the last few days. I knew he wouldn't mind me reaching out to him just as much as I knew I wanted him to reach back to me.

It was just before 8pm when my phone beeped and I saw his message. A cool: 'Hey' – just hanging there. Friendly. Intimate. I imagined him saying it – his deep voice, whispering close to my ear. I felt something shudder deep inside me. I had to remind myself to play it cool.

Hi. How are you?

Okay, all things considered.

I'm glad to hear it.

I considered adding a smiley face but decided against it. As I did against putting an x after my sentence.

I'm sure the police will get to the bottom of it all soon. Leave you to grieve in peace.

I do too, Emily. I feel sick every time I hear his name. People feeling sorry for him now? It's almost as if Rose never existed.

Stay strong, and I'm here if you need to chat.

I wondered if I should tell him about Ingrid Devlin and her horrible insinuations.

Thanks. I hope you don't mind me offloading to you. There aren't many people who understand. It's nice to feel someone is on my side.

Don't worry about it.

I decided to stay quiet. He trusted in me. I didn't want that to change just yet.

I'd like to talk to you more. I was thinking since last week went south so fast – what with me making a complete idiot of myself in public – maybe we could try again? Dinner this time, perhaps?

I may have squealed with delight, just a little bit.

I'd like that.

We chatted some more. Decided Saturday night would suit, only if I didn't have any other plans, you know, like seeing my boyfriend or anything? I told him I didn't have a boyfriend to see. I was rewarded with another smiley emoticon, which I tried not to read anything into. He asked what kind of food I liked and I replied that anything other than seafood was good by me.

He suggested The Red Door, a nice little eatery just across the border into Donegal. Far enough outside of town to avoid gossipy locals. I agreed, of course. I knew the restaurant he mentioned – it had a good reputation and the seating was such that we wouldn't be sitting on top of the other guests, we would have space to talk privately. In other circumstances, it could even have been considered romantic.

We signed off our conversation and maybe high on the thought of seeing Cian for dinner and buoyed by the several glasses of wine I had consumed, I opened my laptop and clicked into my email.

I knew it would still be there. His old email address. BenCullen76@gmail.com.

I could do this, you know. I could face my worst fears. I

could prove Simon and my mother, and even Maud, that I could deal with things myself.

And if necessary I could get proof that he had been trying to get in touch with me. It was something, at least, to go on.

I typed a quick message.

Ben,

You wanted to get in touch? I got your friend request. I'm sure you understand why I rejected it. What do you want from me?

Hitting the send button, I vowed that I wouldn't let myself be so scared of Ben again.

Chapter Twenty-One

Rose

2012

Rose Grahame: Today's the day! We finally move into our dream home! The next step of our life together – and proof that hard work and talent pay off. Housewarming party details to follow later when we're unpacked and settled. So excited! #Newhome #Blessed #WhereDidIPacktheKettle?

'You know we won't be having a housewarming?' Cian laughed, looking over my shoulder.

'Not even a little one?' I asked him. 'Close friends and family?'

He sniffed. 'People just looking for a nosy around the house? Let them look at the magazine spread when it's done – we don't need them snooping in the bathroom cupboards.'

'Close family and friends don't care what brand of shampoo we use, Cian,' I mocked, but he didn't laugh back. He was becoming a little more reclusive these days – the pressure of book three was building. He wanted *From Darkness Comes Light* to be his breakthrough book – the one that won him awards, recognition from the literary community. His second book had earned him the sales he wanted – but the reviews from his peers weren't always kind. He'd have swapped the first for the second.

'Maybe when the book's done,' he said. 'I don't need to worry about a party and everyone asking how my writing is going before then.'

I couldn't help but feel a bit deflated – this house was more than I could have dreamed of. It was beautiful, filled with character. A home that I could see us raising a family in. I was standing in our new kitchen – which was bigger than my first flat – looking at the new furniture that had been delivered and how good it all looked and of course I wanted to show it off. Maybe it did make me shallow, like Cian said, but I was proud of what we had achieved.

'But my parents can call round, and my sisters?' I asked, knowing my mother was dying to get a look around and I wouldn't be able to hold her off for long.

He shrugged his shoulders. 'I suppose I can't stop them,' he said. 'But you know the pressure I'm under, so can you make it quick? We'll do something more when the book is done. Promise.'

I tried to understand. I tried, if I'm honest, to reassure myself it was only going to be great when this blasted book was finished. Although I couldn't tell him I was starting to resent his dedication to writing – how he put it above everything else. How would that make me look? When he had just bought us this big house on the proceeds of his dazzling career? Like the ungrateful cow he had said I was when I had complained of his long hours before.

'Try not to look so sad about it,' Cian said, a hint of frustration in his voice. 'I know you'd love to have everyone round. I'm just asking you to hold off for a bit, Rose. Not nail the door shut. If it makes you feel better, I thought I could invite Greg and Lucy over for dinner? You can do all your showing off then.'

Greg and Lucy, his agent and his publisher. People I liked, I suppose, but didn't really have anything in common with. They didn't find tales from the dental surgery or want to talk about the soaps, and as much as I had tried to widen my reading I still found I preferred lighter reads, reads that didn't make me feel stupid. Neither Greg nor Lucy lived nearby so a visit was a big deal – a huge deal in fact. If we had a fatted calf it would be slaughtered for the occasion. I would play hostess rather than relax over a glass or three of wine. It wouldn't be the house-warming I'd dreamed of.

'I'll ask them if they want to stay over in the spare rooms – sure there's a chance for you to get them decorated – done up just right. I want to impress them, Rose. Make them think I'm in control and not scrabbling around with the soggy middle of this bloody novel.'

He looked sad, stressed – and I suppose my heart ached for him a little. My job was easy in comparison, as he reminded me. His book – and the need for it to be even better than the last – was with him always.

'The book will be brilliant, Cian. I have every faith in you,' I said, wrapping my arms around him.

He kissed the top of my head, pulled me closer. 'I don't know how you put up with me,' he said, 'but I'm glad you do. Look, how about I take a day off this weekend? We can go shopping together? Look for bits for those spare rooms? And on Sunday invite your parents and sisters around? Have an afternoon tea? I think the weather is meant to be nice – we'll go and get some furniture for the garden? You can all make an afternoon of it while I languish in my office.'

'That sounds lovely, Cian. Some time together, just the two

of us. Making this house our home. The break from writing might do you good too – give you a chance to recharge.'

'Maybe,' he said. 'But let's not think about it all too much today. This should be a happy day.'

'It is,' I told him, looking up into his eyes, trying to find that carefree affection that used to be there. 'How about I hunt out the kettle and make us both a cup of tea and we can unpack some more after?'

'I like the sound of a cup of tea,' he said, 'but would you mind if I did even an hour's work after?'

'Of course not,' I said, resigning myself to unpacking the kitchen on my own. Hoping I did it just right. 'You do what you have to do.'

'I'm lucky to have you, Rose Grahame,' he said. 'And when this is all done, we'll celebrate with champagne. We'll have the biggest party imaginable. I promise.'

I knew we wouldn't, but for a moment or two, while I kissed him and counted the blessings in front of me – the house, the more secure income – I let myself believe we would.

Chapter Twenty-Two

Emily

My phone had been my constant companion since I emailed Ben. So far he hadn't responded but that didn't stop me jumping every time a notification arrived. So I jumped when my Messenger pinged that Saturday at 4pm – relaxing only when I saw that the message was from Cian. No doubt it would be about dinner. I'd had my hair and make-up done and bought a new dress (a forties-style tea dress that hugged my curves in a nice but not over the top manner).

My heart sank when I saw the first line.

Sorry to do this so last minute. Look, Jack is a little unsettled today and to be honest getting a sitter has been difficult. Not everyone understands how I'm going out so soon after Rose's death – especially for dinner with a female friend.

I felt tears well in my eyes before I read on.

So if you don't mind, I thought why don't you come round to my house instead? I can throw something tasty together and we can still chat. I know it's not a posh dinner, and my attempts at thanking you for being such a good listener seem to be cursed, but I hope you understand? Besides, I'm sure Jack would really like to see you.

My first reaction was to be relieved that he wasn't cancelling altogether, but I did also feel disappointed – I had been looking forward to being wined and dined in a nice restaurant. I touched my hand to my perfectly waved and set hair, thought of the dress that was hanging on the back of my bedroom door. It deserved to be shown off. But I could hardly argue with him, could I? This wasn't a date. This was a meal between friends and friends understood when other friends who had recently lost their wives couldn't get babysitters and needed to stay in instead.

I tried to convince myself this could actually work in my favour. It would be just Cian and me, in his house (with Jack of course, but toddlers slept; they were famous for it). It would be more intimate. Maybe we would sit on the rug in front of a blazing fire after and sip wine, and while I had no (serious) expectations anything would happen – maybe there would be a moment when he would look at me and there would be some sort of connection that would lay the foundations for something else?

I typed back that I would love to come over for dinner and I would see him later. Then I changed into my new dress anyway because, well, I didn't really have an alternative. I was hardly going to show up in my lounge wear, with my newly coiffed hair tied back in a scrunchie.

Jack was already asleep when I got there.

'He was just worn out,' Cian said, looking a little on the worn out side himself although his hair was damp, suggesting he had just showered. He was dressed casually in jeans and a fresh white T-shirt, in a look not dissimilar to the one he sported in the big family portrait. I instantly felt over-dressed.

As Cian helped me out of my coat, I felt his breath, briefly, on the back of my neck and I closed my eyes, breathed in the smell of his musky cologne.

'I was going to wear this out for dinner,' I said. 'Almost everything else is in the wash,' I lied.

'You look lovely, Emily,' he said, staring straight at me, taking me in from head to toe. I felt something in the pit of my stomach tighten. 'And you've done something different with your hair?'

I touched my hand to my soft curls. 'Thank you. It was time for a bit of a change,' I said.

'It suits you. I like it.'

He led me through to the kitchen where there was a distinct lack of cooking smells. There was however a bottle of red open and breathing on the island, with two glasses beside it. He started to pour. 'Here's my confession,' he said. 'I'm a terrible, and I mean awful, cook. I'm just about scraping by with Jack by living off the pity casseroles people have been dropping over since Rose died. That and a good line in Potato Waffles and Fish Fingers.'

He was blushing as he handed me the glass of wine. 'But I do have a fine selection of takeaway menus – everything from pizza to Indian and even a leaflet from the Thai place in town – but I wouldn't recommend it unless you fancy spending tomorrow chucking up your guts.'

He laughed a little, his whole face changing as he did so, and I laughed too.

'Best avoid that then,' I said.

'Is there anything that takes your fancy?' he asked, opening the drawer in the island and pulling out what was indeed a stellar collection of takeaway menus and spreading them in front of me, his hand briefly brushing mine as I lifted the leaflet for the Mandarin Palace Chinese. I wondered whether he felt the same spark I did, in fact I allowed myself to believe just for a moment that he did. In believing that, I was able to put thoughts of what had been said at work – how Owen was, how it all was – to the back of my mind. I'd enjoy dinner with him. With a friend. A friend I hoped might be more.

★

It wasn't quite a rug in front of a roaring fire, but Cian and I sat on opposite sides of that big squashy sofa and chatted after we'd eaten. We had abandoned the red wine in favour of a dry white with our dinner, and I was on my second glass and feeling myself relax more and more in his company. I had kicked off my heels and tucked my legs up under me and we were both sitting facing each other. Cian looked less tired, less strained, than he had done in my company before. If it weren't for the massive picture of Rose looking down on us, I could almost, almost make believe she had never existed.

So when Cian started to speak of the renewed police interest in her death I felt, I don't know, disappointed? Irritated?

'I just want it to be all over and done with. So Jack and I can get on with our lives. It feels like there's a big cloud hanging over both our heads,' he said sadly.

'And the police – have they told you anything at all?'

He shook his head. 'They don't seem to want to share any information with me. They say it's "not relevant to Rose's case" and then they ask more questions. They're contradicting themselves left, right and centre. They keep asking if I ever met Kevin McDaid. Keep asking about my relationship with Rose – like I haven't told them, told the whole bloody world – how I felt about her. She was my wife – the mother of my son.' He sat forward, buried his head in his hands for a moment. I didn't know what to do – part of me wanted to reach out and touch him. Comfort him. Just as the urge began to get too much, he sat up again, ran his fingers through his hair and looked at me. His eyes were narrowed, burning with rage.

'Do you know my solicitor has warned me they may search

the house? The case isn't relevant to Rose's case – but they may search my fucking house? May seize my computer? How will I even be able to work if they seize my computer? Not that I can write my name at the minute but still. That's my life's work, and they want to take it and rip it all to pieces trying to find what? Some imaginary Tweet I sent to Kevin McDaid asking him to kill my wife? Offering him money to do it. It's ludicrous!'

I sat back. Stunned for a second. Cian was angry now. His eyes dark. I could see the muscles in his hands tense.

'I'm sure it'll all get cleared up soon,' I soothed. 'They can't make stuff up. They can't accuse you of something you didn't do, or wouldn't do.'

'But mud sticks, Emily. Don't you realise that? Once the rumours start, people will start to believe them. And there are people out there who want to believe it. People who would love to see me get brought down a peg or two.'

'I'm sure that's not true,' I said.

'Oh Emily, you sweet, naive creature. Of course it's true. Nothing gets people off round here like seeing someone who made something of themselves have it all come crashing down around them. We lie – pretend we're proud of our success stories – but that's bullshit, Emily. At the end of the day, we're all supposed to know our place. Not have ideas above our station. As the old saying goes "Once shite gets up, it's hard to beat down." Well there are plenty who think I'm nothing but a piece of shit – me and my pretentious ways and my big words and my literary awards. My lovely house, and my beautiful son and my perfect wife. People like to hate me for that. People want to hate me. To destroy me. They think pinning this on me will do it – but the truth is I'm already destroyed. I was destroyed the moment she died. But that's not enough – people are cruel, Emily.'

I knew that only too well – the cruelty of others was seared on my brain. But people could be good too – I had to believe that.

'A lot of people love you – you and Jack – and they want to help.'

He snorted. 'Yeah. That's why the one person I can confide in is someone I've only known a couple of weeks?' There was a laugh – hollow, cold. It stung a little.

'You've friends. The staff at Scott's speak very highly of you.'

'Even Owen?' His eyebrow was raised.

I paused. 'Owen keeps himself to himself. I don't really speak to him too much.'

'It's not like Owen to be solitary. Normally he likes to be all over everyone else's business.'

'What do you mean?' I asked.

Suddenly Cian was standing up, his hands in his hair again, walking across the room – or more accurately stomping. I could see his hands clenching on his head. He walked to the far end of the kitchen, stood with his back to me, his hands on the worktop, his head hung low. I didn't know what to say or do, so I sipped from my wine glass, the wine now tasting warm and bitter. My stomach was clenching. I realised I was still nervous – but now it wasn't in a good way.

After a time – maybe thirty seconds, which of course felt like much more – he turned to look at me again. His face sad again. Traces of anger gone. 'Can I trust you, Emily?' he said.

'Of course,' I replied.

'I mean, really trust you?' He was walking towards me, I turned to face him head on, pulling my legs out from under me and putting my feet flat on the floor.

'You know you can,' I said.

He took a deep breath. 'Rose and Owen have known each for a long time. Long before Rose started working for him.

167

They met when Rose was a student working a Saturday job in Tesco. He was working there too, subsidising his university years. They became friends – good friends – but that's all it ever was, for Rose anyway. Owen, however, he always had a thing for her. I mean, I can't blame him. She is – was – a beautiful woman. So beautiful. She wasn't interested in him in that way though. Owen Scott would never be Rose's type. He was much too "safe" – too boring for her. I mean, a dentist?' Cian's mouth curled up at the edges as he said the word 'dentist', as if he could imagine nothing more boring, more sedate, more uninspiring. 'He wasn't happy when she turned him down, but Rose being Rose, they stayed friends, you know. Then when Rose and I met – well, Owen couldn't have made it clearer that he didn't think I was good enough for her. I was an aspiring writer, in his eyes I was a layabout who was living in cloud cuckoo land. Rose started working for him – and she was the breadwinner then – he never missed an opportunity to remind me of that. Remind me I wasn't treating Rose the way he could. He was sly about it though – he wouldn't say it in front of Rose. He would tell her he admired that I was chasing my dream while rubbing my nose in my lack of success. Paying Rose a "bonus" that would cover the rent, saying that's what friends did. I felt totally emasculated by him. So you can imagine how pissed off he was when my books started to sell. And when they started to garner critical acclaim too and interest from film producers. He realised the one thing he had over me – the security, the money – he didn't have any more. It made him angry. Rose said he had been getting increasingly shitty with her in work. She was considering handing in her notice. I wanted her to do it, we definitely didn't need the money any more. She had stayed on because she enjoyed the work and had friends there, but he was making her miserable, in fact. She told me, you know, that she was scared of how he would react when she told him she was leaving . . .'

I was dumbfounded. Although I had seen that darker, angry side of Owen lately. But still, this was something else. Something beyond my comprehension. 'You're not suggesting he was angry enough to want to hurt Rose though, are you? It doesn't seem like him. Not really. He can be moody – but not this . . .'

Cian shook his head. 'No, no I don't think he would have hurt her. He wouldn't have the balls to do anything like that. Mr Goody Two Shoes,' he almost spat the sentence out, before laughing a distorted, angry laugh. 'But it keeps me awake at night . . . just wondering . . . would he have asked someone to do it for him?'

Thoughts of what Ingrid Devlin had told me – that money and been deposited in Kevin McDaid's account – jumped into my head. Had she been telling the truth about that? My head hurt – a combination of the wine and trying to take it all in.

'You do believe me, don't you, Emily?' Cian said, taking my hands in his. He looked directly into my eyes, his expression soft, pleading. I thought of how broken he was. How he seemed to be just coping and no more. 'It's important that you believe me. I feel as if no one is on my side – even Rose's family have been cold with me. As if they believe that I would hurt her. Can you imagine how that feels, Emily? They were my family too and now they've cut me off. We talk through mutual friends about visitation to Jack. Everything has changed.'

I watched as a tear rolled down his cheek – instinctively, I pulled my hand from his and wiped the tear away with my thumb, holding my hand to his cheek. He closed his eyes, rested his head on my hand as if he hadn't rested properly in weeks. 'I need to know someone believes me,' he whispered.

I would have to trust my instincts, which may have been influenced by the wine, and the handsome man with his face

169

in my hands, his tears wet on my wrist. My instincts, I realised as I felt my pulse quicken, were also influenced greatly by my heart, which in that moment just wanted to comfort Cian. He opened his eyes and looked at me, blinking back tears, waiting for my response.

'I believe you,' I whispered, and he turned his head and rewarded my faith in him with the softest brush of his lips against my palm.

I pulled my hand back, not because I wanted to, but because I was afraid that if I didn't – in that very moment – I would be lost to him. I would do something stupid, try to kiss him properly or something equally daft that would send him running. His wife was only dead a couple of months and she had been the love of his life. Who was I? Someone he could talk to?

'I'd better go,' I said.

'I've asked too much of you,' he said softly. 'I've said too much.'

I shook my head, slipped my feet back into my heels and started looking in my bag for my mobile to call a taxi. Anything that would have me looking in a direction that was not at him. 'It's not that at all,' I said. 'You haven't asked too much of me. I believe you.' I turned to look at him. 'I believe in you.'

'Don't go,' he said. 'Stay with me, please.'

I looked at him. I wondered whether he'd been drinking before I arrived. He certainly hadn't drunk enough over dinner to have him making silly propositions. 'I'm not sure,' I said, although that damn gut and that damned heart of mine, as well as that coiled spring deep inside me, was screaming at me to say yes. 'It's late, and you're emotional. It's been a difficult time.'

'There's a spare room,' he said. 'It would just be nice to know you're here. I've hated waking up alone. I can get you something to sleep in. I can drive you home in the morning.'

Ah, just friends. I felt a mixture of relief and disappointment but the thought of being close to him was so appealing and my head was still aching.

'Please,' he said, taking my mobile from my hand and slipping it back into my bag. 'It would mean a lot to me.'

I nodded, found my voice and said 'okay' and was rewarded with a smile.

'I know this seems strange,' he said, as he topped up my wine glass, his mood suddenly elevated, 'but nothing about the last two months hasn't been strange so I've learned to just go with it. My instincts tell me you're a good person to have in my corner.'

I wondered as he drained his own glass and poured another if his instincts were as intrinsically messed up as mine.

Chapter Twenty-Three

It was still dark when I woke. I lifted my phone, prayed the battery hadn't run down, and checked the time. It was just after 7am. I had 10% left of battery life. Enough to last while I got up, dressed and called a taxi.

It felt strange now, in the morning, and not necessarily good strange. I had slept relatively well – an extra glass of wine followed by a shot or two (or was it three?) of finest Scotch ensured that. I had kept my wits about me though – steered the conversation back to the everyday. Or was it Cian that had steered the conversation away from the big issues?

It had become a bit hazy. I remembered him playing music through his iPad on a fancy Bluetooth sound system that probably cost more than I earned in a month. He had said it was the first time since Rose died that he could see what normal was – feel what normal was.

He had pulled me to my feet and we had danced and sung, probably too loudly, to 'Wonderwall' by Oasis. Jack woke up, fussed a bit. Cian had gone upstairs and settled him, singing the lyrics to him as he drifted back to sleep and I remembered my heart swelling with affection for him.

I had been sat on the sofa, finishing my drink, suddenly beyond tired and feeling my eyes start to droop. The room had been warm. I was buzzing on the alcohol. Content. My earlier concerns that anything about this was strange were gone – because we were just two lonely people spending time together. Two broken people. Of course, he didn't know I was broken – but I was. Although then, in that blissfully hazy moment, I was hopeful I might finally be on my way to getting healed.

My eyes had jolted open when I felt his hands on my shoulder. 'Sleepyhead,' he'd said. 'Maybe we should call it a night? I think we made it through the full Oasis back catalogue anyway – at least the songs that were worth remembering.'

I had smiled, nodded. The thought of sleep exquisite. 'That would be good,' I'd said, standing up, carrying my glass to the sink and rinsing it.

'It's the second door on the right upstairs,' Cian had said. 'There's an en-suite bathroom and fresh towels. There's even a spare toothbrush in the bathroom cabinet. Rose always liked to be prepared for guests. She was renowned for her hospitality. Had to have everything just so.'

'She sounds like a great woman,' I'd said.

'Yes,' he had replied. 'She was. If you go on up, I'll bring you a T-shirt to sleep in.'

Then I had nodded, padded up the stairs to the second room on the right. There was no doubt Rose had exquisite taste. The room was decked out in classic black and white – spotless, clean. A cream carpet, cream walls. A dressing table complete with sample-sized creams and potions. Almost like a hotel room.

The bathroom was no less hotel-like. The end of the toilet paper had even been folded to a neat triangle. This was much nicer than my flat could ever be. In fact it was nicer than most of the hotels I had ever stayed in. I had washed my face – a little terrified of Cian seeing me without my make-up but more terrified of leaving make-up stains on the pristine white Egyptian cotton bedding on the guest bed. Then I had taken one of the three new toothbrushes in the bathroom cabinet and brushed my teeth. I was just finishing when I'd heard a knock on the bedroom door.

In the soft lamplight of the guest room, Cian Grahame had looked even more handsome than he ever had before – more dishevelled than he had been earlier – but it was a look that worked well on him. His T-shirt was creased and had come untucked from his jeans in one section. The thought of slipping my hand under the cool cotton and touching him flashed across my mind. I pushed it back.

'I brought these for you,' he'd said, holding out a T-shirt towards me with one hand and a glass of iced water with the other. 'You might get thirsty in the night.'. There should be some aspirin in the bathroom cabinet if you feel a headache coming on.'

'Thank you,' I'd said, taking both from him. 'You think of everything.'

'It's important to get the details right.' He had smiled, his eyes fixed on mine. We were stood a foot apart, maybe two at most. The urge to feel the roughness of his beard on my hand again had almost overwhelmed me. In fact, I had swooned – actually swooned – when he'd leant over and kissed me softly on the cheek, whispering in my ear that he hoped I slept well. I couldn't find my voice to say anything in response, so I nodded and it was only after he had closed the door and I could hear him walking away, presumably to his room – the room he had shared with Rose – that I'd realised I had been holding my breath.

I was used to waking during the night but I was not used to hearing footsteps in my room. Drowsy, my eyes and limbs heavy with the weight of a sleep brought on by wine, I had struggled to pull myself into consciousness as the footsteps moved ever closer. I had heard breathing, deep and low, and could make out a shadow in the darkness. Croaking a hello, I'd forced myself to sit up, pulling the duvet around me. My heart had been racing, my brain fuzzy. Fear – first of all. A gut response. Years of waiting for revenge to hit me. Sleeping with one eye always open. The footsteps had been heavy, my brain was struggling to focus. To remember I wasn't in my flat. I was with Cian. Cian – at the very thought my eyes pinged open and there he had been at the bottom of the bed, looking at me.

'I'm sorry,' he had whispered. 'I just thought . . .'

I had pulled the duvet tighter but while I knew I should feel scared, I didn't. My eyes instead had been drawn to him. Standing just feet from me, wearing only a pair of low slung pyjama bottoms. His chest was toned, with a light smattering of dark hair that looked as though it would be soft and warm to touch, but which, even in the darkness, I could see ran down his abdomen until it disappeared under the waistband of his pyjama bottoms. I had felt my breath quicken. I couldn't speak, so I just looked at him.

'I'm lonely, Emily. I'm so lonely and I just thought . . . well, I thought you might be lonely too. And you might allow me to hold you?'

I had nodded. Of course I would allow him to hold me. It had been such a long time since anyone held me. And this was Cian Grahame, handsome, talented, loving and in pain, and he needed human contact. He had moved to the side of the bed and climbed in; I lay down and allowed him to spoon against me – his arms wrapped around my waist. The warmth of his body against mine. The feel of his breath on my neck. The rhythm of his breathing. The calmness of this room with the weight of a man's arm – Cian's arm, on my waist. I had felt my breathing fall in with his and I drifted off to sleep.

175

When I woke at seven, even though it was still dark, I could sense immediately that he was gone. I wondered if I had dreamt it – but when I turned around the imprint of him was there on the other side of the bed. I reached my hand over, could feel the indentation of where his head had been. I lay there for a moment, thinking how strange it had been. Lovely at the time – but strange. To have him come in and hold me, sleep beside me, and then disappear. I couldn't hear another noise in the house – I wondered was he still asleep, having crawled back into his own bed? Perhaps guilt-ridden. Was that what I was feeling? Guilt? Did I feel I had betrayed Rose? All I knew was that I wanted to leave.

If I got dressed quickly and quietly, I was sure I could sneak downstairs and out the front door – where I could call a taxi from the end of the street. Of course it would still be a walk of shame of sorts, but I reminded myself I hadn't done anything wrong. We were just friends. Even the dancing and the drinking and the way he had kissed my cheek before I went to sleep. Even the spooning.

I kept my heels off so that I could creep downstairs and across the marble hall without making too much noise. I was two steps from the bottom when I heard Cian walk down the hall.

'Morning, sunshine,' he said with a smile, before glancing at my shoes in my hand and my bag slung over my shoulder. 'You weren't leaving, were you?'

'Erm,' I muttered, 'I didn't want to wake you so I thought I would just sneak out. I have plans with my parents today.' I was lying, of course, but he didn't need to know that.

'Oh, we're always up early here. Young Jack makes sure no one sleeps after 6am. Please don't rush out – I have coffee,' he said, nodding in the direction of the kitchen. 'And freshly baked croissants – I mean, not that I actually baked them myself but

I have some par-baked ones that will be fully baked in a few minutes. Jack and I won't get through them just the two of us – please, stay for breakfast at least?'

He turned his back, assuming I was following I suppose, and well, the smell of the croissants baking, mixed with the smell of freshly brewed coffee and the noise of Jack chattering and laughing to himself in the kitchen was all very alluring. Cian, in his jeans, a white shirt rolled up at the sleeves, and with the top two buttons undone, was also alluring.

Jack smiled at me as I walked into the room, waved his chubby hands at me from where he sat in his high chair. The room was pristine – all traces of dinner and drinks the night before gone. Clearly Cian wasn't a man to lie down under a hangover. Then again, he was so organised he had probably drunk the recommended pint of water before bed and taken his aspirin as a precaution – a move I wish I had pulled myself.

'I would have helped you clean up,' I offered, tickling Jack under the chin and sitting down at the kitchen island.

'Before or after you sneaked out?' he said with a smile.

I had the good grace to blush. 'Sorry – I just thought it would be easier to leave you to your day.'

'It's easier to start the day with someone other than just Jack here,' he said, opening the fridge and taking out a bottle of fresh orange juice. Suddenly I was very thirsty and when he offered me a glass I nodded and gulped it down – it tasted so good.

'You didn't drink your water last night, did you?' he laughed.

I shook my head. 'I was so tired, I think I passed out.'

'Good thing you didn't get a taxi home then. I would have worried about you being in a taxi on your own that late at night. There are bad people out there, Emily. As we both know. Besides, it was nice to have you here.'

'All's well that ends well,' I said as he topped up my orange juice before taking the croissants, flaky and crispy, from the oven.

'Thankfully,' he said and smiled.

We ate breakfast together over the course of an hour, neither of us mentioning his middle-of-the-night visit, and then he drove me home.

At that stage I probably could have been talked into spending the rest of the day with him – but I could hardly admit that I had lied about going to see my parents, could I?

When he left me at my apartment – on his way to take Jack to the park – he told me he would be in touch. He thanked me for listening. For helping him feel like him again. Then he kissed me, on the cheek again. But it lingered just a second or two longer than before. I was sure I heard him take a deep breath as he pulled away from me – and I was sure, well, almost sure – I saw a certain longing in his eyes before he turned his head away from mine.

★

I couldn't look at Owen the same way when I went back to work on Monday morning. I couldn't get what Cian had told me out of my head. An obsessive who had become angry because Rose didn't love him? That she was telling him she was going to leave? That Cian believed he could have possibly paid Kevin McDaid to hurt her? It was beyond comprehension. Then again, Ben had fooled so many people; it was hardly beyond the realm of possibility that Owen could as well.

I messaged Cian in my lunch break – told him I was finding it hard to even look at Owen, knowing what I knew.

'He's not worth your anxiety,' Cian had messaged me back. 'But if you need to de-stress, come over after work. Jack will be with Rose's family tonight. If I'm honest, I could use a bit of company to get through it.'

The pull was strong. I knew before I'd even finished reading the message that I would go.

That was the reason, as I walked home from the surgery, mentally planning what I would wear and how I would fix my hair, that I was smiling. That was until I heard someone call my name and I looked around to see Ingrid Devlin hot on my heels again.

Chapter Twenty-Four

I turned my back on her as soon as I saw her and walked off. I had nothing I wanted or needed to say to her. The further she was from me, the better, as far as I was concerned.

'Emily!' she called again. 'Emily, hang on. Please, let me explain.'

'There's nothing to explain,' I called over my shoulder, still walking. 'I've you figured out and I don't want anything to do with you.'

I could hear her footsteps get closer. She was persistent as hell. 'You don't want anything to do with me? Is that because you're trying to protect Cian Grahame? You and he seem very cosy these days?'

I stopped, my heart thumping and turned to find her just a few feet behind me. 'I don't know what you think you're talking about but you have no idea about Cian Grahame. Or me, for that matter.'

'I would think someone who left his house early on a Sunday morning would have some sort of a notion about Cian Grahame,' she said, shrugging her shoulders.

'That's none of your business,' I stammered, while part of me wondered how she knew.

'Maybe – but our readers would still be interested in hearing how the grieving widower of Rose Grahame was sleeping with the woman who took over her job? It's tabloid gold. And that's before we even throw in the police investigation.'

When I first saw Ingrid Devlin I thought her an attractive woman – composed, measured, professional. Now all I could see was ugly, snide and sneaky.

'How would you know about people leaving Cian Grahame's house? That's a bit scumbag reporter isn't it?' I bit back.

'You say that like it would offend me,' she said, moving a step closer, dangerously close to invading my personal space. I could feel my pulse quicken and the sheen of a cool sweat break out across my forehead. 'But what you call acting like a scumbag, I call uncovering news.'

'Well you uncovered it wrong. We're just friends, that's all.'

'With benefits,' she snorted.

'It's not like that at all,' I said, aware that I wanted it to be like that. Or even more than that. That I had been walking home thinking about my underwear choice for tonight. 'And you've no right to be spying on ordinary people going about their business. How dare you?'

'You are awfully touchy,' she said. 'Look, Emily—'

'That's another thing,' I interrupted her. 'How do you know my name? I didn't tell you my name last time.'

'Facebook is a great thing,' she said, 'and I'd make for a pretty rubbish journalist if I couldn't use it to suss out your name. Facebook friends with Cian too, I noticed. But that's by the by – Emily, I'm not trying to catch you out. I'm not saying Cian is the bad guy in all this, but I was being honest when I told you I needed a fresh line on this story. Something no one else can get – and I know you can help me get it. You can be my in to Cian. He has turned down all requests from the media so far – each and every one. Perhaps you could get him to talk to me?' She raised one perfectly plucked and shaped eyebrow and waited for my response. For a second I was gobsmacked. Could she really be serious?

'Why on earth do you think I would help you?' I asked. 'You've lied to me, stalked me, chased after me in the street! Why would I talk to you?'

"Well the thing is, Emily, it's quite funny you mention all that lying and stalking and chasing – because it's usually you doing that sort of thing, isn't it? At least according to your ex. A formal caution and a non-molestation order, isn't that how it ended? I uncovered that too – maybe in a scumbag way, as you would put it. But you really wouldn't want people up here – away from all that nastiness – finding out about that, would you?'

I felt the air rush from my lungs. It was as though I crumpled, folded in on myself – every ounce of shame and embarrassment and humiliation washing over me. She'd spoken to Ben? Ben who hadn't responded to my email? 'You've no right to nosy into my personal life . . .' I whispered, with not even half enough conviction.

'Maybe not,' she said, 'but still, I wonder would Cian want you around baby Jack if he knew your form?'

'You don't understand.'

'No, I suppose I don't. I suppose that isn't what it looked like either. Just like you and Cian looking very much the little family climbing into his car yesterday morning.'

I felt panic surge, tears spring to my eyes. 'What did I ever do to you to make you do this to me?'

'I've not done anything, Emily. I've just told you what I know. It's entirely up to you what I do with that information. But getting me closer to Cian? That might just make me forget certain things.'

I blinked at her – felt the tears I had been trying to hold in slide down my face.

'I know there is a lot to think about, Emily. But there's no reason we can't be friends. We can make this work for both of us, can't we? Here,' she said, reaching into her pocket, 'take my card. You can contact me on that number at any time. And if you do talk to Cian about me – and I sincerely hope you do – you can tell him it doesn't do him any harm either to have someone from the press on his side.'

She turned on her pointed leather heel and walked away – leaving me shaking, crying in the street. Memories battering me from all sides. It might not have been in the way I had feared, but my past had still caught up with me and it was threatening to destroy everything all over again.

*

Two anti-anxiety pills, a glass of wine, a sob in the shower and a stern talking to and I had assembled something that resembled an attractive female. I had pulled on a pair of jeans and an off the shoulder, slouchy sweatshirt along with a pair of black boots. It screamed relaxed chic. I tousled my hair and slicked some lipstick and mascara on. I layered some concealer under my eyes, which were still red from crying.

While I dressed I pretended I was Maud – all five foot two of her, petite, thick dark hair, face framed by a chunky fringe. The kind of person who looked effortlessly cool. Maud rarely got flustered. Maud would have this sorted in an instant.

I figured I would be honest with Cian – well, a little honest. There was no need to tell him everything. I'd tell him Ingrid Devlin wanted to speak to him. That she had been hearing whispers and wanted to give him a chance to tell his side of the story. I wouldn't tell him that I didn't trust her. That she was threatening me. I sure as hell would not be telling him what she was threatening me about. Even though I knew the truth of what had happened with Ben, I didn't want any of that mess to colour what he thought of me. It was everything that wasn't Rose. A lack of perfection he wouldn't fall for. The haze of the pills and the glass of wine would allow me to present to him what I needed him to see, and get him to agree to what I needed him to agree to.

As my taxi pulled into the drive, the front door opened and there he was, a smile on his face. As the car stopped, he walked across the gravel and pulled open the door for me, greeting me with a kiss on the cheek as I stood up. As he took my hand and led me towards the house I wanted to pull my hand away, wondering if anyone was watching me arrive. He must have sensed my reticence as we were no sooner in the house and the door closed that he asked if everything was okay.

'You look stressed,' he said as he opened a bottle of the same white wine we had drunk on Saturday night and poured two large glasses. On the coffee table in front of the sofa he had arranged an array of tapas that looked as though it was straight from a high-class restaurant.

'I had this brought in,' he said, as he sat down. 'You like tapas?'

I nodded, sipped from my wine. 'I do. This is great. Thanks. There was no need to go to any trouble.'

'It's not trouble at all,' he said. 'I just phoned the restaurant and they came and set it up and everything. All I had to do was open the door and pay the bill.'

I forced a smiled, and he looked at me quizzically. 'You really are stressed, aren't you?'

'It's been a long day. I suppose I'm just tired.'

'And I forced you to come out? I bet you wish you were relaxing at home instead of providing a listening ear to me?' He looked genuinely concerned.

I reached out and touched his hand. 'No. No, don't worry about that. Wouldn't it be worse if I was going home and brooding alone? At least here I have company.'

'I'm sure you have company most nights, Emily,' he said, putting his hand on top of mine. There it was again. That sense of being grounded – weighted to the here and now. With Cian.

'Not so much,' I said, unable to hide my blush. 'But look, I'm here now – and this wine is lovely and the food too. How has your day been? I feel churlish giving out about how tired I am when you have so much to deal with.'

'Well, to be honest, it's actually nice to talk about something that's not directly related to Rose for a change and to someone who didn't know her. I get tired of all the sad looks and the eulogies about how perfect she was – not that she wasn't everything – but you know . . . it's hard living with the ghost of a saint. Sometimes I want to just be me. To have a normal day. Does that sound awful?' He ran his fingers through his hair, then turned and looked at me. 'But look, let's just have some of this tapas and drink some of this wine and we can start on the Blur back catalogue – if you don't mind hanging round for a while.'

I nodded although this should have been the moment I told him about Ingrid Devlin and her request, but in that moment I wanted what he wanted – just to be somebody in a room with someone else. Without the ghosts of the past, mine or his, around me.

'I don't mind at all,' I said. 'Now, tell me what all this is,' I said, gesturing to the table in front of me.

*

Everything became a little hazy after the third glass of wine. The kind of hazy where time becomes fluid and you experience things in moments and sensations without worrying about anything linear. I'm not entirely sure how we ended up kissing – but we did. I remember that we had been talking for a couple of hours. Cian had said he was incredibly lonely, I'd told him that I knew what that felt like. He said he couldn't believe someone like me could ever find myself lonely. I'd told him when the time was right he might feel he could move on – not replace Rose but find someone who could ease his loneliness.

I hadn't been expecting his kiss, even as he put his hand to my face, then in my hair. Even as he looked deep into my eyes and I could feel his breath, warm and sweet, close to my face. I don't think I was even expecting his kiss as his lips brushed mine. Or as his hand moved behind my head and pulled me closer to him, kissed me more deeply. As his tongue met mine and I felt my body respond. As my hand touched his chest, then moved to the roughness of his stubble. Even as we pulled apart, and I heard a sigh loaded with desire slip from his mouth before he pulled me to him again, I don't think I really believed what was happening.

His hand slipped under my sweater, his thumb brushing against my nipple over the thin material of my bra sending a shockwave of desire straight to my core. It was the kind of shockwave that overruled any doubts I had about what I was doing – what we were doing. I felt him lean over me, the heat from his body on mine as his mouth moved to my neck. I'm not sure if I was more intoxicated from the wine or lust – but I knew the combination of both was lethal. There was no way I could fight it.

In those moments when all I could feel were my nerve endings fizzing to life, I knew I was a lost cause. So when he whispered that he wanted to take me to bed, I was powerless to resist. I went with my instincts – let him lead me from the room and up the stairs where he kissed me again before taking me to the guest room and pressing me against the wall so I could feel his body, hard and hot against mine. I was lost then – there was no going back. I didn't care about anything that was happening in that very moment except the physical sensations coursing through my body.

And as we lay together in bed, him inside me, the weight of him on top of me, moving over me – my body feeling alive, my heart beating fast, our sweat mingling together, our eyes locked, our mouths hungry for each other – I was sure that I was doing the right thing and that this was exactly how things were always meant to work out. Fate was a strange puppet master. Not that that crossed my mind as my orgasm surged inside me and made me cry out against his chest.

★

I woke sometime in the night with no idea what time it was. Cian was, to my surprise, still beside me in the bed, his arm draped across my waist. I lay there for a moment, trying to focus my eyes on him in the darkness of the room. I don't know what I had expected – for him to scream immediately after sex that he had made a huge mistake and kick me out? For him to scurry off to his own bedroom leaving me to wonder what the hell had just happened as I lay in the guest room wondering if and when I should leave? But instead he had pulled me close to him and whispered 'Stay, please stay' as his eyes fluttered closed. I was too sated, too drunk and too comfortable to argue with him and it wasn't long before I drifted off too. But now, in the small hours – feeling sober – I wondered what all of this meant? I knew better than to wake him and ask him, so I let myself enjoy just being close to him, our skin touching, my body aching in all the right places from our lovemaking. It was lovemaking, wasn't it? Not just sex?

Still I knew this little haze of happiness couldn't last

forever – I had to work in the morning and it would be entirely inappropriate to land into work in my sexy sweatshirt, jeans and the previous day's underwear. Not to mention the fact that my make-up was now resoundingly streaked across my face and my hair had a definite bed-head vibe going on – the kind of vibe that would get people talking. My heart sank a little when I thought of Ingrid Devlin – who could well be judging me as I lay there with Cian. I hadn't spoken to him about her – the right moment hadn't arrived. I was sure that as soon as I told him that a journalist really needed to speak to him and I was her contact, he would show me the door.

It certainly wasn't a conversation I wanted to have with him while naked. I crept around the room as quietly as I could, picking up my clothes before creeping into the bathroom and getting dressed. I looked in the mirror – my cheeks were flushed, my eyes bright despite the early hour. I wondered why it had to be so complicated, and in that moment I was angry beyond words at Ingrid Devlin who was about to make me ruin it all.

I brushed my teeth, washed my face and tousled my hair. Then I crept back into the bedroom and sat on the edge of the bed while I put on my socks and boots.

'You leaving?' I heard his voice from behind me and I turned to look at him, his eyes fixed on me even in the darkness.

'I have to work – so I need to go home to get ready,' I said.

'Stay,' he said, patting the bed beside him. 'Take the day off. Call in a sickie. They don't deserve you anyway.'

'I won't get paid if I don't go in,' I told him. 'I'm still on probation and my rent needs to be paid.'

'I'll cover your day's pay,' he said, 'please, just don't go. We've had such a nice evening, such a nice night. You don't know what it means to me to feel normal for a bit.'

'I can't let you cover my wages, Cian. You know that. And

Jack will be back from his granny's this morning. You really don't want Rose's mother arriving and finding me here.'

At the mention of Rose's name, he lay back flat on the bed and put his hands in his hair.

'You think I'm a total bastard, don't you?'

'What? No! Why would I?'

'Sleeping with you, being with you, and Rose isn't long dead. You think I'm disrespecting her memory, don't you?' His voice sounded strange, angry, but as if he could break down at any second.

'No. Cian, no. That's not it at all. I slept with you too – I made that choice too. How could I judge you for it?'

'Because people do, Emily. People have made their minds up about me. They won't understand how I could love Rose so much, miss her so much but still enjoy . . . still need . . . to be with someone else.'

Me. Did he 'need' to be with me? I reached across the bed and took his hand in mine – feeling my nerve endings fizz as we touched. 'I don't judge you, Cian. I take people as I find them and with you, I like what I find. I don't want you to feel I'm pushing you or forcing you into being anything more than friends . . .'

'I think it's clear we're more than friends,' he said, placing my hand on his chest so that I could feel his heart beating. 'We were meant to be together, Emily. I know you feel it too.'

I nodded and he pulled me to him, before pressing his lips against mine so that I was lost again in the touch and taste of him. When we pulled apart, breathless, he asked me again to stay with him and I agreed and I allowed myself to push any thoughts of Ingrid Devlin to the back of my mind as he peeled my clothes off and made me lose control.

It was light when we woke again. I'm not sure of the time – but I was aware of a persistent ringing of the doorbell, followed by a few impatient knocks. I jumped awake, nudging Cian who sat up bleary-eyed.

'Will that be Jack back?' I asked, as I hurriedly pulled my clothes back on.

'He's not due back until lunchtime,' Cian said, running his fingers through his hair and sitting up. The doorbell rang again, as Cian pulled on his jeans.

'Mr Grahame,' a deep male voice rang out. 'This is the police. Can we talk to you?'

Chapter Twenty-Five

2014

Rose

Rose Grahame: An award and Hollywood beckons. I promise I'll remember you all when I'm partying with the celebs! So proud of Cian!

A film deal! It was so incredibly exciting. Cian was like a new man – walking about, chest inflated like a proud peacock. I could hear him chatting to various journalists on the phone – saying he wanted to retain artistic control of the script and have a say in casting.

'It's very important that the story retains its integrity,' he said. 'I feel very strongly about that – I wouldn't want to have the story made into something it's not. It's more nuanced than the average detective story – multi-layered. It would be important that it doesn't get the full blockbuster treatment. I can think of nothing worse.'

I was impressed listening to his confidence in his work – it was such a transformation from the shy author I'd met seven years before who lacked self-belief and felt too nervous to share his work.

Now he'd talk openly about his achievements, his 'craft', his opinions on the literary world. I would never say it to him, but sometimes he came across as a bit pompous. I'd learned to keep quiet though – it was the best way. Don't wake the Kraken. Don't poke the bear. Just smile and nod, and make cups of tea, or pour glasses of wine and serve food at dinner parties in our home. Make sure the guest room was always in tip-top condition. Make sure he had peace to write – that he felt cherished and spoiled when he was in creative mode.

Even if it meant throwing the odd sickie at work to be there and be 'his muse'. Even if it meant hiding my own reading habits from him like they were a dirty secret. Even if it meant being the butt of his jokes at times. 'Oh, Rose wouldn't get that. She prefers something a bit lighter – don't you Rose? I feel grateful if she agrees to read my books.'

Everyone had laughed – so I had too. I didn't see the point in correcting Cian. No good would come of it.

This was his author persona – the person he had to be to be a success. And I wanted him to be a success, didn't I? I wanted him to win awards, to get the film deal. I enjoyed basking in his success – he said. I got my pay off – the nice house, the nice car, the jewellery, the fancy dinners out. The kind of lifestyle I could only have dreamed of when I was younger. He'd lifted me – lifted us – out of a crappy flat and into a lifestyle where it was entirely possible we could end up on the red carpet at the Oscars. 'I'm giving you everything,' he said and he was. So it would be churlish of me to be anything but grateful.

And who could I talk to about it? Who would understand? Poor Rose, in her double-fronted house with her designer kitchen and her Mulberry handbag and her hair coloured at the best hairdressers in town. And isn't she just back from a weekend in London, eating at all the fancy restaurants, appearing in the newspapers? Yes, poor Rose, I'll listen to her tell her problems while I'm trying to pay the bills and feed my children.

Cian was right; they'd get sick listening to me. My complaining would be pathetic. What would I tell them anyway? Admit what it was really like? Admit what he was really like? Admit what he did or more to the point what I let him do? What I let him get away with, because I did. I let him get away with it. All of it. I set the standard for how he treated me. How I bent over backwards to keep him happy. To try and keep him happy. It was my fault, because I didn't challenge him. It was easier to keep the peace.

Maybe the house, and the clothes, and the status appealed to me too much to stand up to him?

I had to put up or shut up.

Chapter Twenty-Six

Emily

I watched as Cian pulled on the wrinkled T-shirt that I had pulled off him and thrown on the floor the night before. I didn't know what to do or what to say.

The voice echoed out again through the letterbox while the doorbell rang – much too loudly. Cian didn't bother putting on his socks or shoes. He paused at the door for a moment, turned to look at me. 'Emily, you trust me, don't you?'

I nodded. 'Of course,' I said, and I meant it. I trusted him implicitly.

'You believe I would never, ever hurt Rose?'

'Of course I believe you,' I told him.

'Then help me, Emily. Please.' He held out a hand to me as if he wanted me to come with him. Slowly, unsure of myself, I reached out to him and he turned and led me downstairs just as a third call came through the door.

'I'm coming,' Cian shouted, a hint of irritation in his voice. Although I was dressed, I felt exposed. It would be clear to whoever saw that we had been sleeping, and perhaps much more. We were dishevelled at best. My hair was no better than it had been earlier – but at least I had washed

194

my well-worn make-up off and brushed my teeth. I expected Cian to let go of my hand and to shoo me into the kitchen. When he said he wanted me to help him, I assumed he wanted me to cover up whatever had gone on between us but he made no such move. Still holding my hand, he opened his front door to three police officers on his front step – one of whom I immediately recognised as DS Bradley. Our eyes met briefly, his widening just a little, before he looked back to Cian.

'Mr Grahame, is it okay if we come in? We have a development in your wife's case we'd like to talk to you about?'

He stood back and let go of my hand. 'Detective Bradley, come in,' he said, gesturing to the living room. 'This is my friend, Emily D'Arcy. Emily, DS Bradley – he's been overseeing the investigation into Rose's death.'

I nodded, briefly, in DS Bradley's direction.

'We've met,' he said.

'At the dentists – Scott's,' I said by way of explanation to Cian, before offering to make tea or coffee for him, DS Bradley and his colleagues.

'Tea would be nice,' DS Bradley said.

'Could you make a pot of coffee too?' Cian asked me, before planting a kiss on the top of my head and leading the three men through to the kitchen.

I was off kilter then. Not sure what was going on. But he had asked me to help him and I'd said I would. I'd said I trusted him, and I did. So I followed him through to the kitchen where I quickly lifted the empty wine bottles and glasses from the table, binning the bottles and rinsed the glasses.

Cian straightened the cushions on the sofa before inviting the police to sit down while I blushed at the memory of his hands skimming over my breasts as he kissed me deeply the night before on that very sofa. I boiled the kettle and put on a pot of coffee to percolate. I took cups from the cupboard and set up a tray.

'There are biscuits in the cupboard to the right of the cooker,' Cian called behind to me as I heard them make small talk. Small talk about me.

'Emily has been a good friend to me in recent weeks,' Cian said. 'I'm not sure how I'd have got through this nightmare without her support.'

'I'm glad you have a support network. I imagine that's very important,' DS Bradley said, as I handed him his cup of tea and cleared the remaining dishes from the previous night onto the tray. I picked up my phone, which was blinking at me from the table, and went back to the kitchen where I loaded the dirty plates and bowls into the dishwasher and pretended I wasn't listening to them.

'I don't have to be here if this is private,' I offered.

'DS Bradley can say anything he needs to in front of you,' Cian said softly, smiling at the three police officers.

'Well, Mr Grahame—'

'Cian, please. I've told you to call me Cian.'

'Well, Cian, as you know we have suspected there was more to Rose's death than just an accident. We now have significant reason to believe this is true and that your wife may have been killed intentionally. Further to that, we also believe foul play was involved in the death of Kevin McDaid. There's no easy way to tell you this, but both inquiries have been upgraded to murder investigations.'

I heard Cian swear as my breath caught in my throat. I felt dizzy.

'No. No. We know what happened to Rose. It was an accident. This is madness,' Cian said angrily. 'And that animal McDaid took his own life. How can you have a murder inquiry when someone threw themselves off a bridge? Is that not the worst use of police resources ever?'

'Cian, you know we have discussed our concerns about the incident in which Rose died. I'm sorry, I know this can't be easy for you at all. As for McDaid, you'll appreciate we are not at liberty to go into details except to say at this stage the evidence presented to us would lead us to believe that Kevin McDaid did not take his own life.'

'So someone threw him off the bridge? A grown man? Who, if the rumours are to be believed, sent a message, apologising for what he was about to do, to Kevin's mother? I write fiction for a living and I can tell you now, my editor wouldn't let that one go. And none of this, even if true, points to foul play being involved in Rose's death. No one would hurt her. No one.'

DS Bradley coughed and looked at his colleagues who were both staring directly at Cian. Bradley spoke again: 'Mr Grahame.'

'Cian. I said to fucking call me Cian!'

'There's no need for that language, Cian,' DS Bradley said, softly, warmly. I wanted to cling to that feeling of softness in his voice. It made what was being said to us slightly more bearable. 'Our investigations are at a delicate stage – and because of that we have some questions we would like to ask you.'

'You don't seriously think I had anything to do with this?' My heart jumped in my chest.

'We simply just want to ask some questions. It's important we get what information we can from you. We can do this now, or we can do this at an arranged time at the police station. It might be easier just to have a chat now.'

'It might be easier if you told me what exactly you think happened to my wife.'

'As I said, we are at a very sensitive stage of the investigation but information has come to light that we really would like to talk to you about. Now at this stage we are asking you to voluntarily help us with our enquiries, but yes, we will be interviewing you under caution.'

'Then I'm going to have to ask that my solicitor is present.'

'That's certainly your right,' DS Bradley said.

'It's more than my right. It's the only way to protect myself from whatever nonsense you lot are trying to pin on me. I write crime novels, Detective Bradley. I know that interviews under caution only happen if police believe that the interviewee is suspected of a crime. It would therefore be fair for me to surmise that you suspect me of hurting my own wife – who had my son with her at the time of her death. And that further to that, you might suspect me of wasting my energy and my breath on that scrote, Kevin McDaid, who, if you lot had been more effective, would never have been out on the streets, driving like a maniac and mowing down innocent people. So I think I will take what I am legally entitled to take. I'm not afraid to answer questions, DS Bradley, but let's not pretend this is just a cosy chat over tea and biscuits.'

'I'm sorry you feel that way,' Detective Bradley said, sitting back in his seat and brushing invisible crumbs off his trousers. 'In that case, we'll see you at the station, Cian. Can we expect to see you and your solicitor there at what, noon?'

'If I can arrange alternative childcare for my son, then you can,' Cian said. 'But I'm sure you're aware these things don't just sort themselves out.'

'No, I imagine they don't. But while we're here,' DS Bradley said, his tone much cooler than before, 'perhaps you wouldn't mind if my officers had a look in some of your computer files? Perhaps a look around your office?'

Cian snorted. 'You have to be out of your mind,' he said. 'Detective, without a warrant, I am under no obligation to allow you or your officers any access to my home or my personal files so I'm going to ask very nicely that you, and your . . . minions . . . leave.'

DS Bradley stood up. 'I have to say, I'm disappointed that

you aren't being more co-operative. I thought we were all on the same side here. That we wanted to get to the bottom of what happened to your wife.'

'But we know what happened to my wife,' Cian said, his voice shaky. 'I identified her body for Christ's sake. I saw the dents in her head. I saw the bruising. I saw how her arm was twisted. I saw where the blood had congealed around her mouth. So I know what happened to my wife and I damn well know who did it as well.'

I could hear that he was starting to get upset. He was still grieving and here were the police, for all intents and purposes, casting aspersions as if he were the villain of the piece. This gentle man who had let me in and showed me his vulnerable side – who cried over his wife and wondered if he was raising his son right and just wanted to be held at the end of the day when he felt lonely. A man who was trying to get his wife away from a work situation that had become almost unbearable for her. A man who had only known me a couple of weeks and who was already trying to protect me. Who already wanted me.

'I think in that instance, it really is better that we do continue this conversation at the station,' DS Bradley said, nodding a goodbye in my direction and turning towards the door.

'I think so,' Cian said. 'But I'm telling you now, you have it wrong. I would never have hurt my wife. And as for McDaid? The only time I ever saw his pathetic face was on his day in court and I'd have been happy never to have seen him ever again. I actually wish that on the night that bastard grew a conscience and threw himself off a bridge, I had been there to see him hit the water. But instead I was here, with Emily trying to convince me that I had reasons not to take my own life.'

★

199

My head was spinning but I was doing my best to try and make sense of what had just happened. Cian had asked me to help him. He had said it just before we had walked down the stairs. He had said it after he kissed me. After a night in which he had kissed every inch of my body and made me feel alive in a way I hadn't in years. If ever. He had asked me to help him after he told me how he could confide in me. How he believed fate had brought us together.

I didn't know what he meant when he asked me. All I knew was that I would help him in whatever way I could. So when he told the police I had been with him on the night Kevin McDaid died I had nodded without thinking too much. They were walking out of the room anyway and all I had to do was hold it together until they had left the house. I had to keep a look of nonchalance on my face as if this wasn't at all news to me. As if he hadn't just dropped it in there without warning and expected me to react appropriately.

And a double murder inquiry? This all felt so messy and the hangover that had been threatening to take hold swooped in, making my head ache.

As I looked at DS Bradley, saw him look back at me, I was sure I felt my cheeks colouring. I felt as if my discomfort was written all over my face, and probably across my chest too, which had a lovely habit of flushing when I was nervous. The off-the-shoulder look couldn't hide the pink hue creeping up towards my neck.

As soon as they left the room, I turned to the sink, put the cool water on full and splashed it on my face, patted the back of my neck. I could feel my legs shake and the rush of blood through my body threaten to deafen me.

I jumped as I felt Cian's arms thread around my waist, and him pull me back towards him, kissing my head and then the side of my neck. 'I'm sorry for landing you in it,' he said, his voice contrite. 'I panicked. Emily, I can see where this is going and I'm so scared.' His voice cracked and as it did, so did my resolve to ask what the fuck just happened. I turned around so that I was looking him directly in the eyes. He was crying and my heart contracted. Putting my hands to his face, I used my thumbs to brush his tears across his cheeks.

'It'll be okay, Cian. It will.'

'But you saw them. You heard them. They have it in for me. I panicked. I knew the first thing they would ask me was where I had been the night he died – and what was I to say? Home alone? They never believe that. Jack wasn't even here that night – he was with his grandparents. They'll have me arrested and in front of the courts before I can blink – for Kevin's death and for Rose's. Jesus, Emily – as if I would, as if I could . . .'

He looked at me so intensely. His eyes burning into mine. His arms around my waist. The only thing I could do was to comfort him and shush him and assure him it would be okay. I pulled him into a hug, worried he would feel the thumping of my heart against his chest.

Then it occurred to me that there was something else I could do to help him – something that might just help me too. 'There's someone you should talk to,' I said, pulling away from him and reaching into my bag for Ingrid Devlin's business card.

★

I surprised myself at how focused I suddenly became. I told Cian to call his solicitor, and arrange for him to be there at the police station. I suggested he call Rose's mother and ask her to keep Jack for another night – then it dawned on me that mightn't be the best move. If the investigation into Rose's death was to be reopened – with the finger of suspicion not directly pointing at Cian but certainly swirling around in his general direction – it was possible that the Grahame family could start being less than co-operative. No, it was better that Cian get Jack back as quickly as he could.

'But I can hardly take him to the police station with me,' Cian had said.

'I'll look after him,' I said. 'You go and pick him up – now – and I'll stay and look after him while you talk to the police. I'm sure you won't be long.'

He nodded. 'And this woman, Ingrid Devlin? How does she fit in?'

'You say people want to believe you're guilty? That they love to see someone who has achieved success get brought down a peg or two? Up until now, you've kept yourself from the press. You closed ranks when Rose died – now it's time to open up. Get the media on your side. Tell them your truth, Cian. Tell them all the things you've told me – about the lonely nights and how Jack still cries for his mammy. Tell them how you hurt and make them see the person I see . . . the person Rose saw. Gentle and loving and protective. Don't let the gossip mongers demonise you.'

I stopped myself from saying 'like they did me'. The irony that if I didn't get Cian to speak to Ingrid, she, and Ben, would demonise the hell out of my past was not lost on me. I felt the unfairness of it all seep from my bones. I didn't get a fair ending with Ben, but Cian could make sure things ended well for him.

There was no way he was going to be framed for something he didn't do. If it meant giving Ingrid Devlin exactly what she wanted on a silver platter then I would give it to her – and trust that karma would have its own way of dealing with her in the future.

By the time Cian's solicitor picked him up to accompany him to the station, Jack and I were sitting on the floor in the living room playing with building blocks. I had called work, left a message in a suitably croaky voice with Tori that I was sick and wasn't sure when I would be back in. I had also listened as Cian phoned Ingrid Devlin and arranged for her to call round later that day with a photographer in tow. He had looked disappointed when I said I didn't think it would be a good idea if I was present when Ingrid arrived – I didn't want her making any assumptions about our friendship – but said he understood. Not everyone would understand, in the way we did, that you can't always choose when someone comes into your life.

I didn't want to do anything that would pose a risk to Cian's reputation, and as I played with Jack, stacking the wooden blocks one on top of the other, I realised it wasn't just our future I was trying to protect. This child – this beautiful baby – had already lost so much. He was still so young, still in nappies. Still looked for a bottle of milk when he was sleepy. He was still teething, a stream of drool running from his mouth onto his bandana-style bib while we stacked the blocks together, singing nursery rhymes. I wondered would he have any memory at all of his mother? I doubted that he would. He would never remember her voice, her feel, the smell of her perfume. Or how she had pushed his buggy to safety as she was mown down. He couldn't lose anyone else, least of all his daddy. It would be beyond cruel.

Suddenly overwhelmed with emotion, I pulled him onto my knee, tickled his tummy and watched him wriggle and laugh – delighting in the infectious sound of his giggles. Then I pulled him to me, revelled in how he lay his head against my chest and looked up at me, his blue eyes wide, framed by the longest most luscious lashes. He touched my cheek with his pudgy hand and instinctively I kissed it, and rocked him back and forth gently singing Twinkle Twinkle to him as his eyes grew heavy and he drifted off to sleep. I wondered how many times Rose had done this and if she had appreciated it every time as much as I appreciated it right then. If she appreciated him – or did she ever lose her temper? Did she ever get cross when she hadn't had enough sleep and he was cutting teeth? Did she ever look at the stretch marks on her body and think they looked horrid? Did she ever not see them as her war wounds – marks that she was a mother? Did she ever curse under her breath when she couldn't go out with her friends at a moment's notice because of her responsibilities to Jack? Did she ever, even for a moment, regret becoming a mother or wish she could turn back time?

Was she really perfect, when all was said and done? All I knew was that if this baby, the baby that had trusted me enough to fall asleep right there in my arms, was mine, I would never take him for granted. Nor would I take Cian for granted. I would appreciate each and every second with my family.

I kissed his head, rocked him gently though he slept, and sang on about diamonds in the sky, all the while hoping that Cian would be home to us soon. Where he belonged.

Chapter Twenty-Seven

Rose

2015

Rose Grahame: This is Cian posting. Baby Jack born this morning. 6lbs 9oz. Mum and baby doing well. So proud of my amazing wife, who has given me the greatest gift in the world, a perfect baby son. I never dreamed I could be this lucky.

He was perfect. This little baby in my arms. Beautiful and innocent. Long eyelashes – his eyes a dark blue – wide and blinking at me, as if he had been here before. As if he had the wisdom of the world already inside him. His tiny fingers were wrapped around my index finger – even though, in reality, I knew it was me who was wrapped around his and always would be.

Our baby. My baby. I was shocked by the strength of maternal love I felt for him. The strength of feeling that I needed to protect him. I needed to make his life happy. Somewhere between pushing him into the world and holding him in my arms for the first time – my life had come into sharp focus.

This boy – this baby. He was the love of my life. No one else could be. He was all that mattered. Not the big house. Not the fancy car. Not the successful husband. Not the increasingly tiring battle to try and make Cian happy – to make him love me again the way he used to. The battle to make him feel less disgusted with me.

Because that's what I saw when I looked in his eyes. Disgust. Or something like it. Something that told me I was less than he was. I had my place and I had no doubt – none – that he loved me in his own way but it wasn't a love I wanted a part of. It could be cruel.

Maybe this baby would change that? This gorgeous, innocent creature that was half me and half him. Maybe it would soothe whatever had gone wrong between us.

He had cried when he held him for the first time. Kissed his head. Cooed at the midwife, asking her was he not the most beautiful baby she had ever seen. He had told me I was a clever girl. That he loved me. That I amazed him. He had kissed me, my forehead, and his tears had dropped onto my cheek and I – flushed from the exertion of labour and childbirth – had to fight the urge to push him away. I felt myself start to shake, my lungs fighting as they gasped for air.

'This happens sometimes,' the midwife had said, soothingly, as my panic turned into me retching and emptying whatever stale water had been lying in my stomach into a kidney bowl. 'The body goes into shock.'

She took the gas and air from me, attached some oxygen, gave me an antiemetic, which left me woozy, but so desperately wanting to hold my baby – needing to hold my baby – but not being able to.

I watched Cian walk around the room with him and my gut instinct screamed that I wanted him to give that baby to me. My baby. My protectiveness overwhelmed me.

When the midwife left and just the three of us remained, Cian sat down beside me and he cried again – rocking back and forward, holding Jack as if he was the most fragile thing in the world. He apologised over and over for his behaviour over the last few months. He told me he knew he had been wrong. He knew he had hurt me. He knew he needed help.

'I'll get it, Rose. For you and for Jack. I'll change. Please believe me that I'll change. Give me the chance to do it. For us, for him.'

He nodded to my baby – our baby – and I knew he deserved the chance to try. Didn't he? Every baby deserved a father and he seemed so contrite. This could be the wake-up call we had been waiting for. He had more than me to lose now.

And he could change – I knew that, believed it deep inside. After all, he hadn't always been difficult to live with. He hadn't always been so angry. He had loved me once – desperately and passionately. There was something there to make me fall so deeply in love with him so fast. I had to believe he could be that man I met that day in the library again. The Cian who made me laugh. The Cian who kissed my freckles. Who told me I was his everything.

'Jack deserves for us to keep trying, doesn't he?' he said. 'We can come through this. Our imperfections will make us more perfect in the long run, Rose. He's all that matters now. This baby. Jack. We have to put him first – do what we need to do for him.'

He was right – I needed to put Jack first. I needed to give him the chance to have the father I knew Cian could be.

Chapter Twenty-Eight

Emily

My flat felt less like home that afternoon. It felt cold, too quiet. Lonely. Not that it hadn't been lonely before – but it felt more so now.

Everything had changed in the last twenty-four hours. Changed utterly – isn't that how the saying goes? Even though the towel I had used to dry my hair the night before was still lying, damp, on the bedroom floor. Even though my make-up was still scattered around my dressing table, my work uniform discarded over the back of my chair. Even though the alarm clock in my room was still set twenty minutes too fast – a habit I started at university and had never got out of. Even though my fridge still had just half a pint of milk, two eggs and some ham – which had curled a little at the side. Even though the curtains in the living room were still pulled closed, everything felt out of sync. As if it didn't quite fit any more. This was no longer the only place I felt at home. There was somewhere else – and someone else who would become a home to me.

It had felt like a wrench to leave Cian when he had come home from the police station. I could see he was tired – drained by what he had heard. He had stalked in, his tie loosened, his shirt sleeves unbuttoned and rolled up to his elbows. He had walked straight to Jack, who was lost in an episode of Bing, and had pulled him onto his knee and sobbed into his hair. The poor child had looked stricken – scared by the outpouring of emotion from his father – and had burst into a flood of tears, kicking and flailing to get away from his father, which only served to put Cian into worse form.

'Jack,' he bawled. 'Sit still, for Christ's sake.' The child just wailed harder, slipping from Cian's knee and toddling to where I stood, wrapping himself around my legs. I lifted him, jiggled him up and down while all the time looking at Cian, trying to judge if he would divert his anger and frustration in my direction.

'Ssh, baby,' I soothed. 'Daddy just wants a cuddle from his best boy. He isn't cross with you, not one bit.'

Jack peeked out at his daddy, sniffing and hiccuping as I continued to jiggle him.

'I'm not cross, baby. Not with you, never with you.' Cian stood up and walked to where I stood and put his arms out for his son, who, if a little reluctantly, reached over and jumped into his father's arms. 'Why don't you show me what you and Emily have been doing while I've been out?' He put Jack down, and knelt beside him, their two heads bowed together over the building blocks. Once Jack was happily playing with his toys Cian looked to me, his face still tense, and said it had been worse than he thought it could be.

'They think I paid Kevin McDaid to kill Rose. And then they think I killed him too.'

'What? How? Are they charging you?' I asked, my eyes wide, my heart thumping, or breaking, or something I didn't understand.

He shook his head. 'No. Or at least not yet, they said. That Bradley one was so bloody smug about it. They don't have

209

evidence, my solicitor said – not enough to charge me anyway but that doesn't stop them putting the pressure on. But they asked me about money. They say they want to see my financial records. They say they have evidence money was paid into Kevin McDaid's bank account.'

Ingrid Devlin had told me the same – that money was involved somewhere in the equation but I had dismissed what she said as another of her lies. Now it was all sickeningly real – except that none of it made sense.

'But this is madness. What motive would you have for killing Rose? For the love of God, you adored that woman. Everyone with a set of eyes in their head could see that.'

'That's what I said to them. It makes me sick to the very pit of my stomach that they think I could have hurt her. That they think I would have paid some messed up little shite like McDaid to kill her? I never would have. I only ever wanted the very best for Rose. I gave her everything – the house, the car, the clothes, the jewellery. She wanted for nothing. I gave her the world and I'd have given her the moon and stars too if I could have.' He shook his head and walked to the kitchen area where he put on the kettle. 'You know what, Emily? You're right – sometimes people just want to believe the worst of you, no matter what evidence they have in front of them to the contrary. The police are taking the lazy approach. It's often the husband or partner therefore it must be the husband in this case. The detectives in my books could do a better job, and they're bloody fictional.'

'And McDaid? How? How would you be involved?'

Cian shook his head. 'I've no idea,' he said, turning to take two cups out of the cupboard, dropping tea bags into them. 'All I know is that I didn't pay that man any money. I wouldn't have pissed on him if he was on fire.'

He looked so utterly forlorn that I walked over and hugged

him. I felt the weight of his head rest on top of mine, and then a soft kiss on my hair. 'I thought I had been through the worst of this nightmare,' he said. 'But it looks like it's only just beginning.'

'You can get through all this,' I said pulling back to look in his eyes. 'I'm here to help you. And Ingrid Devlin will get your story out there for anyone who is prepared to listen. The greatest form of defence is attack – keep calm and let people know the real you.'

Cian had hugged me again and we drank our tea before he called a taxi to take me home. I wondered now, as I pottered around the flat, if Ingrid Devlin was there yet. Was he coping? I wished I could be there to support him, but I knew that wouldn't look right. I had to put his needs first. It was such a shame Rose's family weren't behind him. They should be speaking up for the man their daughter loved. But Cian had told me things had been strained between him and his in-laws for a long time. Just like Owen had, Rose's parents had thought their daughter could do much better than an aspiring writer. Of course, they had tried to build bridges when he became a success but Rose had told him she wasn't going to forgive them that easily. They could take their snobbery and stick it, she had told him. She allowed them access to Jack, but, as Cian said, that was more to do with the goodness of her heart rather than as a result of anything they had done.

Cian's own parents both suffered with health woes, and had relocated to a small village in Cork. They only made the trip north when they absolutely had to. (The funeral of their daughter-in-law was not considered necessary travel – although they had sent a floral tribute and offered Cian and Jack a room to escape to for a while.)

So Cian was essentially alone and my heart ached for him – as it did for my own loneliness.

★

The headline that Cian Grahame just wanted to be left to live in peace to grieve for his wife had been splashed all over the internet by early morning. A picture of him holding that same blasted picture of Rose that stared down from me from the wall in work had been shared widely over social media with click bait links urging people to click to find out 'the haunting story not even this award-winning writer could make up'.

I had clicked on the link – of course I had. Desperate to read what the article said.

It was painful to read his story, and not just because of the sadness that was evident in every word, but also because it was so very clear she would always be a massive part of his life.

Maybe sadness isn't the right word though. Maybe jealousy was?

On my walk to work I stopped to buy a hard copy of the paper – wanting to hold it in my hands, have it to keep. Of course, the story was the talk of the newsagent. An old woman with pursed lips and her arms folded over her ample bosom was talking about how it was 'a sin that the wee baby was getting caught up in the middle of such a mess'.

The newsagent was saying it was terrible that Cian was having his name dragged through the mud, just because he was someone who had done well for himself. This garnered a few nods. A harassed-looking mother, trying to placate a child in a buggy with a bag of crisps, said the police would be better fixed trying to catch the 'real bad guys' – like whoever it was that had burgled her house a few weeks ago, taking her Christmas money and leaving her seven-year-old so traumatised he had started wetting the bed.

'He's a handsome devil all the same,' the large-bosomed woman exclaimed. 'He won't be short of female company to help him raise that wee boy.'

'I'm sure he'd rather have his wife back,' the newsagent said and they all nodded sagely, muttering that it was just terrible and awful and fierce.

I just stood silently, taking it all in. I had felt a little smug when the old woman had commented on how handsome Cian was – thinking that I knew exactly how handsome he was. How his body was sculpted under the striped shirt and jeans he was wearing in that picture. How his arms were strong and toned and made me feel so very safe. How he looked his most handsome when he was falling asleep, his long lashes just like Jack's, fluttering closed.

As expected, when I got to work the majority of the staff were talking about the article, crowded in the staffroom over a copy of the paper.

Tori read out a passage and they made the appropriate sympathetic noises. A few wiped away tears. 'I never realised the police were giving him such a hard time,' another said. 'That's so unfair.'

The nods of agreement ran around the room while I stood, a small – hopefully discreet – smile on my face. While meeting Ingrid Devlin had brought my greatest fears into focus, it seemed it was a good thing after all. She had made Cian sound like more of a saint than Rose.

Donna had scolded us for gossiping but had a good read of the article herself, turning to ask no one in particular: 'So they really think he had something to do with Rose's death? I wonder what evidence they have?'

The article had been light on the details of any police claims about evidence, running only the official line that the investigations had been upgraded and police were following several lines of inquiry. It would be 'inappropriate' to comment further at this stage, a police spokesperson had said.

I opened my mouth to comment on the money police had found in McDaid's bank account but at the last minute caught myself. We had decided not to go public about our friendship for a reason – because we didn't want to be judged and I was under no illusions that the person or people who would judge us most were those who worked in this building.

'God knows,' I muttered instead, 'but they must have something if they made him go to the station.'

Donna shook her head and made to fold the paper up just as Owen walked in and tore it from her hands. 'Let me make this very clear,' he said, turning to make sure we were all looking directly at him. 'I do not want to see any of this rubbish in this office. I do not want it discussed. I do not want to find out that any of you are speaking to the papers, or chatting about this on social media, or coming up with your own twisted theories about what happened. If I find out that any of you speak to the press, you will be fired, with immediate effect. It would do you all well to remember this isn't some stupid soap opera for your entertainment. Rose was our friend. Our loyalty to her goes above and beyond any loyalty that we should have for her husband. If the police are knocking on his door, I trust they have good reason to. I'm not going to pussyfoot around this any more – that man is not welcome in this building. Now, how about you all get yourselves to your work stations and get on with your jobs – which is, after all, what you are paid to do.'

He turned on his heel and stalked out of the room again into his office, slamming the door with such a bang that a child in the waiting area starting to wail.

'I'll go and smooth that over – bring that poor pet an extra sticker or ten,' Tori said, heading for reception while the rest of the staff rinsed teacups in awkward silence. As I walked to reception, I saw Donna knock tentatively on Owen's door before going in.

It was only a matter of seconds before Owen's raised voice

was heard over the surgery. 'Just get on with your work, Donna. Do you have to be there, beside me, every time I look around? I can't think. Let alone breathe with you in my face all the time.'

I quickly switched on the radio to smother the noise of his ranting, but it was a bit too late. Donna was already making her way out of the office, her face blazing and her eyes wide as if she feared to blink lest she started to cry. I watched as she took a deep, shuddering breath, and turned back to the staff kitchen.

'Can you manage here for a moment?' I whispered to Tori, who had adopted the falsest of smiles and cheeriest of voices to assure our clients that everything was entirely normal and running as planned, while I chased down the corridor towards the kitchen to soothe Donna. I was angry, I realised. Angry at Owen and how he had spoken to us and how he had spoken to Donna most of all. She had been bending over backwards these last few weeks to be as kind and supportive to him as she possibly could, even though, God knows, she had enough of her own worries to be dealing with. She didn't need Owen acting like an overgrown, stroppy teen. Or worse, a huffy, manipulative, bossy grown-up. The kind of man Cian told me he was. The kind of man who could act in a truly loathsome manner if he didn't get his own way.

Chapter Twenty-Nine

Donna was emptying her locker – tossing pieces of paper into a waste paper bin, the rest of her belongings into a carrier bag. She stopped every few seconds to wipe tears from her face or to sniff loudly.

'I've had enough,' she gulped between sobs. 'I can't put up with him talking to me like that any more. He can stick his job.'

'Donna!' I said. 'Don't let him get to you like that. He's not worth it. He's just upset about everything,' I soothed, reaching into my pocket for a tissue and handing it to her. 'It's not something to be walking away from your job over. Not with children to feed and clothe.'

'He's not the only person allowed to be upset,' she said, her chest heaving with sobs. 'He doesn't own grief, you know. He isn't the only person caught up in this fucking mess. He's no right to speak to any of us like that – least of all me.' Her face was still blazing with embarrassment after such a public talking to. She roughly wiped her eyes and pushed a strand of her auburn hair that had come loose from her ponytail behind her ear and resumed packing her things.

'There's only so much a person can take,' she sobbed. 'I've tried to understand. I've done everything I could to be as good as she was. To make sure this place kept running smoothly. I've been the one who worked on when everyone else went home – even though I was going home to three boys who wouldn't know how to boil a fucking egg never mind cook a dinner for themselves or for me. I was the one who made sure we didn't miss appointments. That arranged the bloody flowers for her funeral. It was me! Everything I do has been for him. But what do I get in return? Shouted at – and I know you all heard. Jesus Christ, I'm surprised Rose didn't wake from the dead with the commotion!' she said, sniffing loudly. 'Do you know how humiliating that is? They'll all be talking and laughing. They'll all think "Donna's a laughing stock". And the thing is, he won't apologise for it. He'll just carry on as always not thinking about what he does to people. I've had enough, Emily. I really have.'

At that her fight left her, replaced only by her sorrow and humiliation as she crumpled with emotion and I pulled her into a hug – her sobs shuddering through her and my shoulder growing wet with her tears.

'Take deep breaths,' I urged her. 'Everyone here loves you – you *do* hold the place together and if he can't see it now it's his problem. Don't let him have you walk out – what would that achieve?'

I was so angry I was tempted to storm in myself and tell him exactly what I thought of the way in which he had spoken to her. I was even tempted to tell him I knew exactly what way he had treated Rose too. He was nothing more than a spoiled child of a man. A bully. And you didn't let bullies win.

'Put your things back in your locker. I'll make you a tea and if himself asks me about it, I'll tell him outright he owes you an apology. I'll cover for you in surgery with him while you

217

compose yourself. Redo your make-up and hold your head high. Don't walk out on your job – your income.'

She gave me a watery smile and let me make her a cup of tea while she sat mopping up the tears that kept falling. Slowly they stopped and a calm washed over her.

'Thank you, Emily,' she said, sipping from the mug of hot tea. 'Thank you for talking me down. I don't know what I would have done. Would I have walked out on my job and left myself without any money to look after my children? Oh God . . .'

'Look, you're still here. You're going to get through this, okay?'

'I don't know what I'd do without you,' she said, and the warmth in her voice made me in turn feel warm inside.

'It goes both ways,' I said.

*

With how I felt that morning I would have been happy to never work directly with Owen again – but I told myself if he had lost his temper so quickly with Donna that morning he must be on edge.

Perhaps the news that the police were moving forward with their investigation had rattled him. It was, after all, possible that he knew it was only a matter of time before the evidence pointed them in his direction.

I thought of how I'd seen Owen lift Kevin McDaid's file. I wondered, had he put it back? I'd check later I told myself as I took my seat in the surgery and waited for the first patient to arrive.

I tried to focus on the positive – if there was such a thing as a positive in this situation. The more rattled Owen became, the more the evidence pointed to him, the less it pointed to Ben. The less it pointed to me being the intended target. I clung to that thought while everything else seemed such a mess.

Owen stalked into the room and sighed deeply as he looked at the records of our next patient. 'Where's Donna?' he asked. 'We've a root canal after this and it's beyond your ability.' His voice was sharp and I bristled.

'She's helping out with a problem in reception. I said I'd cover for her until it was sorted. You know Donna, she knows that computer system better than the rest of us. She'll have it sorted quickly,' I lied. I wouldn't let him know he had succeeded in upsetting her.

He sighed again. 'I suppose I should apologise to her,' he said. I raised an eyebrow.

'I was out of line just now. I know that. It's not like me to lose my temper.' (I held in the words: 'that's not what I've heard'.) 'It's just seeing him all over the paper – smiling like butter wouldn't melt. If only the world knew what he was really like,' he said, before leaving the room to call in our first patient. There was no point in my telling him that the whole point of the article was to show the world exactly what Cian was like – the real, loving, caring, Cian. Owen wanted to believe what Owen wanted to believe and that was all there was to it.

He walked back in with a nervous-looking teenager who was due a check-up.

'I brushed my teeth three times this morning,' the spotty-faced youth said. 'So they should be extra clean.'

'We'll have a look and see then,' Owen said, his trademark friendly smile back on his face, as if he hadn't just upset almost everyone who worked for him, and led one of his most loyal staff members to consider quitting on the spot.

★

At lunchtime I declined the usual sandwich from the deli and said I was nipping out to get a bit of fresh air instead. I walked

219

down Shipquay Street to the Peace Park, just across the road from the Guildhall. Sitting down on one of the park's benches, I took my phone out to call Cian.

I had been itching to talk to him all day – to fill him in on what had been said in the newsagents but also to tell him that Owen seemed to be unravelling. I knew that would make him happy and I wanted more than anything to make him happy. I also wanted to hear how he was. He had been so devastated the day before.

I scrolled through my contacts and dialled his number. He answered the phone after three rings, but his tone was sharp.

'Emily, can I help you?' he almost barked. No hello. No softness. No hint of 'I've only got through the last week or two because of you'. It was as if I was an unwanted disturbance to him.

I felt wrong-footed. For the briefest of moments I wondered had I dialled the right number? But it definitely was Cian's voice on the other end of the line.

'I was just . . . calling to . . . see how you are,' I stuttered. 'After the article . . . and everything.'

He sighed, deeply. 'I'm right in the middle of something. I'll call you later.' He hung up without a goodbye, leaving me sat on the bench, wondering what on earth had just happened.

I found it hard to force a smile on my face as I put my phone back in my bag and slowly made my way back up Shipquay Street and onto the Sandwich Company to grab a salad that I didn't really have the appetite for and a coffee that I didn't really want to drink. At least Donna seemed brighter when I walked into the staff room. She was sitting on her own, sipping a coffee and reading a magazine. She smiled as I sat down opposite her and stared at my lunch.

'He apologised,' she said, her eyes glittering. 'Profusely. Said he didn't mean to take out his frustration on me. He even bought me a bunch of flowers from the corner shop,' she said, nodding towards the sink where a sorry-looking bunch of carnations were resting in some water. 'Okay, they don't look like much, but it's the thought that counts. We should probably cut him some slack. He *is* under a lot of pressure.'

'We all are,' I said, sitting down and staring at the salad in front of me, knowing there was no way I'd eat it.

'You seem out of sorts,' Donna said, reaching over and squeezing my hand. 'It's not like you, Emily. You're the one who keeps us all smiling – what's wrong?'

To my shame I felt tears prick at my eyes but there was no way I could tell her what was upsetting me. She wouldn't understand. I did feel soothed by her telling me that I made people smile. But that only made me want to cry a little bit more. I hastily wiped a tear from my eye.

'Oh, nothing. Just PMT or something. You know me, soft as they come. Been feeling a little out of sorts all day.'

Donna smiled and reached into her bag. 'I have just the thing for you then,' she said, pulling out a bar of Dairy Milk. 'I was saving this for home time but your need is greater than mine.'

'No,' I said, shaking my head, 'I'm fine really.'

But she opened the packet, broke off a square and pushed it into my hand before sitting the rest of the bar in front of me.

'Don't be silly. It's medicinal, I insist,' she said.

Not wanting to offend, or perhaps not having the energy to offend, I lifted the piece of chocolate and popped it in my mouth where it melted – sickly, sweet, sticky.

Donna raised an eyebrow. 'Maybe you're still sick, from yesterday?' she said. 'You shouldn't have come in, you poor thing. Look, why not take the rest of the day off? Go home, have a good cry and a good rest and I guarantee tomorrow you'll feel better.'

Once again I didn't feel I had the energy to argue with her so, deflated and suddenly exhausted, I lifted my bag – leaving the salad and the remaining chocolate on the table – and set off for home, feeling as if my legs were slowly turning to lead.

★

When I got home, I downed three anti-anxiety pills with a long glass of water. I knew from experience this would calm me down enough to allow me to fight off the darkest of thoughts. If I was lucky – really lucky – they would make me drowsy enough to have a sleep, to escape watching my phone to see if Cian would call back. To escape the urge to call him again and ask him what was going on. He had sounded so cold. The familiar feeling of being a nuisance to someone – a head-ache they couldn't get rid of with two paracetamols and a glass of water – was starting to wash over me and I didn't like it.

Soon, I could feel the blissful haziness of the pills start to unfurl through me, so I wandered to my bedroom and stripped to my underwear, throwing my uniform that I had so carefully ironed that morning onto the floor in an undignified heap. Without washing my make-up off, I climbed into bed and pulled my duvet up over my head, hoping to escape into a blissful, numb sleep.

When I woke, fuzzy-headed, mouth dry, disorientated as to what time of day or year it was, I reached for my phone. Blinking and trying to focus, I looked at the screen in front of me.

A flashing email notification and three missed calls. Clicking straight into the missed calls, I offered up a silent prayer. Please let them be from Cian. Please let them all be him phoning me to explain. To say he was sorry. To ask me to call over.

But the calls weren't from Cian. One was from a private number. One was from Donna's mobile and the other from Scott's landline.

There were two messages left on my voicemail. Was it too much to hope Cian was calling me from a private number? I dialled into my voicemail and listened with decreasing patience as the automated voice read out the number that had left the first of the messages. It was Donna.

'You're probably sleeping. I didn't want to call and not leave a message and have you worrying what I was calling about. I was just calling with gossip really – but I've heard the police have just conducted a search on Cian Grahame's house. He must be hiding something, Emily. He must have been fooling us all. I'll let you know if I hear any more. Get a good rest. See you tomorrow!'

She sounded cheerful. Euphoric even – at complete odds with the horrible feeling in the pit of my stomach. I listened on to the next call. Tori this time. Less cheerful. Positively not euphoric.

'Erm, Emily. The police have just been here. That Detective Bradley? He was looking to talk to you? In relation to the investigation? He asked a few questions about you, Emily. How long we'd known you, etc.? Anyway, Owen gave him your contact details and I think you should expect a call if not a visit.'

The horrible feeling in the pit of my stomach grew and rose up, spilling out all over my bedroom carpet.

Chapter Thirty

I ran the shower – cold so that it would shock me into waking up. Shock me into being fully aware of what was happening. Shock me into being with it enough to be able to deal with what was to come next.

It wasn't so much that the police could well be on their way to my flat right that very moment – I had known that was likely as soon as Cian had given my name as an alibi.

It was more that they had visited Scott's and spoken to staff there and let them know they were going to speak to me. That would make no sense, none at all, to my colleagues. As far as they were concerned I was a blow in. A new start who took over the job left behind by Rose. I was someone who knew nothing, except what they told me, of how she died. Someone who only knew Cian because of his visit to the surgery. Someone who couldn't possibly be linked to the nightmare that had unfolded since Rose had pushed that buggy out of the lift and walked into the path of Kevin McDaid.

They would think the worst of me. Owen – God only knows what Owen would think. God only knows what Owen would do. If, as Cian suspected, he was in some way involved in Rose's death – would I be putting myself in danger by consorting with the man he hated most of all?

The cold water stung as it hit my skin, turning it red, then blue with the cold. My teeth chattering, I turned it off and pulled a towel from the rail. Dressing in yoga pants and a baggy sweatshirt, I pulled a hairbrush through my hair, made a large coffee and waited for the doorbell to ring.

While I waited, I tried to phone Cian. If the police were searching his house I could understand why he was so off with me before. He must be going through hell. The article didn't work. It didn't put the police off at all. It didn't slow them down. They were continuing to look for information to put him in the frame.

I wondered why they didn't look elsewhere? Why they hadn't invited Owen in for a chat? Surely Cian had told them what kind of a man he was? Surely Cian had access to messages he had sent Rose? Something that proved he felt aggrieved? Surely that would be enough to have the police sniffing around him too? Maybe I'd mention that? Maybe I'd tell them they were barking up the wrong tree with Cian and they should look elsewhere.

Cian's phone went straight to voicemail. I left a short message, telling him the police were looking for me. Asking him to call me. Saying I hoped he was okay. I tried to hide the hint of desperation from my voice.

The blinking email notification flashed at me again and I clicked in, my heart stopping to see it was a reply from Ben. It was as if he timed these things for maximum impact. I threw the phone to the floor, resisted the urge to kick it under the sofa. I couldn't, just could not, find the strength on top of everything else to read it just then. I nudged it just out of view under my coffee table.

I jolted when the buzzer went at the door. As expected,

when I answered it was DS Bradley and one of his colleagues, wondering if they could talk to me.

Should I call a solicitor? I had used one before. With Ben. I could get her number if I needed to, but she was in Belfast. Not likely to be interested. I chewed on my thumbnail as I buzzed the police in through the main door and waited for them to arrive at my flat. I wondered if I should have put on make-up. War paint. Something akin to armour. To give me the courage to lie.

It was okay to lie when it was for the greater good, wasn't it?

DS Bradley offered me a small, tight smile when he arrived. He had a female officer with him who looked like she should still be in sixth form. She stood swamped in her heavy boots and full uniform, looking deeply uncomfortable.

'Please, have a seat,' I said to them both, probably a little too formally, before making my own way to the armchair, where I sat down, suddenly feeling as if my limbs were inordinately large and clumsy. I pushed my hair behind my ears and looked at them both as they sat down and the young female officer pulled a notebook from her pocket.

'We seem to keep running into each other,' DS Bradley said, his tone neutral.

'That will happen if you call to my house,' I said, trying to keep my voice light. Making our conversation sound like banter, belying the nerves that were jangling through my body.

He smiled. 'I suppose so. But at the Grahame house. And Scott's? And if I'm not mistaken, outside Kevin McDaid's wake? You keep yourself busy. Did you know Kevin McDaid?'

I felt heat start to rise at the back of my neck, I put my hand to it. 'Not really,' I said. 'I mean, I knew one of his cousins. So I was there for them,' I lied.

DS Bradley nodded. 'Coincidence all the same – given the

Scott's connection and Rose, and of course your friendship with Cian.'

'They do say truth is stranger than fiction, don't they?' I said, rubbing my neck. 'Is this an official interview? You know, like Cian had? Under caution?'

DS Bradley shook his head. 'Not at this stage,' he said. 'This is just a chat, Ms D'Arcy. Nothing to be worried about. It's just part of our ongoing investigation. We may ask you to make a formal statement at some stage but for now, we just want to ask a few questions.'

The female officer nodded at me, smiled as if this was all perfectly normal everyday stuff.

'And how long have you known Mr Grahame for?'

'About a month,' I said – trying to ignore how he raised his eyebrows at my admission. 'He came into the surgery with his son, and we got talking.'

'Quite a connection really, to be so close that within a very short time you were trying to counsel him to stop him taking his own life?'

I prayed I wasn't blushing. 'We clicked,' I said. 'He needed someone to talk to. People tend to open up to me.'

'Did you know Mrs Grahame – Rose?'

I shook my head. 'No. I didn't know her. I told you that at Scott's.'

'And you were with Cian the night Kevin McDaid died?'

I nodded. I didn't speak. Maybe if I didn't actually say the words it wouldn't be lying. I could get away with it.

'He was upset and you were counselling him?' He repeated the question he had asked just a few moments before. Was he trying to catch me out?

I nodded. 'He's been finding life very tough. When you add people pointing the finger at him to the mix, it's not hard to see why he would be close to breaking point.' I hoped I had made my point, but DS Bradley just nodded and looked to the female officer beside him who was scribbling in her notebook. She hadn't spoken at all since they arrived at my flat.

'Has Mr Grahame indicated to you anyone he feels would have or could have hurt his wife?'

I thought of Owen. Who had given me my second chance and had welcomed me into the surgery and been a kind and fair boss – that is until the last week. He'd shown how he could behave when he was stressed, but could he really be the kind of man who would have someone killed?

I suppose anything is possible if you feel scorned enough. If you felt betrayed and hurt. If you wanted to hurt someone else – not just Rose, but the man who had taken her for ever.

I swallowed. 'He did tell me that Owen Scott had been infatuated with Rose. Was angry, even, when she didn't return his advances.'

'Owen Scott, your boss?'

I nodded.

'And has there been any talk of Owen's relationship with Rose among your work colleagues since you started there?'

I shook my head. I couldn't in good conscience say there had been – nothing negative anyway. 'No,' I said, feeling increasingly uncomfortable. I wrapped my arms around my tummy and took a deep breath to try and steady myself.

'Are you feeling okay, Ms D'Arcy? Your work colleague told me you had gone home sick today – still sick from yesterday, she said.'

I blushed deeper – cringed. He knew that yesterday I had been perfectly well and in Cian's house, making tea for him. Being caught lying was one thing. Being caught lying by a policeman was something else. Especially when he looked at me with the hint of a smile on his face. He'd be handsome, I guessed, if I didn't feel so intimidated by him.

'Well, actually today I don't feel so well – but yesterday, yes – well, it's not against the law to fake the odd sickie.' I attempted a quick laugh but it sounded fake and the lie rolled around the room like giant balls of tumbleweed.

DS Bradley cleared his throat. 'No. It isn't. We'd be rushed off our feet if it was,' he said, calm, collected, playing the good cop. 'When it comes to work, can I ask, has anyone spoken ill of Rose? Has there been any chat that would indicate she – Mr Scott aside – had any enemies?'

Inwardly I wished she did. It would make all of this easier. 'No,' I told him honestly. 'I'd say if they had it in their power they would have put her forward for a sainthood. She seems to have been completely faultless.'

'We all have our faults,' DS Bradley said, looking at me pointedly – making me feel as if my faults were written all over my face.

'Yes, I suppose we do,' I replied.

'Well, Ms D'Arcy—'

'Emily, please call me Emily,' I said, in a last-ditch attempt to try and make things less awkward between us. If I could hold on to him in good cop mode maybe things wouldn't be so bad.

He nodded again. 'Well, Emily, I think that's all we need from you for now. As I said before we may well invite you in to make a formal statement in the near future but in the meantime, if you can think of anything – anything at all – that might be of use to the investigation, perhaps you could give me a call?' He reached into his jacket pocket and took out a business card.

'I will,' I said, standing up and taking it from him, itching to get them out of my flat as soon as possible.

The still mute female officer nodded at me and headed for the door – while DS Bradley stopped, turned back to me and spoke.

'Emily, it might be worth really thinking about any details that might help this investigation. Perhaps you're mistaken about what night you were with Mr Grahame – counselling him? It can be easy to mix up evenings, the things we do. Life is so busy these days. So if you find you have misremembered things – maybe you could get in touch?' His expression was soft, his voice gentle.

I didn't know what to say. I didn't know how to react. Did he know I was lying? Did he want me to tell him – categorically – that Cian had been on his own when McDaid died because it would fit in with the version of events he wanted for that night? Whatever the reason, it was clear he had his sights firmly set on Cian and he was taking aim and getting ready to fire.

★

I looked out of my living room window until I could see DS Bradley and his colleague drive off. I admit my paranoia was at an all-time high. I'd probably watched too many corny crime movies. I wondered if he would have left a bug somewhere and then gave myself a good shake. Told myself to wise up. Told myself what had just happened was nothing more than a routine chat as part of an ongoing investigation. If it was something more, DS Bradley would have played a full-on bad cop. He would have hauled me over the coals for lying to work. He would have questioned me more about being at McDaid's wake. But he hadn't. Not yet anyway. He had smirked a bit, yes. Been formal, of course. But there had also been a kindness there.

Still, my flat suddenly felt claustrophobic and my options for people to call on to reassure me were even more limited than they had ever been. My phone, and the email from Ben, was still taunting me from under the coffee table. I was afraid to look at it, as if it would summon him directly into my living room.

I realised I had no one to reach out to – no one except the one person in this world who would understand the hell of this investigation. The only person who would, or could, understand was Cian.

I picked up my phone and dialled through, swearing to myself as it went once again to his voicemail. In my anger I threw my phone on the sofa before picking it back up, thinking the evening was unlikely to improve anyway and I might as well just rip the giant Ben-sized plaster off there and then.

He'd written only a couple of lines, which blurred in front of my eyes before I was able to read them.

Emily,

I don't know why I sent that friend request. Except I was thinking about you and about us and I'd had a few drinks. I shouldn't have. We're both much better off without being in each other's lives.

A journalist has been in touch asking about our relationship. Emily, I've moved on. I know I fucked up back then. We both did, but please don't rake up the past. Let's just get on with our lives.

Ben

So that was that. All that fear, all those worries, boiling down to a short email in which he said he'd had too much to drink and was better off out of my life. God, I knew he was right. There wasn't a part of me that wanted him in my life again. But somehow the part that should have been doing cartwheels of joy that he wasn't about to show up on my doorstep and that he was as scared of Ingrid Devlin as I was, was still and silent.

I felt a deep sense of shame to realise that a part of me felt rejected again. Irrational, I know, but I felt tears well up and start to run down my cheeks.

In that moment I felt the need to be held and to be loved and to be told I mattered to someone.

So I went into my bedroom, slipped on a pair of trainers. I pulled my still damp hair back into a loose ponytail and grabbed my chunky cardigan from the back of the bedroom door. Grabbing my phone, my purse and my keys, I left the flat, jumped into my car and set off for Cian's house.

I kept the radio off. The noise of it annoyed me. Everything annoyed me, to be honest. The red lights. The slow drivers. The rain that started to fall in sheets making visibility so poor I was forced to slow down myself, while my stupid car started to steam up. At every junction, at every red light, I checked my phone – which was laying on the passenger seat – to see if he had called me back. But if the call had gone to voicemail, would he even know I had been calling him in the first place? I tried to reassure myself that of course he wouldn't – because if he did, he *would* have called me back. He would have understood how desperately I needed to talk to him.

Arriving at his house, I was relieved to see the lights on. I tried not to think about him being home and why he wouldn't have called me. I tried not to get stressed about the car I didn't recognise, sitting alongside his in the drive. Wrapping my cardigan tight around my body, I jumped from my car, into the pouring rain and ran to his front door. Shivering, I rang the doorbell, then rapped on the door with my fist.

The rain was taking no time at all to fall, the deluge leaving water running down my face and from the end of my nose when the door creaked open and Cian, looking distinctly unstressed, peeked out.

232

'Emily?' He said, not stepping backwards enough to allow me in.

'I needed to see you, Cian. The police have been round.'

I wanted him to pull me into house, into his arms and hug me and tell me everything would be okay, but he just looked at me blankly before speaking. 'I have someone with me just now, Emily. I'm not sure this is the best time to talk.'

Someone with him? I looked at him – in his loose jeans, bare foot. A white T-shirt, which highlighted his toned frame. He was holding a glass of red wine in his hand.

I started shivering violently. The cold seeping through to my bones. 'Please, Cian. I'm scared and I need to know what to do. They asked about the night Kevin McDaid died.'

He stared at me again, a hint of disdain on his face, which I told myself was just my paranoia at play. Then, as if a switch had been flipped inside his head, he stood back.

'Oh Emily, you poor thing, come in,' he said, maybe a little too loudly, ushering me in. 'You must be freezing. Hang on,' he said, turning to walk down the hall but stopping, turning back and kissing me lightly on the tip of my nose. He walked off again and I stood, rain dripping from the ends of my hair to the floor. I sniffed loudly, dragged my sleeve across my face in an attempt to dry myself off only to discover the cardigan was well and truly soaked through too.

I watched as he walked back into the hall from the kitchen. A bundle of towels in his hand. 'Fresh out of the drier,' he said. 'Still warm. Come and get a shower. Get warmed up and dried off.'

'The police, Cian. They asked all sorts of questions,' I said as he took my hand.

'The most important thing is to get you out of those wet clothes before you catch your death. Get a warm shower. We can talk then.'

'But your guest?'

'She'll be fine for a few minutes,' he said and I tried not to feel any hint of jealously at the word 'she'. He led me upstairs, back to the guest bedroom with the beautiful en-suite where he pulled the curtains, switched on the lamp on the side table, before walking into the bathroom and starting to run the shower.

'This will make you feel better,' he said putting the towels on the bed. 'If you give me those wet clothes, I'll put them in the drier for you. I'll leave a dressing gown here for you to wear while they're drying. You've gotten yourself into such a state. You shouldn't worry. There's no way the police can know we weren't together that night unless you tell them.'

'I won't,' I said, still shivering.

Then, very tenderly, he walked towards me and put his hands to my face, tipping my head back so that I was looking directly at him. He bent his head towards mine and kissed me gently – before sliding his hands down my neck and slowly pulling my cardigan from my shoulders, letting it pool on the floor behind us. I shivered again, but it wasn't from the cold this time.

'Let me undress you,' he whispered in my ear, the roughness of his stubble brushing against my cheek. The smell of his cologne invading my senses. I felt his hands slip under my sweatshirt – felt them hot on my cold skin.

'You've had a tough day. You poor thing. You're so cold,' he whispered, brushing my neck with his lips – forcing a soft moan to escape from my mouth as his hands moved upwards and he peeled my sweatshirt from my body. He drew one long, strong finger from my collarbone down between my breasts and I inhaled deeply as he moved his hands lower. 'You're beautiful, Emily,' he said as his hands circled my waist. As he kissed me again I kicked off my trainers, closing my eyes as he dropped to his knees, kissing my stomach as he pulled my yoga pants down and I stepped out of them – grateful at least that I was wearing half-decent underwear. His mouth was on me, for the briefest, most blissful of moments, kissing me through my lace knickers. His hands, warm on my body had me desperate to pull him closer, hold him to me – to lose myself – and all the worries of the last few hours in him. But he stood up again, brushing his hands along the length of my body – close but not close enough to where I wanted them to be and he gave me a wicked smile.

'Oh Emily, you've no idea what you do to me,' he said, his eyes dark. 'If you don't get in the shower right now, I'm going to lose control of myself and I have a guest downstairs.' He kissed me lightly, scooped up my clothes from the floor and turned and left – leaving me confused, with no chance not to get in the shower straight away and allow him to lose control of himself. I stripped off my underwear and climbed under the hot streams of water, shook any negative feelings out of my head. He still needed me. He called me beautiful. Things were good, I reassured myself. I would make him lose control as soon as I got the chance.

Chapter Thirty-One

I dried myself off, slipped my underwear back on and saw that Cian had left a dressing gown for me, as he said he would. It was white and fluffy. I wondered was it his? Or had it been Rose's? I slipped it on and tied the belt and after stopping, briefly, to look in the mirror and tousle my hair to look less like a drowned rat, I padded downstairs and into the kitchen.

The sound of laughter – easy, relaxed – greeted me, as did the sight of the fire blazing, and Ingrid Devlin sitting on the sofa, her shoes kicked off, her legs curled under her sipping from a glass of red wine. A notebook and pen sat in front of her – but the page was blank. Cian was at the opposite end of the sofa, but his body was angled towards her – his arm outstretched over the back of the sofa. I wasn't a body language expert but everything about how they sat screamed too close for comfort at me. I pulled the belt tighter on the dressing gown, feeling exposed.

It was Ingrid who saw me first, who looked up and smiled. 'Oh Emily, come in. Will I pour you a glass of wine?'

She was speaking to me as if her natural place was in that kitchen, on that sofa, beside Cian. In charge of pouring his wine and entertaining his guests. Should it not have been *me* topping up *her* glass?

I bit my tongue. Dampened down my feelings of jealousy. 'That would be nice,' I said.

'Great,' Ingrid said. 'Cian brought a glass over here for you while you were showering.' She lifted the bottle from the table and poured a large measure into a glass that was sitting beside it. 'I hope you're warmed up now,' she said as she poured. 'Cian said you were soaked through.'

'I was but I feel much better now, thanks,' I said, as Cian looked round and offered me a smile.

'You look much better too,' he said. 'Warmer, anyway.' He reached out to me and took my hand in his, guiding me around to the armchair to his right. I sat down, pulling a cushion in front of me to cover my stomach.

'Cian tells me the police called with you today?' Ingrid said.

I nodded. 'They asked me about Rose. About work. About Cian − if I was with him the night Kevin McDaid died.'

'I couldn't have got through that night without you,' Cian said − the ease of his lie both reassuring and disarming. 'She was brilliant,' he said, turning to smile at Ingrid.

'A friend in need is a friend indeed,' she said, putting her own wine glass down on the table.

An awkward silence followed − and I was the first to break it. 'The article was very well received,' I said. 'I heard a lot of people talking about it.'

'Not well received enough to stop the police coming with a warrant to search the house, gain access to my financial records,' Cian said bitterly.

'It's shocking,' Ingrid said, and I wished she would just disappear. It didn't matter that her article had helped Cian right now. I just wanted her and her conniving ways gone. I wanted to be alone with Cian so I could ask him about the fact I had lied to the police for him. I wanted to talk to him about the things only we should know. 'Poor Jack was very upset.'

'The baby was here?' I asked, then something whirred in my brain. 'You were here?'

Ingrid nodded. 'Once the police arrived, Cian called me. He asked me to come over – to witness what he was being subjected to.'

He called Ingrid Devlin – but he didn't call me.

'I thought maybe Ingrid could do a follow-up story – you know, stay on the case,' Cian said.

'You should have called me,' I said, trying to keep my tone light. 'I would have come over.'

'But you were at work – and I doubt Owen would have understood. Besides, what could you have done?'

I could have soothed him. Kept him calm. I could have put Jack in his buggy and taken him to the park to distract him from the intimidating sight of burly police officers in his home. I could have just been there.

I shrugged my shoulders. I didn't want to answer him in that way. Not in front of Ingrid anyway.

'So you've been here all day?' I asked her.

'No,' Cian cut in. 'She was here when the police called and then I invited her over for some dinner. As a thank you. And to allow us to put the finer points on a follow-up story.'

I bristled. Sipped from my wine again. A thank-you dinner. He was fond of those, it seems. I took a breath, chided myself for being silly. Thought of how he had undressed me, kissed me, pulled me to him, his breath ragged, upstairs. I had nothing to fear from this woman.

'It'll be a good piece,' Ingrid said, cutting through my thoughts. 'Especially when we mention how distraught Jack was. Maybe get a picture of him crying? That's good optics – horrible for Jack, of course – but great to get the readers onside.'

238

'How is Jack now?' I asked Cian. 'Did he settle down easy enough?'

'He took a bit of time – needed some extra cuddles, but he's sound out now. Not a peep from him.' He nodded to the baby monitor on the shelf by the door, illuminated with the standby light – no crackles of tears breaking through.

We fell into an awkward silence again. 'Emily, perhaps you might want to think about talking to me at some point too?' Ingrid said.

'I really don't think . . . I'm not sure people would understand. Not so soon after Rose died.'

'Cian's allowed to have friends,' Ingrid said. 'People would understand that.'

I realised that it was what I had told her when we first met. If she suspected any different, and I think she did, she was goading me now. All this talk of friends in need being friends indeed. Did she want me to tell her it was more? Did she want Cian to say it? Did I want Cian to say it? I knew that to the public, it would look bad for him. Still, it stung that I couldn't put her in her place – especially as she looked so cosy beside him.

'I think having someone tell us he had an alibi for that night, on the record, it would really shift public opinion – any that wasn't already in his corner anyway.'

'I'm not sure,' I said, also thinking of Owen's order that none of us talk to the press – his stating that we would get fired. But then again, did I owe Owen any loyalty? Especially if he was the monster Cian said he was. 'I need time to think.'

Ingrid sat straight up, followed by Cian. 'That's the thing,' Ingrid said. 'We might not have a lot of time to wait. If the police arrest and charge Cian, my hands are tied. Things become *sub judice* – no newspaper or media outlet in the world would touch him. Not until after a trial anyway.'

'But if he's innocent? Surely getting the truth out is all that matters?' I said, my stomach twisting at the thought of him being arrested. Paraded in handcuffs. Sent to jail. And what about Jack? Rose's family would claim him for their own and God only knows if they would let him have any access if they believed he had hurt their daughter.

'The law is the law,' Ingrid said. 'Even if I wrote the piece, there is no way my editor would publish it. We'd be hauled before the courts ourselves on contempt charges. To be honest, we're probably sailing close to the wind as it is, with a live investigation under way. My editor was only persuaded because of Cian's profile.'

Cian leant forward, put his head in his hands. 'This is a nightmare. It's all a fucking nightmare.'

I reached forward and touched his knee. 'We can get through this, Cian.'

'I'm going to lose everything. I've already lost Rose and now I'm going to lose everything else. My reputation. My freedom. My son. I can't lose him.'

I noticed Ingrid sit forward too, touch his other knee and I pulled back. 'I'm going to do everything I can Cian. I promise,' she said. He looked up at her and thanked her while I sat feeling like a third wheel.

The beep of the drier saved me. 'I imagine those are my clothes,' I said, getting up to walk to the utility room. As I left I heard Ingrid say she had better be on her way – a story to file and all. She called a cheery goodbye to me, as I pulled off the dressing gown and dressed in my still-warm clothes. I called my goodbyes, never so glad as to see someone leave. Perhaps now Cian and I could talk properly.

When I walked back into the room, Cian had just returned from where, I presumed, he had seen Ingrid to the door. 'She's a decent sort,' he said, gesturing to me to fill the spot she had left on the sofa. 'Where did you say you knew her from again?'

'I don't think I did,' I said, sipping from my wine glass to give myself time to think. I was hardly likely to tell him she had blackmailed me over my troubled past. 'She did a story on a friend of mine a couple of years back. My friend always spoke highly of her. Said she was a good journalist.' I hoped he didn't see the blush on my cheeks, or if he did he put it down to being close to him.

'Well, I'm glad you gave me her details. She's about the only thing I have going for me at the moment. DS Bradley pulled no punches when he was here earlier. Said he would find out whatever I was hiding.'

'Well,' I said, shifting closer to him – feeling a need to be as close to him as I could possibly be. 'You know what they say, if you've nothing to hide . . .'

Feeling emboldened by Ingrid's leaving, and the half-glass of wine I'd had – on an empty stomach – I pulled as close to him as I could, before standing up, turning and straddling him where he sat. 'And you have nothing to hide, so you have nothing to worry about,' I said, bending my head towards his, pressing my lips to his full mouth – waiting for him to kiss me back, to finish what he had started upstairs. But instead of a hot, passionate kiss he pulled back. Putting his hand to my cheek, he rubbed his thumb over my lips. I closed my eyes, tried to savour the moment as his hand moved from my cheek to the back of my neck. I felt him move closer – his breath hot on my neck, his hand twisting my hair until he tugged it, forcing my head back, my eyes springing open in shock and pain. Then his mouth, warm at my ear, the sensation of his teeth biting, tugging. Strong enough to make me wince, instinc-tively try to pull away. 'Poor naive girl,' he said, his other arm pulling me tighter to him, pushing himself, hard, against me.

241

'Don't you realise, once people want you, they will get you whatever it takes?'

★

It was passion. Lust. That's what I told myself when I woke the next morning, in my own bed, my head spinning from what had happened. He'd had a tough day – his nerves were on edge. And I had come on to him – strongly. I mean, I had straddled him, kissed him. He'd just responded, passionately. He had warned me earlier that I could make him lose control of himself. It was just that I wasn't expecting that. What he did. How he did it. I felt the sting at the skin on my neck, the skin wasn't quite broken but it still smarted. My breasts ached from where he had pulled and kneaded them, my arms ached from where he had held them behind me, made me powerless in front of him. The top of my thighs were tender from where he had driven himself into me, hard, fast, animalistic, primal. I'd expected some of the tenderness we had shared a few nights before – the way we had sought comfort in each other.

Lust. It had to be lust.

After, he had shown me some tenderness. He had stroked my back as I lay, stunned, across his chest. He had kissed my hair. He had told me I was beautiful. That I was perfect in his eyes. That I was his saviour. I would help him find his way through this nightmare.

My eyes had been heavy with sleep when he had shifted below me. 'You should probably head for home before it gets much later,' he had said. I'd blinked up at him, confused. I wanted to sleep there, with him. I needed to feel comfort from him. I needed to not be alone.

'You've work in the morning – you probably don't want to be late,' he had said, sitting up and pulling on his jeans.

I could have argued, I supposed, but he was right. I did have work in the morning – and it was going to be tough enough as it was without adding being late to the mix.

'What will I tell them when they ask why the police came to see me?' I'd asked him.

He shrugged his shoulders. 'I won't tell you want to say, Emily. That's up to you.'

As I had started to dress, feeling very self-conscious, I looked at him. 'If I told them we were together?' I offered.

He'd stilled for a moment, looked directly at me in a way that made me want to cross my arms over my chest – hide myself a little. Then, again as if a switch had been flicked, he had moved towards me and kissed the top of my head. 'If you want to tell them that, it's okay with me.' He'd pulled me to standing, then wrapped his arms warmly around me in a hug that pressed my head against his still bare chest. 'Because we are together, aren't we, Emily? We're in this together.'

So I found myself driving home, through the still pouring rain, at close to midnight feeling uneasy about everything that happened that day. I noticed I had a missed Skype call from Maud, and I was tempted to call her back. She would be home from work, probably getting her dinner or getting ready to go to some fancy Manhattan bar and sip cocktails with friends. But I knew she would stall her plans to talk to me. I knew I could rely on her. Rely on her to listen and to advise. Yet, something held me back. Pride perhaps. She had told me to be careful and now I was in over my head. Falling in love with a man who had recently lost his wife. Lying for him – because I believed, deep down, in his innocence.

Didn't I?

★

I figured if I acted like there was nothing unsettling about the police calling to speak to me – everything would be fine. So

I took a few deep breaths, pushed open the door to Scott's and walked in with my head held high.

'Morning,' I said to Tori. 'I'll be out in five. Just let me grab a coffee.'

She nodded, and I ignored the look of confusion on her face. As I walked on she called that she was glad I was feeling better. The staff room was, thankfully, empty so I made my coffee in peace, locked my bag and coat in my locker and downed my drink while trying not to look at the picture of Rose. Although I knew if she was the person everyone said she was, she would have wanted Cian to be happy and she would have moved heaven and earth to make sure Jack was okay.

Still I probably finished my coffee quicker than I normally would to escape from under her gaze. I took my seat beside Tori with no comment. Looked up the appointment list for the day and called our first client through to see Sarah. I then focused directly on my screen, catching up on orders, appointments and referrals. I kept my head down, tried to avoid any unnecessary conversation. Each time Tori tried to speak to me, I would lift the phone and fake a very important call, or suddenly remember that I promised to get a glass of water for someone, or send an email with information about our cosmetic procedures. I managed to avoid any conversation about anything non-work related until just before 11am when the phone on my desk buzzed to life, and the call came from Owen's surgery. I answered and asked him if he was ready for his next client while I clicked into the system to see who to call.

'Emily, could you come in and see me for a minute?' he asked.

Of course I had to. I couldn't say no. So I stood up and, trying to ignore the thumping of my heart, reminded myself again that I had done nothing wrong. Nothing that Owen knew about anyway. With my best professional smile on my face, I knocked on his door and waited for him to call 'Come in'.

He was sat by his workbench and he gestured to me to sit down on the stool opposite him.

'I think we need to talk,' he said softly.

'Is there something wrong with my work?' I asked, taking my seat. If I made this about work, it would be harder for Owen to talk about anything else.

'No. Not at all. You've settled in remarkably well. You've become a valued member of staff.'

I couldn't help but smile. 'That's good,' I said, straightening my tunic and brushing my hair back behind my ears, before remembering that I had been trying to hide the bruising from the night before. I brushed it forward again and looked at Owen.

'Look, this is a bit awkward and I'm not quite sure where to start . . .' He shifted on his seat. He looked uncertain of himself.

'At the very beginning?' I said, forcing my voice to remain calm, my tone light. Act normal and it will be normal, I told myself.

'You'll be aware Detective Bradley was here again yesterday,' he said.

'Yes, I know. I believe the police are asking a lot of questions. Of a lot of people,' I said.

'Yes, they are. It's heartening to see them take it all so seriously. It's beyond comprehension, you know. That they think someone hurt her on purpose. That someone could be capable of hurting a person like Rose.'

I nodded but inside I was getting a little heartsore of hearing about Saint Rose. People like Rose, good people, had bad things happen to them all the time. It wasn't that unbelievable.

'Look, Emily. I know the police were looking to ask you questions about your relationship with Cian Grahame. They asked me whether you'd ever mentioned that you and Cian were close.'

I didn't know what to say, so I said nothing. I just stared at him while my brain tried to think of something to say that wouldn't make things more uncomfortable.

'We've not known each other long,' I said, 'just since the first time he called in here.'

'Look . . . I know it's none of my business who you keep company with outside of work and maybe I'm crossing a line here but Emily, I like you. You seem like a nice person. A decent person. And I think you should think about what you're getting yourself into.'

'I know he is grieving for Rose – and Jack is too. We talk about that a lot, you know. About Rose and her life.' I met his eyes with mine. Looked him straight in the face as I told him – hoping that he would understand from what I was saying that I knew a lot about Rose. About things that had hurt Rose. About men who had been obsessed with her – who had made her perfect life hell.

He moved again, looked down to his hands and back at me. 'Emily, Cian Grahame isn't all he portrays himself to be. That article yesterday? The follow-up today? That's not the real Cian.'

It dawned on me that I hadn't seen today's piece yet, but I knew how Ingrid would have written about him. From what I had seen the night before she was besotted with him.

'From what I know of him, they show him exactly as he is,' I said defensively. 'A man who feels hounded after his wife was murdered. A man who has to deal with others being jealous of what he has achieved – so much so that it prevents them from showing him an ounce of human decency.'

To my surprise Owen laughed. A short, brittle laugh. Then he shook his head. 'He's done a number on you, hasn't he?' he asked. 'He is just so good at creating fiction, I'll give him that.'

I felt myself bristle at his response. He − who had bullied Rose − who had threatened her. Who, for all I knew, had been the one responsible for her death. I wouldn't have thought it possible when I first met him. But now it felt like he was showing himself to be everything Cian had warned me he was.

'He told me you would do everything you could to blacken his name,' I said, trying to keep my voice calm.

'Cian Grahame needs no help blackening his name,' Owen said. 'Have you never wondered why he doesn't have a stream of friends battering down his door to help him in his hour of need? Why his own family aren't around? He's not a nice person, Emily.'

'I take people as I find them,' I said defensively. 'People don't understand Cian. They want to bring him down.'

'Oh, the patented "feel sorry for me, Cian Grahame" speech,' he said. 'He hasn't grown out of it, then?'

I stood up. 'Owen, I appreciate your concern, if that's what it is, but if you are happy with me and my work then I don't think we have anything more to discuss here. So, as you know, we are very busy today and I'd like to get back to doing my job well, which is the only thing that should concern you about me.'

I got up and turned to walk to the door. I wasn't even halfway across the room when I felt him grab my arm − tightly, so much so that it hurt − before spinning me round towards him.

'You don't seem to understand, Emily,' he said, as I squirmed to get out of his grip.

'You're hurting me,' I said as he spoke, his grip pulling on my already sore and tired muscles. 'Please let go.'

'I can't,' he said. 'Not until you understand exactly the kind of man you're getting dangerously close to.'

I shrugged as hard as I could but he held on. 'The only dangerous man I'm near is you, Owen.'

He let go as if my words had burned him and I immediately started to rub my arm.

'I'm sorry,' he said, reaching out to rub my arm too but I pulled away. 'I'm so sorry. Look Emily, you don't understand. He's not what he seems. What he put Rose through . . . you need to listen.'

'No!' I said, backing away from him. 'He told me you would say all this. He told me you would lie about him. You would do everything to hurt him because he had the one thing you wanted but couldn't have. He told me you made her life miserable!' I started to cry – my voice started to break and I willed myself to be able to keep talking without losing it all together. 'I didn't want to believe him, Owen, but look at you! Look how you're acting!'

'It's because I don't want him destroying someone else like he did her,' he said.

'He didn't destroy her!' I shouted. 'He had nothing to do with her death.'

I watched as he laughed again. Actually laughed, then cried. 'Rose was dead a long time before she stepped in front of that car, Emily. And it was everything – every little thing – to do with Cian.'

Chapter Thirty-Two

Rose

2017

Rose Grahame: has a secret smile :)

I knew I was playing with fire updating my status like that, but I had to let a little something out.

I did have a secret smile. I was excited after a long time of not really being excited about anything. After a long time of not really allowing myself to feel anything. For months after Jack's birth I felt like I was plodding through mud, or fog or something that made me feel nothing like me. Nothing at all. I wondered if I even know who I was any more.

Cian, I suppose, did his best at first. Or he tried. He did seem to try and change like he said he would. He would let me sleep. Tell me to rest up and heal. He would tell me he loved me. Loved our son.

That kept me going in those early days. Gave me faith that the old him was back – that all he had promised would come to pass.

But it seemed the old him was just a passing visitor. His

patience wore thin. His compassion ran out. His deadline approached and it was not the done thing to have a wife lying down under the pressure of new motherhood. He wanted me to get back to the 'old me' – and in the end he tried to drag me there kicking and screaming.

He wanted a better mother for his son.

A better wife for him.

A glitzier trophy on his arm. 'You used to be so beautiful – so vibrant. Where did that go?'

Someone who loved him more – loved him enough to be everything for him whenever he wanted it. However he wanted it.

Someone to keep his home perfect.

Make him tea and bring him biscuits when he was writing.

Keep the baby quiet.

Look beautiful.

Let him climb on top of me and thrust himself into me when he needed to release tension.

I'd become an accessory – and for a long time I believed that was all I was good for.

For a long time I told myself I bruised too easy. It wasn't that he was too rough, it was that my blood vessels – the living cells and tissue that made me who I was – were too weak. They bled easy, they didn't withstand anything other than a gentle touch. They weren't compatible with difficult times.

It wasn't that he needed to be more gentle – softer – it was that I needed to be harder. Tougher.

So I stood up to him. I stood up to him when he demanded I leave my job. I took what he threw at me (some choice words, a cup, his fist) but I stood my ground. I'd lost enough of myself. I didn't want to lose any more. I told him if he didn't let up, he would lose me. I warned him.

That gave me the strength. That and then, finally, unexpectedly, feeling what it was like to be really loved. Realising I wasn't too soft. I didn't need to change. I was good enough – as I was. I didn't have to act. I didn't have to fit anyone's mould other than my own. I was loveable.

I can't say how freeing that was – that realisation. That I was worthy of being loved and that love wasn't what I had been led to believe it was over the last decade. Love could be all I hoped it would be.

So I have a secret smile, but if he asked me what the status was about, which he would – he always did – I'd lie.

I'd become quite adept at lying.

Anybody looking in would think I was ridiculously happy. I wasn't. But I would be.

Chapter Thirty-Three

Emily

Owen's words stopped me in my tracks.

I didn't know how to react. He was looking at me, shock written across his face, as if he couldn't believe he had said what he had.

'You're being ridiculous,' I said, my voice a whisper. It was the only thing that explained all this. 'Your jealousy is making you say stupid things. Point the finger at an innocent man. Is this what you've told the police as well? That he's a bad man? It would be laughable, Owen, if you weren't destroying people's lives.'

I turned to leave because I didn't want to listen to him any more – the way he threw out stupid accusations with nothing – nothing at all to back them up.

'The bruise on your neck, Emily,' he said as I walked to the door.

I stopped.

'I've seen it,' he said.

'It has nothing to do with you,' I said, my face blazing, as I put my hand to my neck, annoyed that my attempts to cover it up hadn't been successful.

'I've seen bruises like that before,' he said.

'I imagine any of us who was ever a teenager has seen bruises like that, Owen,' I said, but with a shake in my voice that I couldn't hide. I remember how Cian had bitten my earlobe, bitten my neck, became rougher, his hands groping, pulling, pinching. Passion, I thought. But the feel of his teeth on my skin, biting – more pain than pleasure. A sensation that could never be pleasurable.

'He treated Rose like that. Owned her. Used her. Controlled her. Don't you understand that? He was an abusive husband. That's why I hate him. That's why the sight of him makes my skin crawl because I know what he did to her.'

'You're a liar, Owen. And don't worry, I've told the police just who it was that controlled her, abused her and made her life hell and we both know it wasn't Cian. You can stick your toxic, hateful job and your lies. I don't want any part of them any more.'

I turned and walked out of the surgery, every part of my body shaking. I felt the bruise on my arm smart, my skin burning from the friction of sleeve against skin. I walked as quickly as I could to the staff room where I emptied the few items I had in my locker into my bag and walked out without speaking to anyone. I didn't even make eye contact because I would have lost it – one way or the other. I would have cried, or shouted, or called Owen out publicly, not caring who heard. I didn't look back.

I stopped at a small coffee shop, ordered a latte and took out my phone.

I'd call three people, I decided.

First of all I'd call DS Bradley, tell him about Owen's outburst – how he had left me bruised. How I felt unsafe with him.

Then I'd call Cian – tell him I had stormed out of work. That I was scared and sore. I'd allow him to soothe me. God,

I hoped he would soothe me. I hoped he would hold me, gently caress me. Tell me he was glad I had stood up to Owen.

And finally, if I had enough courage, I would call Maud and tell her that I was in well over my head. I had done it again. And not in a quirky Britney Spears kind of a way – in a spectacular, fucked up, confusing, violent way that meant I didn't understand anything any more about anyone.

Roughly brushing my tears from my face, I felt embarrassed to be so exposed in public. So I lifted a newspaper from the magazine rack in the café, hid behind it, and started to read Ingrid Devlin's piece in which Cian Grahame was vowing he would never love again.

'Only one woman could ever make me feel as whole and complete as Rose did. You don't get that twice in a lifetime – I don't even see the point in looking,' he said.

My heart sank and I put the notion of calling him and asking him to reassure me out of my head. I cried a little harder too – until, not a single phone call made, and my coffee not touched, I lifted my bags and headed back into the rain again.

I couldn't face the thought of going home, so I took out my car keys and climbed into my car, switching on the engine and the fans to clear the steam on the windscreen. I paused to light and smoke a cigarette – allowing the plumes of warm smoke to calm me. I wouldn't think about the fact that, again, I had no job. No income. I had been making friends at Scott's – but those friendships were not well enough established to continue when I wasn't working there any more. Especially when I had all but told Owen I believed he had abused and hurt Rose. I had stopped just short of telling him I believed he had been responsible for her death. But only just.

I lit a second cigarette and dialled the number DS Bradley had given me, swearing when it went to his answer service. I rattled off a quick message, asking him to call me. Telling him

I might have information – or maybe not. But a suspicion. I had a suspicion. And if he could call me, that would be great. I left my number, even though I knew he had my number already.

I looked at my phone, at Maud's number. I did a calculation – it would be about 6am in New York. She would be up and getting ready for work – maybe even at the gym.

She would help me; I knew she would. But would she judge me too? There had to be times – had to be – when she rolled her eyes to heaven and wished I would just disappear.

The thought hit me like a sobering slap to the face. I stubbed out my cigarette, slipped my phone into my bag, put the car into first gear and drove off.

★

I drove around for an hour before I decided to head towards Tullagh Bay, a secluded beach on the Atlantic coast about forty minutes from Derry. I could lose myself to my thoughts there without interruption. And I did lose myself there. Sat for an hour or more on the beach. I had taken off my shoes and my socks and buried my toes in the damp sand – trying to ignore the cold seeping into my body. The rain had turned to a fine mist – the kind that looks as though it couldn't do much damage but that soaks through to your skin in seconds.

I watched the waves roll in – the foam crashing and curling before reaching further and further up the shore towards me. Watching the sea never ceased to ground me. It was unchangeable. It was constant. Whatever happened – whatever seasons came and went, whatever way the wind blew, whatever was going on in the world, whatever was going on in the lives of the people who walked along the shores – the waves always just did what they did best. They came and went.

I wondered how many people had sat where I sat now, contemplating their lives.

I thought about everything that had happened since that first day when Rose and I had travelled down in an elevator together. How things had spiralled.

I wondered had Rose visited this beach? Maybe with Cian. Maybe with Jack. Had she found comfort from the tides? I rubbed my arm, it didn't hurt so much now – but I was still aware of it. Still felt his grip as I turned to leave. He seemed too convinced Cian was a bad person. A dangerous person. But was he just protecting himself?

I had to trust my gut. I thought of Rose – the bubbly persona on Facebook. Her declarations of love for Cian. The happy pictures she shared of them together. How proud she said she was of him and his achievements. There was never an ounce of negativity on her page. Only happiness. Only a smile that would light up the world.

I thought of her pictures hanging in their home. Again that smile – bright and genuine. Those moments we shared together too – in the lift as it travelled down the four floors to the bottom of the shopping centre. I closed my eyes and tried to recall every second of it. The doors opening. Her smiling. A chubby-fisted wave from Jack. Bags hanging on the back of the buggy. A funky coloured changing bag hanging there too – a soft blue teddy peeping out. Rose, hair in a loose bun. Leather jacket. Skinny jeans and heavy boots. A maroon T-shirt – I remembered that. Remembered how the maroon T-shirt and the blood merged together when she hit the ground. A scarf, white, with black swallows. She looked so stylish. I remembered thinking that. A real yummy mummy with a baby that looked like he should have been in a Baby Gap advertising campaign. We reached for the button for the ground floor together. Laughed – that little polite laugh people do in these situations.

'Done with your shopping for today?' I'd asked her.

A silly question. She was heading to the bottom floor – to the exit.

'All done.' She had smiled at me. 'We're all done, aren't we, Jack?'

He'd cooed at her and she'd smiled brightly at him.

'Best to get this wee man home for tea,' I'd said.

'Actually, we're going to a friend's house, aren't we Jack?' She was glowing with happiness. With contentment. I'd smiled and she'd turned her attention fully to Jack, singing softly to him as we descended. When the doors had opened, I'd smiled. Gestured at her to go first. Wished her a lovely evening with her friend.

She had smiled back. 'Thank you. I know it will be,' she'd said – and she walked out, across the hall, through the automatic doors and into the street. Onto the road.

You couldn't fake that level of happiness, could you? Not the kind of happiness that glistens in your eyes. She was luminous.

I climbed to my feet, lifted my shoes and carried them by my side as I walked back up the sand, towards my car. I decided to drive to see Cian. Where I hoped he could make me as happy as he had made Rose.

★

He answered the door with Jack in his arms. Jack squealed with delight and hurled himself at me and I took him in my arms and told him it was lovely to see him too.

Cian was smiling too. That gentle smile that I loved so much. Loved. It dawned on me. I smiled back, content with the realisation.

'This is an unexpected surprise,' he said, bending forward to kiss me on the cheek.

'Oh, I was just passing and thought I would call in,' I lied.

'But you're soaked through again,' he said, peeking out and seeing my car. 'Is it just your preferred state these days?'

He turned before I could answer him, and led the way to the kitchen where I sat Jack down on the mat in front of his wooden toy garage and smiled as he lifted a little blue car and watched it speed down a ramp.

I made to sit down on the sofa but he baulked.

'No,' Cian said. 'Don't sit there. You're soaking. You'll wreck the fabric.' I jumped up at the harshness in his voice.

'I'm sorry,' I said. 'I didn't think.'

'It's okay,' he said, going to the utility room and carrying through a couple of towels. 'Why not get dried off? Or better still a quick shower? Warm up a bit?'

'I'm fine, really,' I said, taking my coat off. 'My coat took the worst of it – and my hair – I'm sure I look like a drowned rat.' I made to dry my hair with one of the towels, but he stopped me.

'Emily, go and get a shower. Tidy yourself up.' His voice was soft – but there was a curl to his lip, a determined edge to his words that made me realise it was best not to argue. I should have gone home and changed first. Showered. Reapplied my make-up. Not shown up like a bag lady at his door.

'Okay,' I said.

'I left the robe you were wearing in the guest room, hanging on the back of the door,' he said.

I nodded and padded up the stairs – wondering whether he'd ever invite me into his room. Or into the family bathroom. Perhaps that would be too difficult for him – his shared space with her? I had to give him time to cope with his grief, I reminded myself. Besides, I did love this guest room, had started to see it as my own space. And it didn't feel as if Rose was all over it. Sure, he said it was she who had made certain it was always sitting hotel perfect – but it had no pictures of her staring at me. Her half-empty bottles of shower gel weren't in the shower. No ornaments or clutter sat on any surface. It was as anonymous as any hotel room and I liked that – in a house where Rose smiled down from every wall.

I stripped off, showered and pulled the dressing gown back on but not before looking at my reflection in the mirror in the bathroom. The bruise on my neck had turned a dark purple. There were bruises on my thighs from where he had gripped them tight – where I had made him lose control.

I padded downstairs to where he had changed Jack into his pyjamas and packed away his toys. Jack was cuddled into his chest, his hand to his daddy's face while Cian kissed his hand and gave him his bottle of milk. I watched from the doorway for a bit – it was such a beautiful, tender scene. Jack's eyelids grew heavy, fluttering closed while Cian soothed him, whispered that he loved him and he would never let anyone hurt him. He would never leave him. His would never let anyone take him from him.

I dared not speak and break their precious moments together. I watched them until Cian turned to look at me, and smiled. 'I'll just take him up,' he said. 'You pour the wine and we can talk.'

When he came back downstairs, I had poured two glasses of white wine. He sat turned towards me and sipped from his glass.

'You look unsettled by something,' he said. 'Was it the article? The things I said about not finding love again? You know I have to make people think there is no way in heaven I would have hurt her. We did talk about this. It was your idea, of course, to keep quiet about us. You said people wouldn't understand.'

When he put it like that it was churlish of me to tell him I had been upset by it. It was all part of the game he had to play to make sure he wasn't taken from Jack. 'No, it's not that,' I said. 'Owen pulled me aside today.'

His face darkened at the mention of Owen's name.

'And?' he said.

'He said he wanted to warn me about you. He said you were a dangerous man.'

I watched as Cian stiffened, his jawline taut, his hands clenched. He shook his head. 'What else did that waste of space say?'

'I told him he was the one who was dangerous,' I offered. Keen to soothe him.

'But what did *he* say?' Cian asked, his tone angrier.

'He said . . . he said Rose had died long before she stepped out in front of that car and that you were to blame.'

The sound of the wine glass smashing on the wall made me jump. Cian jumped to his feet, paced the room. 'Jesus, he has some cheek. Some fucking gall. We were happy. We were making things work. We were trying for another baby, for the love of God. What did you say to him?'

'I told him he could stick his job,' I said meekly. 'Then I stormed out. I've been driving around since, trying to figure things out, and I came here because I needed to see you.'

He sat down beside me, took my face in his hands. 'You did the right thing, Emily. You know that, don't you?'

I nodded. 'I called DS Bradley, left a message. I want to tell him how Owen was with me. His temper.' I reached for my arm, but decided not to tell Cian. Was I afraid of how he would react? 'So yes, I did the right thing. Even though I haven't a clue how my rent is going to be paid . . .' I tried to put on a brave face. 'But sure there are other jobs.'

'There are,' he said. He let go of my face and stood up and paced the room again. 'Work for me,' he said. 'Come here. Be my housekeeper. Jack's nanny. I don't like sending him to nursery. I don't want Rose's family poisoning him against me. You could do it, Emily. He loves you. You're so good with him. And you get me. You understand.'

'Work here?'

'It's a perfect solution,' he said. 'You could keep your flat — or you could live in,' he said, still pacing, but his voice faster. Excited even.

Live in? Was he asking me to move in with him? Staff or lover? Housekeeper or friend?

'You like the guest room, don't you?' he rattled on. 'You can make it your own. Until we know where we're going? Me and you? If we could be a proper thing? A family?'

A family. It was all I had ever wanted — and yes, I had fallen hook, line and sinker for Jack already; not to mention Cian.

I wanted to throw myself into his arms. I wanted to kiss his face. See, he could make me happy. He was doing it right now.

Chapter Thirty-Four

I didn't stay with Cian that night. I drank my glass of wine while he got on the phone to his solicitor, and to Ingrid Devlin to tell them both what had happened with Owen and me. I heard him tell his solicitor that I was just waiting for DS Bradley to call me back, and I saw him smile as his solicitor spoke. Clearly Owen's loss of temper could only be a good thing. It showed he wasn't the calm, cool and collected man people thought he was.

Ingrid Devlin, well, he spoke more quietly to her. In hushed tones. Said that he might be employing me. As his housekeeper – so anyone who wanted to ask questions about why I was staying over could be told it was a professional relationship.

He had been so happy when he finished on the phone – as if there was a light at the end of the tunnel. He had kissed me and then he sat, fidgeting on the sofa, sipping his wine, jiggling his leg, occasionally smiling at me.

'Would you mind if I wrote for a bit?' he asked. 'I feel inspired. God, Emily, do you understand? I feel inspired for the first time since she died. I want to write – to lose myself for hours in it. My hands are almost itching with the need to write.'

'Of course I don't mind,' I said.

'I may be some time – hours maybe. When the mood takes me . . .'

He looked so excited that even though I had hoped he would take me to him and hold me tenderly and make me feel cherished, I couldn't be annoyed. His expression was so joyous. So animated. It was endearing. Shades of Jack when presented with his favourite toy.

'You have to write when the notion takes you,' I said, smiling. 'I know how you've struggled. Look, Cian, I'll go home. Leave you to it. It's been a long and stressful day all round.'

'You don't mind?' he asked, his eyebrow raised.

'Not at all,' I said, leaning over to kiss him. Even though a part of me did mind because when we were alone like this – kissing, drinking wine – I could pretend everything was perfect.

So I dressed, drove home. Looked around my flat. Considered Cian's offer.

I could leave behind the saggy sofa. The heating that rattled in the middle of the night. The taps that either delivered freezing cold or boiling water and nothing in between – to live in a house that looked like it belonged in an interior design magazine. With a handsome, successful man. And a beautiful baby boy.

I was changing out of my uniform, debating whether to simply bin it or launder it and take it back to Scott's, when my phone rang. Donna's name flashed up and I answered.

'Emily, are you at home? Can I come over? I need to talk to you.'

'I was just getting ready for bed,' I lied. I wasn't sure I was in the mood for Donna to come around and try to persuade me that Owen was actually just misunderstood.

'It's important that I talk to you,' she said. 'Really important.' Her voice was shaky.

'Are you okay, Donna?'

'I'm fine, except that I really, really need to talk to you. And the sooner the better.'

I sighed. Donna had been nothing but kind to me. I didn't want to brush her off. I had a feeling people brushed her off a lot. 'Okay,' I said.

'Great. I'll be with you in ten,' she said, hanging up.

★

Just over ten minutes later the buzzer went on my door and I hit the button to let Donna in. I opened the door to the flat waiting for her to come up the stairs.

What I was not expecting – not at all – was that she would be accompanied by Owen. When I saw him, my heart quickened. 'No,' I said without even thinking about it. 'I didn't say he could come over. I don't want him here.' I moved to push the door shut but Donna was too quick for me, getting her hand, and her weight, behind it before I could close it. I pushed as hard as I could but when Owen put his hand to the door, pushing it too, I was no match for them.

I stumbled backwards. 'I'll call the police,' I said, my hands shaking, heart thumping trying to remember where I'd left my phone. I had got changed in my bedroom – had I left it there? It was on the other side of the flat and they were in front of me. Blocking my path.

'There's no need for that,' Donna said calmly. 'We're here to help you, Emily. We're your friends.'

'Please,' Owen said. 'Just let us explain. I know I got things wrong earlier.'

I thought of how he had grabbed my arm. I had told him he was hurting me. I didn't want him in my space. This was all wrong and I felt a surge of panic build up inside me until I couldn't quite catch my breath and I started to feel dizzy.

Everywhere I looked, they were there. I couldn't get past them. I couldn't breathe. I wanted to run. I wanted to open a window. Suck in air, or throw myself out of it.

'Please, Emily,' I heard Donna's voice – still calm. 'Just breathe. I promise we're on your side. Owen begged me to come with him so you wouldn't be scared. Oh Emily, he feels wretched – but when you know why – when you understand why he reacted the way he did, you'll understand.'

'You scared me,' I said to Owen, with a sob I hadn't expected.

'I'm so, so sorry, Emily. Truly,' Owen said. 'I promise I never meant to hurt you. I'm so ashamed.'

I felt Donna's hand take mine. 'Come and sit down, pet,' she said, leading me to the sofa. 'Take some deep breaths. Owen, get a glass of water. I'm sorry for springing this on you but if I'd told you he was coming with me you wouldn't have let me come over.'

I nodded.

'But what he has to tell you, it's important. You need to know the truth about Rose. And about Cian. And about Owen too for that matter.'

She sounded so sincere and her touch was so reassuring that I felt my breathing start to slow and steady. Still, I felt nervous when Owen came back into the room and handed me a glass of tap water. 'Just a sip,' he said. 'Take your time.'

He walked across the room and sat on the armchair opposite us. I was thankful for that – for him giving me the space to breathe. I sipped the water, felt Donna's hand in mine and centred myself.

'So you wanted to talk to me,' I said when I found my voice.

I felt Donna tense a little. Owen took a deep breath. 'I'm not proud of all of this,' he said. 'I want you to know that. I never thought I would be a man who fell in love with a married woman.'

So Cian was right – Owen had harboured feelings for Rose.

'I certainly never expected her to love me back – but the thing is, Emily, she did.' I straightened my back, tried to make sense of what he was saying. 'We tried to fight it for a long time. We didn't intend to hurt anyone. You have to believe that Rose was the sweetest, most gentle creature you could ever meet. Everything she did was with the intention of helping others. She was the kind of woman who would have gone hungry to make sure everyone else was fed. That's why I fell in love with her – and I was the luckiest man in the world when she fell in love with me too.'

'That's not Cian's version of events,' I said.

'No – well Cian has always had his own world view, Emily. Rose did love him – at one stage. I'm not even going to try and deny that. But in the end, Emily, she was terrified of him. He controlled every aspect of her life – everything. What she wore. Who she spoke to. Where she worked. He even posted on her social media accounts for her. He pulled all the strings and she was too scared to fight back. He isolated her from her family – kept them at arm's reach. She learned it was easier just to go along with what he wanted – and when Jack was born, everything got worse. It was like she lost her fight. She told me she didn't want her baby being caught up in their arguments so she allowed him to have whatever he wanted. But when she was at work, well, things were different. That was our own stupid bubble of happiness. I don't know if he suspected something between us, but he became insistent she quit, stayed home to raise Jack. He thought it looked bad for "a successful literary author to have his wife out slaving in a dental surgery". That he sent his son out to a nursery when he was more than able to provide enough to have her at home caring for him. She fought him on it. That was the last straw for her. She knew if she gave up working she would spend her

266

days in that big house, at his whim and she would lose what little of herself she had left. And it would be impossible for us to ever see each other. He would be always be there – always.'

I shook my head. 'No. They were happy. They were trying for another baby. Cian is devastated by all this. He misses her so much. He's broken.'

'He doesn't know broken!' Owen said. 'Jesus, he is such a good actor. But that's all it is. He was losing her anyway, so he had to do it on his terms. We were going to start again. The two of us. When he started pushing her more and more to leave work, we made the decision we didn't want to wait any more. We couldn't risk waiting any more. She was leaving him anyway, Emily.'

My head hurt. Donna was squeezing my hand tightly. I looked to her. 'He's telling you the truth, Emily. They were together and yes, Owen made her very happy.' Donna's eyes were sad, her words sounded so genuine. 'She was hopeful for the future. She didn't want to be scared any more.'

'He's a bully,' Owen cut in. 'Nothing more . . .' He looked directly at me when he said that. Tilted his head just a little – an almost imperceptible nod towards my neck and the bruises he had seen. 'He said he loved her – cherished her – but he treated her like she was his possession. If you haven't seen that side of him yet, Emily, it's only a matter of time. Don't confuse control with passion. Don't excuse bad behaviour because he's grieving. Most of all, don't think you can fix him – or that he will change. Rose made so many excuses for him – tried so hard to fix what was wrong in her marriage. But she never really had a say in any of it. He was always in control.'

I thought of his home. Even with a toddler running around, it was always show-home perfect. Everything in its place. Permanently photoshoot ready. Did that make him a bad person? Was it just that he liked nice things and he liked them kept nice? Imagine how I would have felt if I had arrived to find the place with overflowing bins, plastic toys scattered everywhere, a washing pile that had taken on a life of its own? I was supposed to think he was an abusive control freak because his house was clean? But then I thought of how he had reacted when I had gone to sit on the sofa in my wet coat. How when he told me to make myself presentable there was a hint of distaste, or was it disgust, in his voice? How he had reacted strangely when I had showed up at his door – how he had been with me on the phone when I told him the police had spoken to me. How he didn't correct Ingrid when she said we were just friends. How cosy he looked with her. How she looked at me with the same dismissive look on her face as he had. Each memory hit me like a slap. I desperately wanted to push them down again but they kept floating to the top. No – it wasn't possible that I had been blind to a man's control once again. Then again, maybe I just wanted my happy ending and I would take less than perfect to get that.

Even if less than perfect bordered on abusive.

I shivered, felt tears prick at my eyes. I didn't want any of this to be true. I was scrambling for ways to ignore what they were telling me. I thought of all the things Cian had told me. He had appeared so sincere.

'He said you were the abusive one. That Rose was leaving work and she was scared of how you would react because you were obsessed with her. He said she couldn't work there any more because you were making her life miserable.' I whispered the next bit. I felt so fucked up putting it out there. 'Owen, he thinks you might be responsible for hiring Kevin McDaid.'

Owen swore under his breath, shook his head. Donna pulled her hand from mine. 'I'll make tea,' she said, standing up and walking to the kitchen. 'I can see we might be some time.'

'Oh Emily, for fuck's sake, he is so full of it,' Owen began. 'I would never, ever have hurt her.'

'But he told me the same – *he* would never hurt her,' I said.

'And you believe that? I saw the bruise, Emily. I bet it's not the only one,' he whispered, so that Donna wouldn't hear.

'No, it's not. There's a bruise on my arm too. The one you left,' I said, rubbing my temples. I didn't have a clue who to trust, if anyone. I thought life was complicated enough with Ben. This was a whole new level of messed up.

'I'm sorry. I can't apologise enough for that,' he said. 'I'll regret that for the rest of my days. But you have to believe me that I'm telling the truth. The day she died she was on her way to me. We were supposed to meet for dinner and then we were going to go and view a house – a place we could share together. Somewhere out of town – somewhere he wouldn't know. She was so excited. Cian was away at a book event so for once she had the freedom to do something without him. It was all she could talk about – she was already planning how to decorate the house. Bright colours. Cushions. Upcycled furniture. Vintage-style trinkets – the kinds of things he would never let her have no matter how much she wanted them. She was so creative – artistic. She wanted to make things. She wanted a home – Cian kept a show house. We had spoken just half an hour before on the phone. She said she had picked up a few design brochures, bought a few funky photo frames. She couldn't wait to show them to me.' He looked up at me, his eyes filled with tears. 'We were so excited. So happy. I wanted to give her everything he didn't. Then it all ended – just like that. In a split second. As if that wasn't nightmare enough, Cian is trying to push the blame onto me? Jesus Christ!'

My mind flashed back to that day – to how happy Rose had looked. How she was going to 'meet a friend' for dinner.

How she knew she would have a lovely evening. She had a glint in her eye. She looked beautiful – glowing.

'She was happy,' I stuttered. 'She was so happy that she was going to meet you.'

I could see the confusion written all over his face. I needed to tell him she had been happy until that very last moment. If what he was telling me was true, he deserved that comfort.

I took a deep breath. 'I maybe should have told you before. But I didn't know how – and I didn't want you to judge me. I just wanted to be happy – and your workplace – you all looked so happy. Rose looked so happy in all her pictures with your staff.'

Donna had walked back into the room carrying two mugs of tea, which she put down on my coffee table before she sat down – the look on her face mirroring the look on Owen's.

'I was with Rose when she died. Or just before she died. I travelled down in the lift with her and Jack. We chatted, briefly.' I looked at Owen, his eyes wide. 'She told me she was on her way to meet a friend and she knew she would have a lovely evening. When the lift stopped, I told her to go ahead. To walk out ahead of me. She had a buggy and shopping bags and I just wanted to let her go first – so she did. She walked through the hall onto the street. She was singing to Jack. And then . . . she stepped onto that road and . . .' My voice was shaking. I closed my eyes as the memory of the impact assaulted me again. As did all those nights I had woken after dreaming of Rose, twisted and bloodied, telling me it should have been me.

'Was it instant?' Owen asked, blinking back tears. 'Like they said? Did she suffer? I know they said she didn't, but they would say that. I've wondered, all this time, were they lying?'

'They weren't lying. She was there and then she was gone and I wish, I really wish, that she wasn't. I wish it had been me. All this time, all I can do is blame myself. If I hadn't let

270

her go first . . . if I had walked out first, then I'd have been the one who was hit by the car. It should have been me. It always should have been me. I even convinced myself that my ex – a man as controlling as you say Cian is, was behind it all. I was crippled with guilt because if it had been me who had died, nobody would have cared. Not really.'

I saw Owen recoil a little.

'I'm sure that's not true,' he offered. I appreciated his words. I was sure he was wishing that it had been me even as he tried to comfort me.

'Oh, it's true, Owen. I'm not saying it to get any sympathy – I'm telling you to explain. I carried that around with me – that feeling that the wrong woman was dead. I still carry it with me. But anyway, I looked her up on Facebook and I saw this happy woman – who was so loved and cherished and had everything I'd ever wanted and I . . . God this sounds awful . . . I wanted some of that happiness. It wasn't all that deliberate at first. I was out of work. I needed something. I didn't want just another job that paid the rent but gave me nothing else. I was so lonely,' I said, the tears that had been threatening started to fall – cooling my cheeks, which were burning with shame. 'So when the job was advertised I applied for it because Rose looked so happy – and she had friends and I wanted that. I wanted it so much and I was sure, when you offered me that job, that I was getting my second chance.'

Owen put his heads in his hands. Donna sat as if frozen. I'm sure they were running over everything that had happened in the last few weeks – even down to my friendship with Cian – and wondering just how unhinged I was. Saying it out loud – thinking of how I had kept it from Maud, from my parents – maybe I *was* unhinged? There was no way to spin this in a positive way.

'I thought I'd finally got it right for once in my stupid life.

I was actually happy – and now, now I don't know who I am any more. I don't know who to trust, or what to believe. For all his faults – and you mightn't want to hear this – I know Cian did love Rose very much. And Jack, I don't see that he would ever risk Jack. I just don't see it.'

'It was a lie though,' Owen said. 'What you saw of Rose and her life – that was an illusion he made sure she put out there. He said he wanted to help her win friends and influence people – but it was more sinister than that.'

Flashes of memories, wedding plans, pictures, the perfect relationship I had painted online with Ben – while everything was going wrong. But no – Rose looked happier than that. It looked genuine. Cian wrote her long love messages – messages she replied to. Heart emojis and smiley faces. Ben had never done that. Never engaged with me online. Not the Facebook type, I told people. I pinched the bridge of my nose, realised Owen was still talking.

'He has a twisted idea of what love is. He may have loved her – but not in the right way. Not in a healthy way. I don't think he knows how to love any differently than that. But Jack? That's the one thing I can't get my head around – when the police said it was on purpose – how he could risk his son? I didn't think even Cian Grahame was that much of a monster.'

My head hurt and even though I don't think I believed what I was saying any more, I said, 'He's not a monster though. I need to believe he's not a monster.'

Donna took my hand. 'Emily, please. Believe me, he is a monster. And I can prove it.'

Chapter Thirty-Five

'When Rose died, before Cian came to get her things from work, I cleared out her locker for him. I knew she had plans – and whatever had happened, I didn't want him thinking badly of her, finding out what was going on. I owed that to her memory,' Donna said. 'It was the very least I could do for her.'

'You kept her stuff?' Owen asked.

'Only the incriminating things,' Donna said, looking directly at him. He paled. We both knew the incriminating stuff would have been related to their relationship.

'What kind of incriminating things?' I blurted out. 'And how do they prove Cian is a monster?'

'She kept a journal – she wrote in it that it was the one place he couldn't control her thoughts. And she kept her pills there too.'

'Pills?' I asked.

'Birth control pills,' Donna said, blushing. 'There was no way Rose wanted to have another baby – not now. Not with Cian. She couldn't keep the pills at home though – not even in her bag. He'd have found them. He checked everything.'

'Did she mention me?' Owen's voice was soft, desperate even.

'She said she loved you. And she knew you loved her too, she never doubted that. You made her happy.' Donna's voice was low, almost a whisper. She couldn't make eye contact with him.

I expected – well I don't know what I expected – maybe I imagined he would have been happy at the news but he wasn't. He looked more broken than before – and then a wave of something, anger maybe, washed over him.

'Donna, you know the police have been asking me all sorts of questions. You know Cian has been feeding them lies – has had Emily feed them lies . . .'

I bristled at his words but I couldn't defend myself.

'All the time, the proof was there that Cian was treating her badly and that she was happy with me. That could have changed everything. Weeks ago.'

'I thought I was protecting you,' Donna protested. 'Everyone thought it was an accident – a horrible, tragic accident, and I wanted to protect you from Cian. I wanted to make sure he didn't take his grief and his anger out on you. And I felt a duty to protect her memory as well. I didn't want people – not Cian, not the world – raking over her life. Painting her as a victim. Painting her as a slut.'

The word slut made Owen wince. 'Rose was nowhere near a slut,' he hissed.

'*I* know that and *you* know that,' Donna said hastily. 'But would the world see it differently? If Cian got hold of her journal, if he spun it the way he wanted to spin it . . .'

'But if she *was* cheating on him?' I offered . . . desperately clinging on to what minute hope I had left that there was an explanation other than him being a monster for all this.

'Emily, wake up,' Owen said. 'Stop trying to find decency in *that man*.'

'I'll show you the journals,' Donna said. 'I'll bring them to work in the morning.'

'But . . .' I started, remembering how I had stormed out. Work was not my work. Not any more.

Owen cut through my thoughts. 'You reacted to how I treated you. And I'm so very sorry for that. It makes me no better than him. Your job's still there for you if you want it, Emily.'

'I need to think,' I said.

'Come in tomorrow. See the journal. At least keep yourself safe,' Owen said.

Donna squeezed my hand and I felt a fresh wave of tears rise up. I had opened up to these people. I had told them I had watched Rose die, I had taken her job – and they still wanted to protect me. Not like my family, who had been so embarrassed by me that we barely spoke.

'I know this is all overwhelming,' Owen said. 'But our intentions are good. I promise you.'

'You don't have to do this,' I told them. 'You don't have to be nice to me. I'd understand. I lied to you. I've made such a mess of everything.'

'Emily, we've all made a mess of this,' Owen said, a look of resignation on his face. 'We'll all have our guilt over this until the day we die, I imagine. Now we have to do what we can to make sure she gets the justice she deserves.'

I nodded and they stood up, made to leave. Suddenly it was as if every ounce of energy drained from my body and all I wanted to do was sleep.

'It's a busy day tomorrow – so come in after 5pm, or call any time you need to. Think about your job – about staying,' Owen said.

I just nodded because I was too tired to speak. Owen shook my hand, his touch so gentle as if trying to make up for the way he had handled me earlier. He stood back and Donna hugged me. 'Are you okay?' she whispered. 'Do you want me to stay?'

I did. I really did. I wanted that sense of security of knowing someone else was there – but no – I needed time to think. To sleep. To have space.

'I'll see you tomorrow,' I said, nodding at her. There was a hint of something in her eyes – but I had to ignore it. I didn't have anything more to give anyone else just now. It was all I could do to hang on to my own sanity. They left and I stumbled into my bedroom and threw myself down on top of my bed. Blissfully, I was asleep within minutes.

*

The cold woke me. I lay there trying to get my body to catch up with my brain. It was freezing. I wondered if the heating had packed in – although it had been a mild enough night before and this was the kind of cold that seeps right into your bones. By the soft glow of the street lamp that illuminated my bedroom window I could see that steam was rising from my mouth with every exhalation. I tried to reach out to pull my duvet around me, cursing myself for falling asleep on top of the covers but my limbs felt heavy, weighed down. No matter how I tried to force them they would not move and I was sure it was getting colder.

There was a creak by my door. The squeaky floorboard outside my bedroom sighed loudly – the way it did when someone stood on it. My heart started thumping – so loud I could hear it; so loud that I could feel it in my ears. I was afraid to open my eyes, to move my head. Was that a shadow? I wanted to move again – but I couldn't. I opened my eyes slightly – my curtain was billowing – the window open, the cold air rushing in. Another creak.

A shadow. Was it just headlights passing outside? Everything had a haze. And still I couldn't move. Should I play dead? Was that absurd? Did I have a choice? Whatever, it was impossible – the curls of warm breath steaming in the air above me would give me away in seconds. I felt my finger twitch – tried again to move. Had I been restrained? I tried to sense if my wrists were bound but I could barely feel them. Even through the cold I felt myself start to sweat. I tried to call out for help but when I opened my mouth the faintest of noises came out. A pitiful, hoarse whisper of 'Help'.

The window seemed wider and the breeze was picking up. If I got up, if I could, would I be able to run? I calculated my escape routes – through the door, through the window? I was on the second floor – not likely to die from a fall but likely to hurt myself all the same. There was another shadow and the sound of breathing. I wasn't sure any more if it was my breathing or someone else. There was a rattle to it. I tried to hold my breath to listen but even when I did all I could hear was the thumping of my own heart. Loud. Invasive – both a part of me and not.

A cold hand – ice cold – on my leg. It was soft, damp. I felt cold fingers walk up to my knee then, a single icy cold, hard, bony finger ran back down to my ankle. I tried to call out again. But I still couldn't make a noise. I started to cry – felt the sobs rise from my rib cage and stutter from my throat, the strength of them threatening to choke me.

A voice. Soft. Singing. Gently. 'Twinkle, twinkle, little star . . .' I knew whose voice that was and my chest contracted with fear until I could not force air into my lungs. Please, I begged my limbs, start working. Please, I begged my chest, relax and breathe. Please, I begged my voice, let me scream for help. I felt the weight shift as she sat on my bed, continuing with her song. 'How I wonder what you are . . .' She finished. She took a breath and it grew colder again.

I felt that ice-cold hand on my face, followed by her other hand on the other side of my face as she turned me towards her. I forced my eyes closed. Felt her breath on my face, the gentle brush of her hair on my cheek. Her lips brushing my ear. 'Look at me,' she whispered, before pulling back.

And I did – and it was Rose Grahame. Beautiful. Perfect. Dead. Her neck still twisted. Blood dried from where she had spluttered as her last breaths left her body. Her skin was grey now, mottled. I felt the power return to my limbs and I sat up, staring at her.

'I'm sorry,' I told her.

She put her finger to my lips. Shushed me.

'Don't let it be you,' she said.

I reached out to hug her. I needed to hug her, but instead I woke. The room was warm, the window closed. I was lying just as I had been when I went to sleep. I spoke just to see if my voice worked. Sat up just to check that my limbs were not seized. And I sat, hugging my knees and crying for Rose and the happy ending she never got to have.

When Cian rang in the morning, I ignored his call.

★

Everything had shifted, in just a matter of days. In a matter of hours. I didn't know who I was any more – and I didn't know what to believe. I would never be able to unknow what I now did about Cian – but I wanted to believe in some goodness in him. I clicked into Rose's Facebook page, read over her posts, read over his letters to her. When I considered what Owen and Donna had told me, they all took on such a sinister tone. Even after she died, he still held onto her. Controlled how people grieved for her. Claimed her as his – and not as a person in her own right. True love or obsession? Where does one end and the other begin? Was the line blurred, or just so fine that the slightest nick would allow one to spill into the other?

Cian tried calling again at 10am. At 11am he sent a text message asking me to call him back ASAP. I looked at it – considered, briefly, calling him – but decided I didn't know what to think, let alone what to say to him.

Donna texted just to check that I was okay and ask if I could call into the surgery after 5pm. I replied a very quick 'Yes' and then pushed my phone to the other side of the sofa as if the distance between me and it would protect me from whatever calls came on it. Of course, nosiness became too much for me and each time it beeped, or buzzed or rang I turned the phone face up to see who it was.

When the name on the screen read 'Detective Bradley' I took a deep breath and answered.

'DS Bradley,' I answered.

'Emily,' he said. 'I'm sorry it's taken me a while to get back to you. Things have been moving fast here.'

My skin prickled. I almost laughed. A silly, hysterical laugh that screamed 'not half as fast as they have moved here'.

'So, how can I help you?' he asked.

'I think I have new information – about Cian and Rose.'

'You think you have new information?' He sounded wary. I didn't blame him. It was dawning on me just what a sad case I must look in his eyes.

'Can you meet me at Scott's just after 5pm?' I asked. 'I have something to show you. You want information relevant to your inquiry about Cian?'

DS Bradley took a deep breath. 'I'll send one of my officers.'

'Please,' I said. 'Please can you come? I trust you. All of this is scary to me.'

'Emily, do you feel as if you are in danger?' He sounded concerned.

Was I in danger? I didn't actually know any more. I had never felt more adrift. 'I don't know,' I said.

'I'll see you soon after 5pm,' he said. 'But if you feel in danger, at all, you call us. You have my number – but if you feel immediately threatened, call 999.'

I could hardly speak – so I nodded, made a vaguely affirmative sound.

'Take care of yourself, Emily,' he said before he hung up.

I pushed my phone back to the safe distance of the other side of the sofa and I lifted my laptop and switched it on. I clicked into my email and started sending an email to Maud – one that explained everything. One that apologised for everything. That said everything I had been too proud or blind or ashamed to say. I hovered over the send button – knowing that sending it would finally, completely confirm that I was once again a walking disaster. I closed my eyes and pressed send, then slammed my laptop lid down and leaving it and my phone exactly where they were I got up, pulled on a sweater and some trainers and went for a walk. Fresh air would help. It would give me some sense of clarity. If nothing else it would get me out of my flat and away from thinking about Rose and how I had dreamt of her sitting on my bed.

Chapter Thirty-Six

By 5pm I had walked into the city centre. In town I had sat on a bench outside of the bottom entrance of the Foyleside Shopping Centre – watched the traffic drive up the one-way street towards the old two-decked Craigavon Bridge and away from the multi-storey car park that blocked the view of the river from the shopping centre. I watched the people walk in and out of the automatic doors, distracted by their plans, their families, their phones. There was a wilted bunch of flowers Sellotaped to a street light. It was only the obvious sign there had ever been a tragedy here. No one really paid any attention. They had moved on even though it hadn't even been two months.

I walked slowly back across Foyle Street, through the now quiet Waterloo Place and over along the Strand Road towards home to see I had missed another two calls from Cian, and three missed calls from Maud. Neither of them had left a voicemail but Maud had sent a text saying she hoped I was okay and if I could just call her as soon as possible so she could hear my actual voice to know if I was really fine.

I got ready to walk to Scott's, not that it took much effort.

I simply didn't have the energy to change my clothes, to fix my hair or to put make-up on. It was hard enough putting one foot in front of the other so Donna and Owen would have to take me just as they found me. The idea almost made me laugh — if only I believed anyone in the world would accept me just as I actually was, I wouldn't be in this mess.

Tori did her very best not to look shocked at my appearance when I arrived just as she was switching off her computer. 'I don't know what is going on but Owen has been like a cat on a hot tin roof all day,' she said, her eyebrow raised as if she expected me to fill her in on everything. I just shrugged before asking if he was in.

'In his office,' she said, 'along with Donna — who has been on edge too. It's been a fun day.' She rolled her eyes at the word fun.

I nodded and walked towards the office, leaving Tori none the wiser — and definitely unimpressed by my reluctance to gossip.

Owen and Donna were already sitting when I walked in, full cups of coffee in front of them along with an open storage box. Owen looked about as bad as I did. Tired, his eyes red rimmed. His hands were resting, palms down, on a floral, bound notebook. Donna's face was serious, her hands clasped, her usually perfectly manicured red nails chipped, bitten down. The perfect façade of our perfect workplace was crumbling.

'Can I see it?' I asked. Owen sat up straight, lifted his hands away and I reached down and picked up the book. I wasn't expecting to feel so strongly just holding it. But knowing it was something she would have held in her hand — a place she would feel safe to share her feelings — it made something in me contract. I almost didn't want to read her words, it would make it all so real in a way it hadn't been before, but I knew I had to. There was something so, so visceral about seeing the swirls and loops of her handwriting. The smudges. The crossed-out words – the notes hastily scrawled in the margins. I ran my hand over the soft indentations her pen had made on the page. This was the most real Rose Grahame would ever be to me.

★

I need to put this somewhere. Somewhere he can't read it.

Can't control it.

Can't edit it.

Somewhere where I can tell the truth. The real truth. Not his version of the truth. The first thing I've wanted to say for so long now is I've been acting a part. I've been playing the dutiful wife not because I wanted to but because I had no choice. He still says he loves me, but he has killed any love I had for him over the years. And I did love him once. I loved him with all my heart. I can't believe I was ever so stupid.

When everyone is jealous of me, I want to scream at them not to be. That it's not what it seems. I wonder, sometimes, how they can't see it. The way he controls everything. The way he grips my arm a little too tightly. The way he is always there. Always. He'll pick me up from nights out – or worse still, invite himself along and everyone loves him. Of course they do. The charming, bestselling author. And he's good looking. Although it's true that the more you know a person the more it affects how you see them. I don't see him as handsome any more. I don't see him as sexy.

I hate him.

And I'm sorry, Jack, if some day you read this and you read that I hate your daddy – but I do. I hate that he lied to me. Told me he loved me. Made me believe love was his brand of love. Controlling me. Stripping away everything that made me me, until I don't think I knew who I was any more. Not really.

And everyone was jealous. That was the biggest joke of all.

*He is a good daddy to Jack, though. I can't take that from him.
Although I live in fear of Jack growing up and thinking how his daddy
treats women is the right way to treat women. I don't want Jack to
treat any girlfriends like this. I don't want him to control them. To make
them change into what he wants rather than who they really are.*

*Cian says I'm ungrateful. He has 'given me everything'. I suppose
he has. The house. The car. The baby. The stupidly expensive wedding
ring on my finger, which I hate wearing. He upgraded my plain, gold
band – which my granny had worn and had given to me before our
wedding – when he won The Simpson Award. I didn't want the new
band. Platinum. Diamonds. Blingy. All the girls were mad about it.
Said he must really love me. I hated it. A loud 'I own you' shouting
from my finger. All status. All 'look at how great I am'. Look at what
I have. Look what I treat my wife to.*

*None of that 'look how I treat my wife'. He put my granny's ring
in a box in a drawer in his office. Under lock and key. He'd keep it
safe, he said. No one would take it.*

Not even me.

*Perhaps I brought it on myself. Because I wanted him. When we
first met. Then again, he was different then. Didn't have a pot to piss
in, as he would say. We were equals, I suppose. And God, he loved
me. Cherished me. Treated me to simple romantic things – a picnic on
the rug in front of the fire. A glass of wine and a hot bath waiting
for me when I came home from work. I loved the claustrophobic nature
of his love at first. I was young. Stupid. I still hadn't figured out that
Heathcliff wasn't so much a romantic hero as a psychopath who
controlled and destroyed everything he loved.*

I remember he sneered when I told him that Wuthering Heights
was my favourite book. It wasn't even my favourite book. Light a
Penny Candle *was – but even then I knew Cian Grahame would
choke if I admitted a love of something so popular. So 'common'. He
wouldn't care if I tried to argue it was brilliant, before its time, funny
and sad and beautiful. So I thought of the literary books I had read*

284

– which really didn't amount to much. GCSE English. I had enjoyed Wuthering Heights. *I found it all moody and dark and Heathcliff sexy and fierce. My teenage hormones rampant, I loved the thought of a man being driven mad by his love of me.*

I was so fucking stupid.

I believed ours was true love. That he wanted me, needed me so passionately because I was his everything. But really, I was just another thing to him. Something to own. A character in one of his books – and he tried to edit me, rewrite me and decide my plot twists.

All I needed was for him to love me. Me. The real me. The me I was before we met. The me I thought was a good person. A nice person. I know I was never going to change the world. I didn't have any standout talents. Finding the cure for cancer wasn't in my destiny. But I believe I was good. I was kind. I was pretty in my own way. I was funny in my own way. I was caring. I was loving. Yes, I laughed too loud when I found something funny. I cried over ads on TV. Ones nobody else cried over. I loved watching Ant and Dec. I loved reading funny, well-written, beautiful books with pink covers. I was the kind of person people confided in. The kind of person who could be relied on to always have paracetamol in my handbag, spare hairgrips, Vaseline and clear nail polish in case of ladders-in-tights emergencies. I liked to wear sweatshirts and tie my hair up in a ponytail. I didn't really care about brand names and labels. I probably ate too much chocolate. I could be extraordinarily grumpy when tired. But I was a good person. I hope I can still be a good person.

Just not good enough for Cian Grahame, bestselling author. Mr Success. Mr Has-to-keep-a-public-profile. Did he change, or did I? Did he change me? Sometimes I don't know what happened any more. Or how it happened. Or whose fault it was, or is.

I don't even know when. Not really. There wasn't a changing point – an explosion. There wasn't a kick to my stomach or a slap across my face. There wasn't a push to my back as I walked up or down stairs. There wasn't a moment when I looked at him, shocked, devastated at what he'd done. I didn't even realise it at first. I'm that stupid. What was romantic and protective became possessive and claustrophobic. I realised it had been a few weeks since I'd seen my parents or my sisters. Then my friends stopped calling round so much. Definitely not when he was home – and he's a writer, he's always at home.

He wanted me to leave work – especially when I fell pregnant. He told me most women dream of living a life of luxury, of being ladies who lunch. I couldn't imagine it – couldn't want it. Anyway, I didn't have ladies to lunch with any more. I only had Cian and where once the thought of the two of us existing in our little bubble together was everything I could have wanted, by then it made me feel scared. Terrified. I could see my life disappearing. I could see me blending into the background, like the wallpaper in his office. Expensive. Pretty. But just decoration. Without real purpose. Except to make him happy. Quietly.

He told me I was ungrateful. Unsupportive. He told me I was a bad mother – before I even held Jack in my arms. How could a mother have a baby and plan to give the baby to someone else to mind while she went out to work? I told him he could look after the baby. It was a moment of rebellion on my part – one that I paid for after. Not with cuts or bruises. But it still hurt. The names. The insinuations. The way he looked at me as if I was nothing. Then he would make a big fuss – go and buy all the nursery furniture we could possibly need and more. Promise me it would be better. He would be better. We started painting that room – our baby's room – filled with the things he chose. He dabbed paint on my nose and laughed and I tried – I really tried – to love him again. He took my picture and I smiled for him and part of it was genuine. I promise.

But when I said my back was aching, my ankles swelling, he tutted. Accused me of ruining the day. Accused me of not caring about the baby. Told me we never should have even considered having a family in the first place. I felt Jack kick and wriggle in my stomach and he asked was there still time to get an abortion? We could tell everyone it was a miscarriage. I pleaded with him to stop. I told him I was

286

sorry. I lied. I lied and told him I loved him and I loved our baby and I carried on painting even though my pregnant belly ached, and my ankles hurt and my head pounded and I wanted to cry.

As quick as his anger had arrived, it passed. He called me to him later, showed me where he had posted the picture of me, nose daubed with paint, to my Facebook account. He kissed me, and my tummy, and it was as if nothing had happened. It was as if he hadn't suggested killing our baby.

And that was before he started to become 'clumsy' around me, accidentally knocking me into the worktops, saying he hadn't seen me as he closed the door trapping my fingers, getting a bit too lost in 'passion' and leaving little bruises . . . After a while, I couldn't deny there was more to what he was doing than being clumsy.

The thing is, even though I know he isn't a good person, I know I have to accept I'm not a good person either.

A good person doesn't cheat. A good person doesn't give up on their marriage. Even if the for-better-or-worse bit is now worse the vast majority of the time. Even if they fall in love with someone else. Maybe Cian was right all along. Maybe I was ungrateful. A weak person. A person who doesn't deserve his love. Or what he gave me.

I'd leave. I'd let him win. If it wasn't for Jack.

Owen says I deserve more. He says I never deserve to feel anything but love. I should be happy – and waking up every day smiling and assured that I am enough.

I don't think Owen really knows me though. How can he when I don't know myself?

*

I went back on the pill today. I had to see the doctor in my lunch break – pick up my prescription from the chemist, hide the pills in the back of my locker. I don't see any choice. I can't get an implant – he'd know. I'd be afraid he'd know even if I had the coil fitted. This seems the safest option because I can't fall pregnant. I can't have another baby — not with him. It would end everything. I can't keep taking the morning after pill. I can't risk having to see if someone could get the abortion pill smuggled into the country for me. I can't travel to England for a termination. He'd know. I can't hide a pregnancy — he is there, waving the pregnancy testing kit in my face every twenty-eight days. Sitting on the edge of the bath while I pee in a cup and he dips the stick in. There's no way I could hide it. None.

This is the only thing I can think of to be in control of my own life. I always thought I'd have a house full of babies, and if things were different I would have. If he was more like the man he was when we met — then maybe? That man wouldn't shout at me the way he does. He wouldn't tell me I could never understand what it was like to be him. I wasn't like him. I'm ordinary. Boring. I couldn't create anything if my life depended on it.

Except his babies, apparently. But I don't want to. Not now.

I'm scared of him.

His moods are getting darker. He's more controlling. Everything has to be just so. I left one of Jack's bottles in the nursery — I was tired and it was the middle of the night — and he accused me of being lazy. Of trying to annoy him. Of being ungrateful for the house we lived in, the lifestyle he gave me. I cried. I told him I had just been tired and he had sneered. Told me I wouldn't be so tired if I didn't insist on going out to work.

But how would I even see Owen? I can't tell Cian that Owen's the only thing that makes me feel like I want to go on. He makes me feel loved. Strange, isn't it? You can work alongside someone for years. Know them as a friend and then, one day, everything changes and you wonder how you never, ever knew before? Then again, I never saw the bad in Cian. Not at first. Now it's all I see.

So it's entirely possible the opposite could be true of Owen. I never saw how amazing he is. Now, it is everything. That sounds really cheesy, doesn't it? But I feel a bit cheesy when I think of him.

★

I'm in love. Properly in love. Like I've never been in love before. And he loves me back. Cherishes me. And I have to put that here because I can't say it out loud anywhere. I can't shout it from the rooftops, which is what I want to do. I want to be a complete madly-in-love eejit and wear a T-shirt that says 'I love Owen & Owen loves me' on it. I want to feel the way I feel when I am with him forever. This is happiness. This is love. This is everything. He is everything. And he's so sexy – I mean . . . God, he drives me wild. (I'm blushing as I write this but I want there to be a time when we don't have to worry about snatched moments and secret trysts and we can shag on the kitchen counter or on the sofa or anywhere we want.) No one has ever made me feel like he does. No one has ever made me want them as much as I want him. His mind, his body (oh, God, his body!!! I know, I'm like a schoolgirl with a crush!), his heart. Most of all his heart. His beautiful, loving, tender heart. Capable of fixing me. All things considered, I'm such a lucky, lucky girl!!

*

I'm going to do it!!!

I'm going to leave him. I'm going to go and be with Owen. Take Jack. Start again.

Owen has been amazing. He's helped me feel brave enough. We've talked about it so much – planned it. Now I just have to do it. Leave Cian and hope he feels strongly enough about his public image that he won't make a big scene.

I know he'll be hurt – but it's his turn to feel hurt. I've done it for long enough. I want to be happy. I'm young. I need to live my life. With Owen and Jack.

*

I tried to let the words settle. Sink in. I tried to marry them with the smiling selfies, the life-affirming quotes, the posts about how happy she was – how she was blessed. I only needed to see the grief tearing strips from Owen second by second, moment by moment, to know it was true. He was rocking, slowly — small movements — barely perceptible but it was almost as if, the more I read, the more I knew, the more it was 'out there', the more real it became. To all of us. To Owen most of all. He'd known she had been unhappy, of course. He'd known how Cian had treated her. He had known how she had wanted to escape. How they thought they were going to escape together. Somewhere new. A fresh beginning where he would help her heal again. But seeing the face of others as we read her words? It was as if pain had become visible — and it was all I could see when I looked at Owen's face.

'I should have done more,' he whispered.

'You were taking her away from it all,' I said. 'You were giving her a new beginning.'

'Not enough, it wasn't enough. We weren't quick enough. I didn't get her out of there fast enough.'

I was trying to think of something to say when a rattle of the shutters outside made us jump. Donna looked at me, wide-eyed and scared.

'DS Bradley,' I said, shaking my head as if trying to shake the words out of it. 'I meant to tell you, I asked him to meet me here. I want to talk to him.'

'Here?' Donna asked, twisting her hands tighter.

'I think he needs to see this diary, don't you? Don't you think he needs to know about Cian? The real Cian?'

'Of course he does,' Owen said.

'But won't I get in trouble?' Donna asked, as the rattle on the shutter grew louder.

'How? Why?'

'Because I kept it from him — isn't that obstructing justice or something?' she said. She looked genuinely terrified.

'We don't have to tell him you had it,' Owen said. 'Say we found it yesterday . . . or today . . .'

A third rattle, loud, almost deafening made Donna jump again. 'But I need to get home to the boys. Won't he ask questions? The boys will be worried. They won't know where I am. I don't have time to stand here and talk to the police. I can't risk getting into trouble. I'm all they have.'

I didn't know what to say, and I didn't want to keep DS Bradley waiting any longer.

'Just go home,' I heard Owen say. 'We'll deal with this. I'll deal with this, Donna. It's about time I took more responsibility for it all.'

I heard a mumbled response as I unlocked the front door and raised the shutters to let DS Bradley in.

'I was about to leave,' he said, his face serious, a hint of irritation in his voice. 'I've told you things are busy at the moment, Emily, so if we can get to the point, that would be good.'

'Of course,' I said. 'I've something to show you and something to tell you.'

He followed me into Owen's office. Donna had already left and Owen was holding onto the journal for dear life. I suppose I hadn't thought of how hard it would be for him to get to see something that was such a part of Rose for such a short time, only to have to let go of it again.

He stood up, shook DS Bradley's hand. 'Emily hadn't told me you were coming, but she's right – you need to see this. It's a journal Rose kept – it's her own words about how things were between her and Cian. It's what I told you – but in her words, her writing.'

His words were like a slap in the face to me. He had told DS Bradley about how Rose was treated, about his affair with her and all the time Detective Bradley was talking to me, was telling me to think carefully about things, he knew of the allegations made against Cian. I watched as Owen pushed the book across the desk. DS Bradley pulled some latex gloves from his pocket, put them on and lifted it.

'And where has this been until this time?' he asked.

'Here,' Owen said. 'I was sorting out some of our filing yesterday – found it in the back of a drawer.'

'And you waited to pass it over until today?'

Owen shifted in his seat. 'When you read it, when you take it . . . you'll see it contains a lot of personal information. Not just about Cian – but about me. About her feelings towards me. About what we had together.' His voice broke a little. He coughed. Cleared his throat. 'I just wanted the chance to see it. To read it. To spend some time with her words.'

DS Bradley opened the book, flicking through it, scanning the words. He tutted. Shook his head. Sighed but stayed silent.

'So you can go get him now?' Owen said. 'Doesn't this show motive? Doesn't it show form?'

'It's definitely something to add to the investigation,' DS Bradley said.

'No. It has to be more than that,' Owen said. 'It has to be enough to show what he did to her.'

'Much as I would like it to be, Owen, it doesn't fall into the category of hard evidence. It's useful – definitely – but it's nothing more than circumstantial. Any defence counsel would argue that it's a big leap from a few scribblings in a diary saying she was scared of him to him having her killed – especially given the wealth of stuff posted on her own social media accounts.'

'Which he posted for her,' Owen said, anger in his voice.

'Look, Owen, you know as well as I do that I want to nail this bastard. I don't know how, and the pieces haven't fit together yet but I have no doubt he has something to do with her death.'

I felt my face blaze hotter and hotter as they spoke. If a man of DS Bradley's calibre suspected Cian Grahame of being involved – what must he think of me? The poor misfortunate under his thumb now? Had he known all along that Cian had been controlling towards Rose – had he thought that was what was waiting for me? I shuddered at the thought. How I had trusted him. Loved him. Maybe I was sick? Maybe I was as bad as him? I was desperate for DS Bradley to know that I wasn't.

'I lied,' I blurted and both men looked at me. 'I lied when I said I was with him the night Kevin McDaid was killed. I wasn't. I didn't know he was going to say that,' I said, my eyes pleading with DS Bradley to believe me. 'When he told you that day in his house – I didn't know and he had pleaded with me to help him. Said he was desperate. Scared of losing Jack. I panicked when he said it and I should have told you afterwards. But no, I wasn't with him. I had only just met him that day, when he had come in with Jack to the surgery – to register him.' I nodded to Owen to confirm this. He nodded back.

'You'd never even spoken to him before then?' DS Bradley asked.

I rubbed my temples. 'No. I mean I had read what he'd written on Rose's Facebook page . . .'

'Rose's Facebook page? Were you friends with her? I thought you said you didn't know her?'

I felt my face burn. I wanted the floor to swallow me up. All my lies. All my pathetic-ness was being laid bare now to the police and to Owen and the right thing to do was face it, even if I wanted to run from it.

'No. No. Her page has no privacy settings – or very poor ones. After she died, I looked her up. I saw what he wrote. I couldn't help but think of him as a decent man who was grieving.'

'And do you look up the Facebook pages of many people who have died?' DS Bradley asked.

'No,' I said, staring at my shoes. I noticed the leather at the front of my right trainer was scuffed. A deep score – not the kind that would wash off or would be easily covered. 'It was different with Rose, because I was there when she died. I was on the street. I saw it happen.'

Chapter Thirty-Seven

I don't know what reaction I expected. Handcuffs to be whipped out at lightning speed, perhaps? My rights to be read to me there and then before I was dragged away? Withholding evidence? Obstructing the course of justice? Was I guilty of both – probably. Actually, most definitely.

But DS Bradley didn't arrest me. He told me seeing such an accident must have been very traumatic. I had given a sad, pathetic laugh. Even 'very traumatic' seemed like the biggest understatement in the world.

'You will make a statement to the affect that you were not with Cian on the night Kevin McDaid died, won't you?' It was posed as a question but we knew the only answer I could possibly give was yes. I nodded.

'You're willing to put in your statement that you had only met him for the first time that afternoon?'

I nodded again. 'He did message me that night. On Facebook. But we definitely did not meet up.'

'But that's good, isn't it?' Owen said. 'Do you still have the message? It would prove you weren't together. That would be enough, wouldn't it? To get him?' He looked at DS Bradley.

DS Bradley nodded. 'It will certainly help us. Emily, we'll need a copy of those messages. We've been moving as fast as we can but we're getting knocked back at every turn. We've been able to rule out of a lot of McDaid's cohorts – his friends and enemies – from the investigation. If we can use this to prove Cian has lied about who was with him that night, it puts a different slant on it.'

'But it doesn't prove he was responsible for killing Rose,' Owen said, defeated.

'No. It doesn't. But leave that with us – we've a few other irons in the fire. We might know something sooner rather than later.'

'Like what?' Owen asked.

DS Bradley shook his head. 'Look, I like you Owen and because of that, well, I've probably said too much as it is. I'm not saying anything else. Emily, can we take a written statement from you later – tonight or tomorrow?'

My head was still spinning and I wanted it to be clear. I wanted to get it right. I wanted to not mess this up – for Rose and for Owen and for Jack. But for me too. Because a little seed of anger was growing inside me that Cian had used me. Lied to me. Made me, briefly, believe that things could work out – and then snatched it all from me again.

'Tomorrow morning?' I said. 'I can come in first thing. Will I need a solicitor or anything?'

He shook his head. 'I don't think that will be necessary. But I think it goes without saying that this information is kept from Cian? We need whatever element of surprise we can get.'

I nodded and felt myself exhale. Suddenly I wanted to cry. I felt it well up inside me but I refused to give in to it. While Owen saw DS Bradley out, I sat looking around this office – this place that had become so important to me and I thought of all the drama, the broken hearts, the lies, the secrets that were held within these walls.

'Are you okay?' I heard Owen ask. I looked up at him – at how wretched he looked.

'About as okay as you, by the looks of it,' I said with a weak smile.

I was met with one in return. 'You know, if we get him – it will go a long way to making things easier,' he said. 'That's all I want now for her – to have him done for this.'

'You really do think it was him, don't you?' I asked.

'I can't think of any other plausible explanation,' he said. 'Maybe he found out she was leaving – maybe it was too much for his ego to take?'

'And you think he killed Kevin McDaid too?'

Owen shrugged. 'I wouldn't put anything past him. Not any more.'

He offered me a lift back to my flat, but I said I would rather walk to try and lift my headache. He told me to be careful as he locked up and I made to set off. I was a few steps down the road when he called me back.

'Emily,' he said. 'You should know that it was true. We were a happy place to work. These are good people. We watch out for each other. That part of her online persona was real – she was happy with us. And she, more than anyone, would understand why someone else would want to try and find happiness.'

I nodded and turned again to walk away.

'Don't be too late in tomorrow,' he called after me. 'As soon as you're done with DS Bradley. We need you on our team.'

★

I sent Donna a text on my way back to the flat. Told her everything was okay and she was absolutely not to worry.

I told her I hoped the boys were okay and that I would see her in work the next day. She responded with a 'Thank you' and a little kiss at the end.

It made me feel a little better and I did my best to hold onto that feeling as I climbed the stairs to my flat and let myself in. Although I was tired, I was a little scared to sleep after the dream about Rose the night before. I decided to try and unwind with a soak in the bath and when I was in fresh pyjamas, fluffy bed socks and had given my hair a very quick blow dry I heated some milk in the microwave. I craved the simple things. Comforting things. A book to read before bedtime and a cup of warm milk to soothe me. The same ordinary things that used to comfort me as a child. A part of me even craved my mother – a hug, the smell of her perfume, the feeling of being small and protected.

When the buzzer for my flat went, its shrill tone made me jump. It had gone 10pm. People didn't call here after 10pm. People didn't call here at all, really, and certainly not without messaging first to let me know. My stomach lurched as I thought it might be DS Bradley, perhaps back to arrest me for lying to him. Perhaps he was over the good cop thing and was now onto the bad cop bit.

I lifted the handset and said hello.

'Emily. It's Cian. I need to talk to you. Let me in.'

If the thought of it being DS Bradley had made my stomach turn, the thought of Cian Grahame, with all I now knew about him, made it do backflips. I took a deep breath. I had answered the damned door buzzer. He knew I was in. I looked across the room to where I left my phone. Should I call DS Bradley now? Tell him Cian was here?

What would or could he do anyway? I bit my lip, and tried to make my voice sound as normal as possible. 'This is unexpected. Come up.'

I hit the door release button and listened for the sound of his footsteps tramping up the stairs towards me. If I could just concentrate on behaving normally, I would be okay.

I plastered a smile on my face and opened my door as I heard him approach. 'This is a nice surprise,' I said as he came into view. He wasn't smiling – but then I realised smiling wasn't something that came easy to Cian. He preferred mean and moody, sad and intense. If he smiled it always made him look a little less like him.

I moved to kiss him, even though Rose's words were running around my head. Once she had only seen the good – then she could only see the bad. The mask had slipped and I didn't want to breathe the same air as him, let alone kiss him, but I had to act as normally as I could.

As it happened he pushed me away – and walked straight into my flat, leaving me standing by the door wishing I had my phone in my hand after all.

'Would you like a cup of tea? A glass of water? I'm afraid I don't have much in,' I said.

He shook his head and paced the length of my living room – pulling back the curtain and looking out of the window into the front street. When he turned to look at me it was as if I could see that switch hit again. Nice Cian was coming to play. Maybe.

'I'm sorry for being brusque,' he said, moving to sit on the sofa – beside my phone – which he lifted and sat on the side table before patting the seat beside him. 'I've been trying to get in touch with you all day. You were so upset about work yesterday and I wanted to make sure you were okay.'

'Well, I'm fine – you can see that. I just had a few things to do. Had to go and visit my parents,' I lied. 'And I forgot my phone here. I'm such an eejit.'

He patted the sofa again and I sat beside him. He took my

hands in his – those hands of his that had made me so weak with desire – but now I wondered what on earth they were really capable of. Writing great books. Pinching someone tightly to inflict pain. Pushing. Shoving. Handing over cash to pay for someone to be killed? Killing someone?

'You're shaking,' he said.

'Am I?' I said, trying to take my hands from his and finding them holding on tight.

'You are. Maybe you're cold. Let me warm them for you,' he said, lifting his hands, cupped over mine, to his lips and blowing gently on them. It was an intimate gesture – the kind of gesture that would have made me go to pieces just a day or two before – but now it made me want to run.

'You have to know, Emily, that you worried me. You can't do that – behave that way,' he said.

I looked at him blankly – afraid to speak in case I said the wrong thing.

'Go missing. Not be contactable. It makes me uneasy.'

'Sure it was only for a few hours and you're here now. All's well that ends well.'

'Well I wasn't to know that. All I knew was that I couldn't get in touch with you. Not here. Not even on Facebook. You should have realised that would have me on edge.' The warmth in his voice was tinged with something darker.

'I'm sorry,' I muttered.

'You should be,' he said, his eyes blazing. 'The last time . . . the last time I couldn't get in touch with someone – someone who should have been there for me always – was the day Rose died. I tried and tried to call her and got no response. None at all. No news until the police arrived at the book festival and broke the news. Didn't you realise I would worry?'

He released my hands, brushed my cheek with his fingers, twisted a lock of my hair around them before pushing the hair behind my ears – his hand then moving to the base of my neck. He moved closer still, his eyes locked on mine. I felt his breath on my face – a faint trace of whisky assaulting my nostrils. I willed myself not to pull away – not to react to the flight signals my brain was sending me. He moved his other hand to the centre of my chest – placed his palm flat against me. 'Your heart is beating too fast,' he whispered, his voice husky.

'It's you,' I said, forcing a tone to my voice that I did not feel. 'You do things to me, Cian, you know that.'

His lips brushed with mine – again I tried not to recoil. Tried to respond to him. I needn't have worried too much – his lips may have grazed mine but he quickly moved his mouth to my ear. I felt him wind my hair around his fist at the nape of my neck. I heard his breathing grow more urgent – as if he was turned on, as if he needed me desperately. I took a deep breath, which I let out in one loud, sharp gasp as he pulled my hair violently, jolting my head backwards while he whispered in my ear – so close I could feel the specks of spittle land on my skin, turning my stomach. 'Never do that again, Emily. Do you hear me?'

I couldn't find my voice, so I tried to nod but I couldn't. His grip was too tight – so tight it brought tears to my eyes.

'You do hear me, don't you, Emily?' he asked.

I choked out a yes and as quickly as he had pulled on my hair, he let it go and my head fell forward – a tear plopping onto my pyjama bottoms.

'Good girl,' he said, his voice immediately softer. 'Oh Emily, Emily, please look at me?'

Afraid to defy him, I lifted my head to look at him. He lifted his hand again and as much as I tried, I couldn't help myself but flinch a little.

Stroking my cheek, brushing my tears away, he spoke softly.

'Oh Emily, don't cry. Don't be upset. All's well that ends well, isn't it? That's what you said. You're okay. You were only away seeing your parents. It was maybe a little silly of me to be so worried – it's only because of what has happened with Rose. You understand that, don't you? You understand why I would get so upset and why you should've been in touch?'

'Yes,' I said, fake smile plastered on again.

'Good. Good. Because when you move in, you can't have me worrying about you. Or about Jack.'

It struck me that it was late.

'Where is Jack, anyway?' I asked, hoping he wasn't outside sleeping in the car. It was too cold – he would be too vulnerable.

'I got someone to mind him,' he said.

Something in me wanted to ask who – was that mad? Even though he had just hurt me, even though I knew who he was, I felt possessive and, dare I say it, angry at the thought of someone else being with Jack. I didn't ask him though – didn't want to give him anything else to feel angry about. This – this walking on eggshells – I knew how to do it well. When I was with Ben, I had become adept at causing as little damage as possible to any and all eggshells I walked on. I hated the person I was then – and that familiar self-loathing wasn't far from my sights right now.

'He missed you today,' Cian said. 'That's another thing, Emily. If you're going to be in his life, you have to be a constant. You have to put him first. You know that, don't you? I mean Rose – I loved her so much. I do love her – but she didn't put him first . . . not when she was working.'

'At least she was handing in her notice,' I said, watching his face carefully for a response.

A moment of nothing, of indifference even, before he nodded. 'Yes. Of course. To spend more time with Jack and our new baby, whenever we would be blessed. The thought of Jack growing up as an only child, or with too much space between him and a brother or sister, it makes me sad, you know?'

He looked at me and I wished things were different. I wished he was the man he made himself out to be. I wished what happened to Rose had been nothing more than a very tragic accident. I wished what he was telling me now was true. That he wanted me to be everything to him and to Jack.

'Cian,' I said, desperate to have him out of my space. 'I'm very tired. It's been a long day you know – visiting mum and dad. There was the driving, and the weather was bad so the roads were horrible. I was just going to bed when you called round. Would you mind if I just went to sleep? I've a bit of a headache.'

He looked at me as if he couldn't quite get a read of my face. The Emily he knew would probably be doing everything she could to get him into bed. She was a bit of a desperate character, if the truth be told.

'You'll come and see us tomorrow?' he asked.

I nodded. 'Of course. I look forward to it.'

'Can we expect you first thing?'

'I have a doctor's appointment. I'll see you around 11am maybe?' It surprised me how easy I was able to lie to him.

'Okay. Okay, that sounds good,' he said, still looking at me strangely. He leant towards me again and I closed my eyes until I felt the softest touch of his lips on the tip of my nose. 'Sleep well, sweet girl,' he said, standing up and walking over to the door, letting himself out.

I sat, frozen to my sofa, until I heard the sound of a car engine starting and him driving away. It was silly of me to tell him I would see him tomorrow. I didn't have a notion of how I would get out of that – but I knew I didn't want to be with him again. I never wanted to see his face. I never wanted to feel his touch. And as for my dream of a happy ever after with him and Jack? That was well and truly gone and my heart ached with loneliness and disappointment.

Chapter Thirty-Eight

I pulled my coat a little tighter as I stood outside the police station on Strand Road and pressed the intercom button. The thick iron gate seemed to be situated in just the right spot to catch the breeze blowing off the river and I couldn't help but shiver as I waited for a response.

I think I expected someone to talk to me – I prepared my little spiel. 'Emily D'Arcy, here to see DS Bradley regarding the Rose Grahame investigation' – but I didn't need it – no disembodied voice spoke to me through the intercom. The gate just gave a heavy clunk and started opening automatically, squealing as it did so, the sound of iron grating on concrete.

I peeped my head through and walked in. There was no sign of life – just a tall, bland building – windows reinforced, of course – hiding behind the tall surrounding walls. A throw-back to more difficult times – times that were etched in the bullet marks on the walls. I walked through the car park to the non-descript brownstoned building. Up the steps past a smattering of discarded cigarette butts into the bleak reception where a row of plastic chairs sat empty against a wall adorned with anti-crime messages and information about due process for speaking to officers.

The reception desk itself featured a large, dark, Perspex screen, which I could barely see behind, but I vaguely detected some form of movement. I walked to it, stood and bent my head down a little towards the gaps designed to allow sound to carry from one side to the other and tried to see more clearly what was behind.

I was met with the less than friendly gaze of a uniformed police officer who appeared to be performing some sort of risk assessment on me.

'Can I help you?' he asked, his tone suggesting he would rather do anything else with his day than help me.

'I'm Emily D'Arcy. I've an appointment to see DS Bradley – to make a statement for the Grahame investigation?'

He looked at me again, but didn't speak. Just slowly turned away and walked back to his desk where, when I crouched down to look, I could see him lift his phone and dial an extension.

I just about made out that he was speaking to DS Bradley, announcing my arrival when he shuffled back, and told me to take a seat.

I'd been in a police station before, of course. Being interviewed under caution. Being actually cautioned. Listening to the PSNI officers talk to me but not really hearing them speak. I was too zoned out. Too broken. Sitting there now, even though I was scared and even though I felt like the life I thought I'd have was being ripped away from me, it dawned on me that I didn't feel broken by it. Battered, yes. Bruised. A little cracked around the edges – perhaps. But not broken.

A door to the right of the reception desk opened and DS Bradley walked through – the same silent officer who was with him when he called to my flat was following him.

'It's nice to see you Emily,' he said with a smile that seemed genuine, or at least genuine enough to make me feel safe and comfortable in what was an otherwise totally surreal situation. 'Are you happy to go ahead?'

I nodded. 'Yes. I am.'

'Great, Constable Wilson here will bring you through to the interview room. Get you a cup of tea or a coffee if you want? I'll be with you shortly.'

Constable Wilson smiled and said 'Follow me' and I did as I was told, following her through a maze of doors and narrow corridors until we arrived at a small rectangular room – one plastic chair in front of a table and two more behind it. There were no windows, but an air conditioning vent overhead whirred, spluttering a dusty scented coolness into the air.

I asked for a glass of water, which she brought, and moments later we were joined by DS Bradley, who took the remaining seat and offered me another warm, reassuring smile. It struck me that in any other situation I might find him attractive and I almost laughed at the absurdity of that thought coming into my head at that precise time.

He explained he was going to ask me all that I knew about Cian Grahame and in particular his whereabouts on certain key dates. I nodded that I understood and he told me that if I needed a break at any time, I was just to let him know. I told him I was sure I would be fine, but before we spoke, I needed some advice.

'Cian came to see me last night,' I told him. I watched as he and Constable Wilson exchanged a look. 'He said he was worried because he hadn't heard from me yesterday – and of course you wanted me not to tell him anything about any of this. I lied and told him I was at my parents. But . . .' I felt my voice crack. 'He became, well, not exactly violent but agitated.'

'Did he hurt you, Emily?' DS Bradley asked.

I had a flashback to the sharp pull on my hair, how my head was forced backwards. How I was unable to move. How he hissed in my ear. How my head hurt last night, how my neck felt tender. How I had cried and he told me not to get upset.

'He scared me,' I mumbled. 'And yes, he hurt me.'

'We can take a statement, Emily. Have you any bruises? Did he leave a mark? We can have the police doctor look at you? We could make a case against him on this.'

I thought of the bruise on my neck – was that assault or consensual sex? It was rougher than I would have liked – but I hadn't fought him off. Hadn't said no. I hadn't fought him off last night either. I had even allowed him to kiss me – but that didn't mean I consented to his behaviour. It meant I was trying to preserve myself.

I lowered the collar on my uniform – showed the bruise while my face blazed with shame. Told them how he had pulled my hair the night before.

'We'll keep you safe, Emily. Please don't worry,' DS Bradley said, with a tone so reassuring that I believed that he would.

They took my statement. Asked so many questions I felt myself get dizzy. They took a separate statement about the assault – assuring me it *was* assault. 'If more women came forward, less men would get away with this kind of behaviour,' Constable Wilson said. I wondered whether Rose ever thought of coming forward? Then again – she was under his charm, wasn't she? He had done to her what Ben did to me – made her feel as if she brought his tempers and controlling behaviour on herself.

I wondered about Ben. Was he with someone now? Had he changed? Was it really the case that I had just brought the worst out in him? Was there something in me that did that? Brought out the worst in people – drove them to the extremes of behaviour? Or had I just made it too easy for him, and for Cian too, to mould me and use me? I'd change now, I vowed. I'd go to counselling. I'd not let this break me.

As long as Cian didn't get to me first.

When I was finished, it had already passed 11am – already passed the time I told Cian I would be at his house. 'I'm not sure what to do,' I confided in Constable Wilson.

'I will get a car to take you where you want to go,' she said, softly, reassuringly. 'A couple of officers will be keeping Cian busy for a few hours, so try not to worry about that now. If you have somewhere else you could stay tonight, that might be an idea – just until things settle?'

I tried not to think about how my options were severely limited – I just nodded. I would sort something out.

'Are you going to arrest him?' I asked.

'We're going to talk to him about what you've said. We also have enough from the journal to ask him more questions. We have to see how it goes from there.' She handed me her card – told me to call her if I needed her or, in an emergency, to dial 999 and someone would be with me straight away. I tried not to feel sick at that thought.

'Try not to let it worry you too much – with people like Cian, sometimes all it takes is someone to stand up to him to scare him off. He has a lot to lose, Emily. He'll do his best not to risk that. Now let me walk you out.' She led the way back through the maze of corridors and doors and out into the soulless waiting area again. 'If you just wait there I'll get you some leaflets for support services,' she said. Just as she turned to leave me, the door opened again and DS Bradley peered out. 'Constable Wilson, can you come with me please? We've just got the CCTV footage – you'll want to see this, and perhaps, Emily – could you wait around a bit? We might need you to verify the identity of someone.'

They disappeared, leaving me to sit on the red plastic chairs wondering what exactly they had found. What CCTV footage were they looking at? From the accident that wasn't an accident? From the night Kevin McDaid died?

I took my phone from my bag and felt my stomach constrict at the sight of a missed call from Cian at 11.05am. He was already looking for me. I had already broken his rules.

Chapter Thirty-Nine

They were gone about ten minutes before I heard the door open again and saw Detective Bradley approach me. 'Emily, I wonder, could we ask you to look at some footage for us?'

'Of course,' I said, although I was trembling and the very last thing I wanted to do was to walk back through that door.

'Thank you,' he said. 'I'll lead the way.'

We went to a different room this time, one where a number of officers stood around a collection of screens. 'Emily, we've been trying to find out who might have paid a considerable amount of money into Kevin McDaid's bank account – but the bank they used records over their CCTV footage once a month and by the time we requested the film from the day in question it had already been overwritten. We had to turn to the City Centre Initiative, and their CCTV cameras, to see if we could capture someone entering the bank at the relevant time.'

'We knew a female had paid the money in,' Constable Wilson said, her face a little flushed. 'If I'm honest, Emily, we thought it might have been you.'

'I didn't. I couldn't have. I didn't even know him. I didn't know any of them – not before . . .'

'We saw you at McDaid's wake,' Detective Bradley said. 'And then when we saw you at Scott's and again at the Grahame house . . .'

I blanched. Realising just how incriminating my behaviour had been. Until now I thought it just painted me as a bit of a crazy – but to realise I had unwittingly been putting myself in the frame for a murder investigation – it made me feel ill.

'I had nothing to do with it. I swear,' I said, panic rising again. I put my hand to the back of a chair to steady myself.

'Emily, it's okay. We have ruled you out of our investigation – but if you could help us with this . . .'

A young officer with short, dark hair and thick-rimmed glasses hit a few buttons on a computer and a grainy black and white image came into view of The Diamond – one of the city's landmarks. The video was taken looking directly across the old War Monument at the bank on the corner of The Diamond and Butcher Street – one of the city's busiest thoroughfares – and there were lots of people walking along the pavement, parking outside the bank and crossing the road.

'Can you zoom in?' DS Bradley asked, and the young officer pulled the image in closer to the bank. Many of those walking had their hoods up or carried umbrellas against the rain, but occasionally I got a glimpse of a face, none of which I recognised. The young officer pulled in a little tighter.

'Can you run it forward a bit, to 2.42pm?' DS Bradley asked. 'There, that's it,' he said. 'Emily, can you look at this figure approaching the bank from Butcher Street? Is there anything familiar about the person you see? The image isn't great, so really we're just looking to see if you can confirm our suspicions?'

I moved closer to the screen, squinted to focus. Saw a figure in a trench coat, a dark scarf wrapped around her neck, an umbrella obscuring a clear view of her face. But the familiar white trousers peeping out at the bottom of her coat made me uneasy. When she came to the door – lowered the umbrella to take it down before walking into the bank, she looked upwards at the sky and, even though the image was grainy, there was no mistaking who it was. My hand flew to my mouth and I looked at DS Bradley and Constable Wilson who were staring at me expectantly.

'That's Donna,' I said.

'That's what we suspected,' DS Bradley replied.

★

Donna. Sweet Donna. Put-upon Donna. None of it made sense. Why on earth would she have deposited money into Kevin McDaid's bank account? Why would she be involved in any of this? She had sat with me last night – with Owen and me – showing us Rose's diaries. Showing me proof that Cian was a bully and a control freak. Pointing the finger at him. Unless that was all part of the plan – point the finger at Cian, make the evidence stack up in his favour and away from her? But it would never have been pointed in her direction anyway. Who would ever have thought Donna – who had to run the gamut between work and parent/teacher meetings with her boys – could ever be tied up in something so sinister? Donna who would regale us with tales of how she spent the previous evening doing nothing more exciting than catching up on the soaps and occasionally looking at the latest loser uploads on online dating sites?

Donna who had cried almost every day about Rose. Who said Rose was one of her best friends. I felt as if the carpet had been whipped out from under me again. If Donna was involved – did that mean Cian was innocent after all? Yes, he might be a horrible person but he wasn't a murderer by proxy, was he? Did it mean that Owen could be involved after all? Those two had been thick as thieves these last few weeks – Donna always knocking on his office door or insisting she assist him in the surgery.

Donna.

The police officers talked around me – I barely took it in but I knew they were going to bring Donna in for questioning. A big part of me – and I don't quite know why – wanted to lift my phone and call her and tell her to run. Warn her. Tell her to call a solicitor. I thought of how fragile she seemed lately and I worried this would break her. But was it all an act? Was everyone in this sad state of affairs acting? Were they all pretending to be someone they weren't? Was it possible I was the most sane among them all?

The buzzing of my phone jolted me into the here and now. I lifted it to see another missed call from Cian and a text from Owen saying he hoped I was okay and he hoped he would see me soon – but what was I to do? Go to work? Go to Cian's? Go home? Run away to the States and Maud and hope she would give me a sofa to sleep on?

My mind just kept drifting back to Donna. She would be so scared. I knew she would. I felt for her. None of this was right. No, I would go to work and at least, when the police arrived, I could offer her a slice of comfort maybe? Then again, maybe she didn't deserve it. She had, or so it looked, been responsible for killing a woman, and risking the life of a baby in the process.

I left the police station, turning down the offer of a lift, and walked back into the cold across the street to the walkway that ran the length of the old Quay. I walked to the water's edge – stood there looking in. Thinking of Kevin McDaid and how

314

he had met his end there. So many lives had been destroyed already and I wondered how many more would be before this was all over. I would say it was the wind that brought tears to my eyes but I think it was much more.

★

When the police arrived at Scott's, they thankfully decided to keep their presence low key. DS Bradley nodded at me as he arrived and I told him I would bring him through to Owen's office – and then bring Donna to him. There was no way to stop this being horrible for everyone – but they would at least try to be as sensitive as possible. None of this was going to look good for Scott's anyway. The word would spread quickly.

My hand was shaking hard as I knocked on the surgery door and pushed down the handle to see Donna and Owen huddled around the computer screen looking at dental X-rays for the next client. A perfectly normal day was about to take a horrible turn. They both looked at me as I walked in. Despite my best efforts, I wasn't able to hide how I was feeling.

'Emily, what's wrong?' Owen asked. 'You look like you've seen a ghost. Is Cian here? Are you okay?' He stood up to walk towards me, and his genuine concern made me want to weep and shield him from what was about to happen.

'Donna,' I said, keeping my voice as steady as I could. 'There are some people here to see you.'

She looked at me without blinking. She was like a rabbit caught in the headlights – unable to move. Stunned. Terrified.

'People?' Owen asked, looking from me to Donna and back again.

'Police,' I said, in little more than a whisper.

There was a low moan, as Donna clutched her stomach and folded in on herself. I felt myself give in to tears.

'What on earth would the police want to see you about, Donna?' Owen asked, his face a picture of perfect confusion.

'DS Bradley and his colleagues are waiting for you in Owen's office,' I said to Donna as she sucked in her breath and tried to stop keening.

'Bradley? This isn't about Rose?' Owen asked. 'Donna?' His confusion was almost as hard to watch as Donna's fear. It was clear nothing about this made sense to him.

'They know?' she asked me and in that moment I knew it was true. It might not have made any sense but it was true.

I nodded.

'They know what?' Owen asked, his voice impatient now. 'What on earth is going on?'

Donna turned to him and took his hands in hers while he looked on completely bemused. Gulping back sobs, she spoke. 'I'm so, so sorry, Owen. So sorry. He wasn't meant to kill her. He was only meant to hurt her. To delay things – to stop you moving in together. To give her time to think. To give me time to think. If I'd known what would happen . . . if I'd known Jack would be there. It wasn't meant to be like this. She wasn't meant to die.'

I watched as the severity of the situation registered on Owen's face. He threw her hands from his as if they were on fire – and she jumped backwards as if it was she who had been burned.

'She just had everything, Owen, and I had nothing,' she said, pleading with him to understand. 'I just wanted something for me for a change. A chance to let you get to know the real me – to realise *we* could have been happy. She had Cian and they had their problems but they could work through it. Why would you throw all that away?' She was sobbing loudly now – attracting the attention from staff and clients alike. DS Bradley and Constable Wilson came out of the office and when she saw them she looked wide-eyed from them, to me, to Owen.

'All I wanted was you to love me like I loved you. You know I love you, Owen. You know I've loved you for a long time. She was in the way – but he wasn't meant to kill her. Just hurt her or scare her. Just hit the pause button. I thought I was being careful. If I had known what would happen, I never would have . . .' As her voice trailed off, DS Bradley walked past me and started telling her, in his calm voice, that she was under arrest in connection with the murder of Rose Grahame. I saw the faces of our colleagues first register shock, then crumple with grief. As he read her rights, she continued to plead with Owen, who could do nothing but watch as this nightmare scene played out in front of us. 'Why should she be the one to get everything? Why didn't I deserve to be happy? I just wanted to be happy, Owen. I just wanted us to be happy. I'm so sorry. I'm so, so sorry. She wasn't meant to die.'

Although I am sure there was noise around us as she was lead out of the surgery and into the police car that was parked outside, I couldn't hear it. I couldn't hear anything except for her pleading and sobbing. It was only when the door was closed, and the car had pulled off that the noise of ringing phones and hushed whispers and the sobs of co-workers struggling to come to terms with what had happened crashed back in.

I looked at Owen, who was standing with his back to me – his hands resting on the work surface in the surgery, his shoulders shaking, his knuckles white. I saw him bough and break and curl into himself. The sound of his wail echo around the room.

Very gently I pulled the door closed and walked back into the main waiting area. 'I'm very sorry,' I announced to our waiting clients, 'I'm sure you can understand why, but we will be closing now and we will reschedule your appointments for a suitable time. I'm very sorry for the inconvenience.'

No one argued. No one tutted. No one called us useless. The clients just stood, lifted their belongings and quietly left, nodding to us as you would to someone at a wake as they walked out. As I locked the door behind them, I saw that most of them had already lifted their phones and were tapping on the screens or making calls. The news would be out there – and soon.

'Tori, can you get me Donna's next of kin information please? We should make sure someone is there for her boys?'

Tori nodded, sniffing loudly, but went to retrieve Donna's HR file.

The rest of us huddled around, not sure what to say or do.

The sound of the surgery door opening made us all jump. Owen came out and walked towards us all. He opened his mouth to speak, but I imagine he couldn't find the words either. Sarah walked towards him and hugged him. Tori followed. As did all the other staff members, one by one, until I found myself clinging on to a shell-shocked community of workers myself.

'Go home everyone,' Owen said. 'Go home to your families and your loved ones and just, well, just go home. I'll keep you updated on how things are. I think you know – no, I know you know, not to talk to the media. The press will probably descend on us as soon as they hear – we'll close until next week.'

'I'll stay and help you get messages out to our clients,' I said.

'Me too,' said Tori.

Owen nodded, and walked back to his office.

Funnily enough, the whole episode had distracted me from

the persistent buzzing of my phone, which was vibrating for all its worth in my locker as Cian tried and tried to get in touch with me.

Chapter Forty

The only way to quiet the ringing of the phones was to switch on the auto-answer service. Tori recorded a new message saying the surgery was closed due to unforeseen circumstances and all clients would be informed of any changes to their appointments.

We put a sign saying the same in our window, but it didn't stop the banging against the shutters – shouts from eager journalists looking for comment. Business cards were slid through the letter box along with hastily scribbled notes on jotter pages asking for exclusivity in return for money and/or a sensitive approach to the story.

Owen became more agitated with the arrival of each one – so Tori and I simply stopped telling him about them, tearing them up and throwing them in the bin. As we worked together through the client list for the following few days, we sat mostly in silence. I suppose it was one of those situations where there was so much to say that none of us knew where to start.

Owen locked himself in his office. Told us he needed some space. He'd get some paperwork cleared up, he said. He looked utterly broken but we respected his wishes to be left alone.

'Do you think . . .' Tori asked as we neared the end of our list, 'do you think this means she was involved in Kevin McDaid's death too?'

I shrugged my shoulders. It seemed unthinkable – but then again the thought that she had been in anyway responsible for Rose's death seemed so completely far-fetched as well.

'I don't understand any of it. I suppose, maybe? But it all seems so unlike her.'

'I know what you mean,' Tori said. 'I just can't get my head around it all, Emily. None of it. That she would do that? But maybe if he had been blackmailing her or something? I mean, if she paid him to hurt Rose and then he wanted more money? You can't trust people like that. I suppose you'd do anything if you were desperate. But still . . .'

Anything if you were desperate. How scared must Donna have been when it all went so spectacularly wrong? She must have been crucifying herself with guilt all this time. Or maybe she wasn't? Maybe she was delighted she had Owen all to herself now? To think she could have been involved in killing Kevin McDaid – that was up close and personal. That moved her to a whole other level. I shuddered at the thought of how I was welcoming her into my life, craving friendship with her, trusting her and feeling sorry for her and meanwhile she could have been plotting all sorts. If Rose, her best friend, hadn't been safe, who could be?

'You never really know people, Tori,' I said. 'But maybe we shouldn't try and guess what happened – I'm sure now she's with the police it will all come out.'

'She'll go to prison for a long time,' Tori said, shaking her head and then, lost in her thoughts, she went back to her work.

After an hour and a half, we were almost done. I told Tori she could head home if she wanted and I would finish things off. She was only too keen to leave, and did so sneaking out

321

of the back door to avoid any random journos waiting in the street, but not before hugging me tightly and telling me to take care of myself.

Gingerly I knocked on the door of Owen's office – thought I would see how he was, offer him a tea or coffee, tell him we were almost done. He called back that I could come in and when I did he was sitting at his desk, files in front of him, mess everywhere. His eyes red rimmed and tired.

'We're almost done here,' I said. 'Tori has just gone and I'm going to finish clearing up. I was just going to get a cup of tea first. Can I get you anything?'

He shook his head before looking at me and giving a weak, strangled laugh. 'A time machine?'

'If only,' I said.

'I can't get my head around it,' he said. 'And I'll never forgive myself.'

'Forgive yourself? There's nothing to forgive.'

'Why didn't I notice something was off with Donna? If I did – if I had realised, maybe Rose would be here. But I didn't. Isn't that just the kicker in all of this? It wasn't that bastard of a husband, it was Donna. Who was in love with me.' He shook his head, as if the notion was unthinkable. 'I knew she was a bit clingy – but love me? I never thought. I was so wrapped up in Rose. Christ, Emily. If I had just left well enough alone, she would still be here. Donna wouldn't be in the police station. She wouldn't have done that . . .' He shook his head.

'Owen, you can't help who you fall in love with. You didn't have bad intentions and I read those journals too – I saw how hopeful and happy you made her. Do you think, even if she'd known how things would work out, that she would have changed that?' I pulled a chair up and sat opposite him. 'You don't get the chance to be loved very often,' I said. 'And you know I've made some stupid decisions in my life, just trying

322

to find an ounce of what you and Rose had. Don't regret that, Owen.'

'I miss her,' he said simply.

'If there's one thing I know, it's that it might seem like hell on earth now – and it is hell on earth for you, I'm not trying to say it isn't – but it can get better. You won't ever be the same, and parts will always hurt, but this doesn't have to define you for the rest of your life.' As I said the words something in me clicked. I had been letting so much of what had happened in my past define me – to factor in every decision every day. What happened with Ben was awful. It was humiliating. It was degrading. It had left me in pieces, relying on alcohol and pills and being branded a flake by everyone I knew. But it didn't have to define the rest of my life – I didn't have to let it lead me to make the same mistakes again.

Sitting across from Owen – whose life was crumbling around him – finally made me wake up.

'I'm going to go get a cup of tea,' I said, 'finish up. You should finish up too, Owen. Go home or to your friends or family and let them look after you. Don't shut yourself away.'

He nodded and as I left the room he called me back.

'Milk, two sugars,' he said with a sad smile and I smiled back and walked through to the staff room to put the kettle on.

★

I filled the kettle and while it was boiling, I walked through to the staff room again to get my phone from my locker. I noticed the back door was lying slightly ajar, figured Tori mustn't have pulled it closed just right when she left. I pushed it shut and locked it before turning back to my locker and putting in my combination. I opened the door and was just slipping my hand in to pull out my bag when I felt a blow to the side of my head that unbalanced me. As my head throbbed and spun,

I tried to figure out what had happened. The locker door had been pounded against my head, its cold metal edge cutting into me. I felt a searing pain above my left ear and I reached my hand to it, feeling the warm and sticky sensation of blood on my fingertips. I looked in the direction of the door, trying to get my bearings, and noticed the boots on the ground, the legs, the burly body, the angry face, and the hand that grabbed me by the throat and pushed me hard against the lockers – forcing the air from my lungs.

Cian. His face contorted with anger was all I could see. His face in mine – his breath, hot, sickening on my face. I opened my mouth to call for help and was met with his hand, flat over my mouth and nose – stopping me not only from shouting out but from breathing. I tried to suck air into my lungs, feeling nothing but the suction of his sweaty hand against my face.

'I knew you were a crazy bitch,' he said, 'but this – this, Emily. This takes it to a whole new level.'

My eyes widened with fear. I tried to wriggle from under his touch, fought to escape him, felt the ridges of the lockers rubbing, tearing against my clothes and my skin.

'Were you in on it? Was this one of your crazy fucking moves, Emily? You and Donna, and probably that bastard Owen too. Taking her from me? And then, instead of being told that bitch has been arrested for the murder of my wife – I have the police arrive at my door with some fucking bullshit about how I've assaulted *you*?'

I could feel my lungs straining, every cell in my body trying to absorb what it could, desperate for oxygen, desperate to breathe. The pain growing inside as my body fought to find what wasn't there.

'Oh sweet, naive, stupid little Emily, you have no idea what an assault is. You've no idea what I'm capable of. I can make you disappear – just like I made Kevin McDaid disappear.'

He took his hand from my face and I gasped, swallowed lungfuls of air as his grasp on my neck loosened.

'So you stay quiet, Emily. Or I will. I promise I will – and no one will ever guess. They'll just think that stupid, lonely, crazy woman topped herself. Which, really, if you think about it, is what you should have done years ago . . .' He put his finger to my lips. 'Oh, Ingrid has told me all about you,' he said, trailing that finger across my mouth, before cupping his hand under my chin and pushing my head back against the lockers. 'A real basket case. She spoke to your ex. Did she tell you that? You're quite the disaster, aren't you? Do you think anyone would care if you just vanished? Went for a wee swim like McDaid did? I'd say you'd be easier to deal with than him. He fought me at first, you know. You should have seen the look on his face when I cornered him, forced him into my car. He tried to tell me he was sorry – like that would be enough. Hit like a girl. Cried like a girl too. Begged me not to make him do it. Told me he was going to be a dad. Well, that just made me even more angry, you see. Because Rose – well, she was a mother. She could have been a mother again. After that, he didn't really have a chance. I don't think he believed I would actually do it though. But he took her away from me, Emily, and you know I couldn't let him away with that. So, yes, I roughed him up a bit – but I gave him the chance to do the decent thing. Jump himself. I told him to be a man. Even walked him to the centre of the bridge, helped him take his shoes and coat off. I folded it for him you know, while he stood and cried like a baby. Pissed his trousers. He tried to run – so he forced me in the end. He forced me to do it. He could have done it himself but no, he made me push him – tip him over the barrier, smash my fist down on his fingers when he tried to cling on. He didn't deserve to cling on. Anyone would have done the same. The only fly in the ointment was that the bastard wouldn't tell me who put him up to it. Said he didn't want anyone else getting hurt. Some decency in him after all maybe or just no honour among touts. It wouldn't have made any difference anyway. He wasn't getting out of it alive. People don't wrong me and get away with it, Emily.'

My legs were shaking, my hands fisting, trying to grab onto something — adrenaline making all my senses keener. The smell of him. The sound of him. The thump of my heart, the sound of blood pulsing around my body, whooshing in my ears, the sensation of blood from the cut on my head trickling down my neck.

'And no one is getting out of this, Emily. No one involved in taking her from me.' He loosened his grip but stood in front of me, in my personal space, so close I could hear his heart pounding along with my own. His face softened, his head tilted to one side. 'Because I did love her, Emily. I adored her. I would have given her anything she wanted. I *did* give her everything she wanted — but she was just so fucking ungrateful. Preferred that boring fucking dentist over me. But I would have forgiven her. I would have — we'd have had our baby and we would have been happy again.'

He was crying and for the briefest of moments I saw a glimpse of the man I had fallen for in front of me again. A man who loved his wife. Yes, in a twisted way — but it was love. A dangerous love. One that had tempted me, even if the warning signals had been there.

'I know you loved her,' I croaked. 'You're a good person, Cian,' I said, trying to appeal to the man I knew was in there somewhere. 'Think of Jack. You don't have to make this worse. You can walk away and I'll drop any charges, and I won't tell anyone what you told me about Kevin. I'll tell the police I lied. I'll give you that alibi.'

He looked at me for a moment, contemplating what I was

326

saying. 'Emily D'Arcy,' he said, sing-songing my voice. 'Emily D'Arcy – desperate little Emily. Sad little Emily. I really trusted you, you know. I never thought you'd have the balls to tell the police you weren't with me that night. I thought I'd chosen well when I chose you. You were so . . . so . . . nothing.' He moved closer again, pressing himself against me, his hands around my face, in my hair. He pulled one hand back, looked at the blood on it – a lip curl of disgust forming on his face – before smearing my own blood over my face.

'You were so, are so, nondescript but oh, so mouldable. You wanted to be her, Emily. You stepped into her shoes in work. Didn't waste any time trying to be her. Do you think I didn't notice how you lightened your hair, just like hers? How you so desperately wanted to slip into our lives? Mine and Jack's – so yes, I used you. I thought I could rely on you,' he started grinding against me and I felt my stomach turn, fear rising. 'But you used me too,' he said, pulling away just slightly – not enough to allow me to escape. 'It was never me you wanted – it was what you thought I was. What I represented. What you thought I was with Rose – but I could never be that man with you. I could never love you, even though I know that you would be easier to manage than she was. Easier to control. You were so desperate for it. So grateful for whatever crumbs I could throw at you. You made it so easy. *You* were so easy. A sad little slut. Do you ever think I could fall for you? Just because you dropped your knickers? Come on! You're a smart girl. You know how the world works. A fuck is a fuck. Yours came with an alibi – which was good. It came with the promise of some childcare and a housekeeper. A win-win. Then Ingrid told me about your very sad past. Just how much you would put up with,' he laughed, grabbed my face again, whispered in my ear again.

'You'd have played the game better, Emily. You're so fucking sad, you'd have let me get away with more. You'd have loved the chance to be paraded around – to boast about me on Facebook. Create another web of lies about how life could be perfect. You wouldn't have argued like she did – or at least that's what I thought. Until now. Until you ruined it all by going to the police. And you're back here? In *his* uniform? Oh Emily, you have disappointed me so much.'

'I'm sorry,' I whispered, desperate to get away, willing to do almost anything to get away – but aware that behind me was a locked door. The shutters were down at the front of the surgery. The only other person in the building was Owen – who was lost in a world of his own grief in an office where he wouldn't hear what was going on all the way back here. And even if he could – would I want to put him in front of Cian – knowing just exactly what he had done to Kevin McDaid? No, Cian could do anything he wanted to me, right there, and there was nothing I could do to stop him. 'I'm sorry,' I whispered again, tears flowing, head thumping, legs shaking.

'Kevin McDaid said that too,' Cian said. 'But I don't think he really was. If he was he would have told me about Donna, wouldn't he? But you – you would do whatever you were told because that's the kind of person you are. Pathetic. I'd pity you if you hadn't tried to destroy me.'

'Please, Cian. Don't do this!'

'You have to know I can't stop now,' he said, pushing my hair back from my face, curling it behind my ear. 'I can't trust you. No matter what you say. If I'm going to be destroyed – well, what is it they say? Might as well be hung for a sheep as a lamb?' He reached behind me, pulling my jacket out from the locker. 'Put it on,' he barked and I knew this was the endgame. I suppose, just as Rose watched that car approach her at speed, just how she looked as if this was always going to be how it ended – I knew this was how it was going to end for me. I had always known it should have been me – and it would be me.

Crying, gulping in air, I zipped up my coat, watched as Cian pulled my belongings from the locker.

'Where are we going?' I asked him. 'The press have been coming and going all day – someone will see us.'

'Not if we go out this back door,' he said. 'Don't underestimate me. Unlock the door.'

'I can't,' I said, and I wasn't lying. I don't think I ever really understood the true meaning of frozen with fear until that moment. My arms wouldn't work. My hands wouldn't move. I could barely keep standing.

'For fuck's sake,' he swore, pushing me roughly to the side so he could reach the door.

He had just turned the key in the lock when I heard a crash beside me, looked down and saw a cup in shards at Cian's feet. Another thud, and Cian swearing, his hand rising to his head. A plate. A cup. Enough to disarm him – to surprise him – to gain the upper hand. I saw flashes of Owen. Tried to process his words. The police were on their way. Cian turning to rush at him – my body jolting to life, stretching my foot in front of him, tripping him, watching him stumble and try to find his feet, pushing him over, watching him fall, giving Owen enough time to fell him to the ground, enough time for me to follow through and grab his hands, push them flat into his back.

'You don't get to hurt anyone else,' Owen shouted, raising his fist and punching Cian as hard as he could before falling back, sitting on the floor and just looking at Cian Grahame – this man who had ruined so many lives, directly and indirectly, and shaking his head. 'You had everything. Cian. You threw it all away.'

The sound of footsteps, heavy and urgent outside. The door pushing open. Police officers, armed, tall, dark, looming, everywhere. Someone, DS Bradley lifting me back, holding me to him, telling me it would be okay. He rocked me as I cried and shook and watched Cian be led away. He whispered that I would be okay over and over again until I started to believe it.

I would be okay.

Epilogue

One year later

This was my favourite spot in the world. This desk, looking out of the sash windows over the vista of the Donegal coastline. I lifted another sheet of paper and continued writing my letter. There was little as rewarding as seeing the pages fill with the handwritten word, before folding the crisp white sheets, putting them in an envelope and carefully writing the address on the outside.

It had become my Sunday morning hobby. Relaxing in my living room, taking time to catch up on my letters. Although my life was one I no longer wanted to escape from, it was different from what I thought it would be – but it was rewarding and calm and happy.

Most of all I felt content. I felt as if I finally knew what was important and what was real. I'd taken my lead from Rose – I suppose – when I closed down my social media accounts, and decided to return to traditional letter writing. Maud had thought I had finally cracked at first – but in a good way. A nice way. I had heard her laugh when I told her to watch out for her post. It hadn't taken long for her to admit she loved it – loved getting something other than bills landing in her mailbox. Now she looked forward to my weekly missives greatly. Of course we still spoke on the phone, and occasionally we exchanged emails, but the real emotions, the reality of life was poured out onto paper each Sunday morning.

I had even reconnected with my parents – written to them and explained everything that had happened. I apologised if I had hurt them and they had come to see me, held me close. They told me they were most annoyed and angered that I hadn't asked them for help. They didn't know how to reach out to me. I realised as much as they had shut me out, I had shut them out too. It wasn't easy and there were bumps in the road – but we were on that road at least. It felt so good.

Folding their letter, I slipped it into the envelope and wrote their address – the house where I grew up – on the front of it. Then I sat back for a moment, sipped from my coffee cup, listened to the crackle of the logs on the wood fire. I watched the rhythm of the sea and it was no longer something that promised to wash me away from it all. It was back to being a beautiful, timeless, reassuring reminder that life goes on.

I wondered a little about Jack. I hoped he was happy. After Cian's arrest, Rose's family had been able to gain custody. There was some benefit to Cian not staying in touch with his family, I supposed. I had seen him once. He was in the ice-cream parlour, his face sticky with cream and jelly, and was laughing at his grandmother singing songs to him. I knew, despite the horrible deck life had dealt him, he would always be loved.

It's all any of us can wish for. Certainly, I hoped that if the day came when I was blessed enough to have a baby of my own, that baby would always know he or she was loved.

I'd love to tell you Cian suffered greatly – as he deserved

to, but life is funny. Ingrid Devlin stepped in where I stepped out, it seemed. Although looking back, I'm pretty sure she had already stepped in even when Cian and I were technically together. She has stood by him – strongly and publicly. He's been painted as a romantic hero – a man who killed the man who stole his wife from him. A crime of passion by a man who simply loved too much. And people have bought it, because, as we all know Cian Grahame is very good at painting a false impression of himself. I heard Ingrid was, with his help, writing a book on it – had a deal signed and all. I believe there is talk of a movie. Apparently, he gets a lot of fan mail from poor deluded women – women just like I was – who think he is a broken man they can fix. I wish I could tell them all he is not a man who can be put back together, but I have had to let that go. My counsellor said it was the best thing I could do. Let go of what I couldn't control.

She has been a star – even if at times I have had to be dragged almost kicking and screaming through the door to her. I didn't want to give up my crutches you see – the pills and the booze – but I needed to feel again. I needed to live.

It's Donna who has my sympathy in all this. I know that sounds strange, given what she was responsible for. But I do believe her when she said it was never meant to be like that. Rose was never meant to die. I believed her when she said if she had wanted to really hurt Rose, she would have told Cian – but she didn't want to risk that. She knew what he could be like, and that he would take his anger out on both Rose and her beloved Owen.

Donna had a hard life. All she wanted was to be loved and she thought she had that with Owen. Even if it was only ever really a figment of her imagination. Her life was so tough – such a relentless circle of never feeling appreciated – she felt desperate. Desperate enough to empty the savings account she had kept for her boys' university days to pay Kevin McDaid.

She never denied the charge. She admitted it and she wept in court and said she would never be able to say enough how sorry she was. I had felt heartsore for her. I understood that desperation to be loved.

I don't think she had many people standing behind her to support her. Her boys were mortified, horrified by their mother's actions. I had to keep in touch with her – let her know that she wasn't worthless. She wasn't a terrible person, even if she had done a terrible thing.

I didn't tell Owen that I wrote to her though. I don't think he would understand. He is a good man – an honest, caring man – but he can't yet find it in his heart to forgive her. He might do someday, he said, but it was still a little too raw. I think it will be raw for him for a long time. Rose was the love of his life. As much as he doesn't look so worn out, so beaten down by life every day – as much as he can laugh and smile with us in work on occasion – it is clear there is a part of him missing.

He has become a good friend to me, someone I can confide in. Someone who does, on occasion, kick my ass into going to my counselling sessions. He even helped me find my new home, arranged the moving van and helped load and unload my belongings. He's a good man. The best. I hope – really hope – he will find happiness at some stage, or contentment at least. Isn't that all that we really want?

Clicking the lid back on my pen, I heard the scrabble of paws on the wood floor following my footsteps. It was time for walkies. A stroll along the beach. The door to the study pushed open and in ran Buster, his tail wagging wildly behind him. He proceeded to charge around in circles as if urging me to get up and get a move on. 'Okay, boy,' I said, petting him, ruffling his fur. 'Let me get ready and I'll grab your lead.'

I glanced at the clock. It was almost midday and I was definitely cutting it fine. 'I won't be long, I promise,' I said as I walked past him into the hall, where I pulled on my coat and boots and lifted his lead down from its hook. Wrapping my scarf around my neck, I clipped his lead on and headed to my front door, down my garden path and across the road to the beach.

It was quiet at this time of day, especially given that winter was still making itself felt. A few stragglers walked up and down the sand. Dogs running, dipping in and out of the water.

I saw him in the distance – his tall frame making me smile. Bonnie, his golden Labrador ran, off lead, beside him, bounding on the sand. I raised my hand to wave to him, saw him wave in response and watched as Buster took off in his direction.

'It's a cold one today,' he said, smiling. 'I was almost tempted to call you and cancel.'

'A bit of cold doesn't bother a big, burly man like you, does it?'

He laughed, his blue eyes sparkling. 'I prefer the heat if truth be told. But Bonnie would never forgive me if I was late for one of her walks with Buster.'

'Good for Bonnie,' I said, looping my arm in his.

'To tell the truth, I think I would be annoyed at myself if I missed my date with you too,' he said kissing the top of my head.

'And so you should be. Now – the full length of this beach and back – and then back to mine, where I have a nice fire burning and a roast in the oven.'

'You're spoiling me,' he said.

I stopped and looked up at him, drinking in his features. This man – who had helped me, soothed me, protected me and who was slowly but surely teaching me what real love could be. My heart fluttered and I stood up on my tiptoes to kiss him gently on the lips.

'You deserve it,' I said with a smile. 'Now, last one to that rock is a rotten egg,' I said, taking off at speed – enjoying the sound of DS David Bradley's laugh in my wake.

Acknowledgements

First of all, my thanks must go to my editor Phoebe Morgan for taking on a former women's fiction author trying to break into a new genre. Thanks for your enthusiasm, encouragement and guidance which helped polish this book to what it is now. I will be eternally grateful to you and all the team at Avon for taking a chance on me and for showing 'Rose' so much love and dedication.

In a similar vein, my agent Ger Nichol who played match-maker and found me this wonderful new home, thank you. We've been through a lot together but you have steadfastly been on my side and offered friendship as well as guidance. Thank you.

Pulling this book together took a lot of research and hard work. Changing genres from women's fiction to thrillers required a leap of faith and I can't thank the friends, in writing and otherwise, who offered guidance and assured me all along that I could do it.

Most especially thanks to Fionnuala Kearney, beta reader extraordinaire, FaceTime legend and one of the best friends a girl could have, and to Margaret Scott and Caroline Finnerty for always being there. Always. Day and night. Even when I was hysterical.

Thanks also to Emma Hannigan, Melissa Hill, Sheila O'Flanagan, Rowan Coleman, Cally Taylor, Brian McGilloway, Claire Hennessy, Caroline Grace Cassidy and Shirley Benton.

Massive thanks to Marian Keyes for encouragement and her wonderful and generous endorsement of this book – and to her Himself, Tony Baines, for his support also. Marian, you always have been and will continue to be a huge inspiration in my life.

To my beta readers, Jacintha O'Reilly Mooney, Julie-Anne Campbell (just be, my friend!) and Margaret Bonass Madden for helping iron out the early crises and for informing me when it all got a bit 'too Derry'.

My friends, especial Vicki, also one of the very best friends a girl could have. We've come a long way baby.

To the former 'Journal' girls who made a leap of faith with me – thank you, Bernie, Catherine and especially Erin for continued faith in me when I had little in myself.

And to the women who helped me find the confidence to be the person I always wanted to be, Carey Ann and Sandra, my cheerleaders and friends.

Writing makes for a solitary life – so to those Twitter friends who are my online work colleagues during the day thank you for the laughs, distractions, understanding and friendship. From the writers, to the readers, the *Strictly* watchers, the fellow spoonies, the crochet fans and all those randomers I have encountered along the way, thank you. There are too many of you to name individually but I hope you know who you are. Mention must go to my Twitter muse Lesley Price, who has become a true and hilariously bad-ass friend. I'd be lost without your sense of humour and your take on inspirational quotes.

And to Stevie, aka Mr S, the man in the hat, for talking sense and enjoying the banter when I need a laugh.

When it comes to closer to home, I may get emotional so I'll try and keep this tight and to the point. To my husband, thank you for having the faith in me to encourage and support me while I took a big chance on this whole writing thing. I love you.

To my children, in the words of Bryan Adams, everything I do, I do it for you. I love you both with all my heart and I thank you for all the times you understood when Mum was 'writing that book again'.

To my wider family, I love you. Thank you especially to Marie-Louise, Auntie Raine and Mimi for supporting me and believing in me.

To my siblings, Lisa, Peter and Emma and assorted partners, children, dogs and cats. Thank you for enduring life with a tortured artiste.

To all the 'Roses' and 'Emilys' of the world who have shared their stories with me over the years. Thank you for your honesty and your bravery.

To my readers, who I hope enjoy the change of pace. All the booksellers, librarians, publishing people and lovely journalists and bloggers, thank you.

And finally, to my parents, to whom this book is dedicated – it's been a long time coming but you have never, for one second, doubted me. I love you both with all my heart and I couldn't have asked for better.

Book Club Questions

1. Why do you think Rose tries so hard to maintain an image of perfection throughout the book?
2. Who do you think is the victim of this story?
3. How do you think the men in this novel are portrayed?
4. The use of social media and how we show ourselves to others is a theme in this book. Do you think social media makes people more competitive with each other?
5. What did you think of the title of the book? Do you think it ties in well with the themes of domestic abuse? Would you have given the book a different title?
6. Cian comes across as a sympathetic character to both Rose and Emily when they meet him. Particularly in the case of Rose, do you think he always had controlling tendencies but was able to keep them hidden until the relationship was well established?
7. What did you think of the portrayal of Donna in the book? Do you think she was as close to Rose as she stated, or was their friendship marred by jealousy?
8. This book deals with some very dark themes – notably the

issue of suicidal thoughts and depression. Do you think these issues were handled sensitively?

9. The book is set in the author's home town of Derry~Londonderry in Northern Ireland. Do you think the location added anything to the story?

If you are struggling with any of the issues covered in this book, the contact details for Women's Aid and The Samaritans are listed below.

Women's Aid: 0808 2000 247 (24 hour free-phone)
helpine@womensaid.org.uk

The Samaritans: 116 123 (UK & ROI)
jo@samaritans.org

There is no bond greater than blood . . .

The number one bestseller is back.

Here are two things I know about my mother:
1. She had dark hair, like mine.
2. She wasn't very happy at the end.

DISCARDED
From Nashville Public Library

'A rollercoaster of a read'
LISA HALL

'Highly recommended'
T M LOGAN

11
MISSED CALLS

ELISABETH CARPENTER

Elisabeth Carpenter returns with another
twisty, unputdownable thriller . . .